ALSO BY MICHAEL DOWNING

A Narrow Time

Mother of God

Michael Downing

Simon and Schuster

New York   London   Toronto   Sydney   Tokyo   Singapore

Simon and Schuster
Simon & Schuster Building
Rockefeller Center
1230 Avenue of the Americas
New York, New York 10020

SIMON AND SCHUSTER and colophon are registered trademarks
of Simon & Schuster Inc.

Designed by Irving Perkins Associates
Manufactured in the United States of America

1 3 5 7 9 10 8 6 4 2

Library of Congress Cataloging in Publication Data
Downing, Michael.
Mother of God / Michael Downing.
p. cm.
I. Title.
PS3554.O9346M6   1990   89–49767
813'.54—dc20   CIP
ISBN 0–671–69506–1

This is for Joseph, who paid my passage.

In the world you will have trouble,
but be brave: I have conquered the world.

Jesus, as given by John

\

Preconceptions

I

ARTHUR ADAMSKI LEARNED the disadvantages of being a man one by lumbering one. He invented routines to protect and sustain what few pleasures survived his education. As he had every Saturday for more than twenty years, he'd got himself out of bed after Sylvia left for morning Mass. Perched on the narrow bench in the built-in alcove that barely accommodated his six-foot frame, he hunched over the painted plywood table and read the *Pittsfield Courier*. Here, despite the odds, he enjoyed a temporary sense of possession over the house he'd provided his family in Pittsfield's best neighborhood.

The house no longer housed a family. His elder daughter, Jane, lived somewhere in New York City. Alison and her husband and children lived within three blocks of this stucco house on Holmes Road, but the distance wasn't stable; it fed itself on time and grew. Artie—"Arthur junior hardly," according to his father—worked with juvenile delinquents in Pennsylvania, and had given up on the house even as a home for the holidays.

By rights, it should have been Stephen's home. But since the youngest Adamski had decided not to return for his junior year at the University of Massachusetts, he'd lived in a private place, a strangely inaccessible corner of whatever room he wandered through.

The morning newspaper for the eighth of October, 1983, made public the fact that Stephen had wandered away to a new, if temporary, residence. Arthur could just picture his skinny blond son seated on a bench not unlike the bench in the alcove, his eyes fixed on a point of no interest to anyone else who might be in the room with him. Arthur held to this picture of Stephen as he reread the first few paragraphs of the newspaper story about the local youth who had vandalized the Temple Beth Israel and subsequently stood in front of a

11

local judge and refused to answer the charges on the grounds that his kingdom was not of this world. Arthur hoped he could make sense of the story as a sort of caption for his image of Stephen in a local jail cell.

But the story made no sense to Arthur. And the image of his displaced, unreachable son was not startling or compelling. For weeks now, Arthur had spoken to Stephen across a vast expanse, with no confirmation that his requests and cajolings had been received. "Are you thinking about a job you might like to take on, Steve? Are you going to get a refund for the first semester tuition we sent down to Amherst? It seems you've lost some weight, Steve. Or maybe I'm not used to how tall you are. I don't know which it is. How about it?"

Arthur covered the story with his hands, then raised one hand as a fist and slammed it against the newsprint, to obliterate the incident. As if Stephen might be lurking out of sight in the living room, Arthur addressed him. "Well, what do you want me to do? You tell everyone you won't see visitors. You won't let me make bail for you. What?"

Accustomed to Stephen's silence, he waited hopelessly for an answer. Frustration faded to sadness as he folded the newspaper's front page in on itself to hide Stephen's story. Inventing a sense of urgency, he resolved to penetrate Stephen's privacy, reach in with his stronger arm and extricate him.

Attempting to stand before he'd slid to the end of the bench, Arthur got his leg jammed between the table top and the wall. Instinctively, he reached his hands under the table and began to leverage it off its base. A sharp snap alerted him to what he was about to do. Embarrassed and alarmed, he stared accusingly at his hands, slid out of the alcove. From a few feet away, the table looked unharmed. But Arthur could see the newspaper had unfolded itself, exposing Stephen. Defeated, he held his hands out to the story, a kind of introduction. Aloud, matter-of-factly, he said, "My son. The crazy bastard."

II

Sylvia McGill Adamski had begun her weekly walk around the neighborhood of the Church of the Sacred Heart by inventing her alibi: "This morning I had to think about Stephen before I could face God." Rarely had she been accosted by a familiar face and been obliged to provide an explanation for her failure to actually go inside the church, but the precaution was her license.

Sylvia's pace this morning was furious. She wanted to propel herself beyond doubt, to a point where Stephen's actions would be simple, quantifiable. But she couldn't make herself believe that Stephen had left college with the express aim of becoming a petty criminal.

When she circled back to the intersection of Holmes Road and Elm Street, she was sweating, pulling her head back with every breath. Resting at the corner, she watched a large maroon sedan edge past the Holmes Road stoplight. Reflexively, she stepped off the curb and rushed along the faded paint of the pedestrian crosswalk, just in time to force the driver to pump his brakes and jar himself against the steering wheel. As was her pleasure, Sylvia turned to face the driver as this small calamity occurred. Meeting the man's embarrassed stare, she performed a pantomime to convey her relief and then her willingness to forgive and forget his potentially fatal miscalculation.

Sylvia was something of an expert at milking such small successes, but this morning's coup was nothing more than a momentary distraction. Her pace returned her home too soon. She tried to justify a visit with her daughter, thinking of the private meetings Stephen had with Alison's husband (and, as far as anyone could tell, Stephen's self-appointed legal counsel), Roger. Despite his claim that they had only reviewed charges, Roger must have formed a judgment of her son's demeanor.

13

"I have not seen or spoken to my son in three days." Sylvia tried to forecast the effect of such a plaint on her polite son-in-law.

In fact, she was unwilling to increase the stakes just yet. To date, everyone was dealing with the episode as if it were a small disturbance, a youngster's indiscretion. She did not want to be the one to probe beneath the unlikely but tolerable veneer. It was easy for her to see that the safest route was the path of least resistance, which led her to the broad macadam driveway lined with long since deflowered peonies, through the kitchen door, where she and Arthur could pretend that Stephen's strange behavior had no resonance, that he was just another child to be dealt with, that their most prized secrets were hidden at a twenty-year remove and not within their twenty-year-old son.

III

SYLVIA RECOGNIZED ARTHUR's torso and legs, but his head was hidden in the cabinet under the sink. "Are you looking for something I could help you find, Arthur? Or is this just the man's version of sticking your head in the oven?" Sylvia stepped over him and only then heard words among the grunts he was emitting.

"The small wrench? In the sink. Hand it to me?"

Sylvia pulled a large wooden spoon from an encrusted saucepan, handed it to her husband. "Good morning, dear."

Arthur grabbed the spoon and attempted to apply it to the joint of the drainpipe. With his left hand, he held the loose connection together, sensing that at any moment the sludge caught in the trap would escape. "Good morning, already. The wrench in the sink?"

"It was a little joke."

"Thank you, Sylvia. Now, the wrench, if you can manage it?"

She finished filling the metal coffee filter, then opened a cabinet opposite the sink. "The wrench? One second. I was thinking of asking Alison and Roger to dinner tonight, on account of Roger being so good to—"

"Oh for Christ's sake."

Sylvia turned in time to watch water rush out of the pipe, splash down onto the crowded cabinet shelves. Arthur was still holding the U-shaped pipe he'd hoped to reconnect. "Get this shirt off me. It's covered with the stuff."

Sylvia concentrated on not laughing. "First off, Arthur, hand me the pipe. And then we can—"

He threw the drainpipe into the sink, where it banged against the wrench. He shook his arms free of her grasp. "It's not water. It's a whole entire bottle of that drain cleaner. Just take it off from the back and let me get to the shower. And wash your hands. Or run them under water for an hour. You can't touch this stuff like it's just water, Sylvia. Could you get this shirt off my back?"

"They couldn't sell it if it was as bad as all that, Arthur. They can't sell lye as if it's household detergent."

"Have you ever read one of those bottles?" Arthur turned to Sylvia as she pulled off his wet shirt. "Read the label and wash your hands well. I can't believe you don't know that." He seized this opportunity to instruct his wife, holding his arms away from his body, as if she might remove them next. "It's industrial strength and it cannot be used in plastic piping. The whole idea behind a product like this—"

Sylvia couldn't help herself. She laughed. "The whole idea is so you don't have to dismantle the kitchen sink every time a carrot falls down the drain, isn't it?"

He grabbed his shirt, threw it in the garbage pail he'd removed from the cabinet beneath the sink, shook his head to make it clear this was a terrible waste. "Thank you for the wrench. I'm going to shower."

"I'll make coffee, and I promise to wash my hands." She'd adopted a pouty voice, hoping a mock flirtation would eclipse

the minor disaster. Arthur did not respond. She got the coffeepot and, hearing the rush of water to the shower upstairs,
she added, "I notice your arms haven't fallen off yet." She
turned the cold water tap, and before she thought to place the
pot beneath the spigot, several cool quarts cascaded through
the open-ended pipe onto the bricklike linoleum floor. The
stupidity of staring at the disconnected joint in the sink as
water soaked her canvas shoes tipped Sylvia's emotional balance. As if he were a wicked child standing in her way, she
screamed, "Arthur! Arthur, what are you doing?"

She hadn't wiped the floor or even filled the coffeepot when
she heard her husband racing down the stairs.

"What happened? What did you do?"

Arthur's voice came to her across years, not accusingly but
frightened. Confused by his arrival, Sylvia did not move. "I
don't think anything happened. Did it?"

"You screamed."

There was Arthur, holding a small white bath towel as a
weapon he could use to defend his wife. His hair was slicked
back from his face and his skin shone, wet and red. Even in
the calm silence, he stood at the ready, his thick legs set in an
apprehensive crouch. "You're okay." He was disappointed.

"I'm okay." Sylvia repeated the phrase, to convince herself.
In fact, she still was confused by his presence. He looked improbably handsome. What she'd thoughtlessly ascribed to
middle-age weight gain and the inevitable sagging of lines and
angles now seemed to her a ripening. He had informed the
athletic contours of his youth. She could imagine the taut-
ness of his flexed thigh muscles, the slight give of his barrel
chest under the weight of her head.

"You don't sound okay."

She felt ridiculous in his handsome, naked presence. She
was afraid he would see she'd harbored in her mind a weaker,
sadder version of him. "It's Stephen. That's what made me
scream." She simply could not make sense of her desire to be
held by him, to be protected. She had never considered that he
might just be capable of withstanding her dismissals, circum-

venting her refusal to be bound to him. "And I've made something of a mess here. Aren't you cold?"

He just stared at her.

"Maybe I should shower, too. I mean, I'm halfway there as it is."

Arthur wanted to pull her to him. He could see it, the aftermath, his arms crossed against her back. But he was not sure he could do it quickly, with force enough to countermand her reflexive jolt away. He walked slowly to the sink, looked underneath, tied the towel around his waist. "I saw how this was draining too slow. And my first thought was, Who cares? But, even if he is in some real trouble, and even if he doesn't want to deal with us, I have to fix the drain. I have to keep going and hope I think of some way I can help him out. Right?"

The spell was broken. "Fixing a drain is not exactly an act of treason, if that's what you mean." Sylvia did not look at him. She'd found her voice. "But no matter what either of us may admit or think, I hope we can agree on one thing. He does not belong in jail. Whether this is a mistake or Stephen really got it in his head to deface private property is not so important as—"

"What about the kingdom in another world comment? And the moneylenders business the *Courier* couldn't resist?" Arthur immediately regretted his aggressive posture. "Though it could be that Steve was being sarcastic. In fact, that's a good guess, I think."

"Guessing is a great help right now." Sylvia raised her hands and tilted her head, to make it clear she couldn't be blamed for sounding cynical. "I don't know what he's up to exactly. But I can promise you this—I am tired of not having a way into this. I am not going to read about my son in the newspapers for the next month. I am going to make something happen. It's not as if because he won't see us the two of us have to play dead. If he needs help, that's one thing."

Arthur saw she was really years away from him. The arms crossed against her back were a young man's arms. Chastened, he said, "How can he not need help?"

IV

ALISON GREETED HER HUSBAND at the front door. "This is a weekend, for God's sake. Do you know it's after six? My mother invited us for dinner, and since you didn't punch in your direct line at the office I couldn't get through. I left the kids with Liz. We're meant to be there at seven. All right?"

Roger looked at Alison as if she had been speaking a foreign language. The very mention of Sylvia and Arthur caused him to shut down entirely. "I think dinner there is not the best idea, Al." He knew this was no matter for casual dismissal, especially at this late hour, but he hoped a quick kiss and request for sympathy might win him release from the evening's event. "I've spent half the day trying to figure out why the firm took on the contested estate of a Stockbridge dowager who has been dead for more than three years, and the other half on the phone with Jack Pasternini."

Alison recognized the name of the recently elected district attorney. "About Stephen? Talking to Pasternini about Stephen?" She followed her husband to the kitchen at the back of the house.

Roger sat at the kitchen table, waited for his wife to arrive. "Yes, about Stephen. And I really think something can be worked out, though this is really not for publication, Al."

She stemmed the urge to pry. She respected Roger's professional integrity. She even understood his exasperation with her parents' repeated attempts to make him divulge something pertinent about Stephen's version of the events that landed him in jail. But she was increasingly unable to abide Roger's refusal to admit her to the inner sanctum. "Why say you were on the phone with Pasternini at all, then? Play your FBI games, if that's what you think matters."

"Where are the kids? You said something about them earlier."

"Funny, but all day long they wanted to know where you were. I went to see Liz. They're going to spend the night with her and little Lizzie." Alison finally sat opposite her husband. "On account of us going to dinner, I left them there."

Roger practically had conceded dinner, in trade for her silence on the Stephen issue. "How is Liz?"

"Painting like mad. Talking a lot. I don't think she can get a handle on David being dead. Especially him coming back there in the end to, what? To die, I guess."

Roger held Liz responsible for the demise of her marriage to David, and he did not doubt that David's fatal cancer had been incited by the divorce. "I think of David."

"The house is absolutely haunted by him. The couch where he slept all those days, and little Lizzie making crayon pictures—and, the whole thing is too sad." Alison stood, to interrupt herself. She'd been on the verge of describing Liz's new young lover. What Roger did not need was one more objectionable fact about Liz to use against her. "I had a stupid— well, a sort of ugly legal question. For you."

Roger stared at Alison, trying to convey the futility of asking about Stephen's case.

"Is Liz David's widow now?"

Roger smiled, then realized how inappropriate a smile would seem. "No. They were divorced."

"But she is technically widowed by him dying. And, I mean, they lived together, to the extent David was alive."

"You must be hanging around lawyers too much. To the extent he was alive?"

Alison was used to Roger's finding her crass. She counted it among his affectations. "The answer is still, No, I guess."

"Liz was his ex-wife."

Alison sat again. "Death certainly makes fools of people. Honestly, what is the point of divorcing when you'll both end up dead, after all is said and done?"

"That's the long-term wisdom, I guess."

Unthinkingly, Alison disagreed. "No, it's my daily view."

"Of marriage?" Roger was suddenly interested in the topic.

"You know what I mean." Alison said this lightly, believing Roger did understand.

Reassured, he let himself relax. "Stephen probably won't be prosecuted, Al. Please, please—nothing about this tonight. I can tell you more, all I know, really, after I speak to Pasternini again tomorrow. I think that with a promise of counseling, maybe psychiatric evaluation . . ."

Alison recognized this as her opportunity. She warned herself not to overplay her hand. "A court-appointed shrink?"

"I think they'll make that a stipulation, at least the initial conference. But I don't think it's unreasonable for them to demand something long term. Private or otherwise."

Alison pulled two glasses from a cabinet. "You want to split a beer?"

"Yeah, perfect." He smiled, watched her stretch her thin torso and raise her arm above her head. "The truth of it is none of this was my initiative. I mean, Stephen wouldn't let me help him, really. Or talk to me. I just described various outcomes. There must be some pressure on the district attorney's office."

Alison finished pouring before she spoke. "Lucky, I guess." She sensed she was nearing the center of the story. "Political pressure, you mean?"

Roger had forwarded the pressure theory casually. Now he felt stuck with it. "I wouldn't be told, obviously. It's not the sort of thing a new D.A. wants to advertise."

Alison adopted the theory without further scrutiny. She worked to dispel the emotions overtaking her, the familiar anger and humiliation that had never found voice, whose objects had always eluded her. Imitating a movie actress, she delivered the beer to Roger, walked to the counter. With her back to her husband, she said, "It makes you wonder who the powerful people in this city are, doesn't it?"

"I guess so. It is lucky for Stephen, no matter what."

"Isn't it odd that someone wanted to help him out? Even in this indirect way?" Alison was anxious for a reprieve. Without forewarning, she'd come upon an exit ramp, a chance to find her way back to the beginning of the endless road she'd traveled since her family's fall from grace.

Roger sucked at his beer. He'd all but dismissed the likelihood of political pressure. "You never know who is helping whom. Anyway, all that doesn't have to do with Stephen."

Alison countered sharply. "This has everything to do with Stephen. That much is pretty damn clear." She regretted her tone, shrugged her shoulders to distance herself from the outburst. "No matter what the intended effect, though, it is going to help him. Right?"

Roger could not see into Alison's torment. He could only see the surface pain, her frustration. As best he could tell, she was repressing her emotions—embarrassment principal among them—out of loyalty to her brother and as a sort of instructive pose for her parents. "Stephen is going to be all right, Al. I really believe that."

"I'd like to believe what's true. For a change. Let's put on the armor for dinner."

V

SYLVIA STOOD OVER ARTHUR, who was stretched out on the blue divan. In a slightly louder than normal voice, she repeated his name. She knew that, short of shaking him and poking him with the half-empty fifth of rum she'd picked up off the low coffee table, this was her only chance of rousing him. It was a method she'd developed when Jane and Alison became teenagers who could sleep through any alarm or loud noise. They'd dubbed it the Adamski Water Torture. Sylvia used it to save herself a trip upstairs every morning while in the midst of preparing breakfast.

Arthur knew he was not dreaming, but he could not imagine what was making him so uncomfortable. He finally opened his eyes, saw Sylvia's thick, stockinged legs and the lower half of her blue skirt.

"They're on their way, Arthur."

"I'm drunk by now, dear. Just tell them I ate something." He stood slowly, not wanting to wake completely. "I have a funny feeling I might be in the mood for a nap at this time of day. Once I get it in my head I'm going to have the time of my life, you can never get me under the shower, now that you think of it."

Sylvia moved so he could make his wordy way to the bedroom without an annoying detour. She was long since convinced he drank because he was sick. A month or, in this case, a year of sobriety signaled nothing in the way of a cure. She figured if she were an alcoholic, this would be a banner day for getting drunk. In its sad way it made sense to her. It was not even enough of a disappointment to interfere with her dinner plans. She capped the rum and went to the kitchen to check her roast.

"Arthur drank too much and I can hardly blame him." Sylvia formulated this sentence carefully, weeding through a variety of simple, declarative explanations. When she finally spoke it to Roger and Alison, they lost the hearty good cheer they'd worked up for the evening. Seeing her guests deflate, Sylvia suggested they sit and eat without delay, thinking she might capitalize on the realistic atmosphere.

She allowed herself to be engaged in a few minutes of light chat about her daughter's friend Liz, then launched her offensive. "Roger, you'll at least credit me for not asking sooner. Agreed?" Sylvia only paused briefly. Roger had snapped to attention, and she did not want to give him time to set ground rules. "I don't need to know why you chose to get involved on Stephen's behalf. That is your business, after all." She let her voice trail off, avoided Alison's stare.

Roger smiled, tired in advance. "It was Stephen's choice, Sylvia, not mine. There's nothing to explain."

Sylvia had her first answer.

"Mom, you know he'd tell you anything he could. If there was anything to tell." Since her mother would not look at her, Alison turned to Roger. She wanted him to know he owed her nothing here. What she could not translate into a facial expression was her idea that he did owe it to his wife to tell her things first.

"I know you're in a terrible position, Roger." Sylvia offered him a bowl of potatoes. "I don't have to explain what I think of my own position." Here she ventured a quick look at her daughter. "Of course, the entire city of Pittsfield now knows what he said to the judge yesterday. And I guess I could just wait to hear a radio report about his next appearance in court. I mean, for the trial."

"There probably won't be a trial." Alison dismissed the possibility as a hysterical prediction.

Roger watched Sylvia receive this information which betrayed his pose of ignorance. He was revealed, defenseless.

Sylvia let the awkward seconds pass unaided. She shook her head, then laid her knife and fork on the white tablecloth. "I'm being naïve. I'm meant not to know certain things." She stood and lifted her plate. "I'm just going to plug in the coffeepot. Heat the pie." She wouldn't look at either of them.

Roger and Alison exchanged weak smiles. What could be done? Only a plaster wall separated them from Sylvia. It was no time for a strategy session. She might walk back into the room at any minute.

Alison rolled her eyes and folded the linen napkin, her white flag. She would not interfere again. Roger was on his own.

Roger wanted to protect Alison from herself, really. He thought it made sense to confide in Sylvia, seeing that he had nothing but good news. He could make her believe Alison knew nothing, that he alone had withheld information.

Sylvia allowed them to make their presentation without interruption. She even let Alison speculate on the possibility of political pressure on the district attorney. She knew more now. She was convinced that years of patience had been rewarded.

Only to tease herself, to thrill to her secret, Sylvia asked, "I wonder who would do such a thing, though, Alison. Maybe Roger is right. Maybe it doesn't matter at all who did it."

Roger was annoyed to see his offhand suggestion of unfriendly persuasion emerging again. "If anyone did anything unusual."

Sylvia was uninterested in his weak retraction. The presence of Judge Martin Parris in the machinations was beyond Roger's comprehension. Though she'd settled for undisclosed, unacknowledged proof of his existence, Parris had come back into her life.

Alison and Roger were standing at the front door, promising to call with news from Pasternini. Sylvia clung to the doorjamb, certain she would otherwise run out into her yard and prance along Holmes Road. She let herself be kissed, watched her silhouetted guests darken and disappear into the night. Before they were out of range, she yelled, "Have a lovely night. Come again." She kissed her hand and raised it, feeling every bit the grande dame of the Berkshires, the luckiest woman in the world.

VI

SYLVIA WOKE IN A SWEAT. She turned to Arthur. Only his red face was not covered by the blanket. It was Sylvia's contention that a man gives off a disproportionate amount of heat at night, making it impossible for his partner to sleep in comfort. Hoping for a sudden chill of relief, she raised the two windows facing Dorothy Hammerstone's neat brick house. But no exchange occurred. The air was of a piece. She went back and stripped both sheet and blanket from Arthur, draped them over the bedposts to dry.

Arthur did not move.

As far as Sylvia was concerned, a man as handsome as Arthur didn't have to so much as move in this world. Bad luck, shame, suspicion, disfavor—any and even all of life's indignities might attend the handsome man. But he could always retreat, seek repose, and with no additional effort secure his unassailable place in the world. Sylvia knew no man was above reproach, least of all Arthur. But, to her astonishment, to this day, she could discount his faults and frailty, seeing so much beauty.

Quietly, so not to rouse him, but aloud, she said, "Good morning, Arthur. Today is the second Sunday of October. And both of us are still here. What do you make of that?" She showered, dressed, and left for Sunday Mass, the one that counted after all.

Arthur did not open his eyes until she closed the back door. Awake for more than an hour, he went to the open window and looked down as her high-heeled shoes clicked along the drive. He attempted to formulate a prayer on her behalf but he muffed it, ended up begging her forgiveness.

In the kitchen, Arthur found a note from Sylvia under his highball glass. *The drain is working like new. Maybe everything is not beyond repair.* It was her way of excusing if not forgiving him. Arthur factored the note into his batting average. As always, he was hitting around .500, a drunken strikeout balanced against a show of manual dexterity. He knew it was an arguable statistical trick, but he'd learned to live with the umpire's generosity.

Into the empty glass he poured two fingers of cold maple syrup. Bracing himself with one hand on the cool metal lip of the sink, he drank the dose. It required three goes at the glass, peering at the recalcitrant amber clot. This was an antidote Arthur had concocted for drunkenness. As he'd explained it to Sylvia (who since made a habit of setting out the empty glass), drinking the syrup recreated the queasiness of his first encounter with straight rum. It prevented a mistake giving way to a binge.

Arthur rinsed the glass with warm water and wished he could do the same for his mouth. Of course, the aftertaste was part of the effectiveness of the treatment. He did not take a mouthful of water, but neither did he make the supposedly requisite call to his peer counselor, Bob Gastineau. Should Sylvia make a point of asking, he was prepared to pretend he'd spoken to Bob. But never was the wisdom of drinking himself down more compelling than in the midst of a support session.

Years ago, Arthur had succumbed to Sylvia's diagnosis of his weakness. He'd joined fourteen adult alcoholics for a few months of weekly meetings, attended the Berkshire Medical Center's weekend clinic for recovering drunkards (the tough label the staff psychologist applied, as a form of social shock therapy). He'd even called Gastineau a few times, though each conversation was strictly experimental; Arthur tested the healing waters by inventing nights of debauchery. In all, he earned high marks from his rescuers.

Waiting for Sylvia to return with the Sunday paper, to check the level of syrup in the clear glass bottle into which a tin of Vermont's finest had been decanted, Arthur let himself resurrect his parents in the statuette form he loved. He saw the arc of their heads and shoulders from below, as if they were a wave about to break over him. More than any dissenting opinion, Arthur trusted this, his measure of sincerity: He looked at their faces and he felt no shame.

He'd heard all about denial and repression and old-fashioned lying. But when he came down to it, he knew he was not a drunk.

The telephone ringing delivered him to the present. "Hello. Arthur Adamski here."

"Dad? It's Alison. You sound ready for business this morning."

"Why not?"

Alison laughed to expedite things. "Anyway, I was calling to invite us over there. Roger has a good report." She was annoyed her father did not interrupt with surprise or gratitude. "About Stephen, Dad. Roger has good news and we thought we would walk over and talk to you and Mom. We figured you could use some good news today."

Arthur received this as an indictment of his impotence and unconcern: What had he done for his son since the arrest? "Is everything all right? I mean, nothing happened to him in that jail?"

"Is that an invitation? Is Mom there?"

"She should be back from Mass any minute now."

"Are you up for guests? Should we come a little later?"

"Why wouldn't we want you to come?" Arthur did not wait for an answer. "Me, you mean? I'm ready for anything. Nothing a good night's sleep won't cure. Or help, I mean. Do you want to come right now?"

Alison could only wish she'd waited until Sylvia was home. "My God, this is beginning to sound like a meeting of Congress. I'll bring something to eat. Danish?"

"Do you want me to have your mother call you about that?"

Alison shook the receiver in the air, even made faces at the mouthpiece. "Half an hour. With some sweet rolls. It's meant to be good news, Dad."

"We could use some of that. I'll get the coffee going. Are the kids with you?"

"They're staying with Liz for the morning." Alison considered Liz's home a safe house, where her children could wait out the trouble. "Half an hour?"

"Fine then." Arthur hung up, reached for his glass, put it away, out of sight. He picked up the note Sylvia had left, gratuitously ran some water down the drain. Maybe Sylvia was right. Maybe everything could be repaired.

VII

SYLVIA AND ALISON worked quickly to assemble the elements of the ad hoc brunch. They both knew the optimal setting for discussion of Stephen's release called for everyone's being seated at the dining-room table, every utensil and potentially useful condiment within reach.

Arthur appeared from the living room as Sylvia unplugged the percolator and followed Roger and Alison to the dining room. Roger clapped a hand on Arthur's shoulder, sharing a manly bewilderment at the pace of the kitchen performance.

Sylvia was the last to sit. "Well, that was easy."

"Easy?" Roger poured juice for everyone. "You two are frightening in a kitchen together."

"I hate anyone in the kitchen with me but Alison. The way you see some people stare up into their own cupboards as if they can't for the life of them figure out how everything got there?"

"Or the ones who rummage through the garbage?" Alison was ladling fruit into her bowl. "Liz is famous for throwing out some box and then having to dig after it, to figure out how long to boil frozen peas. Or one stirring spoon for four pots? And maybe half the chopped onions were scooped off the floor?"

"I don't know why some people bother to cook at all." Sylvia said so without soliciting further comment. She stood and topped off coffee cups. Her manner was so perfunctory she might just as well have announced her intention to get down to business. The scene had been set. Anticipation peaked.

Alison was a student of her mother's sense of drama. She knew it was hers to cue Roger. "Everyone wants to be the bearer of good news, but Roger has the details straight."

Arthur said, "Is this finally about Stephen?"

"No, Arthur. Roger is making a run for the presidency." Sylvia turned her attention from Arthur to Stephen, and this was enough to alter her mood. Almost pitifully happy, she said, "He's really coming home?"

"Not unconditionally, but yes. As of tomorrow. I think he's scheduled for release around noon. There will be some exit meetings. And an evaluation by a court-appointed psychologist. That's a condition of the release. But Pasternini"—Roger turned to Arthur here—"the new district attorney? He's seeing to it that all charges are dropped. Rabbi Sisitkin is relieved, apparently. He didn't want Stephen persecuted."

Alison nimbly corrected her husband. "Or prosecuted, presumably. It's a Reform congregation."

"What did I say? Persecuted?" Roger let out his trademark giggle. This spoiled his effect, denatured an otherwise reassuring, literal-minded performance. It made people suspect he was toying with them.

Arthur forced a chuckle. "Maybe Stephen would prefer 'persecuted.'" He'd retreated to an ironic distance by default. There was no place for him in the foreground.

"Stephen is being released and the charges are dropped, Arthur. Or weren't you listening?" Sylvia was already planning her reunion with her son. She envisioned introducing him to Martin Parris, the source to which she'd traced the court's leniency, a source only she could name. "I think this ought to give us all a chance to take a deep breath. Stephen has a lot of decisions to make about his future. What with the leave from college and all. Maybe this is his chance to wipe the slate clean. He deserves that much, Arthur."

Alison could see the ancient feud was on again. She knew from experience Sylvia would not allow it to be fought as an open exchange. And neither parent would admit the child, age and loyalty notwithstanding. Years of failed attempts to intervene as either ally or impartial mediator—Alison would have adopted any stance in exchange for the essential facts—had taught her to beware of even witness status. Arthur and Sylvia had spent the better part of their married lives waging holy war. The only convention of this war was absolute secrecy, maintained by both combatants.

After a respectable silence, Roger spoke. "It is true the record will show the charges have been dropped. But the evaluation is mandatory." He considered this for a few seconds. "I mean, this will not follow Stephen. In that sense, it is erased."

Arthur raised his juice glass, a mock toast. "Well, that is very nice. I, for one, am just waiting for someone to figure out how to erase Saturday's newspaper. Maybe erase his wisecrack about kingdoms in another world. Or just . . . erase it all. Everything." From no distance would it be safe to call for erasing Stephen. "But I suppose I'm being negative. Spoiling the fun, as you might say, dear. Spoiling things again." Arthur was virtually talking to himself.

"There is nothing else in the way of facts until I hear from the D.A. I'll pass on exact times and all that. Oh, and Stephen has not been told." Roger jerked his head up, giggled again. "Of course, someone will have to tell him."

Alison laughed, as if she understood the humor. "As of this morning, he didn't know. I'm sure he does by now. I think the idea is not to talk about this, except among ourselves. Until it is official. That is the idea."

Sylvia said, "I'll do my best. Though I'm not so used to keeping happy secrets. Maybe it will be fun. Really." She reached for a small pastry, then handed the tray to Arthur. "Alison, do you remember when you and Roger were trying to keep it quiet about moving back here from Boston? So Roger could . . . was it because he was looking into another firm?"

"It was the one and only firm. I just didn't want Phelps senior and junior to think they could get me cheaply. I guess I was playing hard to get."

Pastry circulated. Brunch resumed. Certain she'd evaded Arthur's attacks and effectively postponed a second assault, Sylvia excused herself to make a pot of coffee, trusting the momentum to sustain itself. From her post in the kitchen, she listened to Roger's unfailingly shocking tales about the ineptitude of T. Scott Phelps, the junior member of the prestigious Phelps & Phelps partnership. Even Arthur was drawn in. As the first of the hot water popped into the plastic hood, Sylvia backed away until she was propped up by the sink. Ordinarily, her successful orchestration of a return to normal relations would have satisfied her. She goaded herself toward happiness with plans for Stephen's return to family life.

It was no use. Something had gone wrong with Stephen, inside Stephen. Tempting as it was, she could not cast him as an impetuous vandal with a penchant for wisecracks. His refusal to see her was his warning, a grenade in his hand. And why hadn't Martin Parris declared himself? Did he believe any number of years could dissemble his presence?

Arthur walked into the kitchen trailed by laughter. He was

beaming. By way of explanation to his startled wife, he said, "More office stories."

Sylvia managed to say, "The coffee."

Still smiling, Arthur whispered, "Who did Roger say it was? Last night? Did he say who arranged this little miracle?"

Sylvia pressed hard against the sink. "Neither of them knows. There may not have been any political pressure on anybody."

"We're not the Rockefellers and Carnegies here, Sylvia. The political weight we carry was bought and paid for. Why don't you give us a guess?"

Sylvia knew what she had to do. She must remember that the hand is quicker than the eye. He mustn't see her move a muscle. In less time than he required to blink, she would reach in and choke off her heart. And she would still look like a woman, still sound like a woman. That was the real magic she had to perform. Like any great trick, it appeared effortless.

"If Roger doesn't know, Sylvia, we could clue him in. Professional courtesy or something. Sylvia?"

"Martin Parris rolled over you once, Arthur. Then he rolled over me a few dozen times. What makes you think he even knows either of us is alive?"

"It has his signature. Doesn't it? The whole thing being nameless. That's why we both know."

Sylvia sensed she had few bloodless seconds left. "Then this is the first time you and I have shared so much as a fact. Have a drink on me, Arthur."

Arthur turned away, ashamed for her and for himself. He ripped the plug out of the wall by jerking the handle of the percolator. Cord and all, he returned to the dining room, said nothing to disturb the frightened, unrewarded silence.

Sylvia let the rush of blood fill her, swayed as her body recovered from the strain she'd caused it. It scared her to know she was still not too old to perform such a trick.

First Trimester

THE DISPOSAL of the land and trees in the largest valley of the Berkshire Hills excites illusions of isolation. Not awesome or austere, the place is snug, its boundary hills never more than a day's hike away. A nearly treeless small plateau rises at the point deemed to be the center, or near enough to merit designation as the center of the city founded here in 1761. Fittingly, the first church is erected on this little height of land, a stone's throw from a lone prodigious tree assigned a civic status as The Old Elm. The area is dubbed Park Square, though topographically it is a circle; and it is widely known, though unregarded, that Old Elm predates Pittsfield and its founders' dreams. Forging a heritage requires men to shape the facts at their disposal.

The Calvinist congregation in First Church enjoys unrivaled stature. Having masterminded the Great Awakening, Jonathan Edwards moves to the Berkshires in his final years to produce his masterpiece, *The Freedom of the Will*. The first book composed in the country, it appears to be the final buttress in the congregation's bid for immortality.

But the Awakening is channeled democratically through the revolutionary nation, reviving Baptists, Lutherans, and Shakers. The plateau at Pittsfield's center becomes a staging ground for temples of increasing splendor. The grander second First Church rings The Old Elm in the company of brethren sects and secular brethren. First Agricultural Bank, Berkshire Medical Institution, and City Hall fill the gaps between the many churches.

Divided by denomination and united under one God by political decree, the faithful work and worship in a circle bordering the unpaved road that rings the fenced-in park. The Old Elm, an artifact of nature and of history, stands enormous in this context.

By 1861, the city is connected to the swelling nation by a railroad and a rift. Before the Pittsfield Centennial is celebrated, the first Western Massachusetts soldiers called to service in the Civil War assemble at Park Square. None of these intrepid men foresees the successfully united states looking past New England, looking south for cheaper textiles, to the West for large-scale farms to feed their growth.

In 1861, a bolt of lightning strikes the isolated Old Elm. Its splintered trunk is dug up, hauled across the split-beam fencing, and dragged down the road a ways.

Abandoned mills and family farms in outlying Berkshire towns back into the future on the merits of the ancient reclaimed legacy of nature. Refashioned as resorts and spas and summer homes, they offer respite from the crowds and clamor of prosperity in Pennsylvania and New York. Towels from the Carolinas, mass-manufactured Texas sheets, and prime beef slaughtered in Chicago acquire country charm in rooms replete with rustic beams, open hearths, and six-over-six wavy windows overlooking static waterwheels and horse-drawn plows.

But lightning struck in Pittsfield. Pioneering patrons of the country's first electric company, Pittsfield's people are not disposed toward the quaint fate of their neighbors. The well-lit city manages to attract attention, and the General Electric company arrives with the twentieth century. And, unnaturally enough, lightning strikes a second time. GE engineers produce one million volts of manmade lightning, win the city headlines as the The High Voltage Capital of the World.

Lightning striking twice: The future looks so bright in artificial light.

But circles and parallel lines are drawn over time by men. Chronological ironies are manmade, too.

In 1961, Pittsfield's bicentennial is heralded by a world-record power-line transmission ignited at the city's second center, the maze of transformer labs and factories. A mile northwest, at Park Square, a second elm is planted. High school bands and decorated fire trucks parade around the park, leading union workers sporting light-bulb tiaras, in homage to that incoherent light source as a symbol of invention.

The marching men have yet to learn that one year earlier the frontier of the future they envision was pierced by a co-herent beam of light shot forward by the world's first success-ful laser.

Even the most durable of their symbols fails them.

Time surrounds Pittsfield. The locals hold their ground as unformed futures travel through them and materialize as the past, as if they are themselves transformers. They pose resis-tance, direct conductance, expend themselves to make some-thing of the unremitting power they receive.

Looking back on what they've made, they see the past is not enough. It fails to represent their efforts and intentions, their ambitions and their fondest hopes. It needs a history.

Dreams do not belong to time. They are created for the future, which will not have them. Seeing them unrealized, the dreamers wrap them around the disappointing past. Like as many gifts, these are delivered to the unreceptive future.

Histories are just dreams of transformation.

Presently, the untransformed plywood table commands Arthur's attention. Picking at the layered paint, he recalls his many promises to sand and refinish the surface. He suspends his excavation when he realizes Sylvia is no longer reading the Saturday *Courier*. She is staring at him. A year after moving his wife and three children to this house on Holmes Road, he's done nothing more than mindlessly pry loose some chips.

He swipes the paper from his wife, rubs his index finger up and down a few columns, then yells, "Here it is!" He pretends to read. "Sources close to Adamski say the end is in sight. All repairs will be completed before the end of 1963." He drops the newspaper to gauge her reaction.

"Oh, the table? The paint, you mean?"

Still hoping to amuse her, he scratches the surface with the blade of his butter knife. "No time like the present."

"It's a start, I suppose." Sylvia smiles her confusion. Three days of similarly awkward, exaggerated exchanges have convinced her she's been found out. So she smiles, daring him to cast a stone at his live-in infidel. She means to warn him, to make him see it would be her pleasure to confess. "You only mean the table, then. I thought you meant something else, about the present."

Sylvia's tactics are lost on Arthur. He barely can look at her, never mind intuit secrets. He has a confession of his own. "Well, for instance, the business isn't exactly running smoothly. To say the least."

"For instance?" Sylvia readies herself, squares her shoulders. Arthur has raised the standard of the business; the name of Martin Parris will be hoisted up above her. She resolves to pledge allegiance to her lover, Arthur's partner.

"I mean, for instance, maybe I was right all along. About not knowing enough to start a company like Insulum. The fact is, I don't actually know the first thing about making better insulation for the core of a transformer. Or even exactly what goes on at the center of a modern transformer. God knows, I've read about it all. I can even give you the impression I get the gist of it, at least. The truth is, I negotiated contracts with the General Electric. I signed documents and made promises and do you know what this adds up to, Sylvia?"

"A year of hard work, a new house, a partnership in a lucrative new venture. That's what you told me a year ago, when you left the GE with Martin. But I'm guessing you've got a new total, right?"

"Right. Only it's a negative number."

Unnerved by his childlike refusal to state his case, Sylvia moves from her defensive posture in the corner of the alcove, slides along the bench until she is facing him directly. "You mean your contract with the General Electric fell through?"

"Oh no."

"You can't afford to fill the orders? Somehow, this Insulum material is too expensive for you to make?"

"Sylvia, we never set out to make it. It's the process for making it, for applying it to existing manufacturing—"

"Yes, Arthur. But semantics aside. The negative numbers?"

"That was just a turn of the phrase. I don't mean we're losing money exactly. I don't think Martin or I expected not to lose some money this year, even next year. When you consider the profits we projected for 1965? We could live with some losses. It's not a money thing, no."

"Arthur? Let's agree on the fact that I am an idiot who knows nothing about business. You don't have to keep laboring at that point." Sylvia is not sure why she's holding on to his hands, except perhaps to shake loose his still undisclosed problem. "But could we skip the part about the accounting futures and tell me what the hell is bothering you?"

He pulls her hands toward him, somehow receives from them assurance of support. "Of course, it made sense that I should be the one signing off on everything. I did it every day while I was at the GE. I was hardly the first product supervisor in history who didn't completely understand the machines and the inner workings of what have you. I *represented* the products for the company." Arthur hopes his emphasis conveys the limits of his expertise. "Martin and I saw our chance to get off on our own and, of course, it would be me initialing spec sheets, drafting the sales pitch. Martin is a lawyer. He forms the company, I represent the material—I mean, the process. You see? How many times did Martin ask me to verify this was a new material, a new process for improving transformer efficiency? Had I been over it with other engineers? Could I guarantee it was proprietary?" Arthur refuses to let Sylvia withdraw her hands. "I am the product supervisor. Martin dug up the engineer with the idea, with the brains. Martin formed a company. And let's face it, Sylvia, he gave up a fat salary as a corporate staff attorney—"

She yanks her hands away, to shut him down. "Martin Parris came to you after he had the parts in place. Martin knew just what he was doing. He had to. He's too smart to throw over a career on a whim, or some technicality. Arthur, in plain language—not as the supervisor, just as yourself—what is going wrong?"

Bolstered by her conviction of his innocence, he relinquishes the simple truth. "Insulum is a direct patent infringement. Apparently it's plain as day. The engineer sold us a fancy package of pirated work. Not only his own work—which was bought and paid for by GE, since he's worked there for about ten years—but it was the collective work of a whole damn department. That is the idea inside the fancy package he sold to us."

"To Martin Parris. Martin sold it to you."

"Me. The product supervisor. You see? Christ, this Insulum material would sell itself. Martin could have signed on with a shoe salesman to pitch this stuff. It sells itself. It was up to me to verify, to be sure it was an authentic, new thing in the world. You see? I signed everything, Sylvia."

"And the upshot of this? Where does it leave you?"

"I guess, in plain language, I've sort of committed fraud. And maybe more, since we have money from this we can't return. I mean, spent money." Arthur feels claustrophobic in the alcove, lowers his voice to a whisper. "It's like I did something really amazing."

"Knowingly? Intentionally?"

"No. You see, that's why it's so amazing. I just don't know what I really meant to do."

Sylvia fails to keep him in focus as an adult, a husband, a partner in a touted new local business. She sees he is another manchild in the world, reluctantly facing his mother. "It's a little hard to believe, Arthur. I mean, either you intended to defraud someone or not. The middle ground is pretty narrow."

"I said that was the amazing part." He hopes she can appreciate how confusing it is to be the subject of such a mystery.

"You can look at me all you want, Arthur. I can hardly tell you what you knew. I can tell you I find it hard to know what to say. Am I supposed to do something?"

"You mean to help me?"

His willingness to be a child undoes her. "No, that's not exactly what I had in mind. I had in mind the fact that we have a fancy new house in a fancy new neighborhood and three children and you damn well better know something soon. And have you got a lawyer is another thing I mean."

"Sylvia, Martin is certainly a better lawyer than—"

"Stop it! Martin Parris?" She is up and out of the alcove; from several feet away, she turns on him. "Life just isn't this amazing by itself, Arthur. Could you at least entertain a doubt about Martin and his intentions?" She is crying. She sees his innocence. "I need to go, get out. The children? What is it? Two o'clock? The girls won't be back till five. Artie? I don't know, stay here?"

"Sylvia, it might not be nearly as bad as it seems. I bet I can work out a deal. Martin is working on some friends right now."

"You just didn't know what you were doing. That's the worst of it right now. Not knowing what you're doing. It's so dangerous." She pulls the keys from a hook under the cabinet and runs out to the car.

The twenty minutes driving herself to Becket, to Martin's country home, are spent in a series of imagined confrontations. Sylvia prepares the accusations she will level, anticipating Parris's responses. In every plausible defense, she detects a phrase or attitude that proves her allegation: Martin betrayed Arthur.

Of course, no imagined degree of prowess or verbosity will deflect attention from her own betrayal. Even in her least evenhanded casting of Martin, she cannot see him being dull enough to overlook the irony of Mrs. Adamski riding on a wave of righteousness.

A woman cannot betray a man. Marriage is just a sacramental betrayal, anyway. At least infidelity is not a crime. A sin of passion is more easily forgiven.

She finds no rationale to vindicate herself, but her conviction is unaltered: Adultery is the natural, forgivable, or at least predictable sin. She's determined that, should inspiration fail her, she will simply state the obvious: Martin's is the grievous sin, as even he must understand.

After she parks in his driveway, behind the noisily idling tractorlike lawnmower, she understands what she has done.

Unwittingly, she has offended the implicit rules of their affair. She has arrived without warning. This makes her feel daring, even brave. Proud of her offense, she climbs aboard the vibrating metal seat of the lawnmower, remembering his prohibition against whims and enthusiasms that might compromise his reputation, his new business, his real life.

Within minutes Martin appears at the propped-open front door of his low white house. He runs to her, reaches up and turns off the rumbling engine. "I just got off the phone with him. Arthur. He called me. I half expected you might be on your way."

Feeling jaunty and happily scandalous, Sylvia swivels on the seat and crosses her legs. "What did the other half expect?"

"Why don't we go inside?" He can see she is giddy. He is familiar with her nervous juggling of moods. He's watched her offer reckless passion, unfounded hope, and ineffable sadness in the first moments of their time alone. It might be the self-conscious draping of his cardigan on the back of Arthur's favorite chair, the way she takes the telephone receiver from its cradle on her way to draw a window shade, or tightening his tie knot and pulling at the shoulders of his blazer: She tosses up her contradictory feelings to distract him while she establishes her presence.

"Why inside? It's the first Saturday of April. Why don't I head off for the south forty?" She is yelling, as if the motor were running.

"I have iced tea. I made it. Real tea."

"With the business collapsing, I figured I'd better learn to do some practical work around here. Something more skilled than my usual services."

"You mean you can do more?" He laughs, embarrassed by his voice, powered up to match her volume. "Why are we yelling?"

She shouts. "Instead of crying, you mean? Because we're adults, like you always say. We're allowed."

Quietly, nodding toward the house and smirking, he says, "Come in."

She's afraid of him now. With a coy shake of his head, a half smile, he will have her in his house, on his terms. He's always doing something friendly with his body or his voice to raise the possibilities. She never can attend to memory in his presence. The confrontations she imagined are irrelevant if she accedes to the shrug of his shoulders, his hand confidently extended.

Martin knows she is resisting. He hears her litany of his previous lovers and sees she'll soon have her three children standing in a line between them. This is her way of claiming distance. If he does not act quickly and convincingly, she'll have the space adorned with tokens of her married years predating his arrival.

"Or, if you don't want to come in, I could teach you how to drive that thing. Anyone who can navigate Route 7 in a station wagon can do it."

"I don't do lawns, Martin." Sylvia dismounts. "Anyway, I didn't come all the way out here for yard work. There's enough of that undone on Holmes Road. Though, from what Arthur tells me, maybe the condition of the lawn and garden is going to be the bank's problem soon. Will the bank get the house?"

"No one is going to lose homes over this." He kicks at a balanced log and catches the freed door, holds it open for her. "Is that what Arthur told you is going to happen?"

From her favorite perch on the low pine table, she waits for him to take his place on the huge white sofa. "Arthur doesn't seem to know what hit him. Do you?"

"Why are you shaking your head like that? Am I supposed to have all the answers? Is that why you came rushing out here? To get the truth about how Arthur and I seem to have paid a lot of money for something that was stolen from the company we want to sell it to? Good luck."

"I get the feeling my luck is running out."

When he's with her in his house, he can see the woman he desires. But the woman Martin wants would have the wit to cut her fate away from Arthur's sagging circumstance. "It doesn't much suit you, Sylvia. Melodrama. Stop posing. Besides which, you seem to have this whole affair a little inflated. Right now, it's just an inquiry. And so maybe we've been had. It's not time for midnight escape plans yet."

"Arthur keeps talking about signing off on contracts, being the one, the product supervisor—"

"I'm supposed to tell you about Arthur's inability to keep things in proportion? Like it's news?"

"You're just supposed to tell me if Arthur was set up to be the victim here." She's willing to believe anything. A quick denial would absolve them both.

"You know what I think about this. I don't want in on your marriage." He doesn't want to countenance her role as Arthur's wife. "I want you. You go figure Arthur, if that's what's eating you. Don't make me the judge of your indiscretions. And any man who is the victim of his circumstances deserves to be."

"Why, Martin, how philosophical of you." Sylvia dreamily repeats the epigram, laying herself out on the table, full-length, at midsentence. "What kind of ass would believe that?"

"What are you? The sacrificial lamb?" He is gone as he says this, returns with two glasses of iced tea. "Drink this. It will calm your nerves."

She won't sit up or take the glass he's placed beside her ear. "My mother had a case of the nerves almost daily. She would announce it, like a curse upon my sister's head. Until I was fourteen or so I used to picture it as a suitcase filled with something alive. A case of the nerves. You know, like in cartoons, when someone stows away in luggage and has to struggle to get out?" Laughing, she sits up, sticks a finger in the glass to taste the tea. "This is good."

"Thank you. I used honey."

"Why tell me? If it's up to me, we'll have Kool-Aid." This strikes her as so funny she has to walk to the windows opposite the couch. She collects the thin curtain in her hand, presses her forehead against the cool glass. "You really need that thing just to cut the grass?"

"Need it?" He stretches out his legs. "I guess not. Not really. But I like it."

"Like these ridiculous chintz curtains, I suppose. It's not as if anyone is around to peek in." She lets the material drift back to the frame. "Got a match?" She's facing him now.

It is a line from their first meeting in his house, from the first month of her first affair. Less than four months later, she is impressed by their traditions—the poses, vows, and jokes they recognize as artifacts. They never tire of these tokens of their history.

"A match. How funny, Sylvia. I didn't know you smoked."

"Smoke? I don't. Why?"

"You asked for a match."

"Oh, that. No. I asked if you have a match. A date, or even a wife. As in, Are you spoken for?"

"Oh, in that case, No."

"Hard to find, a match."

"Not impossible, Sylvia."

"No. By no means. As in, Maybe you've met yours."

And he does not say he knows she is right. And she hangs on to her qualifier, her maybe, like a girl to feigned indifference. And the foreplay is over and successful and recorded: another artifact.

Words brought them together. The chance to be heard, saying anything at all, was irresistible. For more than a year, Sylvia marveled as Arthur's energetic, wiry little lawyer friend fielded after-dinner puns and innuendos gleefully, unerringly. Alternately embarrassed and annoyed, Arthur eventually took to acting as a shield for his new partner. This only heightened the thrill. Martin deftly pitched around his would-be defender. Sylvia bobbed and weaved, lined up her target, and released a volley before Arthur moved to spoil her angle.

Finally, Arthur's interference ceased to amuse them. They wanted head-on contests, with force and endurance as the stakes, not the subtleties of dealing with a third.

One week after the Insulum New Year's party, Martin was

invited to lunch in the kitchen alcove, where Sylvia noticed his scaled-down proportions were more appropriate than her husband's bulk. A few awkward, silent minutes frightened them. Perhaps they'd come to rely on Arthur's well-intentioned interference, or the aspect of suspicion they assigned to him.

Martin said, "Maybe I should leave."

Sylvia said, "I think you're meant to say that afterward."

Thereafter, words did not fail them.

Sitting with her back against the headboard of his bed, Sylvia is watching Martin. He has taken up a post at the curtained windows in his living room. He is naked, his slim arms crossed so that his hands rest just above his buttocks. She's always charmed by his unassuming body at a distance. It seems to her a privilege to know that something precious is inside the rather ordinary frame. When he turns to her, she doesn't tuck her thick legs underneath the quilt or try to rearrange her hair. Here, she makes no use of tricks and illusions acquired by the plain and clever women who read the magazines.

"You're awake at last."

"No one stole your tractor?"

Martin lies across the foot of the bed. "All's well."

"What would you have done if I hadn't come this afternoon?"

"You mean the lawn? Would I have mowed it? Christ, I do that about twice a year. You're really the only one I'd do it for. So we could have a lunch out there without a scythe."

"Well, I'm proving to be quite a bother." She has her hands and forearms buried in a pillowcase. "I never dry-mop before you come. In fact, I never dry-mop anymore. But I meant that more theoretically. If Arthur hadn't called is what I meant, what would you have done? I guess I mean, why did Arthur have to be the one to tell me about Insulum maybe going bust? I feel so calm saying that. This can't be right."

"No, it's right." He likes the softness of her calves, gets his hands tucked under them. When he looks at her, his gaze skids happily along her legs, up and over her heavy breasts. "If you hadn't come, I would've worked myself up to some awful pitch. But it's not the worst . . . it's not the end of the world. These are." He sits up and tugs her legs, presses her cold feet against his chest. "These are the end of the world. The tips of the iceberg." Letting her feet slide down him until they balance on his thighs, he laughs. "What'll we do next?"

"I don't even have to think." But she does think, considers the impossible. "If I could do anything at all? I would stay here. All night. Tonight. Of course, I can't."

He is thrilled, rises to the challenge, massaging her feet and calves.

"What time is it? Five?" She reaches for the wind-up clock beside the bed. "Seven-thirty? Well, this ought to destroy the mystery for Arthur." She is dressing before he moves.

"I am not even asking you to stay. A man of his word. I suppose begging is out of the question?"

She won't even look at him until she's clothed and properly arranged. This is her exit ritual. He looks ridiculous, naked in her respectable presence. "Don't get up. Those curtains in the living room are see-through. Could you call me this week? I'd like a few hours' warning if we're all going to jail."

"Nice talking to you again, Arthur." Martin keeps his back to the bedroom door as she leaves.

"I'm happy I came. Good night. Sweet dreams." This gets her out the door and into damp night air. Before his house is out of sight, she is rousing memory and holding to hope, the opposing molds of her assumed identity.

Turning into her driveway, she sees every room in the house is lit. Both the front and the back doors are open. Annoyed, she rushes toward the back entry and, at close range, sees her elder daughter, Jane, sitting on the stoop.

"Daddy went to the Pittsfield High baseball game. He took Artie with him. The Coswalds picked them up. How was the meeting?" Jane does not move out of her mother's way.

"The meeting? Was fine. But why are the doors open? It's cold tonight, Jane. Come inside. Or put on a sweater." Sylvia suspects Jane is intentionally blocking her progress. "Is your sister home?"

"She didn't want to go to the game either. What was this meeting for, anyway?"

"Jane, do you mind if I go inside? I'm freezing."

Jane turns her head quickly, bends and peeks inside the back hall. "You think it's that cold out?"

"I'll be glad to debate this in the kitchen. Stand up." Sylvia takes her daughter's hand and leads her in. "What did you burn?" She hears cautious footsteps in the dining room. "Was there a fire?"

"I let Alison make grilled cheese. I guess it got burned or something. Was this a Rosary Sodality meeting tonight?" Jane slides along the bench into the corner of the alcove.

"No. It's the hairspray I smell now." Sylvia looks up, as if to see the scent. Suddenly, forcefully, she turns on her daughter. "It's cigarettes, isn't it, young lady? Alison, you get in here this minute. Alison?"

"Coming, Mom."

"Did you have her smoking, too? Jane?"

"I didn't say I smoked. You did. Who cares anyway? It's my business if I want to smoke. I'm sixteen."

Sylvia can't hear her. She is waiting for the younger sister to arrive, to bring the episode to a firm and quick close. "I am coming into the dining room in exactly five seconds, Alison."

From the connecting pantry, Alison says, "Here. I'm right here, Mom." But she doesn't dare enter the kitchen.

"If you're hiding something for your sister, you'll only make matters worse. For both of you. Give me whatever it is. Now. I'm almost out of patience."

From her post in the alcove, Jane cannot resist a jibe. "You call this patience?"

Alison is transporting a saucer filled with soiled water and several butts, as if it is a holy offering. The thirteen-year-old is already reduced to tears.

"Just put that in the sink. I see you were supposed to cover for your sister."

Alison cannot look at Jane. She's betrayed her again. The

mother's wrath is the lesser threat. "I don't smoke, Ma. I don't."

"No, you just play along. It's not much better. Go to your room. I'll come up after I've had a talk with your sister." Sylvia watches Alison run from the spotlight, mortified. "It's a real act of kindness, putting Alison through this, isn't it? You answer me when I ask you a question, young lady."

"If you just let me smoke it wouldn't happen."

Sylvia sees her insolent, skinny daughter and knows her too well. Forced into a corner, she's more spirited at every turn of bad luck. Sylvia knows it falls to her to give Jane access to a more agreeable style, a way of being a woman in the world. But, without fail, Sylvia takes this girl on her own terms, one time battling it out and the next simply expressing dissent. She's entrusted Jane to nothing more consistent or reliable than her own sense of the identity they share.

"For one thing, Jane, the hairspray was truly juvenile. Stupid. It is actually making me sick to my stomach."

"I opened the doors. And I only told Alison not to tell. And I did make her a grilled cheese sandwich."

"Oh, I see. It's all aboveboard." Sylvia moves to the sink, afraid she may get sick.

"All right. The hairspray was stupid. But I had to."

"Stop talking about the hairspray and cheese."

"Well, what am I supposed to say? Ground me. That ought to make a big difference. Carol and Stacey are grounded for the rest of the month. I couldn't care less."

"Grounding for the week goes without saying. We've been through this before." Sylvia runs cold water, splashes some on her face.

"Thanks a lot. I'd like to know what you think I'm supposed to do around this place if I don't smoke. Like there are so many things to do I just can't tell you."

Angrier about the likelihood that she will get sick, Sylvia yells, "Don't you have a brain in your head? You, of all people. If you have to smoke those wretched things, go outside. You have it freezing in here as it is. Why should everyone else have to suffer? And leave your sister out of it. It's bad enough she has to have you as an example—oh, for God's sake. Damn you!" With that, Sylvia is bent over the sink, vomiting.

"What? Are you really sick or something?" Jane is amazed by the sight of her mother heaving. "How did it happen so fast?"

Panting, afraid to leave the sink, Sylvia rears her head. "The fan. It's in your father's closet. Get it and put it in that doorway."

Jane does not want to move while her mother is watching. "You want a fan? Really?"

Concentrating on an image of the fan sucking out the heavy air, Sylvia drops her head forward. She wags a finger above her head. "In the bedroom. The closet near the windows."

Bending toward her mother, Jane can't suppress a giddy smile. "After all that about the cold, you sure you want a fan?"

By now Sylvia has taken in enough of the raw sweetness and soot to lose speech. Dry heaves force her to brace both hands on the counter.

Jane races behind her, returns with the fan. After several barely audible commands, she has the blades whirring at high speed—though, as far as she is concerned, it would be better just to blow in a lot of fresh air. Sensing it is her role to stand guard over the appliance, she moves it flush against the threshold, so her mother can run by and outside. "Maybe you should go outside. You could sit in the car for a while. How would that be?"

"I'm fine now. Thanks, though. See?" Sylvia stands straight, to establish her recovery.

"You don't look good. Your face is all red and your hair is bad."

"Thank you, darling. That's a big help." She mats down her tangled hair, rinses out her mouth. "If you ever use hairspray to cover your tracks again, I will personally shave your

head. I'm going upstairs. Get this smell out of here, somehow. And fast. You hear me?"

"Am I still grounded?"

"You tell me. What do you think?"

Seeing her mother has recovered, Jane relaxes into indignation. "It won't stop me, if that's what you think."

"I'm too angry now, Jane. Please don't. All right? It's not
enough, what it does to you, how ridiculous you look. And
your teeth and yellow fingers. Now I have to be sick and your
sister has to be dragged in?" Sylvia does not want this to
escalate again. She has enough energy to get upstairs without falling over. "I certainly hope you enjoyed what you
smoked tonight. It'll have to last you for a long time, believe
you me."

Sylvia does not return to see what her daughter has kicked
over. She figures it's the fan, which is ancient and sturdy. As
if on cue, the light in Alison's bedroom is extinguished as
Sylvia mounts the top stair. Sylvia can see the child pretending to be asleep, fearing retribution. Alison has none of her
sister's boldness, her mother's wiles. Caught red-handed, Alison is an exaggerated sight, a storybook waif.

Leaning on the painted doorjamb, Sylvia whispers, "You
don't have to turn on the light. I know you love your sister,
Alison. But you don't have to lie for her to prove it. She'll
understand if you just don't go along with her from now on.
You don't have to snitch on her. Just steer clear of her is the
best way."

Crying, of course, Alison hopes to vindicate her soiled reputation. "I was just supposed to get rid of the saucer and air
out the downstairs, and then I could choose the television
programs. And I'm not supposed to say anything about a boy
coming over here in a car tonight, after Dad and Artie left."

"A boy for Jane?" Sylvia considers any hint of social life
involving her diffident daughter—covert or brazen—a sign of
hope. "Did he stay?"

"She'll kill me if she finds out. You know her."

Her delight hidden in the darkness, Sylvia whispers, conspiratorially, "I won't tell. It's a promise." She wants to safeguard the potential romance, and she's not sure she can trust Alison not to confess. "Don't you go telling Jane you told me, will you? We'll keep it between us. God bless."

In her own room, Sylvia undresses but doesn't bother with a nightgown. She tries to reconstruct her day, to account for being so tired, but she preempts that effort as she slips into bed, pretending it's another bed, in an older house, with a larger yard. Amused by her lackluster imagination, she tells herself the wages of sin are exhaustion.

Within the hour, Jane is convinced her work is done. She stuffs the fan into the coat closet under the stairs and, incautious as ever, heads out to the back stoop. She lights a filtertip cigarette. Greedy for the heady atmosphere of rebellion and danger, she drops it midway and lights a fresh one.

Arthur sees the signal ember he often has spotted in the back yard or reflected in a neighboring storm window. Unobserved, he hurries past the driveway with Artie in his arms.

Artie is awake, but lately he has learned to act the role of little boy who fell asleep, to win himself a place against his father's heart. It is a ten-year-old's idea of salvage. This summer, joining other sons and fathers in the bleachers at Waconah Park has become a somber, almost silent ritual. Several innings pass without instructive play-by-play from Arthur or a shout of disapproval at the blind and biased umpires. Arthur sits through home runs, outs called on strikes, and double plays. So Artie follows form—silent, holding to his seat, and staring at the shortstop—hoping that his friends may mistake his father's inattention for a show of expert concentration or discrimination.

Carrying his sleepy son is something Arthur likes to do, a man's job he can manage, another romance of the way it used to be. Both boy and man enjoy proximity, but this is not spontaneous camaraderie. It is a solitary, retrospective pleasure.

After depositing his son in his bed, Arthur takes to his

bedroom. The surprise of hearing Sylvia asleep so early and the oddity of her humming, send him backing out, like an astonished houseguest who stumbled onto something private. Now he is marooned in the hall. Only Jane's bed is unoccupied; he is certain to wake Alison if he enters the room. Least of all does he want to put Jane in a position to confess her transgression. A stolen cigarette in the dark is a part of his romance of youth, one insubstantial piece of his daughter's heart to which he can claim relation. Until he hears the back door close, he is trapped, but happily so; even in a house as big as this, he thinks. Finally, opting for the way of peace, he steals to his wife's side, slips into bed without waking her. He hopes Jane will have the sense to sneak another smoke or two, since no one has to be the wiser.

If even the youngest Adamski announced to the others that he anticipated a miracle in church this Sunday morning, two weeks shy of Easter, his sisters and his parents would take turns disabusing him of his naïveté. The idea, as each of them knows, is that a miracle is like a wish come true; it can be arranged, but only as a private deal.

Arthur escorts his wife and children to their customary pew and returns to join the standing male elite. He propositions Jesus while twisting split ends off the wicker basket he will pass by worshipers during the consecration. In effect, he pledges to confess the sin of perpetrating fraud (he inserts a caveat to explain that he doesn't fully understand the charge), if it will serve as down payment on a Providential intercession to keep him out of jail.

Sylvia begrudgingly admits to her God she deserves the nausea none of her patent medicines would assuage. But she also makes it clear that something less pedestrian might better serve His purpose. If the priest should see her sin and refuse her Holy Communion, she would know He was mindful of her actions and that it was time she made amends.

Alison, her white Leatherette prayer book pressed between her hands, makes a strong and simple case for His consideration. She explains that if He rewound all the clocks, she would

not lie again to protect Jane. It's up to Him to do this without disrupting the entire city. She hasn't time to help Him
out with the practicalities: her mother has noticed her prayer
book is not open. Despite forewarnings, Alison has not kept
pace with the progress of the Latin prayers. Knowing piety
is a prerequisite for miracles, she withdraws her bid and opens
to the Gloria.

Jane keeps herself amused by redesigning hairstyles for the
mothers of her classmates. But Father Harriman's exuberant
recitation of the temptations lurking in the world draws her
attention to the altar. The crucifix suspended over the pulpit
inspires her to invent a method to quit smoking: Think of the
bloody nail wounds as scars from pagans' cigarettes. But, as
she tells Him, that sounds like something some retarded nun
would say. Besides, she's not the kind of girl who goes around
prodding people with a burning butt. And, in case He hasn't
noticed, Father Harriman smokes cigars.

Though he could hardly know his parents and sisters have
lost their weekly bids for something wonderful, Artie assumes
his will not get off the ground. He doesn't even mask it as a
prayer. Standing to recite the Creed phonetically, he holds a
quarter in each hand. He is sure they won't fall to the floor
a second time and provoke another round of shushing from
his sisters. But, wouldn't it be great if, when he opened his
fist high above the basket, everyone could see he'd changed
the quarters into Mallow Cups? After all, he gave them up
for Lent. Wouldn't that be perfect?

Like all Adamski highest hopes, the one about the Mallow
Cups does not pan out. And, except for God, who's all-
forgiving and grants you everything you need, no one is the
wiser.

Reentry into the untransformed world is not unaided. There
is the sausage and pancake breakfast at home, the abundant
Sunday newspaper, the unscheduled afternoon. Sundays have
their rewards.

By midday, the children are dispersed. Arthur has assumed
his cherished pose on the sofa, surrounded by the disarray of

Sunday sections and discarded shoes, socks, jacket and tie, and finally his belt. "Sylvia? You see this cartoon on the editorial page yet?"

Any distraction from her unabated nausea is welcome. "The one about what's inside the pillbox hat?"

"No, this thing with the reporters carrying shovels?"

"I don't think so. Why?" She doesn't turn to him or even obligingly crane her neck, wary as she is about unsettling her body.

"The reporters are sweating and one of them is complaining to the President—no, well I guess it's actually Johnson. Yes, it is Johnson, with the dome they always give him for a head? Johnson is saying the Peace Corps replaced the press corps. Anyway, it struck me as funny. You want to see it?"

"Well, yes. Just hold it open there. Oh, right. Yes." Leaning forward, she enters the lingering cloud of sausage fumes. "I think I'll run upstairs and change." This is all she offers by way of explanation for actually running up to the cool bathroom, where she kneels on the pink linoleum. As she vomits, she reaches over and opens the bathtub spigot. Her instinctive priority is to cover her tracks, escape detection.

Reeling back on her heels to stand, she feels weak beyond repair. To calm the spastic twitching deep inside her, she blows out air in tiny moans. Her voice comes to her sounding strangely low, on warmer air than normal. She knows that she is not alone.

Sylvia is skilled at apprehensive, inconclusive self-examination. She strips, as she has several times in recent weeks, prods her hips and lifts her breasts, presses both hands flat against her crotch and drags them slowly, smoothing back protective hair and inelastic flesh. This is sufficient to support the optimistic diagnosis: Years will intervene between a few distended cycles and her sterile older age. But the mirror on the door also shows her too abundant hips, a waist swelled just beyond the normal arc of abdomen and rib. Dismissively, as if the naked woman in the mirror were an incompetent young nurse, she says, "And you had me worried about menopause.

Are you blind?" Now she knows her body had not failed to
bleed; her blood had run, but deep inside, mapping out another's tiny veins.

She wraps her hands and forearms tight around her hips,
to make her child feel a stronger woman holding them in
place. "You have to understand, we really didn't know you
were here. There might even be some question about who
you are, exactly. We're certainly going to hear some yelling
and screaming about that question, at the very least. One of
the things about children is they have fathers. One father
per child is the rule." She has to suck in air to keep herself
from falling forward. "We'll have a bath. And get to know
each other. I mean, no matter what, I am going to have to
be the mother." Avoiding her reflected eyes, to claim her
final distance from the mother in the mirror, she studies the
heavy hips as they twist, sees the unfamiliar abdomen in profile before she turns away to test the spewing water, press a
stopper into the drain. Lifting her leg over the rim of the
tub, she takes her body weight on her arms, balances on the
cold, curled lip of porcelain. In this ungainly straddled pose
she waits, until the mother in the mirror stands behind her,
then makes her way inside. Her fear is consumed, fuel to feed
her resignation. "Like this is a bath. Those are my clothes.
The ones on the floor over there. I am the mother. For one
reason and another, mothers cry. That's another thing to
know." She lowers herself into the half-full tub, unstops the
drain, and leaves the faucets open. The coursing water pro-
longs her privacy, a well whose limits she has tested.

The dubious paternity provides a queer, distracting joy.
Staring at her stomach, she conjures up an image of the being
in her womb, regards this featureless fetus as an optical illu-
sion that will yield to concentration. But as she lies back in
the churning water, she sees herself falling backward under
Arthur's weight. Arthur is the father.

For years, she'd orchestrated her availability according to
the rhythms charted flawlessly since Artie's birth. Then she
and Martin talked their way upstairs. In lieu of simple depri-

vation for her fertile days (the rule she had imposed on Arthur), she resolved to learn a new technique. At the local library, too daunted to check out *Applying Principles of Psychology to Marriage*, she spent two mornings convincing herself sex could be administered orally.

As illicit as any pharmaceutical, her scheme of oral contraception had a peculiar flaw. One Friday, late in January, Arthur's interest was launched with a roll to his side and a gathering of her hair in his large hand, his customary form of inquiry. She did not mechanically brush away his hand and recollect her hair in a twist along her neck. Rejecting Arthur, despite legitimate preventive motive, would signal too complete a victory for her lover of a few weeks' standing. Though it was only hours since she'd left his house in Becket, she would not accord Martin a proprietary claim. To service Arthur—and it was a service, the minutes with her mouth on Martin's penis assuaged only by the servile pleasure eked from a display of competence—would require explanations, which would take her to the threshold of confession. And Saturday night, Arthur turned to her again, entitled to a second visit in exchange for weeks of unremitting distance.

She knows the father of the child is her weakness, the weakness of her love for Martin and for Arthur. And shame attends the weak: Arthur's humiliating public failure as a private businessman, the prospect of an unpaid mortgage, intimacy withered to a charity bestowed upon an unsuspecting cuckold, an hour with her lover carved from several hours' worth of lies to children and a friend or two. The catalogue of shame tempts her to distrust her diagnosis, and she does attempt to admit the possibility of a miscalculation: Couldn't Martin Parris be the father? But this optimistic doubt would not withstand the months of waiting. Sylvia would not survive the waiting in an outer office while a doctor draws the blood of two men and a child, to divine a lineage without regard for her intentions.

Arms curled around her ample stomach, she feels no room for doubt. She won't wait for someone else to explicate what happened here. But she cannot bear another child out of weakness. Aloud, as if by speaking she can transform a lie into a solemn oath, she says, "We need a stronger father."

Resolve alone does not deliver strength. Nor can she wash away her weakness. In the bath, in the midst of Arthur's whispering about the launching of a criminal investigation, even in the act of telephoning Martin, she feels herself immobilized and rendered ineffective. When she finally speaks to Martin, just before noon on Thursday, she brings to bear no seductive power, feels nothing of the thrill such boldness ordinarily provides. When she says she needs to see him, it is not a simple invitation; it is a prayer for intercession. Sylvia needs Martin to reconceive her child.

Martin rings the doorbell twice, lets himself in, smiles when he sees she's laid a lunch on trays in the living room. "This is a first. Not secreted in the alcove at the back of the house? Is it an anniversary? I wore my summer pinstripes, so I'm ready for a celebration. It's an occasion, anticipating summer. You look awfully serious, Miss Sylvia." He drops his briefcase, walks to her side and kisses her. "What? Am I late?"

She won't stand to welcome him. Hands against her knees, braced for the fall she feels she is about to take, she speaks to test her voice. "You look fine. Did you meet with Arthur today?"

"He told you already? The GE getting a temporary restraining order is pro forma. It doesn't change our situation. We can't do any business until they're ready to do business with us, can we?" He settles on the divan. "Arthur's acting like a fugitive. I'm not about to hang him out to dry. I promise. You have my word."

"So, there is going to be a hanging, after all?"

"Gut reaction? I think Arthur knew more than I did. Or at least sooner. It's not that I expected no protest from the General Electric contracts department when we made the initial offer. Insulum was bound to sound familiar. They virtually invented the transformer, so chances are they'd be familiar with potential enhancements. That's just reasonable. I think all this legal action is part of the negotiation. They'll chip away at us—but they want the formula for Insulum. Arthur may be missing the finer points, but he wasn't unaware that there was precedent for the research."

"I hope you don't really expect me to make sense of whatever it is you just said, Martin." Sylvia is afraid he won't provide an opening for her. "As far as I'm concerned, what Arthur ought to know and what he understands are two unrelated quantities."

Parris seizes the infrequently offered bait. "You should have seen his performance in my office. Like a kid—a Little Leaguer listening to the coach. All ears. I think he believed I was asking him to play along with a scam. That I had set out to hoodwink the GE. He was willing to be a team player, anything not to be cut from the roster."

There is a reason for Sylvia's refusal to admit Arthur to their conversations. In this context, Arthur deserves her patronage. "This all happened this morning?"

"I thought you said Arthur called you."

"You said that, Martin. I was just fishing around when I asked about the meeting."

"It doesn't matter. He would have told you anyway."

"This is remarkable." She is up and away from him, leans on the mantel. "Don't you think maybe you were bound to tell me?" She discards her pose of supplication to accommodate her indignation. "Tell me what you've done to him. Tell me what to expect. I'm not his. Here I am, with you. For you. See?" She holds out her arms.

Even at this distance, Parris feels her strength, wants to be protected, held by her. "I trusted him. And now, his instinct is to fall apart." The picture of Arthur in his office, wrapped in an impervious, willing ignorance, exercises Martin. "He was supposed to know how to make decisions about patents, to document and validate original research. It was his fucking job. Now he's crying in my office? And telling me I had to know what he thought I expected him to do? And did I mention that Forrester—the shyster engineer? The other fucking

Judas I hired? He's nowhere. Gone. And Arthur wants to know the plan? He keeps saying to me, What's the plan? What's the plan? Well, fuck if I know. Fuck if I know anything."

Stronger again, Sylvia looks down on him, determined to taunt him to her level. "Save it for the *Courier*, Martin. I'm not impressed by innocence. You knew just what you were up to." She struts to the low table, pours herself a glass of iced tea. "Have some? It's from a jar, but it's a national brand. Premium." Filling his glass, she shakes her head dismissively. "Bear in mind my partnership with Arthur. It's produced a few insights." She hands him the glass, walks back to the mantel. "Even as you tell it? I believe Arthur. For God's sake, it's vintage Arthur. Not knowing enough."

"Think about it, Sylvia. I am a lawyer. How much do you think I know about transformers? And that is something of a liability if you are meant to be running a company that lives and breathes by transformers. You think maybe hiring Arthur was my way of getting to you?"

"It would be a hell of a compliment if you said so." Frustrated and scared by his refusal to divulge his betrayal of Arthur, in which she still believes, she tries to guess his motives for withholding. "You are afraid. You think I'll side with him. That I'll report to him on what you've done. Right? Is that what this is all about? The one about the wife always returning to the nest?"

"I'd do anything if we could just leave here. Really run away and be alone." He looks up at her, as if she might just be able to arrange this.

Because she refuses to see his weakness, she credits him with coldness. "Don't start a long speech explaining why that terribly original little drama is not on the program, Martin. If this is the beginning of your exit, just pick up your goddamn briefcase and leave the glass on the table."

"Exit?" This brings him to her side. "Sylvia, I'm running scared here. Leave? I need you now, really need you. Is that your plan? Call it off on account of Insulum going bust?" He has her by the shoulders. "Martin loves Sylvia." And with this unprecedented declaration, he gives her what he has hidden from every woman he has known. He offers her his other-worldly twin, his fragile, hopeless self.

Sylvia knows a weaker woman would crumble now, raze her own foundation and pledge herself to days and even years of building up a life on the shaky ground he's dared to show her. "I was just wrong. I was convinced you knew. Or at least that you were engineering the latter half of something gone awry." She turns her head slowly, which he understands as a command to withdraw his hands. "Martin's not an engineer." In his still expectant face she sees the shadow of her overestimation. She can't tolerate the way he looks. He's nothing but a mirror here, reflecting back the weakened woman she discovered only days before. She won't have it. While he stands, dutiful as any child waiting for a scolding, she takes herself in her own hands and presses hard against her womb. She will deliver strength.

"You look so sad." He backs away, takes to the couch again. "Is it so bad? Saying it?"

"Love, you mean? Of course not, Martin." She is walking but she feels herself gliding to his side. "You've always had a way with words." She sips his tea. "But while you were talking nice, well . . . Why do I want to be entertaining just now? To please you?" She walks away, leans back against the door. "I am carrying Arthur's child."

"Pregnant?"

"Well, yes, Martin. That would be a synonym."

"How far along?"

Posed as a serious question, this makes her laugh. "Don't think of it as a project. Think in terms of swimming somewhere. And I'm wet."

"Why isn't it mine?"

"Yours?" She yells this, to snap him to attention, make him look into her eyes. He won't see her move, but she is not immobilized. Without so much as a gasp she has her heart in hand and twists it closed. She laughs, seizes the few bloodless seconds she has wrought. "It wasn't for the thrill I got I learned to take you in my mouth. It wasn't that I thought an old dog better learn new tricks. Is that what you thought, Martin? Well, someone had to be aware. Actions have consequences. I didn't dare interrupt your pleasure, so I took the low road, the woman's route to extramarital bliss. Your child? That's a sweet thought, Martin. Count the days in your average month. And subtract my days at your knees. It all adds up."

"Arthur's child?"

Can he see her time is up? The child has coaxed her body back to life and she is afraid her resolve will falter. "Given the limited options, yes. Arthur's child."

"You want this? His child? Now?"

She relaxes when she sees he won't approach. "Typical of Arthur. He got lucky." Sensing he might mount one last campaign, she speaks quickly. "Don't let's get into my textbook options here, Martin. I have to live with remembering the very night, with Arthur. So he wouldn't get suspicious." She watches him absorb this. "I can live with regret, I think. I'm something of a veteran there. It won't kill me. But killing off this child? That would do it, literally be the death of me."

"Then, I am sorry. As if I am you, Sylvia. Sorry more than you can know."

She won't abide his sorrow. She is beyond him now. She has begun her work, turning pleasure she has sucked from him into an acrid venom she must expiate. She needs his strength, not his sadness or joy. He begins to stand, but she takes a few steps toward him and he slumps into the cushions. Near him but above him, she frames his slight, lithe body in its least affecting pose. His love for her is hidden, like the fragile collarbone beneath the starched and manly armor. No matter where his body's been and what she might have wished on its behalf, he's not the man she had in mind.

Martin watches, waiting for a cue. "Am I supposed to leave? Is that the idea? Is the noble thing to swear I'll never bother you again?"

"The idea is to be strong." And she still believes he has strength, that she must choke off his will to give her only weakness. "I know you can be strong."

"Then you're not hearing me. It's taking all I have to handle Arthur and the company and the—"

"You should be ashamed of yourself." She hadn't meant to dare him so directly, but she is desperate. "Handling Arthur is hardly a full-time job, Martin. I do it as a hobby."

"Stop it. Shut up. It's ugly." He stands, hoping to silence her.

"I like the way it looks."

He grabs her shoulders, but she won't let him pull her to his chest. Gently shaking her, he says, "Don't do this. Hey, it's me. It's Martin."

It's her laughter that undoes him. He drops his right hand quickly and as quickly swings it toward her head.

Reflex turns her, jolts her left hand up to block his swing. Then she lets her arms fall to her side. "Go ahead, Martin. Hammer it home."

He can only tell himself he intended to hit her. He has tried to hurt her.

"My sister never learned to block a punch. Once he hit you, my father had you." She speaks through her rapid breathing, wipes away the sweat released along her face and neck. She knows her body is hot with adrenaline she won't need this time. "I saw my mother beg for more. My sister finally ran for her life." She has to bend forward, to take in air enough to stop her gasping.

"I could never hurt you." He cannot prove this, cannot bring these words to life.

"But, that's what Arthur is. A man who could never hurt me. And with a little rouge, a nice pair of nylons, I'm the girl for him."

"You're so beautiful. Just standing there."

"No, Martin. You're halfway there. You have to admit it is ugly and not despise it. It doesn't want to be pretty. It wanted to be seen and loved. Is that too much?" She holds out her hands, fending off his approach. "Not slapped down. Not pitied or forgiven."

"I'm right here, Sylvia. I can see it all." He wants her to believe he's overcome the distance she has claimed, that he's risen to her challenge. "I see it all. The only woman I ever loved."

She knows he sees her now. She feels herself in full light.

She is revealed. But his greeting troubles her. It is not spoken by Martin Parris in the flesh. This willing, seeing presence is an emissary of the corporate lawyer, public man. She has called forth his better. But once outside this room, beyond their private sphere, he would not bring to bear this shining self that magnifies what's pure and strong in her. He'd wince, pained by the unstable, flinty glare of her illumined imperfections.

They've seen each other in a fragile light. But Martin is a man by virtue of his presence in the world beyond. Out in the pale, diffusive light of day, she'd feel his presence as a shadow.

"I won't let go of you." He is ashamed. He cannot move to her. He can't even bring himself to touch her.

She understands that she could press his hands against the child, teach him how to lay a stronger claim. But he will have to claim her first. And so she lets him go.

Tracing lines haphazardly across her stomach as he drives away, she tells herself he's taking nothing of her with him. To her child, whose presence now is large with hope, she says, "I will father you forth. I'll do his work for him. He'll come to claim us. He saw me at my worst and he said he loves me." This is all the child has to know. Sylvia believes in miracles, in words made flesh.

A car rolling up her driveway starts her running to the door, expecting to see Martin. But the unfamiliar station wagon quickly backs out and chugs away. Scornful of her own impatience, she walks to the kitchen, telephones her husband. She tells him he must come to her immediately. She needs to see him, as she says.

Amiable as ever, Arthur figures she's prepared a special lunch to cheer him up. He claps his hands appreciatively over the undisturbed trays. "Great. I had a cup of soup and a really bad orange at lunch. I'm starved."

"Arthur?" Speaking his name is easier than she imagined. "Arthur, I love you, and I have done something terrible. So terrible, it is amazing."

"You didn't talk to the *Courier* about the investigation? They've had reporters calling all morning." He sits in a chair beside the mantel, expecting the worst.

"You mustn't ask me any questions for a minute. I mean, you can know anything and everything, but first you have to let me go with it. I won't tell you otherwise. I know I won't. What I'm about to tell you is too amazing, even to me." She waits until she sees he is willing to be conducted through the maze. She lets several seconds pass, to test her strength. She must be sure she can hold him. Finally, she edges forward on the divan cushion. "This lunch? I made it for Martin. Martin Parris. Your partner and, since January, my lover." As he invokes the name with disbelief, she yells, "Yes! An affair." She softens when his back and legs go limp, leaving him slumped in his chair. "I know it sounds like I'm bragging or something, but I ended it today. It doesn't forgive or explain a thing, I know. But it is over. I have always loved you, Arthur. And even now I know you know that's true. But the amazing thing we can't just put behind us is that I am sitting here and I am pregnant. It is Martin's child, Arthur. You know how I do my calendar each month, how careful I am about days and dates. It is Martin's child. But I lied to him. I lied and told him it was yours. Because I want it to be yours. No one ever has to know it is not your child."

The Women
and the Well

I

ARTHUR YELLED, "Give him my love, okay?" He waved to Sylvia from his car. She was leaning against the open front door. Her gaze was fixed on him and she was almost smiling, but Arthur felt her attention vault over him toward Stephen and the process of his release.

Arthur had interrupted their silent breakfast, wondering aloud what mayhem his absence from the office might create. Sylvia released him from his promise to accompany her and Roger without so much as a question. An hour later, backing the car out of the drive, Arthur was relieved not to have to face Stephen in the courthouse, and heartbroken to know Sylvia had anticipated his withdrawal.

He headed north, toward the offices of Spectronics, the publishing firm at which he'd spent almost twenty years as director of advertising. Vaunted as the position sounded when offered to him in the wake of the Insulum scandal, it initially required little more than recording the receipt of checks and black-and-white advertisements from manufacturers of laser peripherals in Florida and Texas.

Hetty Marshall, the founder, owner, and publisher of a pioneering trade magazine for the electro-optics industry, had up and moved her tottering business from Albany, New York, to Dalton, Massachusetts, after striking a deal with a failing local print shop. Her ignorance (and, later, her indifference) regarding small-town scandal made it possible for Arthur to secure a job before the Insulum episode concluded. Willing as he was to credit his own good luck, he suspected Sylvia had prevailed on Martin Parris to protect him from prosecution. He never confirmed this. Failure made him superstitious; his freedom was a gift horse, so he kept his eyes averted. He never was called to trial and, unrefuted, his suspicion matured into conviction. He had Sylvia to thank for his job at Spectronics, since even the tunnel-visioned Hetty Marshall could not have disregarded all-out criminal proceedings.

Arthur had made an ineffectual stab at exonerating himself when he interviewed for the position with the fledgling publisher. His prospective employer allowed him only a few minutes.

"But are you ready to take on something new, Adamski? That's what I want to know. Transformers are yesterday. I need a hand now, today. Am I coming through yet?" Standing only an inch shorter than Arthur, and every bit as solidly built, she could have passed as his twin sister. After a brief pause, during which Arthur tried to reformulate his recent past in more honorable terms, Hetty hoisted herself up onto the edge of her desk. Her feet were all but against his shins. "Truth? I'm not expecting dozens of the Berkshires' ad reps to come running. Who is this widow with the laser magazine, anyway? Am I right? Adamski, this is my one shot at it. I put everything Jack and I have left into this magazine. Jack? My late husband. I know I talk like everybody should know his name. But the idea, between you and me—oh, what the hell, I let Jack in on it, too. The idea is three publications by 1970. I mean it. We can do this."

"Are you offering me the job?"

"Are you accepting?"

"Where do I sign?"

"There's your desk." Hetty stood and pointed to a gray desk at the other end of the corrugated metal shell of a headquarters that had previously housed a small tool-and-die business. "I'll give you a client list. Of course, only on new clients do you get the commission."

"Lasers and optics. What I mean is, they're not exactly my strongest suit." Arthur tried to picture a laser, but he only conjured an image of its concentrated light beam.

"You sell ad space in a journal written for and by experts. Leave the understanding to the scientists. That's my motto. I'm not fool enough to think I just hired Albert Einstein." Here she laughed, shouting "ha" a few times. "I look at you and I see a man who can do a job. It's a hunch. I didn't get a rule book when I started this thing going, so I stick with my hunches. Follow me. I'll introduce you around. Three others, so there's no memorizing lots of names and titles. Come on."

Arthur never mastered the technology. Fiber optics, laser fusion studies, microscopic surgical gear, and the myriad attendant techniques and gadgetry advanced and changed measurably by the month. Whereas it had been the innovators and risk-takers who claimed the few big prizes in the world of manufacturing, in the realm of the new technology any adjunct position gave one a share in unprecedented profits and rewards. Arthur mastered his job, nothing more. And, as luck would have it, his job assumed the sleek and enviable contours of the high-tech world.

Social prominence, which had been within reach with the Insulum start-up, was not so easily won. Sylvia reminded Arthur of their lost position in the community, despite his financial recovery and the existence of seven Spectronics periodicals circulating throughout the English-speaking world. "Maybe if they appeared in the stores, or on the stands, Arthur. Instead of just trade magazines. One for people like me." It was Sylvia's idea of what she'd lost, not the health of Spectronics, that motivated this recurrent suggestion.

Still, Arthur could finally invoke the image of his aged parents, stand within the arc of their attention, and again feel no shame. He was reinstated in the world of the good, the realm of the innocent. This he celebrated every morning of late, driving to Dalton via East Street, past the massive gray geometry of Pittsfield's principal employer, and once the largest of the corporate giant's many appendages. Arthur's pleasure was to think of the General Electric's waning interest in its bulky electric works and its pursuit of the electronic future as a late-date vindication of his own professional path.

A left turn at a blinking yellow light led him along a winding, unpaved road known only to employees of the transformer division. From this dangerously narrow single lane, he could measure time.

On either side loomed the irregular checkerboard of thousands of six-by-six window panes. The vast glass expanses were supposed to make conditions inside less unreal, less inhumane. But the windows had been painted black the morning after the Japanese blasted Pearl Harbor. Some admixture of civic pride and rumored threat convinced locals that Pittsfield was fourth on the Axis list of attractive air-raid targets in America. Status as a bomber's bull's-eye seemed a logical conclusion to the process of putting Pittsfield on the map with a new Naval Ordnance plant and the renowned transformer operation. So the factory windows were painted black, concealing round-the-clock activity.

No intrepid enemy pilot capitalized on this rather hastily and incompletely hidden American stronghold. But the occasional brave young teenage rebel would put a rock through a pane or two of blackened glass; a small welding attachment thrown over the head of a man waiting on a suspended work station would knock another hole in the fragile barrier. Forty years of accidents and juvenile crime showed in the translucent, wire-reinforced windows which, within the painted rows, made a kind of crossword puzzle of the glass wall.

Black-glass replacement windows would not have been out of order, to hide the inactivity within. The work force had been halved since 1960; overtime accrued to brokers, lawyers, and accountants, while laborers punched in and out at nine and five, like bankers of a former generation.

This was the new American vulnerability: a vast stockpile of outdated industrial artillery in an armory located light-years from the front. Arthur never quite exhausted his amazement at a simple, unforeseen fact: Had Insulum proved a success as a core material for transformers, the Insulum company would have gone bust before the decade ended. In the age of semiconductors and laser diodes, the huge steel powerhouse transformers and their tethered cruciform transmission lines were receding on the landscape, icons of a lost city.

The Japanese could be accused of decimating local industry at last. Arthur reckoned he was lucky, a survivor of a remotely staged strike. He drove farther north, to his unlikely outpost in the new world, hoping the youngest Adamski would find his way as well. Deprived of any biological connection to Stephen, Arthur tried to convince himself that Stephen's evasion of criminal charges signaled relation of a higher order. He seized the only opportunity left him by the others involved in Stephen's life: He willed the boy the old man's good luck.

II

THE GENTLE PRESSURE of the elderly guard's hand against his back had no effect on Stephen. He entered the Berkshire County Courthouse release room slowly, at his own pace. Deciding not to sit on the solitary wooden chair, he turned to the stout uniformed man. Stephen drained emotion and even simple recognition from his face, a trick he'd worked out to make it clear he was beyond reach.

Without prompting, the elderly gentleman smiled, then bowed his head and snorted. "All right now, son. You're all but out now. Take it easy, tough guy." With a shake of his head, the guard left Stephen alone.

In the oversized window, Stephen saw himself as the guard saw him: too tall, too thin, too young to be any real trouble. But nowhere in that reflected self could he locate the oddball who'd run the two miles to the Temple Beth Israel and sprayed *Jesus Not Jews* with an aerosol can of yellow paint. Four days of solitude had yielded no attachment between Stephen and the still-fresh sense of urgency that found release only after six colored windows had been shattered. No amount of concentration decoded the logic of standing before a local judge and paraphrasing the moneylenders incident from the Bible instead of offering an apology.

Noise in the hall beyond the door alarmed him. He did not know who would arrive to escort him home, but he wanted to make an impression. He lowered the ancient venetian blind, drew the slats tight. Then he sat in his chair, took up the problem of identifying with the vandal, the man of action, the surprising son. Tricky as his memory was, it could not rescind the physical thrill that fueled the running and throwing and testifying. He could not imagine how he'd managed to electrify himself. He simply knew nothing mattered but that he do it again and again.

III

ARTHUR WAITED in his car as Hetty Marshall drove into the Spectronics parking lot. Hetty waved, signaled that she had something to show him. As their respective car doors slammed, she raised a spiral notebook above her head. "Fresh off the press. Literally. It's impressive, all bound together like this. If I were those Brits, I'd want to be bought up by us after reading it."

"An international empire." Arthur was dispirited by his imagined reunion with Stephen.

"Some enthusiasm, Adamski. I get plenty of wet blankets from these Royal Society types." She issued a single "ha."

"You read the thing about Stephen in the paper this weekend?" Arthur was less interested in Hetty's response, which he knew would be dismissive, than he was in measuring the story's currency.

"Is he having a nervous breakdown?" She held the door for Arthur, followed him around the glass-brick wall that defined his office space. "I never really got a sense of what he did. From the story."

"He's being released this morning." Arthur knew this was not an explanation. "The rabbi at the temple is not pressing charges." Arthur looked up at Hetty. "Do kids his age have nervous breakdowns?"

"Nowadays?" Hetty walked around the opaque wall, dragged a chair from the vast reception area already filled with manufacturing representatives and public relations professionals eager to feature their companies in the pages of the appropriate Spectronics monthly. "What about drugs with Stephen?"

"Not the type." Arthur was used to Hetty's complete lack of instinct concerning domestic affairs. It pleased him, this incapacity of hers. In fact, her inability to ask probing questions made her a safe sounding board. Unlike Sylvia and his daughters, Hetty did not appropriate the small territory he claimed in matters of advising and understanding his family. "Now, my daughter Jane? The eldest? The writer?"

"The single daughter. Lives in New York City?"

"Possibly the type. I mean, in her case, I would think seriously about the drug thing. In today's world."

"Stephen's been two years at the University of Massachusetts and you don't think he's ever tried some marijuana?"

Knowingly, Arthur said, "The kids today call it 'grass' or 'dope.'"

"Or sometimes, one of them says to another one—ha!— 'Would you like to smoke a bone?' And that's not to get into the heavy drugs and God knows what nicknames they might have for those."

Arthur laughed as he repeated the bone phrase. The more he thought about this, the funnier it seemed. Laughing so hard he had to yell to force out words, he bellowed, "And joints! Of course, joints and bones."

By then, Hetty was also beyond speech. She stood up, bent over the back of her chair, as if she could physically stop her laughter. "All I can think of—ha! The only thing I can think about is how we used to call this kid—ha! ha! ha!—*bonehead.*"

Arthur leaned back in his chair, howling. Just as he straightened up, he imagined a literal bonehead, and this sent him reeling back in his chair. He wiped his eyes, wheeled his chair back toward his desk cautiously, lest he set off more gales. "If they only knew how ridiculous they sound."

"God, you're funny about your kids, Adamski. Bones." Hetty let a few seconds pass, to be sure she was not prone to a relapse. "Tell the *Courier* to kiss your ass. Your son is coming home. I bet within a month he'll be aching to go back and finish up at college. Why don't you take a personal day and go have it out with him."

Arthur smiled, weakened by her casual reference to his son. He wanted to tell her everything. Day after day they greeted each other, distracted each other, amused and bolstered each other. Age and familiarity had not robbed them of their affection or of their many enduring affectations, including their unfailing use of unadorned surnames. She played tough dame to his good sport. More than once, more or less self-consciously, they'd confessed their mutual love in siblings' terms.

Hetty made of Arthur's long marriage to Sylvia one of the resolute mysteries of life. Arthur held to his outspoken disbelief that she'd not been the object of hundreds of attractive proposals.

Longing played no role in their time together. They recognized each other from the first. But they'd been ill-prepared. Both had known love as a reflector of their weaknesses, a protective pane of glass separating spouses, slid open for infrequent ministrations of the sacrament of reconciliation.

In the modernized warehouse in Dalton, they found themselves in a new sphere, an open-air environment in which prosperity—and its attendant generosity of spirit—thrived. Reflexively, each credited the other with sustaining the atmospheric charm. In Hetty's mind, Arthur had salvaged her incautious determination to succeed where her late husband invariably failed. To Arthur's way of thinking, Hetty had abided and abetted a stupid criminal and given him a second chance. It was simply beyond the bounds of their lived years in the world, the notion that enduring pleasure and reliable welcome could be mutually accomplished.

Surprised by Arthur's dreamy silence, Hetty tried to imagine herself comforting him, reassuring him. Touching him seemed ridiculous, melodramatic. "You're really worried about him. You're worried about Stephen, aren't you?"

Arthur shook his head, another reprimand for not appearing at the courthouse with his wife. "I have this sense that I'm to blame. I mean, in lots of ways I am to blame." He looked to see if she could untangle this. It was clear she could not. "I never told you this, Marshall. The truth is, I never told anyone. No one ever told anyone, so far as I know. Until about a week ago, when I thought it was damn well time he knew." In deference to her, to protect her from his status as a liar, he looked at his watch. "We can talk later. It's a business day around here."

"Some people don't shock easily, Adamski. I don't shock." She crossed her legs. "Being shocked is always a pose."

"Not always, I'm afraid. For instance, Stephen might've been shocked. I guess I know he was. But not so shocked he would have a nervous breakdown, of course. That was not the idea I had in mind." Again, Arthur looked to her, hoping she might intuit the source of his confusion. She simply waited for him to speak, her face unadorned by expectation. "As I said to him, as I said because he really had a right to know, or so I thought. I said, a little less directly than this, I guess. I told him I was not his father in the biological way. In every other way I am, so I am his father. But, biologically, I am not. A man called Martin Parris is the biological father of Stephen." Arthur could look at her, which surprised him. "A few days later he was dropping out of school. And now this. You see, Sylvia was never going to tell anyone. But she didn't treat him normal and I thought he should know why, he should hear it from me, of all people. And now this, and I'm not even there to pick him up. As if maybe I can really pull this off— pretending what I said doesn't have a thing in the world to do with why he is in jail. After twenty years as an obedient, respectful kid."

"Let's go for a drive, Adamski. The printer will have the rest of the reports ready by eleven. We'll head that way." Hetty stood. "Come on. You have six ad reps twiddling their thumbs on my payroll while you do all the grunt work. Give the poor fools a chance to learn the ropes. Come on."

Arthur followed her out of his office, past the expectant appointment holders, into her car. While she let the idling en-

gine ease itself down to a normal pace, Hetty stared straight
ahead. She turned to him as she shifted the car into reverse.
"If we drive directly north for two days or so we'll cross the
Canadian border. We can dump this little yellow wreck in a
river. The Yukon? Anyway, there'll be a couple of packhorses
waiting for us, Adamski. We'll ride at night, to avoid the
Mounties. Once we hit the hills, it's all behind us. What do
you say?"

IV

SYLVIA HAD TRAVELED from her front porch to the office of an
assistant district attorney at the courthouse in a self-induced
trance. Roger's explanation of the meetings to be endured had
not required a response from her. She did take note of the district attorney's willingness to let a subordinate deliver the
terms of Stephen's release; she construed this as an indication
of Roger's lack of standing in the legal community. Throughout the earnest and confidential speech delivered by the young
political appointee, Sylvia nodded, leaving absorption of detail
to her son-in-law. She was primed for one thing only: a glimpse
of, or even an unwitting reference to Martin Parris. Without
that, no degree of solicitousness, no emphasis on the seriousness of the incident at the temple, would deliver Sylvia to the
moment. She had stepped into her vast private waiting room.

Roger was gratified. He'd expected trouble with Sylvia on
this visit. Her passivity seemed to him an act of deference to
his professional standing. He adopted his most officious tone
with the young assistant district attorney, a common affect
for a member of any legal firm in the company of a civil ser-
vant, a way of asserting that collecting usurious fees is of no
consequence in one's decision to opt for private practice.

Roger's large hand on her forearm alerted Sylvia to her inappropriate lack of interest. "What was that?" She hoped to
sound engaged.

"Matthew here wanted to know if anyone has spoken to you

about the doctor Stephen will be involved with." Roger read
Sylvia's confusion as worry. "I know the Paramount program
sounds like a parole, Sylvia. It really isn't, though. And all of
us did agree some kind of therapy was called for." Unaccus-
tomed to her ostensible meekness, Roger lowered his voice.
"We can go over it all again with Stephen. He's just down the
hall. Would you like me to finish up here while you say hello
to him?"

Any excuse to wander around the halls frequented by Martin Parris was thrilling. Sylvia assented. "I would like to go.
Now." As if the two young lawyers might well have read her
mind, she added, "Stephen. I want to see him now. If that's
all right."

Roger led her to the door, pointed out the dark office that
held her younger son. "I'll give you some time alone with
him. Then we can all drive to Paramount together. It's going
to be fine."

Sylvia nodded. She did not move after Roger closed himself
back inside. Not even a custodian was anywhere in sight. She
felt abandoned, a child cast out of a classroom by an impatient teacher. She let the gassy glow of the polished floor
amuse her while she waited to be snapped to attention, called
to account for her presence.

A man in a black suit emerged from the room to which
she'd been directed. He looked to either end of the hall and
finally laughed. Walking toward Sylvia, he said, "I'm afraid
I'm a little confused about where I go next. Could you help
me? My name is Abe. Abe Sisitkin."

Sylvia discovered she could not move. Feeling she was in
danger of being identified as the mother of the vandal, she
could only say, "The rabbi?"

"At Beth Israel. I'm scheduled to meet with Judge Parris,
right about now, I'm afraid. I've got myself disoriented. Is he
in the annex?"

"I'm a visitor." Sylvia was alive. She eluded her urge to
smile. She saw no advantage to be gained by revealing herself
to this man, whom she would likely never meet again. Instead,

she felt she'd been posted here as a guide, a Samaritan. It was hers to protect the holy man who could make of Stephen's crime a fortunate fall, who could make of Stephen a prodigal son.

"I'm sorry, then."

"Nothing in this building is very well marked. Here." Sylvia walked to an open door. "We'll ask." She looked in and waved at the elderly woman behind the desk. "Can you tell me how to find Judge Martin Parris? His office."

The rabbi stood next to her. "I've forgotten where I was to meet him. And, naturally, I am late."

"Come in." The woman stared at Sylvia, annoyed she had not joined the rabbi by the office window. "Please, come in."

"No, thank you. You will help him, though?" Sylvia mimicked Roger's officious tone.

The woman addressed the rabbi. "That's what I collect my check for. I can dial the judge and tell him you're on your way."

Sylvia said, "I hope you'll show him the way as well. Goodbye. Thank you." She closed the door, elated, headed for the release room, eager to make use of her few remaining private minutes with Stephen. Unspecific as were her plans for him, she was confident about her instincts. There was an end in sight.

When her knocking brought no response, she opened the door. In the half-light, she saw her son, seated in the wooden chair, his clothes in a small pile near his feet. He was naked.

She shut the door, pressed her back against it, to deter any other visitors. "Why aren't you dressed? Stephen, you're too skinny. Please dress." She irrationally assigned blame for both his nakedness and his weight loss to the jailers in whose custody he'd spent three days. "They made you strip?"

Stephen smiled, spoke as if he was afraid he might offend her. "They make you strip, to search you before they leave you alone. I can dress as long as you are here. You'll be the witness." He collected his clothes and pulled on his slacks and shirt. With his shoes in his hand, he sat on the floor, his back against the wall beneath the window. "Please, take the chair. Sit down. I'll tie my shoes. You sit in the chair. Please."

Sylvia acquiesced, sensing his embarrassment. "We'll feed you right away, sweetheart. How are you otherwise?"

Stephen wrapped his arms around his legs. "Did you come alone for me?"

"Roger is down the hall."

He stood up, shook his head, walked a full circle around her. "I meant, where is your husband?"

"Why don't you sit here?" Sylvia stood.

"I think you should be sitting in that chair." Stephen clapped his hands. When she sat, he felt a twitch relax his shoulders. He knelt on the floor, near her feet. "I made it dark in here. I thought you might not want to be seen in here with your husband."

Sylvia looked at the door, thinking he was behaving oddly to annoy a guard or court officer who'd look in on them. Seeing no one, she stood again. "Your father sends his love. He had to be at the office."

"That's another question. How many husbands do you think you have, anyway?"

Sylvia could not penetrate this act. The belligerence annoyed her. "Stephen, stop it with the ridiculous questions. You might be grateful. You are being released."

"Why didn't your other husband come?"

As if rationality could take the day, Sylvia calmly said, "I have one husband and he will see you tonight at home."

He stood, clapped his hands, clearly delighted. "Now we're getting somewhere." He clapped again. "Woman? You got more than one husband. Don't you? I know all about your other husband." Watching her walk toward the door panicked him. He wanted her alone, on his territory, where he could elicit the name Arthur refused to give him. "Or are there more than two? You can tell me. I can see it all. You were some kind of whore before my time. That's what I see now."

Sylvia backed herself against the door. "Don't act like a crazy, Stephen. I know better. I know you."

"I am sorry to have to be the one to say it, but you got to know a lot of men in your time."

Sylvia found it impossible to trace the accusations to a source. "Who have you been talking to?"

Stephen felt she was within reach. He molded his voice with comfort. "You can tell me, of all people. No one else has to know. But I have to know. Why else would we be here?"

Sylvia swung the door open and Roger was in the room, a little startled. "Why the blinds?"

Stephen immediately hoisted the slats to the top of the frame. The release of light confused him, as if Roger had burst in on them with a spotlight. He folded his arms across his chest prudishly and stepped behind the chair. A parody of a humiliated, polite child, he said, "Hello, Roger, thank you for coming. Can Mom and I meet you in the hall?"

"I'll wait at the top of the stairs." Roger closed the door as he left.

Stephen's nervous hands found the pockets of his shirt. Elated to discover he was fully dressed, he rubbed his legs and hips and proudly patted his chest.

"Stop doing that with your hands, Stephen. Leave yourself alone."

Sylvia's voice startled him. "What are you doing here?" He was convinced he'd dreamed the minutes naked in her presence.

"More to the point is what you are doing here. You have a long row to hoe, what with the doctors and the lawyers and all. You might try to act like you're sorry for the problems you've caused us all." She did not know what to expect.

Unable to distinguish what he'd done and said from the random urges he privately indulged, Stephen regarded his mother as a threat. "You think you're so smart. You can explain to everybody what happened. Well, you don't know everything."

Sylvia swung the door open, stepped into the hall, afraid to be alone with him.

Behind her, with Roger smiling from a distance, Stephen

whispered, "I didn't really have to undress. I just made that up for some reason."

Sylvia stuck close to Roger, even stopped as she passed through the huge oak doorway, forcing Stephen into his polite public mode. Though she did not believe he could sustain the pose, it was clear he intended the Stephen of record to be the confused and contrite youngster. The other, stranger Stephen, she suspected, would be reserved for her.

Stephen strode quickly ahead. Roger yelled, "To the right, Steve. I parked at my office," and watched Stephen veer away from the broad walk circling Park Square.

When he'd turned the corner into Wendell Avenue, Stephen looked back at Sylvia and Roger as they made their slow way toward him. Once he had their attention, he clapped his hands, then resumed his faster pace.

Sylvia looked to Roger, to see what he made of this. Unrewarded, her gaze traveled to the small raised green of Park Square. "There's a sight for sore eyes." She smiled, looked up at her confused son-in-law. "There are a couple of old-timers on the bench in the middle there. That used to be a place to sit, to really see everyone and everything in this town." She led him around the corner, away from the park. She let her gaze run across the granite courthouse, one last scan for a trace of Martin Parris. "When I was a girl, that park was the hub of the universe. I didn't think people sat there anymore."

Without precedent, Roger put his hand against the small of her back. The coy, wistful way she spoke of herself as a girl was a revelation. But the morning had prepared him for this first glimpse of Sylvia's frailty, her desire to perpetuate memories rather than establish her presence. "Has it changed much? The city?"

Sylvia laughed. "The city? You mean Pittsfield? You know, when the population got to fifty thousand—that must have been the late fifties. Anyway, at that point all the state and local soothsayers were telling us we'd have one hundred thousand people here by nineteen-eighty. We were going to have a big downtown mall. Electric trams to take you from one shop to another. Of course, the numbers haven't grown since. And the mall? They still talk about it. Every time another department store goes bankrupt. What in God's name would we do with a hundred thousand people?"

"They'd have to put condos on Park Square."

"Houseboats on Onota and Pontoosuc lakes?"

"Convert dead space at the GE into lofts for artists?"

"They had a sign in the park when I was a girl. There was some reason it was erected. Wrought iron. Fourth of July in a special year or some anniversary? It said, *You are now at the very heart of the Berkshires.* I used to read that sign and close my eyes and make a wish." Sylvia lowered her voice as they moved into Stephen's range. "I haven't thought about that sign in twenty years."

Stephen climbed into the backseat after Roger unlocked the car doors. "What were you talking about just then, Mom?"

Sylvia stiffened, did not turn to him. "The park. Over the years."

"Someone should write it all down, the history of it. So everyone will know what happened." Stephen advanced this as a friendly, offhand suggestion. He meant to ease himself back inside the borders of her confidence. He'd thought of nice words he could speak to her, apologies for acting bad in public and a plea for her version of the story of his father. But his intentions were not honored. The stranger Stephen stood between them like a filter, transforming *write it down* into a challenge. He saw that Roger, too, had received his words as threats; he eased the stick shift toward reverse as if the gears were made of glass.

Still, Stephen did his best to see his mother in the kindest light, the private ambience of walking hand-in-hand to stores and church, the teasing way she'd wink whenever she confessed a secret about adults in the family or the neighborhood. Stephen kept the faith. He blamed Roger for her silence. What she really thought of Alison or Artie, her distrust of Mrs. Hammerstone next door, the hypocrisy of parish priests, her promises about his growing up to be much stronger than his father—Stephen learned the truth about his family and the outside world as secrets she entrusted to him. He couldn't see her holding back the truth about his father too much longer.

Afraid to speak, lest he upset her accidentally, Stephen reached his hand out, gently tapped his mother's head, assuring her that secrets would be safe with him. This snapped Roger to attention. He eyed Stephen in the rearview mirror. Sylvia leaned forward very slowly, disengaging Stephen's resting hand as if it were a snake poised to writhe around its prey. She hooked her fingers into air vents on the dash and held her body out of striking distance.

Stephen rubbed his fingertips across his palm, to feel what she had felt. He was convinced: In everything he did, the stranger interceded. Hands safely pinned beneath his thighs, he closed his eyes and asked for help from God, reminding Him he ought to have some expertise in matters of good sons and their fake fathers.

V

HETTY MARSHALL WAS AMAZED Arthur remained on the bench in Park Square, especially after Sylvia and Roger disappeared. She stared at him, trying to decipher his passiveness. His elbows were balanced on his thighs, his gaze still fixed on the courthouse door, waiting for Judge Parris to burst out and join the others.

Skeptically, sadly, Arthur said, "She looked right at us."

"Sylvia? She didn't recognize us. We only knew it was her because we were expecting to see her." Hetty imitated Arthur's pose to facilitate conversation. "She would have waved. Or come over here."

"The way she looked back, over her shoulder?" Arthur paused, though not for reassurance. He was waiting for something else to happen. Something definitive. "I didn't even have an urge to go over to them. They looked so relaxed. And normal." He turned his face to Hetty, sensing words alone would not justify his failure to intercede. "When we're all together, in one place? At home, I mean. It's not normal. It's a disaster."

"Will they go home from here?"

"Roger's office is just down the block. Next to the Legion Hall. Maybe they'll go there. Or is it lunch time?"

Responsible for having delivered Arthur to within shouting distance of the courthouse, Hetty tried to arrange for their withdrawal without emphasizing his failure to make use of their strategic placement. "Where would we go for a fancy lunch in the big city?"

Arthur devoted a few seconds to staring at each of the buildings ringing the square: the utility company, the former library appropriated as an annex of the adjacent courthouse, the few remaining churches, the colonial city hall reborn as a bank. "You want to go to lunch around here?"

"That's a ringing endorsement for the idea, Adamski. Would you rather go back to Dalton?"

"We could go anywhere." Arthur announced this as if Hetty might not know they were seated at the center of Pittsfield's principal traffic rotary.

Exasperated by his immobility, she sat back, uttered "ha" a few times. "The troops will starve at this rate."

For Hetty's amusement, he stood and struck a military attitude. He faced South Street, pivoted crisply, scouting the snaggle-toothed array of subdivided buildings, vacant shops, and Pittsfield's one hotel. East, North, and South streets seen, he stopped, forgoing the appropriate conclusion to his mock military inspection. "I can't think about lunch. Look at me. I don't know whether to rush home or just get the hell away from all this."

"How does a quick beer at the Legion sound? Then I'll drop you at home. I can swing by in the morning and we'll drive up to Dalton together." Hetty was up and by him.

Arthur did not want to walk past Roger's office, which ruled out a visit to the new American Legion Hall. "I'll take that

ride. Just the ride." He wouldn't look at her, certain he would
betray his fear.

Just as Arthur caught up with her, Hetty spread her arms to
block his progress. "I said the beer word. Do we have to get
you to Detox right away?" She let her arm swing down behind
him, lightly touched his back. "A little levity. Make 'em laugh.
Come on, I'll take you home." She led him to her car. They
didn't speak.

This was the one liberty Hetty took with Arthur's private
life. She drew on it sparingly, so sparingly she received almost
no nourishment from it. His confession of alcoholism was the
only of Arthur's many astonishing confessions she used against
him—against Sylvia, really.

Initially, this policy was fueled by frustration. Hetty had
lived with the recoveries and relapses of a drinker, her late
husband Jack. Without recourse to the medical evidence of
alcoholism as a disease, which had since made recovery a
noble, open-air affair, she'd taught herself to think of sober
Jack living in a locked corral. With the help of a few other
wives of anonymous alcoholics, she'd learned to love Jack
within his limits.

To shelter Jack from failure—and, eventually, to meet the
mortgage on the six-room saltbox that constituted shelter for
them both—she became his partner and, in effect, his supervisor, in various commercial ventures.

As a result, Hetty's widowhood did not deliver her to the
typical swell of sympathy and support. For her refusal to bring
children into their imperfect union, Hetty won little praise. A
childless widowhood was seen as something of a self-made
scourge. Even longtime friends suspected barrenness was a
punishment she'd courted with her forays into commerce.
Hetty left Albany with a different understanding. In her
scheme, she was victim, not creator, of her fate. Her tentative
but relentless prodding of Arthur's confessed addiction confirmed this destiny for her; she figured she was doomed to be
attracted to alcoholic men.

Then she stumbled onto Arthur in a bar, which brought her nearer to the truth.

Just days shy of her tenth anniversary in Dalton, Hetty was invited to speak to a group of women veterans at a career seminar sponsored by American Legion Post 68. When she arrived at the building on Wendell Avenue, she poked around in several rooms and finally wandered into the large, sparsely decorated lounge to ask for help. At the bar, with a half-empty glass of beer, was Arthur, his attention fixed on a televised Red Sox game.

It was an old nightmare come alive. Hetty literally ran from the bar, eventually found her seminar, delivered a hasty and confusing speech that guaranteed she would never be invited back. She did not even offer to field questions. As she spoke her final words, she collected her briefcase and coat, headed upstairs to the bar. She stared at Arthur's chosen stool and was propelled by the satisfaction of confronting him—Arthur and Jack both—in the act of betrayal.

"What are we drinking tonight, Adamski?"

"Marshall!" Arthur yelled, swung around to face her, thrilled she had turned up. "Ted? Ted, get us another Coke for the boss here." He guided her onto a stool.

Hetty stared at the nearly empty glass of soda in a small puddle of water next to Arthur's tie on the bar. She was tempted to pick it up, sample the contents. "Just a plain soda for you there?" This failed to emerge as accusation or suspicion; it sounded like a suggestion, as if he might do well to add a twist of lemon.

Arthur was still smiling expectantly, waiting for her to launch into a funny story about how she'd landed next to him. "This? Mine? Now it's just a Coke. Earlier I had a glass of beer." He sipped his soda. "I give in like that a couple times a month. No real willpower, I guess. Why are you here?"

Hetty realized she'd brought an arsenal of defensive weapons to do a woman's work. She was overprepared, ready to deal with his anger, his shame, his litany of excuses. She couldn't hold him in focus. As she might stop a vaguely familiar passerby to ask his name, she said, "Aren't you an alcoholic?"

Arthur answered gravely, "And I have to be aware of that when I come in here. Yes." He whisked his tie off the bar, checked it for stains, then displayed it to her. "Should be more careful with the tools of my trade."

Finding no correlation between his behavior and her accusatory pose, she handled her cool glass, staring down at him. Finally, feeling it obligatory, she asked, "Are you drunk, Adamski?"

"Come off it. Once a year maybe. At home. But on the whole, I don't, since I figure I have such a problem with it, with drinking. I can't afford to get drunk all the time." Arthur raised his hand, and the bartender delivered another soda.

Hetty began to suspect she was drunk. She could not get a fix on Arthur Adamski, alcoholic. She was seeing him through a kaleidoscope; every time he spoke or smiled, her image of him got jumbled up. And for nearly two years she returned to this unresolved perspective, even after she and Arthur institutionalized long Friday lunches for private discussion of Spectronics business, during which he would occasionally substitute a beer or two for his standing Coke order.

Finally, she could not tolerate one more attempt to rectify the fractured image. Arthur had finished his third soda at a Friday lunch. He was pitching his idea of contracting an independent advertising representative to cover eastern Canada.

As if the night at the Legion had yet to end, Hetty interrupted him midsentence. "Excuse me. I have to cut in here and this is going to sound ridiculous. This is from left field. I have to say—and I am not exactly a novice here, Adamski. I just have got to tell you I do not leastways believe you are an alcoholic." This was delivered apologetically. Hetty found herself in the odd position of having to justify her disbelief. "You don't act like an alcoholic. You don't lie about drinking. Or hide your beers." Citing reasons animated her. "You don't even drink too much. I've talked to friends about you. I've even asked for advice. I watch you, and I listen to you, and I just don't believe it. Not in the least."

Arthur was surprised by her indiscretion, her admission of devoting so much attention to him. It pleased and embarrassed him. "Well. Thank you. Wherever that came from, thank you. Really." Disposed as he was toward her diagnosis, he'd long since learned that by denying he was an alcoholic he only raised the specter of Denial. In the upside-down modern world, proclaiming himself sick was a symptom of health. "But I am an alcoholic. If you lived with me . . ." Arthur knew it was a sentence he should not finish. It led into their private, unspoiled territory.

Hetty was oblivious to the implications. "I've lived with a drunk. If I lived with you, I would know damn right well you're a man who likes a beer, just a man who—a man like you. Any fool could see as much."

Arthur was stunned. He knew it was up to him to substitute the name of his wife for "any fool."

She had thrown open the gate, stood at the border of the acreage she and Arthur held in sacred trust. Bravely, she set foot on the land. "My opinion is worth something to you here. You have to hear this." She watched Arthur's amazement fade to amusement. He would not follow her. At best, he might extract some pleasure from her transgression. He would not be with her. "There you have it. Hetty Marshall with the News of the World." She slammed the gate, stood overlooking the land beyond, her hand on an old, sturdy post.

Arthur experienced her retreat as relief. It safeguarded his conviction that what Sylvia and Parris had done was unnatural, inhuman. "Anyway, enough about me. What about this ad rep in Toronto?"

Almost ten years later, Hetty was still drawn back to that fence. She'd get herself there with a crack about Arthur's alleged drinking problem. A reference to the beer word was enough to win her a few lovely minutes leaning on the gate. It was not the fate of the land that concerned her. That land would always be there. But leaning on the gatepost gave her a chance to check the timber and the hinges and assure herself she could yet exercise her right of way.

VI

SYLVIA, STEPHEN, AND ROGER stood in unison from the yellow plastic chairs in the Paramount Counseling Service waiting room. Scot Morita smiled, swept the air with his clipboard, urging them to sit down and relax. "I'm just here to get the simplest facts. I'm not the doctor." He dragged a plastic chair from behind a white table at the small room's center. "My name is Scot. I'm an intake counselor. The title is much worse than the job." He dropped the clipboard, picked it up and dropped his pen, a practiced show of clumsiness to defuse apprehension. He rolled the sleeves of his white shirt and loosened his tie. Though he would soon be applying his master's degree in psychology more directly to the patients, for the few remaining days before promotion to professional staff it was his turn to serve as the opening act. He was warming up the crowd.

Roger provided lengthy introductions, including a parenthetical description of his caseload. All the while, Stephen worried he wouldn't manage to control himself. He suspected they'd arranged to have this Scot character guard him while they waited. Just six feet tall, by every other measure Scot was twice as big as Stephen. The implication Stephen drew—supported both by Roger's smug cooperation and his mother's apprehensive manner—was that Scot had clearance to use force to deal with any outburst.

Sylvia was trying to assess the first shock of public embarrassment. The news accounts, the interviews with court officials and police, had not indicted her. But here she was, her crazy son in tow, waiting for a diagnosis of her failure as a mother. Twenty years ago she'd grabbed hold of Arthur and the children, dragged them all inside the house, and locked the door.

But Stephen, whom she'd held nearest to her heart, had broken free of her embrace.

Word was out. He was a rumor of a hidden history. The investigative interest of doctors, lawyers, and reporters was ignited. Twenty years' fermented hope had compromised instinctual response. Instead of rescuing her son and salvaging her home, Sylvia delivered Stephen here to Paramount. The probing of the doctor now would surely fan the flames. Everything would burn.

Still, Sylvia believed that all would not be lost. Parris knew of her predicament. She felt his presence in Stephen's quick release from prison, the retraction of the pending charge. A full-out fire on Holmes Road would bring him to the scene, to rescue what was his.

"Mrs. Adamski? Would you rather fill out the form yourself?" Scot offered her the clipboard.

Sylvia turned to Roger for an explanation. "Was he talking to me?" She looked at Scot, shrugged off her own question. "I wasn't listening to a word you said."

Roger intervened. "I can fill that out for you. It's already been a long day."

Sylvia ignored Roger. She stared at Scot, trying to resolve his Asian features and the accompanying traits and mannerisms, in an attempt to ascertain his ethnic identity. Guessing his height correctly, and gauging his weight at something like two hundred pounds, she concluded he must be Hawaiian. Or Polynesian. She could not remember what she'd once been told about distinctions among cheekbones and eye shapes, so she flirted with several lineages.

With Roger's proficient answers, Scot completed his task. "No more data questions. But we still have a few minutes before Dr. Daye can see you. I could fill you in on the program, answer general questions?" Scot watched Roger turn to Stephen, then to Sylvia, prodding them to seize the initiative. "It's not mandatory. I know this is an odd setting for small talk." Scot did not betray his interest in Stephen, whose case fascinated him; he kept his eyes on Sylvia. "You look a little confused, Mrs. Adamski. Was I unclear about something?"

By now, Sylvia had herself completely confused about this young man, certain only that she found him unusually attractive. "Are your parents Hawaiian? I only ask because you're so tall." She shrugged. "I'm sure you must be asked this all the time." She wanted to make sure he knew it was his fault she'd inquired. "Of course, it's not important." She shunted her interest, to show her willingness to forget the whole episode.

"My parents are both from the northern part of Japan. They grow them bigger in the North. I confuse a lot of people." This was essentially a prerecorded message.

"Japanese." Sylvia said this somberly, a student repeating a lesson, determined to absorb the classification. "Well, I am Irish. My husband is Polish. That makes Stephen—" She needed several seconds to recover from the stupidity of having led herself to this point. "Stephen is his own man. And I do hope you aren't offended by my mention of your race, Mr. Miskita."

"Morita." Scot put a hand to his head, ran it through his hair.

"We have too many names to remember lately." Sylvia saw Stephen swivel in his chair. He was facing her now. "Stephen, I'm sure we could get you a coffee or a soda from a machine."

He patiently waited for her to face him. Then he raised his eyebrows, opened his mouth slightly.

"There is a machine." Scot stood.

"Hello? Can I come in? Whoa! Hello?" The words boomed from the hall. A few kicks to the door followed. "Scot?"

Scot opened the door, closely watched by the others. A handsome man with a bulging stomach and very little hair ran into the room carrying two stacks of overstuffed manila folders, laid his torso and the folders on the table.

"Morning, Doctor. Won't you come in?" Scot stayed by the door.

The doctor was erecting a single tower from the contents of

the folders. "Another ten seconds and I would have kicked the door down. These are yours and they got dumped in my office where there is not room for so much as a potted plant. So you deal with them and make us all feel good about giving you a promotion, which means you'll spend the rest of your days figuring out what the hell to do with your files, and precious little else." He stood straight, turned to his audience. "I am Bill Daye. I don't always make such a tremendous entrance. I don't see why we can't spring for real chairs instead of those." He pointed to Roger, moved toward him. "You're certainly not him? No." He eluded Roger's hand. He sidled toward Stephen. "You're the one. Stephen? Want a coffee?"

Stephen did not look back. He followed Daye from the room, grateful for the rude treatment of his captors.

Scot moved to the table, to stave off the collapse of his towering client records. "I'll get that coffee soon as I get these to my new office, Mrs. Adamski. That was Dr. Daye." Reassuringly, he added, "He is a psychologist. The sessions run an hour. I'm assuming you will wait."

"Roger? I can wait alone."

Annoyed by the incoherence of the morning, Roger said, "I'll stay. And let's see if we can't get some information about exactly what this entails, in the longer term. Right?"

"Oh yes. Exactly." Sylvia had no idea what he might mean. "And just cream in my coffee. Roger?"

"I'll pass on the coffee."

Calmly reassembling his folders, Scot nodded, silently assuring both of them that, had he the bad luck to be related to them, he certainly would break a few laws.

VII

BILL DAYE LED STEPHEN into his rectangular office, ushered him to a black vinyl wingback chair. "Scot gave me your court file this morning, Steve." He moved to an identical chair opposite Stephen, pointed to a red file on the desk behind him. "Your first offense. This business at the Beth Israel?" He dragged a small Lucite table from beside his chair, propped his feet on it. "Relieved to be out?" He glanced at Stephen for the first time, then examined the loose folds of his own stomach, tucked his striped shirt deeper into his trousers. "Am I right you dropped out of college this semester, Steve?"

"My name is Stephen."

"Oh, that's fine with me, then. Stephen it is."

"Stephen it is."

"I don't think of myself as one of those people who like to make mountains out of molehills, Steve. Stephen, I mean. This being your one and only brush with the law." He dragged his feet to the edge of his ad hoc ottoman and shoved it toward Stephen, hoping to distract him. "I'd like you to talk about how you feel."

Stephen reabsorbed the confusion he felt seeping out of him. He could not strangle his interest in the doctor's oddly familiar manner, his almost apologetic approach. "I feel that I know you."

Bill Daye understood this as a compliment, which tapped his enthusiasm. "The same goes for me. Not that we have met, because I know for sure we haven't met until just now. But when I saw you in that room with your mother and—that wasn't your brother?"

"Roger Hibbard."

"Your sister's husband." Daye shook his finger to confirm this, hooked his right foot under the small table and drew it back into his range. "Right, the lawyer." This was progress, establishing the family constellation and Stephen's perception of his place within that arrangement. "You have another sister. And a brother."

"And a mother. And a father. My mother has a husband, too."

Daye laughed, to show his empathy with Stephen's impatience with details. "I can imagine you've heard a lot from all of them. Family advice is unavoidable. Like taxes."

"Death."

Daye shook his head, clapped his hands. "Right. Death and taxes and family advice." He smiled broadly, hungrily, to demonstrate his appetite for humor.

Stephen gave out nothing. He flirted with the doctor's interest, widening his eyes and hunching forward in his chair. "You have to know which stories to believe." He shuddered, as if the words surprised him by forming themselves and securing a bypass that circumvented his reluctance to speak. "Render unto Caesar. That still holds." Stephen tucked his hands beneath his legs, to contain himself. But he was electric again. "What I am telling you is, Do not render him what doesn't belong to him. What happens if Solomon threatens to cut the little baby right in half and nobody speaks up to save the kid? You might say, Fair is fair, and both fathers get a leg and an arm. But that would be a bloody mess. Cut it right through the waist and you can balance both ends on platters. Even though one half would be upside down, the plates would stop the flow of blood." Stephen released his hands, held them out toward the doctor, palms up, as if they were the platters he'd described. Impatient with Daye's silence, he stood, chastised the doctor for his unreadiness to share this burden. "This is the sort of thing I have to imagine. I have to be ready to judge these cases." He swung his arm through the air as a blade. "You've got a world full of people trying to make peace. I have to split the thing in two." He held up his hands again, demonstrating the unsteady counterbalance. "Opposing halves."

Daye just concentrated on Stephen's hands until the severed halves of the child he'd conjured faded and finally disappeared. The scale became hands guided into pockets, then upholstered knobs protruding from the frail curve of the hipbone. The doctor did not raise his head. He gauged his sectional view of the young man, studying the small pleats gathered between each loop by the tightly notched belt, and the spare material drooping above either hip.

Stephen sitting had the effect of displacing the torso with the face in Daye's frame. The doctor considered this a triumph. The patient was coming down, returning. Mindful of the tenuousness of this victory, he offered Stephen a sad, compensatory smile. "Sometimes I think the hardest part of my life is thinking about my choices, or my options. Harder than anything I actually do." He pretended to consider this opinion, as if he hadn't pronounced it to as many patients as he'd seen that month.

Stephen waited for the doctor to approach him. He must have understood; he'd given Stephen signs of their allegiance— ignoring Sylvia and Roger, arranging matched chairs for their meeting, his cozy fussing with the table and his clothes. He'd made himself available and courted Stephen's confidence.

Daye construed this silence as he had the outburst that preceded it, as antagonism. The lack of correspondence between Stephen's inauspicious criminal history and his behavior was not engaging. Mimicked madness, suggestive non sequiturs, and exaggerated pantomimes of pent-up anger were the stock in trade of young men shirking off the blame for their delinquencies. Though he never would have said as much, Daye believed the principal determinant in psychological health was the will to be well. A dozen years of dealing with first-time offenders had cemented this position. Annoyed by the theatrics of a young man whom he took to be a social misfit on the basis of his physical appearance, and whose rather juvenile crime he credited to generations of Catholic anti-Semitism, Daye stood, walked behind his desk. "We won't get anywhere if we don't talk to each other. You don't have to shout to get my attention." He plucked Stephen's red file from his desk. "It says here you're on my docket for three visits a week. Let's agree on one thing. We have enough material to sustain our interest without either one of us resorting to fits and yelling."

Stephen squinted, made the doctor vague and far away, indistinct enough to resemble a bemused professor, Arthur, or the judge presiding at his hearing: another man pretending not to understand.

What would Jesus do?

This was not a facile formulation or delusion of the grandest sort. Stephen lived with Jesus as the precedent for acting as a good man in the world. His belief in miracles, in Word made flesh, was not unreasoned or unique. The faith he brought to bear was not a personal invention. It was the faith professed by millions of Christians. He didn't cage his Jesus or the parables and prophets in fundamental confines. Scripture offered models, metaphors, and ideals to the modern man, to Stephen. Lonely nights in Amherst, whispered stories about Alison's unhappiness with Roger, his brother Artie's unremitting distance—Stephen filtered all of it through faith, a lens that let him see as if through others' eyes, which made the world seem comprehensible, if still unkind.

He had been taught, and he believed, the world itself was good. Jesus saved the world. Of course, goodness could be hidden or disguised. Tempered by his loneliness, the normal wishing for a greater share in popularity and other prizes parceled out unequally along the way, his faith sustained him in his efforts and served as a repository for the relative successes, joys, and unanticipated pleasures he accrued.

Lately, Stephen had been fidgeting with faith, adjusting the lens. He'd discovered it could be inflammatory. But his methods were crude, which made the results impossible to quantify.

Arthur's incomplete confession made this tinkering necessary. Stephen realized he'd overlooked a lot.

In fact, Arthur had delivered Stephen to another world. Lies and secrets animated children and their parents. Accidents displaced intentions. Words were cast as nets, to consolidate a host of contradictory actions. It was a man-made place, a godless world. Still, Stephen's only equipment for investigation was his faith.

He opened his eyes, brought Dr. Daye back. Lodged between two worlds, he gave up hope of rescue and asked for nothing more than solace. "Do you ever touch one of your patients? Like, maybe hug them or anything?"

Daye looked up, following the question Stephen launched. He saw he could receive it as a taunt, an accusation, or a feigned plea issued to entrap him. Hoping to defuse its force, he answered on the basis of setting straight the record. "Let me think, Steve. I mean, no. In the sense that I don't practice interactive therapy. Was that what you meant?" He could see the answer disappointed Stephen. "I'm not trying to avoid you here. What did you want to know?"

Stephen found it unbelievable that this big man did not stand up, take a step or two, and hug him.

VIII

ARTHUR MANAGED TO EXPEND the better part of the afternoon wandering from room to room, repeatedly inspecting the contents of the refrigerator, scanning the bookshelves in the bedrooms, cleaning the small filters that screwed into the base of each spigot. He found nothing worthy of his attention in the girls' bedroom or the dining room, largely because none of the windows in those rooms gave him a post for observing Dorothy Hammerstone as she turned over the summer flower gardens that outlined her backyard. From Stephen's bedroom and from the kitchen, she could be seen at her best, kneeling in profile, occasionally using her knees as a fulcrum and tipping toward the far bank of her suburban moat.

Cursory invasions of Stephen's privacy failed to turn up anything interesting, and Arthur's attempts to imagine himself pronouncing the name *Martin Parris* aloud, to Stephen, were not successful. Flirting with the idea of sauntering out the back door in his chinos and old T-shirt, he would make his way to another window, as if chance alone was charting his course.

Inventing a friendly, covertly seductive interaction with Dorothy was effortless. She always arched her back when he approached her, ran her hands through her short yellow hair and smiled, apologizing for her appearance, then said, "Oh, Art, it's great to see you. Would you like a beer? I've had a couple in the fridge forever."

Whether his ruse involved the borrowing of a rake or alerting her to a cracked storm window, the object of Arthur's forays was singular. Visiting Dorothy was one of his rare indulgences of vanity. He knew, and Sylvia repeatedly told him, Dorothy thought he was handsome. Sylvia would watch Dorothy hanging her linens and, in a mocking nasal voice, whisper, "He's so handsome, Sylvia. How do you stand it?"

The existence of Dorothy's grammar-school-age daughter gave Arthur a haven in his notion of impropriety. And the occasional appearance of one of Dorothy's young admirers in an expensive European car further dimmed his ardor. But the principal deterrent was his worthiness as a mate for Sylvia.

Since their first meeting, Arthur had marked and admired Sylvia's superiority—her quick wit, her rabid acquisition of facts, the way she scoped out people's quirks and ambitions. Added to this was an astonishing reserve of confidence, fed not by pride or even proficiency, but by a simple line of reasoning outfitted with a hook. Whether it was the prospect of raising children or the problem of installing a dishwasher, Sylvia would consider the doubts and concerns expressed by Arthur and then remind him of the tremendous number of people— fools and klutzes among them, as she would point out with brief character histories—who'd managed the very task they were contemplating. Not only was the formula indispensable, it actually mitigated the effects of mistakes and hardships encountered along the way, since the end was clearly not beyond their means. Naturally, Arthur long considered Sylvia his better, not least of all because she so willingly shared this capacity for daily life.

Sylvia showed no sign of weakening until she ran to Martin Parris, as she might have run to greet her father, drawn to danger. Arthur absorbed this offense against their marriage. But, much to his surprise, he found himself incapable of using it against her, or even showing her the horror of its presence in his life. He kept it to himself and found in his resolve to hide it from her a way of giving Sylvia something wonderful, something commensurate with her many gifts. Not accepting a cold beer and getting alone with Dorothy in her tidy brick house was a feature of his desire to correct the balance, to make things even.

But a perfect balance, as Arthur and Sylvia learned, is a peculiar and demanding premise for a marriage. They'd done little more than verify the intervening distance for the better part of twenty years.

IX

AFTER A SILENT LUNCH with Roger, Sylvia and Stephen found Arthur at work in the kitchen. He was replacing the frayed yellow ropes in the two small windows over the sink. Seated on the grooved stainless steel counter, he was surrounded by moldings, screws, a scissors and screwdriver, and a new length of white rope bound around itself to form a noose. With his feet in the sink and a six-pane window on his lap, his impractical impulse to clear out of the kitchen had propelled him into a childlike squat. He looked like an oversized boy awaiting a sponge bath.

Stephen shadowed Sylvia, hiding himself from Arthur, until she crossed the threshold. He clapped loudly. Sylvia swiveled and he slid past her, scooted into the alcove, his back to Arthur.

"Welcome home, Steve. Hello, dear. All's well?" Arthur's attempt to stand only rocked him back onto the counter.

"Don't jump, Arthur." Sylvia edged along the short wall to the living room threshold. "No one has the energy to catch you."

Stephen was facing her, seated on the corner of a built-in bench, his right hand wrapped around the lip of the table. He looked past her, marking the line to the staircase. He held to that line, prepared to rappel to safety should Arthur bound out of the sink and give chase.

Stephen's paranoid readiness was not entirely inappropriate, though Arthur hardly was poised for an attack. In his criminal and public incarnation, Stephen was a threat, keeper of the secret Arthur had hastily exhumed and animated in a fit of sadness. Though his presence struck discordant notes in Sylvia and Arthur, he managed to exact a kind of harmony from the dissonance. Facts notwithstanding, a marriage had been made for twenty years on mutual unbroken vows of secrecy. What Arthur saw in Stephen was his wife's accuser; with Stephen ranting, she was again the infidel. For Sylvia, Stephen represented Arthur's status as a cuckold. They both regarded him as perpetrator of the crimes they had committed.

Stephen could not parse the convoluted grammar of their silence. Still, he felt the twisted, withered strands of shame and yearning arbor and entrap him. His anxiety was animalic, mute. His parents' stillness didn't soothe him. They were not passive, they were waiting on a brutal, predatory instinct.

Stephen tried to stifle a yawn; he closed his mouth, dragged air in through his nose, and water bleared his gaze. Despite this effort, his body let alertness drain away. During his short stay in jail, he had inverted nights and days, sleeping through until midafternoon, to temper the absurdity of physical restraint just as he'd discovered boundless energy. He lurched up and out of the alcove, clapped his hands for cover, ran by his mother, and raced upstairs to bed.

Having braced himself for a physical confrontation with Stephen, Arthur sighed, turned to Sylvia, who walked across the room and lit the burner underneath the kettle. Shuttling between counters, Sylvia made tea as Arthur fiddled with his window. Unworded feelings—raw or insulated, whimsical or visceral—left no wake. Time glided by.

Steeping tea in hand, Sylvia moved around Arthur blithely, cleaning the table and the counters with a damp sponge. Recovered from the paralyzing hope of proximity to Parris, she diffidently resumed her wifely duties. She delivered minimal details about the terms of Stephen's freedom, circumventing Stephen naked in the courthouse, the questions he had raised about her lovers, and his clapping hands. Arthur asked twice, indirectly, about what he did when he first stepped outside the courthouse, to ascertain if he and Hetty had been spied. Sylvia's suspicion was not roused. But the details she withheld from Arthur were magnified. In her unwillingness to represent these weird facts, she recognized the potency of Stephen's problem. Was her son insane or mad or crazy? She chastised herself for possessing only crude and useless measures such as these.

A telephone call from Alison snapped Sylvia to attention. Singular as they had made him, Stephen was not her only child. She brought herself around with several sips of steaming tea, resumed her role as household engineer, handily dispensing with Roger's gloomy recapitulation of the morning's business, and presenting Alison with a schematic of the future which again obscured the secrets old and new that shaped the contours of the family home.

Arthur did not listen to the words she spoke, lulled as he was by her reassuring mother tones. Even Stephen's name, and *court* and *doctor*, were benign, not catalytic. It was only when she said, "Coming here?" and turned to him as if he'd better be prepared for trouble, that the dim pilot light of Arthur's paternal operations was ignited.

After a few perfunctory questions, Sylvia hung up the receiver, glared at her hand accusingly. She didn't look at Arthur. "Alison got a call from her sister. She told her about Stephen. She told Jane."

"And?" Arthur stared through a pane of the repaired window.

"Yes. Exactly. Jane and."

"And what?"

Sylvia shuffled to the refrigerator, dismissed it with a wave of her hand, headed for the back door, pivoted. Failing to find a place to land, she paced in front of Arthur. "They've been in Lenox for a couple days already. And they're coming by tomorrow. They. She's with Regina. Regina Ellington? The mystery girl. Of the 'Regina and I went to Santa Fe or France or . . .' Apparently, Regina has a cousin who owns a house in Lenox."

Arthur had a longstanding policy of refusing to believe his elder daughter was a lesbian. It was not only unimaginable— literally unavailable in his inventory of mental graphics—it was ridiculous. He held to his conviction that making a lesbian of Jane was another of Sylvia's affectations. He believed his wife had issued the diagnosis to demonstrate how up-to-date she was. "Regina is the young woman Jane shares her apartment with in New York? We haven't ever met her, have we?"

"We have never met her. Have we. And she is a professor, or some sort of doctor. At Columbia University. Please be impressed."

"When are they coming? For the day?"

Sylvia was still moving. "Well, I rather doubt they'll ask to spend the night, Arthur. Were you thinking we might get a demonstration?" She anchored her hands to the sink.

Arthur would not respond.

Sylvia leaned forward, looked out on Dorothy's yard. She made no accommodation, friendly or polite, for having stuck her shoulder into the soft flesh of Arthur's side. "It's entirely like her, to turn up with that woman right now. It's as if she can't help it, she just creates uncomfortable situations. Last Easter, when she didn't show up after all? When she'd just published that nice piece in the Sunday magazine? It's all of a piece. It's almost funny."

Arthur eased himself down from his perch without disturbing his wife. "It just occurred to me. One of us ought to call Artie." The disappearance of the one son he could claim confounded Arthur. Artie always got himself to new but unappealing places, into unfamiliar but not adventurous or rewarding situations. Arthur could not defeat the distance from his son with a simple swell of pride or manly admiration.

Arthur once had hoped that Artie's four years at Rutgers majoring in criminal justice would lead to law school or at least would yield some jokes about the Garden State. But Artie spent the intervening summers with his roommate as a counselor for underfunded federal youth-employment programs in Erie, Pennsylvania, which convinced Arthur that his son harbored alien ambitions.

Sylvia ascribed Artie's arcane but unexotic choices to a failure of imagination. But, really, the failure to imagine was her own.

Arthur said, "One of us really ought to call him. Tell him about Stephen." Eight years after Artie's graduation, he still believed he could cajole Sylvia into applying her attractive or persuasive powers to her elder son. After all, Artie had not renounced the family; there were occasional exchanges with his sisters and infrequent greeting cards addressed to the Adamski family. But presently, Arthur feared Sylvia's silence could be construed as a de facto recruitment of his services, so he added, "Of course, what to say? You can't call somebody up out of the blue and say his brother had a fit. I couldn't."

Sylvia did not admit to having sent her son a photocopy of the *Courier* account of Stephen's court appearance. It would only raise her husband's hopes or rancor.

They shared a sense of disappointment; a vague, undocumented failure. Artie was a bit of solder, a resolute remnant of the brittle and eroded seam that used to be a supple lifeline binding their desires and ambitions.

"I have an idea, Arthur. Perhaps we can let Artie know about his brother by having Jane do one of her interviews with Stephen. A profile piece for one of those newsstand magazines."

Arthur claimed the distance Sylvia imposed and used it for his own purposes. "Jane has as much right as anyone to come home. And I, for one, am happy she is coming, too."

Sylvia locked him far away, looking past him to the chat she'd have with Alison to plan a family dinner Tuesday night. Alison's proximity compensated for the distance she required when time came for analysis and binding judgments. Born with her father's temperament, she'd taken more obligingly to Sylvia's confidence and correction. From her early childhood, Alison had heard her mother out. She was not a confidante; Sylvia wasn't in the habit of confessing to mere mortals. Alison's advice was rarely sought and, unlike Jane, she wasn't apt to scrutinize her mother's motives.

Alison was the family archivist, her mother's sympathetic secretary. Overworked and rather badly compensated, Alison enjoyed a sense of power. Like her professional counterparts in offices around the world, Alison felt indispensable, as if her record of all family matters—dates and plans and third-hand stories—formed the I-beam of the overarching structure. Of course, Alison was unaware that Sylvia's idea of shelter for her family was a house of cards.

Alison's escape to college and her early married years in Boston coincided with Stephen's childhood and adolescence. Sylvia was unforthcoming with her daughter while she oversaw the machinations of what amounted to a separate, single-child family. But then, without facilitating the transformation he was born to generate, Stephen left for college (Arthur made a rare appearance in his younger son's life about this time, all but bribing him to go away to Amherst rather than attend the local community college, as Sylvia had arranged; Arthur's need for deliverance proved more desperate than his wife's concern that Stephen would be out of range when lightning struck Holmes Road); Jane reemerged, but out of reach, declared a lesbian for lack of contradicting evidence, and an occasional contributor to general-interest magazines; and Artie's private plan, to stay away forever, had outgrown its benign, forgetful aspect and become a stand-in presence. Sylvia drew Alison back to Pittsfield with tantalizing updates on the status of her wayward siblings. She pleaded for help, if coyly, with long long-distance diatribes against the tyranny of social drinking. She also made a habit of casting the occasional aspersion on the psychological health of her only grandchildren; Alison was teaching English at a junior high school and Sylvia knew her daughter was not safe from self-recrimination on this score.

Words really didn't matter. The voice that named her was enough. It was the tenor of her childhood, of prelapsarian life. That voice cinched Alison's determination to have Roger find a job in Pittsfield. Convinced that both her families would collapse without a greater share of her attentions, she prevailed upon her husband, who was stunned by Alison's display of mettle on this issue. Sylvia had made her strong. But only with her mother, or within her range, could Alison assert herself effectively.

Sylvia spoke with Alison for more than an hour about Jane and Regina. Several unflattering, speculative portraits of Regina were roughed out and worked over. Jane, they felt sure, would appear as she always did, dressed in black.

"Permanent mourning wear." Alison laughed as she said this.

"A widow . . . a widow, but without—" Sylvia gave in to Alison's infectious laughing, laid the receiver on the table and wiped her eyes. "A widow without the fuss!"

Laughter moved them through detailed plans for dinner and the itemized list of proscribed conversation topics. Sylvia was calm again. She and Arthur resumed their friendly postures. They even managed to elicit solace from Stephen's uninterrupted sleep.

As a private show of confidence, Sylvia telephoned Artie's apartment in Erie. Her estimation that he would not have finished his day's work was vindicated. She spoke slowly, somewhat querulously, to his machine: "Artie, dear? The clipping was from me. The *Courier* piece about your brother. Stephen? Or did you not get it yet? This is your mother calling, dear. I don't think I included a letter or even a note with the story. Well, you don't even have it yet. Your brother has had some trouble. It's gotten to be legal—I mean, illegal, really. He has not been feeling very well. Why don't you call me, if you want to, of course. I can always call you again. How are you? Goodbye now, son."

Artie waited for the signal whir and click of his machine, walked across his spare and unrefurbished loft apartment, replayed his mother's message to confirm that she had said, "It's gotten to be legal." He reckoned this malapropism was near enough the truth. Stephen probably had a crack-up in the family car or, more likely, had amassed an intolerably large fine for library books long overdue.

He did not erase the message. He would retire the entire tape eventually, fit it in his shoebox archive of miniature cassettes. He was already charmed by the disparity this one would create in his collection: Stephen's sophomoric plight surrounded by the complement of obscene messages from recently arrested teenagers, pleas for help in locating sons who'd run from homes with fathers' wallets or their .22s, and updates from the Erie police on the whereabouts of another of Artie's parolees infected by a wanderlust.

Artie cultivated such disproportions, and a cryptic sense of irony about them, especially the countervailing misinterpretations of his character. The cops and kids he worked with dreamed about escaping Erie; they considered his migration just another show of silly liberal thinking. But by renting in a lousy neighborhood he'd sparked their admiration. The squatter-students and inventive architects-to-be with whom he shared a massive, saggy rooftop on the smoky summer days suspected Artie was a local, a metal worker come to claim a homesite in the foundry that had employed his father and his brothers. The women he rounded up at dance clubs near the university were impressed by false warnings about his itinerant status and his disaffection with romantic situations.

And he was by now some kind of second-city cowboy, a man without a history or a proper home. The foreground of his life was empty—an arbitrary patch of land from which he kicked away the sagebrush and what tumbleweed the wind deposited nearby.

In Erie, Artie kept his family far away. The Stephen he remembered was a measure of his absence as a brother—excessively polite, unmindful of the Red Sox and the youngish widow in the neighboring brick house. *Illegal Stephen?* Artie tucked this tag line underneath his memory of Stephen bringing him a cup of coffee in the china cup and saucer Sylvia reserved for guests; Stephen had left the living room and twenty minutes later tiptoed back to offer Artie one of the fancy package cookies he'd arranged in two overlapping fans of alternating flavors.

From his span of casement windows, Artie saw Pittsfield in miniature, too tiny to support a life-size family or a criminal of any stature. This made him feel outsized. He figured he would hurt his brother if he reached in with his callused hands to mend the minor mess his mother had reported.

Of course, Artie was pleased his parents were mindful of his lurking presence. Everybody knew there was no doctor in that house; in Artie, they had a veteran practitioner in the wings.

X

STEPHEN WAS ADMIRING his own elegance as he ran along the seamed concrete sidewalk. Each exaggerated step was a slow-motion leap from the center of one white concrete square to the next. He ran for several miles, slowed only by the interruptive jeers of former classmates and television celebrities who stood, hand in hand, at either edge. A woman with a baby perched atop her head laughed and laughed until his confidence gave way. He tiptoed, raised his shoulders with each step to make his body lighter; even so, his black tie shoes cracked the eggshell surface of the path. Mud oozed and painted first his shoes and then his lower legs. Mud sucking at the soles finally displaced the noisy crowd and the geography. He was sure he shouldn't look ahead. He understood he'd got himself marooned, midway along a high, unsteady ridge, sided by precipitous, sheer walls of ferrous rock. He heard a woman yell, "Don't jump!" He looked ahead and saw her, several miles off, straddling the ridge as if it were a balance beam. It was the blond woman who drove the university shuttle bus. Even from this inordinately unfriendly remove, he knew her. She was swinging her legs. She was naked to the waist. Then, as dreamers will, Stephen foreshortened the distance between him and the naked woman with nothing more than an interested stare. At close range, he admired his bare chest and shoulders in the full-length mirror, which he decided was a photograph and not a mirror, hanging on the bathroom door. Unaware of his presence, his mother twisted the knob and pushed at the door with her shoulder. Annoyed the door would not yield, she called to Stephen. Embarrassment, and a wish to end her struggle, afforded him a relocation. He climbed a staircase, met her at the closed oak door and, with no more than a sharp rap, made it swing open. He followed his mother into his college dormitory.

The impossible white light of the dorm room woke Stephen, delivered him abruptly to the unfamiliar midnight of his bedroom on Holmes Road. Fractured amber street light skittered and spun across the glossy planes of Stephen's photographic studies of fruit and household objects. Below the unframed pictures, on shelves shadowed by his bed, he kept his textbooks, canisters of film stacked between two cameras, a printing calculator on a stack of spiral notebooks, and four place settings of cafeteria flatware set inside a white ceramic mug. He kept his meager collection out of sight, to temper his nostalgia. Stephen understood that even his most recent past was relegated to another age. The bookshelves were a reliquary.

The photographs spoke for themselves. Initially, his choice of majors angered Arthur, who suspected Stephen would accrue little in the way of ancient wisdom or commercial skill as a visual studies concentrator. Sylvia withheld her critical assessment, thereby denying Stephen the most pertinent guidance available to an Adamski child.

The oddly askew composition of his photographs—his arranged objects floated listlessly within their frames—revealed his lack of instinct. His technical experiments were primitive, imperfect resolution close-ups obscuring shape and texture so completely as to render citrus, human heads, and flowers indistinguishable, overlapping circles of confusion. Even elementary studies of light were needlessly adorned with fussy textured backdrops or his choice of odd and uninforming angles.

Stephen's efforts were nothing if not testament to his peculiar, sad capacity for self-assessment. He knew he did not measure up. His relative inferiority in workshops did not unsettle him; he was familiar with a place among the lower strata of a group his age. Still, it was redundant confirmation; his photographs, his essays, oral presentations, and the standard tests all failed him. He did not translate well. So he worked twice as hard as classmates, overtaxing his technique. And he unfailingly produced apologetic photographs, images of singular obscurity, the sort instructors pass on in reviews for final grades, in deference to the criticism inherent in the work.

Stephen was accustomed to his failure to fulfill his expectations. He tended not to vent his disappointment, wanting not to seem an ingrate in the face of opportunity. And though his mother's expectations were initially inflated—in fact, they wildly exceeded his performance standards—she did not berate him with her disbelief, the customary payoff on a mother's too-high hopes.

Sylvia exempted Stephen. She isolated him. Of course, isolation from his father was arranged to blunt heredity. Her plan, transmuted over time into a hope and frequently on the verge of devolving into an affectionate whim, retained its nascent shape if not the force of will that gave it birth. She indulged the isolation aspect, even as the likelihood of Martin Parris's interceding waned.

Sylvia diminished Stephen's opportunities for failure. She dismissed as faulty norms he fell below at school and in the neighborhood. Repeatedly, as recently as in her weekly letters to him in the spring semester of his sophomore year at college, she called attention to the higher good: not success but sacrifice, good works above good grades; not laws but love; not life but afterlife. Of course, she sermonized to spare her son the judgments of his betters. And to save herself. She appropriated Jesus and the Bible, drew from it a language to preserve her own peculiar faith. She made Stephen singular. He

couldn't disappoint his mother. What he did accomplish, like
his failures to excel, little mattered. Stephen was to be transformed. She'd staked his life on this, and with it her one hope
for a redemption.

As would anyone who'd bother to invent a new religion,
she'd devised self-serving terms for personal salvation. And
her observance of the principles and tenets wasn't faultless.
Laundry, neighbors, backaches, and the like divert most any
pilgrim. Salvation was not always on her mind, but it was
never barred admission. Whether as a silent *Go to hell* to
Arthur; a *Someday he'll be yours* to Dorothy or Hetty; or just
an undiscerning and approving glance at her reflection in a
mirror, which reliably gave way to a fey smile to acknowledge
the grayed and slightly enlarged Martin she imagined; Sylvia
had kept the faith. Faith returned the favor.

Stephen's childhood and adolescence were recorded by Sylvia and no one else. Perhaps, from his distance as the unofficial stepfather of his middle-aged wife's only child, Arthur
kept himself informed; he certainly saw no cause to intervene. Stephen was spared the harsher, more confusing aspects
of Adamski life. Unlike the older children, he was not sub-
jected to alarums of financial ruin or public censure. The once
contested marriage was allowed to slip into neglected stasis.
His youth was relatively unadulterated. As Sylvia intended,
he'd grown up in a peaceable and uneventful home.

What filtered through to Stephen from the strange and
often silent adult world above him was the Word of God. It
was a tether to his absent sisters and his brother, and a bridge
between the home and city, which he crossed weekly with his
mother. Faithful church attendance led him to faithful recitation of night prayers for absent siblings. Last born, and
often enough last in schoolyard lines or on a list of children
who had learned to multiply with double digits, Stephen was
inclined to stake his hopes on Jesus, who had said the last ones
shall be first. Not only Jesus but his mother said he had the
gift of faith, which was a sort of long-term Midas Touch for

anyone who willingly endured the hardships meted out by untrue friends and overworked, impatient teachers.

Daily, Stephen made a leap or two of faith, hopscotching rather happily from square to numbered square. His peers tossed marker stones adeptly several squares ahead, but he maintained his slower pace. Bending, tossing, leaping one block at a time while balanced on one foot was challenging enough. Increasingly oblivious to others' progress, he made his slow and steady way through high school and two years of college unjostled, if essentially alone.

Then Arthur said, "I'm not your father." Words like rain; the chalk-line boxes disappeared; even those negotiated years before dissolved. Stephen hobbled on one foot, stranded, wishing he were strong enough to pitch his rock straight up to heaven.

A low moan in his parents' room across the hall called Stephen's body to alertness, contracting muscles in his upper back and arms. His eyelids shut, he lay in wait. Arthur growled in his sleep and Stephen laughed aloud, then quickly flexed his legs, retreating into silence as the tension circuited his limbs. He felt he had to move, to let himself be moved. But where?

"Your will not mine be done." He meant these whispered words as prayer, but he spoke ruefully, exasperated by his lately inattentive God. Nor could his agitated mind invent a simple route for late-night walking. Instead, it reproduced two decades' worth of family pictures, including several snapshots of a little boy alone at breakfast in the alcove (unseen, the mother leans against the sink and says she is so lonely, and isn't the house empty since all the children went away?). Relentless memory: Even as he pulled his neatly bundled clothes from underneath the bed and dressed, he was besieged. Distorted half-light flared across his pictures on the wall, just as the lie about his father seared his likeness in invented family portraits.

He headed for the temple, which was not the temple, as his mother said. The body was the temple now. Jewish people still built temples. Catholics built churches, which were different. Stephen reached for the distinction as he tied his shoes. Instead, he got hold of memories of overgenerous meals from holidays, though he knew well his hunger was essential. A fat man serving soup in jail had said, "Proud on the outside, hungry on the inside," and Stephen misconstrued the maxim, made of it a dictum not to eat. Alert and hungry and excited, Stephen made his careful way downstairs, out the door, and then his body fed his thrill, delivered fuel for running, sweating, clapping. Churches were the rock of Peter; this seemed right to Stephen, though he couldn't figure why. Rock of Ages, Rock of Gibraltar, Rock and Roll, or Rock My Soul.

Before he'd crossed abandoned Elm Street, Stephen stopped, opened his mouth, and spit. He bent over to see what he'd spewed out. Unsatisfied, he swallowed carefully, stood straight and closed his eyes. He imagined his torso as an X-ray picture, hoping to identify the strange, illicit taste trailing down his throat to his stomach. He didn't recognize the sweet and acrid signature of bile. He worried he was tasting something filthy that was meant to be secreted. He walked slowly, strangling his urge to swallow. He spit a few times, but eventually regained his courage, gulped, then stopped. A rancid air clouded his neck and head. It was forbidden ether, related to the warm, unperfumed presence of a woman in a dark room; sweat and half-remembered dreams, wet and mingled with the freshness of a linen-service sheet; the scary incense breath of a small man who always smoked a joint before their evening English class.

Stephen ran across the street, ashamed. Abandoning his unfixed temple plans, he opted for the harbor of the pink stucco Church of the Sacred Heart. The doors were locked, but as if it were his home, he sneaked around the side and to the back in search of access, which he felt was owed him. He walked around the church a few times, convinced he had been locked out by design. Finally, he leapt across the ridge of berry bushes, rubbed his palms against the holy, wrinkled skin, begging for admission. He threw his hands up in defeat, indignant and amazed his desperate tactic hadn't made him worthy. He clapped his hands, just to be sure his efforts had not gone unnoticed, marched back to the front, and sat down on the lowest stair.

The driver of a passing car on Elm Street beeped the horn. A young girl in the backseat stuck her head out, yelled, "Everybody up! It's time for church!"

This casual invasion galled him. He was resigned to the indignities of daytime. But here, where anything might happen, Stephen counted on his privacy. Petulance gave way to fear: the driver might report his vigil to his mother or the cops. This carried him across the street, into the neighboring darkness.

Awake in bed, unnerved by what the driver might have seen, he confessed his own uncertainty about the episode to Jesus and as many saints as he could name. Not one of them relented.

No stranger to confusion, Stephen let himself be led.

What was the good of goodness if you made it to the church and it was locked? And what about his mother lying all these years? Did Jane and Artie know? And even Alison and Roger and the kids? And couldn't a professor or a kid from studio just call up Pittsfield, tell everyone they missed him down in Amherst? Someone ought to throw a rock at Arthur. Could he take a picture of the way his mother talked about her kids when they weren't home? He should've stuck a fork into the forearm of that guard who every morning called him Billy Graham, the Preacher Man.

The litany was endless, dizzying, and effortless. This mayhem is what Stephen found at the heart of finding out about his father.

Inadvertently, epitomizing his paternal style, Arthur had led Stephen to his well. It was full of impure thoughts and grand designs, words formed but never spoken, coincidences, superstitions, jealousies, accumulated sadness, and the pulverized ambitions of a young and unassertive man—an olio of urges and ideas deemed bad or inadmissible. The stagnant pool preserved unchosen, unobliging Stephen; a latent, stymied self.

Everyone has a well, is one day driven there or comes upon it dreamily midway along an aimless hike. The waters there are bittersweet. And drinking doesn't slake a thirst (imagine that: the lees of one ingested, then transformed and bodied forth). Still, some will drink, as Stephen did.

The waters were more potent than he could have known. Choices made for him and dreams resigned on his behalf had been fermenting twenty years. He was drunk on what he might have been. And still he drank, greedily. His soul was so thirsty.

The aftershock of the moist and cool October night air sobered Stephen when his body shook spasmodically, demanding his attention. Ruing interruption of his reverie, he stood and traced his hand along the wall. He found his closet, plunged his hands inside the drape of ironed summer shirts and slacks. Rejecting every item as unfit for wear in bed, he stole into the hall. In the room across the way, his mother's gownlike white terry-cloth robe hung over the back of a wicker chair beside her vanity, lit by the unsteady strobing light reflected by her hinged, three-panel mirror.

Excited by the challenge, Stephen moved ahead in half steps, each one followed by a pause to listen for a signal of disturbance. Once he had it in his hands, he pressed it to his chest, testing it against remembered softness. The robe surpassed his memory. Before he made his slow way from the room, he had it on. Circuitous as his route had been, Stephen was convinced the robe was what he'd wanted when he left the house.

It was midmorning before Sylvia resurrected the mystery of the missing robe. Habit had led her blindly from bed to vanity. Unfocused frustration had brought her to her knees, as if the robe might well have slid beneath the bed or flown into the hall.

Seeing Arthur's flannel robe on the bed alerted her to pressing duties. Draped in the red plaid robe, she rushed downstairs to make Arthur breakfast before Hetty came to pick him up for work.

Alison put in the first of several calls. Sylvia spoke briefly with Jane, issued the dinner invitation, even set the dining-room table. Before cooking commenced, she resigned herself to waking Stephen for his early-afternoon session with Dr. Daye. In the rational afterglow of several cups of coffee, it seemed plain enough that Stephen had her robe. On the way to his room, she convinced herself this was a healthy sign, a show of normal familiarity.

Stephen was sitting on his bed, wrapped in the robe. "I took it last night. While you were asleep."

She received this as a threat, and the oddity of him in her clothing, his hands teasing the pockets and sash, undid her. This was not normal. "That's fine, Stephen. It's a warm robe." Her voice was unfamiliar, faint. "I wanted to be sure you were up in time to see the doctor." She'd got herself past his bed, leaned against a low child's bureau. "Would you like some breakfast?" She watched his hands dart beneath the robe, slide across his chest and down his torso, as if the body were an unfamiliar form. Her apprehension escalated, then emerged as anger. "Stop it with the touching yourself like that, Stephen. Please now."

"I could have done anything to you. You were sound asleep."

"I don't think you should go into other people's rooms while they're sleeping. I wouldn't come in here without asking." This seemed a ridiculous stand as she made it.

Her fear inspired him. His travels in the night acquired shape. Everything had been designed to lead him to her room and to this morning meeting with her. "One of the things I had to see was if you had your clothes on in bed or not. I've been giving a lot of thought to how you seduce men with your body."

Sylvia resisted the urge to move. She knew she would go at him, try to shake him free of this obsession with her things, her body. "I don't want to listen to you spout a lot of nonsense."

He rolled his eyes, lifted the spare material gathered at his knees and rubbed it between his hands. "I went to church last night, Mom. At Sacred Heart, like we used to go. Not just out, I went to church. You're so sneaky, I bet you fucked him while I was gone."

She screamed, "Shut up!" This brought her to her feet, but she did not advance. He was staring at her waist and clapping, but she still believed she could reach him. "I am your mother and I am not going to watch you destroy yourself and this family because of some horrible idea you've got into your head. Don't even bother to think you can hurt me or anyone else by running all over this city and acting like a juvenile delinquent with no parents to take care of you. I won't have it." She was speaking to a vision of Stephen pinned to the floor by a large man, then strapped into his bed. "I'll get rid of your socks and shoes so you can't run around like a madman. Do you hear me? I'll have you locked up, if that's what it takes. I won't let a child of mine do this to himself, young man. Do you hear me?"

Stephen hugged himself, rocked back and forth. "I love it when you call me young man. That sends me right over the top."

Revulsion jolted Sylvia's head, shot through her back, and flung her arms out from her sides. To calm herself, she recited her intentions. "I am going to walk out of this room and you will get yourself into some decent clothes for your appointment and this will never happen again." She made it to the door. Then, pleading with him, she whispered, "I love you so much, Stephen."

He held out his left hand, spreading his fingers to enumerate his points. His voice was high and silly, like a young child's voice. "I have to see the doctor, and I have to clean up this shitty room, and I have some other secret things to do, and then I have to do something about this robe, too." He looked at her, hoping she might speak and provoke something else from him. But she was just leaning on the door frame, silently crying. This picture of her calmed him. As if she had explained the source of some great sadness, he smiled ironically. "I know just what you mean."

XI

D<small>R</small>. D<small>AYE</small> <small>CHECKED</small> his watch. He was relieved. He'd exhausted thirty minutes of his session with Stephen Adamski, despite the young man's refusal to answer even the simplest question. He figured he could talk his way through another fifteen or twenty minutes, deliver a closing speech about cooperation, then send Stephen on his way.

Stephen was annoyed by Daye's steadfastness. He was waiting for an outburst of anger from the doctor, to ignite himself. As incentive, he hoisted his loaded camera bag by its long strap and swung it, lariat-style, over his head.

"That's smart, Stephen. You want to break a few more windows?" Daye sat and affected a pose of complete boredom, as if every referral he'd ever counseled had performed this trick.

Stephen lowered the bag to the floor. "I had to take some pictures of my father this morning." He jerked his head up to catch Daye's reaction to this, but his face was unchanged. "Anyway, I have to get them developed. I'm late as it is."

Daye was unresponsive. Stephen's silence made of him one more uncooperative, unremarkable first-time offender. Daye knew his role well: to pose for a couple hours as the ongoing, if waning, presence of lawful, corrective authority. Like the court officers and lawyers who released these unpracticed criminals without effective punishment or even detention, Daye felt his rather weak role afforded him nothing more than a chance to express mild disapproval. "We're not here to discuss your hobbies, Stephen. This is about vandalism and trying to figure out why you want to destroy other people's property."

"I don't think you know who my father is even, Dr. Daye." Stephen still hoped to tease a name out of this man to whom his mother had consigned him. "And what kind of name is that to go around with, anyway? Daye? It's so pretentious." He clapped his hands twice. "Hou would you like it if I called myself Mr. Month? What's your real name?"

"I think making fun of people's names, or their skin color— that's about anger, too. It's about destroying something that's important to someone else because you don't understand it."

Stephen grabbed hold of the camera-bag strap. "I am not the only one confused about this, in case you haven't noticed. Someone has a lot of explaining to do." Stephen had got his voice back into its childish upper register. "Like the man with the clipboard who says he's Japanese only he happens to be about as big as ten Japanese people anybody ever saw? What about that? Or my sister Jane, who just nixed the whole thing with fathers? And I'm supposed to believe her turning up now is just an accident? Come off it. Knock it off. You're certainly not my father, and I've got the pictures to prove it."

Daye suddenly was awake to him. Unnerved by his own sedentary incompetence, he drew himself up in his chair, compensating for his previous inattention. He was reviewing the speech about Solomon and the severed baby for clues, looking for a way into Stephen. Stumbling, he said, "I don't want to make you think I don't take your questions, your ideas, seriously, Steve."

"There you go again with my name. I have the decency to use your stupid name."

"Stephen." Daye smiled, anxious to appease him. "I'm not here to be your father, Stephen."

This was too sad. "That's nothing to brag about. If you knew who he is, you'd want to be him. Mark my words." He panted, to exorcise sadness without crying. He reeled in the bag by the strap, pressed it into his lap. "At least I know what you have to do to find him. I'm getting good at that, at least." He stood, panting.

Apologetically, Daye said, "I'd like you to come by tomorrow, Stephen. Even though we're not scheduled." He had admitted defeat and was hoping to salvage his performance by transferring Stephen to the care of another doctor. "I have a friend I'd like you to meet. Meet with." His hasty inventory of the Paramount staff failed to turn up a candidate.

Stephen was wary of his optimism. "A man or what?" Despite his frustration, he could not bear to think he might choose not to meet the one person who would deliver him to his father. He did not believe in promises anymore. In the inverted world he habited, he relied on accidents and covert meanings masked in angry words of warning. He knew he had the energy to follow many leads. Indirectly, against the will of everyone who traded on the lie, he would learn the name.

Daye said, "Yes, a man. I could tell you his name—"

Stephen yelled, "Don't say it out loud. I'm not ready."

"You can make it, though? At noon, let's say?"

Stephen smiled. "You might just turn out to be a prophet after all. I'll be here all right."

"Noon." Daye figured lunchtime was his best hope for securing a favor from a friend, and he was convinced a single appointment with Stephen would be sufficient to interest any alert colleague. "I could pick you up, if that would make it easier." He wanted to guarantee he would not be responsible for driving Stephen back into the night with a rock in his hand.

"I'll be here." Stephen looked Daye over, trying to assess his motives. "I'll even bring my bag. Just in case." He patted the bag, then snaked his hand in under the loose flap, stroked the soft terry-cloth robe inside.

"Well, then, tomorrow."

Stephen ran from the office without another word. He was inspired to safeguard the robe. Convinced his sister Jane had been called in to discourage him from looking for his father, he wouldn't risk bringing it back to the house. He slung the strap over his shoulder, slowed to a trot, resurrected the memory of the locked church.

He was drawing deeply from the well of curtailed and disavowed emotions. They overwhelmed the channeling mechanics of his brain and body. The elegant assignment of intention to an idea and an action was interrupted; a cruder process operated. Stephen was a sluice for his forbidden energy.

The cotton fabric's nap tickled his palm as his mind regurgitated the doors and windows of the church. This incidental symmetry passed for thought. He would bring the robe as offering, be admitted to the church. His mother's sins of seducing false fathers would be cleansed. Then, the robe would be pleasing to his father.

XII

ALISON JOINED SYLVIA in the kitchen just before seven o'clock. She'd delivered her children to her friend's home again, spent the requisite half hour briefing and cajoling Roger, whom she finally coaxed into an appropriate posture. Minutes after their arrival at Holmes Road she began a perfunctory conversation with her father, which eventually drew a diffident question from Roger. This was Alison's cue to slip out of the room, help her mother with final preparations and pronouncements. But Alison interrupted the familiar routine. She ran upstairs to confirm Arthur's claim that Stephen was napping and might join the party later. She saw her brother cuddling his pillow; his sensible decision not to square off with Jane proved to her he wasn't crazy. She headed downstairs.

"Do you feel like putting together a salad, Alison? Or should we skip it?" Sylvia closed the oven door, moved to the sink.

"A simple one. I'll do it. Are we late?"

"They're meant to arrive at what? Seven-thirty?"

"Jane didn't call again or anything, did she?"

Sylvia was snapping the ends of wax beans donated by her neighbor Dorothy from her final harvest. "Just the one call." This call had been analyzed already. "You know, I am anxious to meet this Regina Everington."

"Ellington, isn't it?"

"That's right. It would be much harder to get through if they were men."

Alison brought a bowl and knife to her mother's side, then deposited vegetables on the counter. "You mean, if it was Artie and a man?" Alison smiled at the thought. "If he ever finds anybody—man, woman, or child—I want to meet her. Or him."

Sylvia was not listening. She was attending to her concerns about Jane. "It's true there have always been lesbians. Lesbos."

"Lesbos?" Alison understood this as name-calling.

"You know, the island of women. Wasn't it part of Greece?"

Alison covered her ignorance. It was a practiced response. "Jane will know all about that. Regina is what interests me."

"Salad, bread, lasagna. And beans? Oh well. I made a pie."

"You said. Lemon meringue. It'll be wonderful."

Sylvia shook the colander under a stream of cold water, tossed the beans a few times, then set the metal colander into the sink. She walked to the alcove slowly, wiping her hands on a towel. "I wish she could settle down and be happy. She makes me feel bad. As if I should do something more for her."

"Maybe she is happy, in her way." This was simply bait, and Alison knew it. She was not above defending her position by invoking her mother's more traditional sensibilities.

"How could she be? Living like that? She certainly never seems very happy. Happy like acting happy, talking and all, yes. But, I mean, when I look at her. I never see her happiness."

The back door swung open and Jane yelled, "Oh, Alison. That's just your car. We were afraid to block it in. Hi. Hello, Mom. I'll just tell Regina to park in the driveway, right?" She walked to Alison, patted her back and kissed her hair. "The pretty sister. My God, Al, you look terrific. I guess maybe I should stop working for a living, too."

Sylvia stood and kissed Jane.

While they held tentatively to each other's hands, Alison said, "Is that a new dress?"

Jane spun around in her black bathrobe of a dress. "I know,

more black. When you look like me, though, the last thing you want to do is start surprising people. Regina?" Jane yelled the name, leaning slightly in the direction of the open door. Again, hopefully, she yelled, "Regina?" She patted Alison again. "I'm so happy you came. Roger, too? Let me get Regina in here before I forget."

From just beyond the door a voice called out. "I left the car. Or am I at the wrong party?" Regina Ellington made her awkward way up the three steps, grabbed the door knob and steadied herself in the small kitchen. "I am Regina and I parked the car in the driveway. Jane can move it if there's a problem. You must be Sylvia."

Sylvia watched Regina approach as she might stare at an oncoming car, knowing bravado was her only hope. A graceless, heavy woman, Regina sort of lumbered, her hands pulling and pressing unhelpfully at her white hair. Sylvia guessed she was at least sixty. In a light-blue mock turtleneck and old-fashioned plaid trousers, this tall, gruff woman presented an irreconcilable physical appearance. Given the expectations she shattered with every step, Regina Ellington's effect was nothing less than astonishing.

Regina took Sylvia in an awkward embrace. "Jane didn't tell you I'm older than she is. I know it's irrelevant, but I also reckon it's a bit of a shock. You're Alison, then?" Regina twisted toward Alison and Jane.

Unbelievably enough, Sylvia heard herself ask, "How old are you?"

Regina pivoted without greeting Alison.

Jane said, "Nice touch, Mom."

Surprised, and a little exhilarated for having asked, Sylvia said, "Well, I'm fifty-nine."

"Sit down then, Sylvia. We celebrated my sixty-third last month."

"This is my sister, Alison. Regina?" Jane had an arm around Alison's shoulder.

Arthur and Roger arrived, and a confusion of greetings and introductions carried everyone into the living room, where wine was served by Arthur, who felt the elderly woman represented a vindication of his understanding of his elder daughter.

"We've heard about you from Jane. But what is it you do, Regina?" Arthur joined Sylvia on the divan.

"Jane mentioned you teach at Columbia." Sylvia raised her eyebrows, to let Regina know Arthur's questions were irrelevant.

"I'm on the faculty at the medical school."

Sylvia ignored the timid expressions of surprise and reverence this drew from her family. "Do you practice as well?"

"I did for decades, but not now."

"Surgical practice?" Sylvia spoke quickly, seriously.

"I practiced with surgeons, but I'm really research-oriented. Oncology."

Sylvia knew Regina would feel the need to clarify this. She preempted her guest. "Cancer. Now you teach full time?"

"A few students. Most of my time now is devoted to people who are outside the traditional arena. I'm doing at lot of behavioral and nutritional work with them."

"As alternatives to chemotherapy and surgery?"

"Alternative and cooperative."

"You must find this fascinating, Jane." Sylvia's deft deflection of attention produced the desired effect. Regina turned an ironic smile to Jane.

"You don't seem bored by the details yourself." Jane lurched out of her seat, grabbed the wine, refilled her glass, and passed the bottle to Alison. "It's the only available anesthetic."

"Everyone liked that article in the Sunday magazine." Arthur failed to remember the subject matter as he spoke. He hoped to avoid a discussion of it. "What are you working on these days?"

"These days? Daddy, you make it sound like you haven't heard from me in years."

Sylvia jumped back in, not to defend Arthur but to join the fray. "He said days, sweetie, not years."

Regina clapped her hands. "Good for you, Sylvia."

Jane raised her glass to her mother, then to Regina. "Now,

that is an unholy alliance. I'm working on a book, Daddy. I always feel like such a braggart saying that. But it's a book, and let's just say it's a novel."

Sylvia scanned her memory for the phrase she wanted. "A roman à clef?"

"How Continental this family is getting." Jane stood, hoping to disengage herself. She distrusted her instinctive attraction to her mother, to Sylvia's challenges. She'd hoped to elude her and it was clear she'd failed. "It's not about me and Regina." She let the shock of this register as if it were being tallied on a digital scoreboard. Then she sat, added to her score. "It's about a straight woman."

Sylvia was not startled. The announcement was a relief. She could see this was not true for everyone. She looked at Jane and saw her best child and her one soul mate. Here was Sylvia's odd, strong, smart, imbalanced heir; another perfect stranger in the world. "A novel? Well, we all look to you for novelty. Now, let's get to that dinner." She said this to Jane, but she said it for Alison and Roger and Arthur, to protect them from the unpleasantly original women whose presence confused and threatened them.

Regina shuffled past Sylvia, lightly touched her back, then said, "Alison, give us something to carry to the table." She led Alison and the two men to the kitchen.

Flatly, Sylvia said, "Just so you know I love you. That's all." She waved, to let Jane know she was free to go.

"Why would I know that? Why in the world would I know that?"

Sylvia knew this was not an accusation. It was a sensible question. "I don't know. A lucky guess?" She waited for a show of emotion, but Jane did not relent. Unlike anyone Sylvia had loved, this daughter offered her no weakness to embrace. Nor would Jane tolerate Sylvia's acknowledgment as a substitute for acceptance. "You do know I love you."

"Of course. That's always been my problem. I know she loves me, so why do I feel like such a wretch? I know she loves me, and I'm afraid to introduce her to the woman I love, who loves me. What's wrong with this picture? What's wrong with me? Or what's wrong with love?" Jane smiled querulously, as if Sylvia might be able to answer her questions.

"Well, you have Regina now."

"Oh, that's good, Mom. But she's not you, or didn't you notice? Regina needs my love, needs me. That puts her in another galaxy, doesn't it?"

"I like her." Sylvia smiled. "I mean, I don't pretend to know what two women are doing—"

"Don't." Jane raised her hands. "I asked for it, I know, but it's enough. What you said. You like her. You'll make sense to each other, by yourselves, I mean. Don't jump in as my mother and tell me about the Church's position, okay?" She stood, stooped to pick up her glass and the nearly empty wine bottle. "I always feel like I bring out the worst in you."

"You see me at my best, and you know it."

"Dinner's ready." Jane nodded toward the dining room, where Alison was lighting candles. She knew the others were pretending to be occupied in the kitchen, waiting for resumption of the interrupted public event.

Sylvia felt a little foolish, a giddy adolescent with her best friend. "We're being rude."

Jane took a step toward the divan, raised her foot and nudged her mother. "We're bad." She tucked the bottle under her arm and extended a hand to Sylvia, pulled her up. "Am I not supposed to ask where Stephen is?"

Sylvia saw Alison look up from her post when Stephen was named. She pulled her hand from Jane's grip, led her to the table reluctantly. Alone with Jane, she could feel herself at full strength, free to wrestle with opposing forces. But, in the dining room, below the room where Stephen slept, she had to live with what this brute force had made of her defenseless family.

Roger and Alison seated themselves across the table from Jane and Regina. Arthur and Sylvia faced each other from opposite ends. This apt and uncomfortable coupling silenced everyone but Arthur, who had attached no significance to the subject of his elder daughter's work in progress. Amiably, he raised his full wineglass. "Here's to Jane's book. I hope it's a big success, honey." He did not drink the wine. Instead, he picked up his water glass and drained it, refilled it from a crystal pitcher, and raised it toward Sylvia, for her approval.

Sylvia nodded obligingly, but she was only momentarily distracted. Her attention was focused on Alison, whose sense of betrayal Sylvia recognized in her curt, excessively polite manner. She watched Alison offer Roger an ironic, almost apologetic smile, signaling her willingness to retreat with him from yet another peculiarity of Adamski life. As a countermeasure, Sylvia asked, "Did you leave the children with Liz, Alison?"

Roger said, "Again."

"There's some debate as to Liz's fitness." Alison said this softly, then carried on for Regina's benefit. "Her husband died only about a month ago. She has a daughter who is our Becky's age. Best friends. She—my friend Liz—she's a painter. She's getting to be successful."

"This is Liz Halstrom?" Jane pointed at her sister. "The one who married the lawyer and wouldn't change her name? That Liz is a painter?"

Roger said, "That's the one."

"I like her. But I thought she was a lawyer, too." Jane turned to Sylvia for clarification.

"And a painter." Sylvia put a hand to Regina's wrist. "You would love this woman, Regina. A real loose cannon, but smart as a whip."

Alison laughed, pointed at Jane. "How smart is a whip?"

"How easy is pie?" Jane punctuated her question by standing up.

Alison took the challenge. "How tough is a tack, though?"

"Big as—no. The best was, Keen as mustard." Jane turned to Sylvia. "You actually used to say that in front of people. Not just family, but people. How keen is mustard, Mom?"

Sylvia effortlessly posed as the mother of a precocious adolescent before answering. "Keep it up, young lady. You'll sing a merry tune."

This brought applause from Alison. Jane bowed to her mother and took her seat. "Perfect. Quick as ever." She nudged Regina. "The 'young lady' part? That was the clincher."

While cajoling her guests to accept seconds, Sylvia managed to deliver Regina to front and center, eliciting stories about her youth as payment-in-kind. Before the group adjourned to the living room for coffee and pie, Sylvia had coaxed long, complicated family and professional tales out of a woman Jane knew to be both intensely private and adept at eluding scrutiny. Alison could see that Regina's responsiveness amazed Jane, as if Sylvia was working some kind of magic.

Finally, when coffee was poured a second time, even Regina seemed to catch on. She stopped herself midsentence in an explanation of her decision to stay at Columbia after a dispute with several colleagues. "Who cares? You'd think I was being paid to talk."

Sylvia wagged her hands. "I would pay to hear these stories. You've had a remarkable life."

Alison looked at Sylvia as she artfully dismissed Regina's protest and wheedled the rest of the story out of her. Improbable as it seemed, Sylvia had successfully resorted to charm. This is what lived behind the intransigent opinions and sheer force of will? And why had Regina Ellington, of all people, induced this reaction?

Alison could make nothing of her confused suspicion. But she wouldn't let it go. She laid it down, smoothed the gauzy surface as best she could. Fragile as it seemed, it was opaque. When she took it up again, she felt ridiculous; it was so flimsy. It was one of many veils her mother wore.

The quiet truce that followed on Regina's story couldn't last. Side by side at one end of the divan, Regina and Jane assumed the quality of strangeness Sylvia had worked to dissemble. Even Arthur saw the meaning in the awkward way his daughter reached across Regina's lap to fill her coffee cup, staring at the others as she did.

"I can make more." Sylvia actually shouted this, afraid that any lapse in amenities would betray the disapproval festering in the silent room. Calmly, she added, "Coffee. Would everyone have another cup?"

Regina said, "It's ten o'clock," turned to Jane.

Jane ignored the hint about Regina's impending bedtime, which she knew had registered with Alison and Roger as another exposé of the lesbian couple. "Stephen is still asleep? Is this normal?"

"Normal?" Alison forced a laugh. "That's a relative term in this family."

"I only meant I'd hoped to see him."

Alison was undeterred. "Have a look at him?"

Jane just stared at her sister until she felt herself go blank again. Several times during the evening she'd felt a poke or prod from Alison and let it pass unchallenged. It was new to her, this caustic younger sister.

Gleeful now, Alison poured more coffee for herself. "Did you want to make an announcement before the entire family, Jane? Because we could get Artie on the phone."

"I'd make more coffee if it weren't so late." Sylvia stood, lifted the cover off the ceramic carafe. "Actually, there is at least another cup or two in here."

Jane held her cup toward her mother. "You've been in Pittsfield too long, Alison. People don't make announcements anymore."

Jane returning Alison's volley had the effect of immobilizing everyone. Sylvia was caught standing, the pot slung at her side.

Stephen's noiseless entrance unlocked the tension. "Hello, everyone." He was neatly dressed, in jeans and a pale yellow shirt. His hair was still damp from a shower. He moved to the center of the room, his back to Alison and Arthur. He smiled at Sylvia, who'd taken to her seat but had not got rid of the coffee pot. "None for me, Mom. I'm meeting some friends." He glanced at his wrist, a private admission of having borrowed the thin silver bracelet watch she kept in a wooden box on her vanity. "Hello, Jane."

Jane stood, opened her arms over the coffee table. "You look great. Must be all that sleep."

Stephen leaned forward, let her kiss his cheek. "I got my days and nights mixed up in jail. You have to do that in jail, to guard your ass. Is this your girlfriend?"

"I'm Regina Ellington." She extended her hand.

To shut him down, Sylvia slid the pot onto the table. "You have an appointment tomorrow, Stephen."

He backed away, stood behind Arthur's chair. "Another candidate. Not until noon, though. I'll be back before then." He put his hands on Arthur's shoulders. "Big date tonight, Art. You interested in a little pokey-pokey?"

Arthur pushed himself out of his chair and Stephen ran to the kitchen. "No one has to tolerate . . ." Arthur stopped yelling when the back door slammed. Confused and humiliated, he followed Stephen's trail as far as the driveway, determined not to return until the visitors were gone.

Roger watched at the front window, behind the divan. "You don't think Arthur is going to try to stop him, do you?"

"That's my son Stephen. I think." Sylvia touched Regina's shoulder as she went to join Roger. "Arthur isn't going after him, Roger. Is that what you asked? What's the point?"

"Are you all right?" Roger had his hand on Sylvia's back. "Who is this new doctor?"

"Let's hope it's Freud." Sylvia turned to free herself, watched Alison walk away toward the kitchen. "Don't you have to collect the children, Roger?"

"Do you want me to stay?" He followed Sylvia, prepared for her to fall back into his arms. "Alison can get the kids home."

"It's time I left." Regina still felt she was on display. She went to the closet under the stairs, extracted her coat. "Unless I could help clean up?"

"I'll stay and do dishes. I can get a cab to Lenox later." Jane picked up several cups to avoid Regina's scrutiny.

Alison returned from the kitchen, stopped to help Regina with her coat. "How about Roger drives you to Lenox, Regina? I just spoke to Liz. She did offer to keep the girls—"

"I'd like them at home tonight. Liz's house is on the way to Lenox." Roger joined Alison at the closet. As if someone had disputed the fact, he giggled, said, "Quite literally on the way. On the road to Lenox. I don't mind at all. It's not a problem for me. Jane can drive Alison home later."

The unlikely pairing of Roger and Regina made for quick and dispirited goodbyes. Once outside, they came upon Arthur, who was leaning against Roger's car. While Jane backed her car out of the driveway, Arthur said, "This can't go on. I mean, how long? It isn't helping him. Good night, all." He waited for Jane at the front door. "I should apologize to your woman friend, Jane. I really am the one to blame for setting him off in the first place."

Sylvia ushered them into the living room. She tried to reconstruct Arthur's brief apology as something other than an inadvertent confession. But it allowed for no misinterpretation. "You?"

Dismissively, Jane said, "It's not a matter of blame, Daddy."

Sylvia said, "Really? You?" But she spoke with so little force that no one acknowledged her question.

"Well, if it's not blame, you tell me the word to use, Jane." Arthur looked at both his daughters. He could not decide if he had exposed himself, the secret he had shared with Stephen. He wanted to retreat, return to his role as bystander. "It's like how you live, Jane. Your lifestyle. You made us face the truth tonight. But it makes me sad, where I wasn't sad before about you, honey. Who's to blame for that?"

"I appreciate the sentiment, whoever is to blame." Jane began to stack saucers, banging them into a pile, one at a time. "And I'll make your apologies to Regina for you. I rather doubt I'll subject her to another evening of Truth or Consequences."

To everyone's amazement, Arthur pursued this. "I think we all made every effort tonight. I'm sure a lot of families would not have been so welcoming, given the fact that—"

"Give it up, please." Jane yelled this, then returned to her cups and saucers. "Save it for Stephen. He's the nut case, or haven't you noticed? Pokey-pokey?"

The words that seemed absurd when Stephen uttered them now struck Alison as hilarious. She broke out laughing. Sylvia was reduced in an instant. When Alison struggled to say, "Honest to God. Pokey?" even Jane relented.

Before the laughter subsided, Arthur said, "Maybe I'm just tired, honey. I'm always happy to see you. Right?"

Jane and Alison waved after their father. Sylvia took longer to recover, but when her daughters began a serious effort to clear dishes, she came around. "Sit for five. I'll make that pot of coffee." She knew it wouldn't last, but she felt young, and irresponsible, and a little goofy. She threw up her hands in mock surrender. "And let's pretend nothing happened. It's a woman's prerogative."

Jane continued to stack. "I meant what I said about Stephen. Just from seeing him tonight. He had your watch on, Mom. I know you saw that."

Sylvia accepted the accusation with a shrug. "Minor-league detail. I can't really think about that. I mean it."

"Well, neither of us is fool enough to think Dad might have an insight, so I don't know who that leaves."

Alison wanted in. "Insight is what it takes? He sees his second shrink tomorrow. The insight professionals are dropping like flies."

"Flies? Well, the point is, Al,"—Jane was making a line of spoons—"you deal with him every day. But from any distance whatsoever, he's . . . the court episode?"

"Nobody thinks it's normal or healthy, Jane. Is that what you're waiting to hear? Look at Mom. Really. Look at her. She's exhausted. But you can't just lock him up. Even in Pittsfield, believe it or not." Alison was staring at Sylvia's bare wrist. "Why would he want to wear your watch?"

"He put on my watch. He's so thin it fit him is all I know." Sylvia felt she was being accused of playing some part in Stephen's performance. "I haven't had much time to devote to

Stephen's motives over the past few days. I've had a hard time just believing what I hear about him, the things he says. I don't really care if he wants to wear my watch. Who does?"

"Why are you so defensive?" Jane collected the spoons, dropped them in a cup. "We all agree it's just a watch. But it does seem evident that he's acting weirder and weirder."

"I don't think you have to use words like *weird* and *nut case*. It's vulgar." Sylvia was crestfallen, seeing what had come of her hopes for a late night with her daughters. "It's bad enough without name-calling."

Alison was still intrigued by the detail of the watch. "Does he go into your room? I mean, like your clothes?"

Badgered, Sylvia turned mean. "One sexual identity problem in this family isn't enough for you, Alison? Or do you think I'm covering for Stephen? That he acts like a lunatic and I try to make him look good for your benefit? It's bad enough I have to listen to Roger's legal wisdom. Please don't you patronize me, too."

"Nice touch, Mom. You want to offend any other relations while we're here? And if Stephen were gay? It would drive him away, not back here. Trust me." Jane took her piled dishes to the kitchen.

Sylvia whispered, "The clothes problem was your suggestion."

Alison was intent on winning a retraction of the slur on Roger. "I hope it has occurred to you how much Roger enjoys associating himself with Stephen in public. I hope it has occurred to you what a boon that is to his career."

Expertly, Sylvia changed tack. "I know I ask too much of both you and Roger. I'm beginning to believe my overreacting makes it impossible for anyone to see clearly. And I'm sure I make it harder for Stephen, who hardly needs more obstacles."

"That's not what I meant. That's not the point."

"It is my point, Alison. You don't need to be shuttling your children here and there every other day."

"Becky and Jennifer think it's a holiday when they go to

Liz's house. She sits around and paints with them or they practice dances from the forties. It leaves me and *Sesame Street* in the dust. Roger isn't worried about the kids. He's got a case about Liz." Alison recorded this, one more willing trade of marital fidelity for a moment of familial intimacy. "You know all that. It's good for him."

Sylvia opened her eyes wide, nodded toward the kitchen. "I guess I sort of blew that."

Alison waved off the concern. "She's a big girl."

Sylvia mouthed the word "Regina," tilted her head.

Alison pressed her face between hands, whispered, "To-morrow."

Pantomiming her reluctance for Alison's enjoyment, Sylvia headed toward Jane in the kitchen. "My parents weren't perfect either."

Jane smiled, barely. "I know. We're all damaged goods. I just felt like sulking for a while."

"Forget the dishes."

"It's therapeutic. You going to bed?"

"I really like Regina."

Jane shook the suds and water from her hands. "This isn't about Regina. This is about me. I make it worse, but it's because I forget when I'm in New York. It's not an issue for me there. It's not an issue for me anywhere else in the world anymore. I get back here and I feel I should have brought a date, a cover story."

"Sweetie, I don't need explanations." Sylvia did not want explanations.

"Coming here, coming out, I guess—"

"I knew. Of course I knew. And Alison." Sylvia still hoped to avoid a discussion of the topic.

"No. You didn't know someone extraordinary loves me." Jane sighed, exasperated that delivering this required tears. "I won't blather on. I promise." She rubbed her face, ran her wet hands through her hair. "I always had this, as a secret. Since I was twelve? I twisted it around, to make it into something I could show you. Something beautiful for you."

"I think you're beautiful." Sylvia traced her fingertips along her daughter's face.

"That's easy for you to say. I look just like you."

Sylvia brought her hands to her own face, pushed her hair back at either side. "You look again." Her voice was strangely musical, suggestive. "You look hard before you go this time." She felt heavy on her feet, as if she were applying pressure from above her body, forcing herself to let Jane see the ugly truth, forcing Jane away for good. She dragged her hands further back along her head, stretching smooth the cheek and eyelid folds. Jane reached up to dispel the mask, but Sylvia resisted her daughter's stronger grip, tensing muscles in her arms and shoulders until her head was in a tremor between her hands. When Jane had seen enough, Sylvia relented.

Jane massaged her mother's palms and forearms, pressing down exercised veins.

Because her daughter wouldn't meet her gaze, Sylvia gently shook her arms, watched the motion pass through their joined hands and travel into Jane. When Jane finally raised her face, she cautiously returned her mother's smile.

Sylvia whispered, "You let her love you," then backed away. "Sylvia's beauty tip for the night. What are the chances you'll at least call before you go back to New York?"

"I've known the odds to be worse. Good night."

Sylvia waved and left the room, then poked her head back around the threshold. "Alison seems to have given up on us."

"She asleep in there?"

"No, no. Gone. She must have walked home."

"Oh, for God's sake." Jane didn't bother to conceal her exasperation or her pity.

"It's two and a half blocks. She's a big girl. Good night."

"Good night, Mom." Jane imagined seeing Alison from above, endlessly walking back and forth between her own house and the family home. Jane tried to see each crossing as her sister's chosen route, but she knew better; the corridor was just her younger sister's lot. The pattern was familiar: Jane upbraided, appeased, rewarded, and released; Alison dutifully pacing.

Still, Jane was disappointed not to have an hour with her sister. Several years had marked her, pretty and obliging as she always was. The impatience with Roger, the allegiance with the impervious Liz Halstrom, and the disappearance of the tether that had bound her to their father—these sustained the tougher, more outspoken mode she had adopted. Alison was more challenging, both troubling and compelling.

It was clear to Jane that Sylvia had been hard at work. Appalling as the effort seemed, Jane could not help but be impressed by the results.

XIII

THE CHURCH of the Sacred Heart was locked. Stephen's methodical examination of the sixteen stained-glass saints proved every window seal was tight. He invented prayers of supplication and recited a litany of all the saints he could string together, halfheartedly hoping he might produce a kind of open sesame. Annoyed he hadn't thought to bring a chair or ladder, he figured he would have to find a rock to break a pane of glass and then climb through to retrieve his mother's robe.

The detail of the chair he might have carried five blocks from his house undid him. It was so easy to imagine: Three teenage boys would walk past him—stare at him and then at each other and then at the chair and back at him—and from just behind he'd hear them laughing. If he got himself inside the church, a priest might rush in, calling out "Hello," and he would have to make a speech about the robe that he was holding. He could see it all, the yellow letters painted on a floor, or waiting, naked, in a chair, his legs uncrossed—he could remember making that decision, not to cross his legs—until someone came to claim him at the courthouse.

What were they thinking when they didn't stop him?

No negative emotion or illicit pleasure preserved in Stephen's well was more commanding than the present image of himself roaming Pittsfield with a chair. It wasn't thrilling. It was silly, as bad as showing off his body to his mother.

His frank assessment of his propensity for looking like a fool in public demystified the other self. He renounced the stranger.

The sad truth was the vandal, like the oddball in the courtroom and the idiot with the chair, was only Stephen. This was the oldest, finest fear; years of vigilance undone in days: He'd shamed himself and publicly embarrassed his entire family.

Stephen wouldn't give himself to sadness. He pressed his tongue up against his palette, snorting short breaths through his nose, to gag the urge to cry. This effort made him dizzy. But, humiliation didn't leak out as his energy was sapped. He was heavy with the knowledge of how easily he'd fooled himself.

He retreated to the church stairs, tried to strike a pose that any passerby would find beyond reproach, as if he'd just walked home his girlfriend and had stopped to wonder if he really liked her. But his body misbehaved, twitching unpredictably. A small truck's noisy passing sent him sliding for the railing, where the driver wouldn't see him.

He was particularly sorry when he thought about the robe he'd stolen from his mother. He hoped at least a bum would wander in and steal it, or a priest would figure it was meant as a donation and add it to the stock of plaid shirts and bell-bottom blue jeans collected for the needy. Any fate would do, so long as his mother didn't have to know what he had done.

He could not believe he'd known how to do so many mean and stupid things. Without recourse to a more sophisticated diagnosis, he regaled himself with the amazing words he'd shouted at his mother, rocks through windows, and three nights in jail. This sequence made him giddy, as would a teacher's story of a bad boy who snapped off car antennas or a girl who showed the boys in junior high her bra.

He only knew that he was misbehaving and he couldn't stop

it. Why hadn't Arthur followed him and dragged him back inside? Wasn't Roger smart enough to figure out a way to keep him locked up for a month?

These were not idle questions. Each one was a poser. His earnest concentration only led to more confounding questions, as a stumper of a riddle will agitate a child's curiosity as much about the process of achieving a solution as it will about the withheld answer.

Frustration led him indirectly to a solid proposition. He could not stay where he was much longer. This quickly gave way to another certainty: His mother wasn't coming after him. Once, Artie tried to run away, when he was ten, and she had said, "You stay here, Artie. It is my turn. I'll run away instead." And, as she always said about his sister Jane, "Someday she's going to learn she can't run away from herself."

Stephen wished he'd written down the stories, especially the parables—the girl who gave a friend a copy of her homework, the little boy who ate an entire box of European chocolates, the leper raised up from the dead, the son who hid his talents in the ground. Unlike myths or made-up stories, these parables attached to real-life people like himself. They brought the world in closer, animating adult siblings, as well as the life-size wooden statues huddled in the hollows of the ornate altar, which now was nothing but a backdrop for the modern marble table used for celebrating Mass.

Of course, the stories had a moral. If he was good (and goodness was an alloy of achievement and obedience), he would be rewarded with the happiness that had eluded his brother and his sisters and, most of all, his father.

Artie's failure to respond to letters mailed to him at college or Jane's forgotten promises of weekends in New York demonstrated that the best intentions by themselves were not sufficient. "I'm sure the proof is in the pudding," his mother would cajole. "They just never get around to making any pudding."

What Stephen wanted was for her to tell him it would be all right, to have her arm around him as she spoke. Then she could tell a joke about how lately he'd cooked up some pretty awful puddings.

Instead, he saw her crying in his bedroom, yelling that she didn't like him in her robe.

What made him make her cry?

Your father doesn't mean to make me cry. Every time she said it, Stephen told himself it wasn't so. Why else would Arthur go no farther than the pantry to snap the fliptop off a hidden beer? Or slam a door when they had guests? Or say he thought a really pretty lady had stopped by the office? What better explanation was there for Arthur suddenly announcing he was not Stephen's father and Stephen's mother was a whore?

Arthur wanted her to cry.

Stephen held his breath, afraid this explanation might be too fragile to endure. He let the breath out with a laugh. Because, if Arthur's story was a lie, then Stephen could be Stephen once again.

His mother had been shocked by what he'd said. She'd never heard of anything so crazy as two husbands or another father. And Arthur hadn't even bothered to invent a name for this other father.

Stephen saw a few of Arthur's words stacked up against the mountain range of every other word he'd ever heard.

Arthur's story was a lie. Arthur wanted her to cry.

Relief arrived with shame. How could he apologize to her? What words did he have? He hadn't meant to make her cry. But that made him no better than his father, which wasn't nearly good enough. He had to start by acting right, go to her with proof of more than just intentions.

Standing from the concrete stairs, determined to make reparations, Stephen drew a breath that shot straight through his lungs. As a hungry child might, he pressed his hands against his stomach, to ascertain if it was really empty. Eating food to fill his stomach struck him as the thing to do. She wanted him to eat.

Excited by the prospect of recovering his status, he ran until he saw a lighted sign for BURGERS PLUS. He was the only customer.

"Say so if you want something from the grill or forever hold your peace." The girl who said this was behind the counter. Her back was pressed to the back of another blond girl, who was scraping a steel spatula across the iron grill. "Now or never." Her voice was friendly, but impatient. "We're busy girls." This last rejoinder made the cook laugh.

"Two cheeseburgers, please?" Stephen looked up to see if the menu was posted. "A soda?" Old wallpaper carried the words *Maria cooks it RIGHT for you!* on long, wavy green pennants. Stephen recognized it from years before, when he would be allowed to ride his bike and buy a sandwich as reward for Saturday chores well done. The restaurant's familiarity in a prior incarnation grounded him. It seemed to him an omen bearing well on his decision to repair himself. This is what he meant when he said, "This place used to be Maria's."

The cook slipped two patties from paper envelopes onto the grill, then cocked her head over her shoulder. "No shit, Sherlock."

The other girl hit the cook on the head with a laminated menu. "Give him a break. You say orange soda?"

He nodded, watched her spill his drink as she carried it to the three-stool counter near the register.

She pointed to the wallpaper. "We're her daughters. She's our mother. Maria. We changed the name to attract more business."

The cook said, "Her brilliant idea. Really working like a charm, huh?" She handed her sister two burgers on white paper plates. "Last meal. I'm cleaning this mother and then we're out of here."

Stephen stood and paid. Right after that, he heard the nicer sister giggle. He ate one of the thin hamburgers quickly, then turned to see what had made her laugh. The cook shoved her sister when she saw his face. Feigning interest in the wallpaper, Stephen tried to overhear the words they whispered, but his ill-disguised attention made them quiet. When he swiveled toward the counter, the sisters started up again. The way they craned their necks to steal a look at him convinced him that they wanted him to notice. He ate his second sandwich slowly, glanced at them only when he stopped to sip his drink. He tried to make it clear he liked the flirting. Finally, made brave by their insistence, he smiled openly at both girls, which sent them running to a room behind the grill, howling and pushing. He heard the cook yell, "Not until he leaves, though." They didn't reappear until he finished eating.

Stephen coughed so they'd come out. He said, "Good night. Thanks for everything. Everything," attempting to extend his pleasure.

The cook moved around the counter and held the door for him. He knew that she was watching when he stepped out onto the curb and balanced before crossing Elm Street. Determined to seize this chance to ask her name, he swung around.

The cook yelled, "Nice watch, buddy," slammed and locked the door. Immediately, the lights went off inside and Stephen heard the sisters laughing.

XIV

JANE KNELT on the divan, staring through her reflected image on the window. Holmes Road was dark and untraveled. She was looking for distraction, a flatbed full of lumber or a moving van from Maine, like those that woke and drew her to this window almost nightly for the two years she had lived here as a girl. She knew she should and wouldn't call Regina. What was she supposed to say? Apologize for her unsophisticated father? Disavow her sister and her husband? She figured she would only agitate Regina, somehow let her know that, in this house, even she'd not seen the gruff, eccentric academic, but a woman older than her mother in beatnik clothing, an aging dyke who talked too much about her work.

This pseudo-Tudor house, which she'd hated from the day

the family moved here from the older, tougher neighborhood two miles to the north, was a haven for the family but for no one else. It was a hideout, not a home. And it was here, no longer sheltered by familiars, whose blind assumptions gave her cover as a normal teenage girl, Jane had learned to fear exposure.

In 1963, in Pittsfield, women who kissed other women on the lips appeared in magazines for men available to drugstore customers who dared to ask for them by name. Besides the salve of light-night traffic, she read novels for the odd suggestion of a Frenchwoman's misbehavior and bought illicit cigarettes from an A&P cashier, Miss Rifkin, who slicked her short hair flat against her head and wore what were reputed to be her dead brother's horn-rimmed glasses, wingtips, and an altered version of his three-piece suit.

Exposure came, but not as Jane had feared it. Before the immodest publicity campaign for Insulum had run its course, Arthur's business fell apart under the weight of rumors of a broken law or two. Then Sylvia announced that she was three months pregnant and intended to go through with it—despite Jane's warnings about giving birth at forty and the cost to an already compromised adolescent social life.

Escape to Boston and New York had made it possible to believe that most of what Jane hated about this house was being sixteen with a secret. She loved her parents. She'd come back this time just to prove her life was indeed an affirmation of the girl they loved in their peculiar way. She could tolerate the telling of the stories of her awkward, angry adolescence, but she wanted the connection drawn between that girl and the woman Regina loved.

The only correlation was marked by Sylvia, as a command and as an accusation: *You let her love you.*

You let her love you. Sylvia decided it was not uncharitable to question why Regina had to be so old. If she had to be a woman, couldn't she be thirty-five or forty? She kept herself awake by testing her intolerance, pretending Regina was five, ten, fifteen years younger than she was. She couldn't locate the point at which she became too old. And Stephen wasn't home yet.

As if she might invade his sleep, Sylvia turned and put a hand on Arthur's shoulder. Touching did not bring her close to him. She was imagining what she might do. But it was simple: Whether she shook him, took him in her arms, or simply made a noise to rouse him, he would turn to her and give her his benign confusion.

She didn't have to wake him to make him tell her why he'd broken silence. In the middle of a dinner or a television movie, he would catch her hand and pull her to attention. "It's just the truth," he'd say. "We can even tell him I adopted him, or just say that I love him anyway." He would say this much urgently, forcefully. Then his power would fall away like a facade. Exposed, ashamed, he'd speak as if to Stephen. "I am not your father. A man called Martin is. Biologically, that is. In every other way I am. Your father. Every other way there is."

She took her hand from Arthur's body. It was done. Sylvia decided Stephen's taunting was not a question but a dare: Speak the name. It was so easy to hear him clapping out a rhythm while he chanted *Martin Parris, Martin Parris, Martin Parris.*

A door below her room slammed shut and she heard Stephen yell, surprised. Next, she heard Jane speak quietly, soothingly. She couldn't make out words, but the conversation calmed him. She believed this signaled a reprieve. She had at least another day. She could get in touch with Martin, deliver Stephen to the future she had dreamed he would inherit.

One day as a counterpoise for twenty sedentary years; the imbalance was preposterous. But Sylvia believed in Stephen, believed he could provide her what she could not secure alone.

Left to her own wits, she was incapable of leaving Arthur and his unqualified love. Unduly, she gave Stephen credit for eliciting from Arthur the story of betrayal, which in twenty years Arthur had never used against her. Moreover, she believed Stephen had attracted Parris's attention. While she disapproved of Stephen's methods, he had successfully asserted a son's right to favor and protection.

Sylvia believed in miracles at any cost. In her debilitated son she saw a power well beyond her own. Buffeted by sadness and remorse at Stephen's suffering, her innocence survived intact, protected by her helplessness. Her efforts to forestall his ravings had proved futile. Her faithfulness to Martin notwithstanding, she really could not blame herself for bringing on the future.

XV

MARTIN PARRIS watched Rabbi Abraham Sisitkin lead two police officers to their car behind the carved granite slab commemorating the building of the Temple Beth Israel. He shook his head, held his hand in half-salute as the cruiser disappeared over the crest of Broad Street.

Sisitkin turned to Parris and hollered, "Everyone wants a guarantee." He didn't move. He didn't want to walk into the black ring fire had burned around the building. The stench of soot was sweet with gasoline, which had been splashed on the front and sides of the brick temple, evidenced by the shadow landscape imprinted on the walls. "What would you do about that smell, Martin?"

Parris walked across the still slick black grass to join him. "The police want to be sure you'll press charges this time."

"That is as polite an *I told you so* as I've heard."

"They can't spend their time chatting up suspects. Not if you're going to retreat again. . . . We've been through all this before."

"If it is the Adamski boy again, then for his sake—and, not least of all for the sake of the property—something should be done."

"You want it both ways, Abe." Parris scuffed his slick soles against the sidewalk. "Even if it wasn't him, you still have a problem out there. You still have to deal with it."

"The problem is always out there, Martin. The only interesting question is, Do I want to fan this little fire to flames?"

Parris coughed. "That's paranoia. We've been here eleven years without an incident. Name a congregation in the Berkshires that's had something like this in the last twenty years. Thirty years. Jew baiting? It just doesn't happen here."

Sisitkin swung his arm in an arc, showing off the damage. "It's everywhere, Martin. But the sad truth is, keeping it out of the *Courier* won't turn the grass green overnight. We've been identified. Hate has eyes to see us now." He flung both arms out, a sardonically grand gesture. "History burns its way into the Berkshires."

"I could make a few calls. Before we go downtown." Parris offered what consolation he could. "I'm not looking to put us back on the front page, Abe."

"You were right, Martin. I didn't help anyone by dropping charges last time. I'm so sorry. And yet I'm not too proud to ask if you will see me through the mess I've made."

"No guarantees, right? Let me speak to the family before we file." Parris looked away, afraid his old friend might see through to his desire to safeguard his personal stake.

"Like it or not, I guess I might have it both ways, after all." He put an arm around Parris's shoulder, led him through the black ring. "If Stephen is our boy, this is just an isolated problem. But I dropped the charges—against advice of counsel, as they say. I gave him a second chance to whip up some supporters. And if it wasn't Stephen? Well, then, we have a little epidemic on our hands."

"Having it both ways. It's just a way of saying you've got it twice as bad." Parris held off saying, *I ought to know.* No son of his would come here with a tank of gas and kneel to strike the match. He had no son. Yet he could see he'd had a hand in bringing forth the son who stooped to set this fire.

XVI

"You want to get over to the left soon, Jane. You take the next left." Arthur had his hand propped against the dashboard of his daughter's unkempt car, anticipating disaster. "You look like you didn't have such a great night. On the couch, I mean."

"Daddy, I'm still trying to work on seeing straight. Stephen came in very late. And talked forever. He claims you don't want to be his father." Annoyed as she was with her father's surrogate driving, she regretted this non sequitur. Apologetically, she added, "He really isn't okay."

"Stephen can say what he likes. It doesn't alter the facts." It was an instantaneous decision. Arthur would deny the truth he'd given Stephen. It took nothing more than the impatience in Jane's voice to convince him denial was the only policy he could maintain. Stephen was sick; he would grant her this, to reinforce his own position. "It wasn't only that your car was blocking mine in the driveway. Why I had to wake you so early. Your mother has to take Stephen to see a doctor this noon. I wanted her to have the car. I know he needs help. I am his father, which I hope you know."

"No one is going to seriously take on the paternity issue, Daddy. It's a question of sanity." Sensing their conversation had degenerated sufficiently to necessitate clarification, she added, "Stephen's. Stephen's sanity, I mean."

Arthur continued at cross-purposes with his daughter, trying to put a stop to questions about Stephen's father. "Are you going to talk to your mother before you go back to Lenox?"

Of course, Jane received this as a command. "I was already planning to stop."

"Don't wake her though, will you? She needs her sleep."

"I thought I might set off a smoke alarm to get things roll-

147

ing for her." She abandoned her conciliatory mode. She knew
where compromise would lead them. Her father would exhort
her to be happy. And he'd tell her that the way she lived made
him sad.

XVII

THE TELEPHONE RINGING woke Sylvia. She stared across the
room, hoping that might be enough to quell the noise. Defeated, she swung her legs over the edge of the bed, shuffled to
her vanity. She took the receiver in hand and pushed her hair
back before she brought it into speaking range. "Yes?" She
turned to read the clock on her nightstand and she heard
Martin Parris introduce himself. But his voice did not register
as real or present. Stephen was asleep in her bed.

She laid the receiver softly onto its cradle, unplugged the
cord, afraid he'd wake if it rang again. She rubbed her hands
up across her face and held her hair back, trying to see him as
Arthur, or see that it was her imagination or a stillborn dream
presenting Stephen there beside her place in bed.

He might have been a vision, calm and silent as he slept, his
hands tucked underneath his chin on Arthur's pillow. But the
silver watch around his wrist was a handcuff binding son and
mother.

She had no words for her confusion. His rhythmic breathing
was a spell, holding her in place against her will. She only
wagged her hands, fending off her sleeping child. She cajoled
herself to move, reducing to mechanics the up and forward
motion of each foot along a narrow floorboard. Her flailing
hands extended at her sides, she inched her body toward the
door, as if she otherwise might lose balance and alert him.

Sylvia looked back across the threshold. In the hall, her distance from him seemed inordinate and sure. She traced the
tightrope line she'd followed, saw the canyon it traversed. It
seemed impossible she'd made the crossing safely. Without a

waking memory to anchor her, she drifted back toward disbelief: Surely she'd have wakened when he passed her nightstand or restored balance to the mattress biased by her weight.

Stephen moaned and rolled, settled on his stomach. The movement startled her. Reflexively, her eyes resolved him in a sharper focus. She took one wary backward step. She saw that it was Stephen in her bed. All that marked the distance now between them was an unseen, ancient line.

A rueful, adolescent sadness took her. She knelt down, wanting to be small and unassailable. Astonished as she was to see he'd crossed the line and crawled into her bed, she was not certain which of them was the transgressor.

Second Trimester

THE BERKSHIRE SPRING is not a season. Winter wanes for months, prolonged by isolated storms of frozen rain that seal and stifle pea-green nodes on ancient elms and lacquer open-pored forsythia. The quantity of light does not increase; the longer-lasting sun wears out reflective tarpaulins of snow and is absorbed by clots of frozen dirt and musty mats of grass. A day devoted to a morning hailstorm and a steamy azure afternoon precipitates a week or two of seamless pewter skies and starless nights. Shooting, blossoming, and blooming are sporadic. The outer edges of the hedges in a single neighborhood deliver crocuses from March through early June.

The herald of the summer is a scimitar of moon attended by the morning star. They rise together from the western run of hills. Four or even five godly days orchestrate the incoherent foliage, extrude and blend the aromatic saps and musks, and wash away the work of winter with a restive wind.

On the final Friday in May, Arthur does not bind himself in lightweight woolen suit and wingtip shoes. He does not post himself at the dining-room table over the morass of contracts and ledgers and dry-run depositions. Nor does he wait on orders from his untrustworthy and irreplaceable field commander, Martin Parris. The second of the perfect days draws Arthur out. In chinos and a sweatshirt, he gathers up the bucket, soap, chamois rags, and polish, to simonize the car.

The car is pink this morning. Sylvia insists it's buff or salmon. It mattered little when they made the purchase last October. Arthur was awaiting the arrival of a black-and-silver 1963 Chevy for himself, a bonus owed him according to the terms of the establishment of Insulum, Incorporated. The special-order Chevy has since been canceled (at a loss of several hundred nonexistent dollars), and Arthur knows the Rambler has to be maintained for several years.

Before he fills the bucket, he spit-polishes a section of the hood, hoping a high-gloss finish may favorably affect the color. But the buffing brings a deeper, blushing shade. He doesn't want to see the Rambler shine.

He backs away, steps up onto the bank of ice impacted with uprooted grass and brittle hunks of pebbled tar. This slick, uneven border left by plows and shovels winds around the drives and sidewalks and the gutters of the neighborhood. It is the seam that binds the winter to the summer. Arthur walks along the mound, pretending to inspect the season's damage. But his objective is a closer look at the unpleasant old woman who owns the neat brick house next door.

Madeline Barker, propped up on her elbows on a blue beach towel in the middle of her lawn, is a fixture of the summer. Arthur figures she's begun her annual attack on dandelions, a fetish requiring her to nag at little Artie when he mows the lawn.

"The weeds! The weeds!" She's apt to scream until Artie cuts the power. "You have to get down on your hands and knees and pluck the roots. Your weeds seed my lawn." This performance is routinely followed by a visit to the Adamski home at dinner time, for a sermon on the evil of the weeds.

Arthur kicks the dirty ice, spraying the painted foundation of her home, just the sort of revenge he would not tolerate from his son. The clatter fails to rouse Madeline Barker. Bucket in hand, Arthur retreats to his house.

"I'm home!" He drops the bucket into the sink, pries off his wet shoes, pretending he's a laborer just in from the night shift. "Children get off to school without a hitch this morning, honey? Love a cup," he continues, pouring cold coffee into the cup he left on the alcove table. "What about we go out and get a couple steaks tonight, do it up?" He saunters to the middle of the kitchen, spins, dances a few steps of a fox trot. "You look mighty good in that yellow dress with your hair all up. We'll ask Mrs. Barker to watch the kids." Arthur dips his imaginary dance partner, the weightless wife he conjures when Sylvia's away conferring with her doctor or chairing meetings of the Sacred Heart Sodality. The ideal other woman utters homey saws repeated weekly by the pretty, skittish actresses around Troy Donahue and Garry Moore. Arthur winks, and then he whispers, "I see I finally got you where I want you."

The woman, who today resembles Mrs. Barker's married daughter, Dorothy, turns her head, embarrassed by her sentimental tears. "Oh, Art, you've made me the happiest woman in the world. What do other women do?"

Arthur shuts his eyes, inventing a riposte. But imagination fails him and his partner slips away. A swig of brackish coffee brings him around completely. Sobered and deflated, he is ready to resume his futile effort to forestall the fall of Insulum.

The files Arthur pores through daily, and the carbon copies held by Parris, are the fetal skin and bones of their stillborn enterprise. The lease on the dismantled suite of offices is paid through June, but the principals—Arthur, Martin, and Larry Forrester, the elusive engineer-inventor—are held together only by a six-week-long restraining order, soon to be replaced by a permanent injunction and several criminal proceedings.

But Arthur's ties to Insulum are particularly knotty. On patent applications and prospective sales agreements is the name *Adamski*, with abbreviated reference to his standing in professional and technical societies. In private meetings with potential clients, and on every document requiring a statement of the company's proprietary right to market the transformer-insulation process, *Adamski* is the engineer of record.

The pending lawsuits charge Insulum with willful violation of copyrighted work and deceptive acts and practices. As Parris sees it—and Arthur trusts his legal vision—in terms admissible in court, Adamski is a synonym for Insulum.

Arthur can't imagine living with a reputation as a criminal. Like storm clouds rolling in from the horizon, the threat defeats his urge to get ahead along another road. Even Sylvia's sermons on the duty of a father to support a household do not move him to addresses in the Help Wanted columns. Instead, he has become an expert winnower, transferring check stubs, memos, catalogues of office furniture, and all inconsequential papers from his files to a row of cardboard boxes on the floor. The few remaining folders on the table are stacked and labeled. The thickest of the three is "Insulum Accounts." On the front of this, he's circled his initials, a mark made after three times through the uncontested records kept by a certified public accountant, whose expert bookkeeping eludes Arthur's rudimentary skill. The second is labeled "Lawyer (Martin Parris)." A week ago, after several halting passes through the legalese he supposes is the accepted language for establishing a company, Arthur made a check mark on the cover, to remind himself the file is in order. Both "Lawyer" and "Accounts" are incidental to the lawsuits. Resignedly, he puts them on the floor beside the boxes. His days of winnowing are behind him now.

The sole remaining file is a dog-eared folder timidly entitled "Information." This is the one he can't relinquish.

Once again, he spills the contents on the maple table. There are fourteen drawings of a standard electrical transformer. For each drawing, Larry Forrester made an overlay on transparent acetate to show how Insulum increases the efficiency of operation. An eight-page narrative explains the process and material in layman's terms. Attached to this are forty pages of trigonometry and chemical equations, the comprehensive manufacturing criteria.

When Arthur signed the reams of documents verifying Insulum six months ago, he alerted no one to his inability to verify these calculations. He overlooked the snags he hit in computation, bolstered by his confidence in Parris, who'd selected him from among the many ranking supervisors employed at GE Pittsfield. Moreover, Larry Forrester had a reputation as a brilliant engineer. His narrative and drawings were proof enough for Arthur that the transformer industry, in which he'd worked for twenty years, had never seen anything like Insulum before.

Six weeks after the restraining order effectively shut down the business, Arthur knows he did not intend to perpetrate a fraud. But how can he defend his actions? He has reviewed the drawings several dozen times: with an overhead projector, Forrester's overlays looming large upon a painted wall; with the pictures taped to window panes and read as if they were a string of X rays. The pictures by themselves prove nothing. He can't defend his application of the term "invention" (which Parris now refers to as "that slight exaggeration"), except to say he wasn't qualified to pass that judgment. While foraging in soggy college textbooks and his legal pads of lecture notes preserved beneath a half-assembled dollhouse in the cellar, Arthur stumbled on this humble vindication. His indexes and glossaries—the synopsis of his formal education—would not yield to pressure he exerted for solutions to Forrester's equations. How could he mastermind a crime he cannot even comprehend? Even if his memory were photographic (and perfect recall did not attend his brief encounters with his college course work), he would not have seen through Forrester's sophisticated presentation.

Twenty research-weighted years in engineering and the science of materials devalued Arthur's professional credentials. But twenty years of affability had their own rewards, as well. A middling student, he went to work at GE unhampered by either the scientist's devotion to research divorced from applications or the technocrat's impatience with a consumer-conscious corporation. Handsomer than most, and grateful for employment with a name-brand company whose products graced his parents' and their neighbors' homes, Arthur won promotion rather easily. Within a few years, he was a manager of engineers and a representative of engineering products. In six years as department supervisor, he made of technical deficiency a style. He managed—managed men and managed to get by—with an emphasis on delegation of authority. He motivated underlings by meting out responsibility other supervisors hoarded. This cultivated loyalty among the engineers who, after all, felt themselves his technical superiors and thus construed his trust as recognition of their greater gifts.

The oddity is that Arthur did not devise this elaborate

strategy. It was an adaptation he succumbed to thoughtlessly. From Arthur's point of view, it was the way things worked.

But with his left hand on the reassembled "Information" file, he looks ahead. The vantage from the ornate witness stand he envisions in the county courthouse offers him an odd perspective. He can see himself as a witness in his own defense.

Arthur swears he's innocent by reason of his ignorance.

Knowledge comes as sadness, as it always will: The vindication of his role at Insulum involves the defamation of a twenty-year career. Now Arthur knows enough to know his innocence is safe, well within the generally accepted borders of what he doesn't understand. He tests his plea, subjecting it to Sylvia's disapproving smile and Martin's nodding disbelief, then to a parade of younger, smarter engineers, who nudge each other as they file past him. These are the witnesses who'll testify on his behalf. Corroborating evidence can be produced in bulk.

"The truth? The truth is I often didn't know what I was doing." When Arthur speaks the words his face and neck warm with a blush that seeps along his shoulders and cascades down his back, until he is relaxed at last. Arthur has come clean.

But who will grant him absolution? Unwitnessed, his confession has no sacramental standing and it will not serve as legal tender.

The silence in the dining room is unforgiving. In the kitchen, he cannot rouse the other woman. Staring through a window just above the sink, he sees only Mrs. Barker. Her back is to him and she doesn't even turn to reach the flouncy broad-brim hat a breeze has lodged against her scrawny privet hedge.

An hour later, sitting in the alcove, he's not waiting for forgiveness any longer. He's wishing he knew someone qualified and willing to refute his first confession.

Sylvia's laughter draws Arthur's attention to the back door. He considers the distance to the dining room, where she'll expect to find him with his work. But she is standing in the back hall before he makes his move.

"Oh, Arthur. Well, you are here." She waves her hand. "He tried the bell. He thought no one was home." To the man Arthur cannot see, she says, "That's the neighbor with the thing for dandelions. Please, come in."

Arthur registers Sylvia's queer, strained voice and her awkward informality. Still, he doesn't move.

She waves both hands, as if to fan herself. "He's inside, Larry. Arthur? Larry Forrester's with me. He and I were on the front lawn talking and I had to convince him you were right here." She guides him past the screen door propped open with her foot, presses a hand to his back as he climbs the two steps to the kitchen. "Arthur? Look who's here."

"Hello, Art. Wanted to have a . . . say a quick 'How are we.' Rang the bell. Front one. Oops." Larry steps to the center of the room as Sylvia brushes by him. "Nice house. This the kitchen? Well, yes, of course. Quiet neighborhood, except for the traffic on Holmes, I guess. Got you at a bad time, Art."

"No, not at all." Arthur does not stand or extend a hand in welcome, which leaves Larry marooned near the sink. Arthur is so grateful Larry is not Martin Parris come home with Sylvia for a confrontation, or news of yet another legal vision he has had, that he simply shakes his head.

Sylvia circles Larry several times, making coffee. "We're very casual around here in the summer, Larry. Please have a seat. Or would we be better in the living room, Arthur?" She knows it's up to her to wake him to the significance of this visit. "The files are all still in the dining room, dear. Though we will have to move them soon." Winning no response from either man, Sylvia again presses her hand against Larry's back. "Please. I'll serve the coffee here. It's cooler back here, anyway."

Larry takes well to her prodding. "Don't mind if I do, then. Nice to have this built-in eating area, I guess."

While Larry's back is to her, Sylvia pats her head with both hands and rears up her shoulders. Arthur knows what she means. Larry's had his prematurely gray head shaved. He sports a brush-topped whiffle. The geometry of the haircut throws into unflattering relief his oversized, indefinitely shaped features. Though several inches shorter than Arthur, he is even less appropriate to the contours of the alcove. The thin table presses in against his stomach and, no matter how he squirms, he cannot cross his legs.

Arthur sympathizes with his problem. "Let's move into the living room." As he speaks, Sylvia leaves a tray of cups and saucers on the table.

Embarrassed, Larry refuses Arthur's offer. "I'm all settled in here, I guess. Anyway, I'm not staying."

"No one's asked you to move in yet, Larry." Sylvia laughs at her own joke, hand on the percolator handle. "Though the idea of taking in boarders has been discussed, of course."

Arthur cannot cast a private, reproving glance in such tight quarters. Instead, he sets out the cups. He can only hope his wife will not continue her performance. He knows this is her idea of best face forward, that she means to court the confidence of their unsuspecting guest. And, to her credit, he believes that in friendlier circumstances—or, at least, in a friendlier woman—this propensity of hers would seem a virtue, the gift of gab.

"Coffee, Larry? Arthur? I think I'll take mine standing up." She carries her cup to the counter by the sink. "Arthur? Is Mrs. Barker tanning?"

"Weeds." He smiles at Larry, who seems happy to carry on without a word explaining his appearance. "Never too soon to stop a weed."

Oblivious to their guest, Sylvia stands on her toes. "She's not moving, though. She's probably laying land mines, to keep the children off her precious lawn. Did I tell you she called the fire department when Teresa Revillio cooked hamburgers on the grill? It was this week. Tuesday."

Impatient with Sylvia, but locked in a stare with Larry Forrester, Arthur suddenly asks the question he can't answer for himself. "What are you doing here, anyway, Larry? What's going on?"

"I'm leaving. Going to Boston in a few days. My brother has a firm there. Real estate. I'm going to take a crack at managing a club he's opened." This is not a response, it is a recitation. He continues, as if otherwise he might forget his next line and be forced back to the beginning. "Let me try the name out on the both of you. Of the club. The Crazy Cossack. It's a big success with the Boston crowd. Listen to this. The girls who sing? Standards, you know?" He turns to Sylvia, an improvised gesture to draw her in. "They're billed as Lenin's Sisters. Like the Lennon Sisters, you see? It's a big hit with everybody, I guess. I'm gonna take a stab at running the place. There's a lot to it, of course. I'm ready for a change, Art. This has all been a lot for me. Linda and me have half a house for now. In Dorchester. Big balcony porch on the second floor, right off the bedroom. It's worth a try. My brother's in real estate for fifteen, twenty years now. He even owns a restaurant on the South Shore. Big place. Seafood . . . the works. You both should call if you make it to Weymouth. And come to the club, by all means. The two of you get to Boston every now and then, right? For a weekend? Sure will be different, all the way around." Larry sips his coffee. "I guess we'd all make it come out different. But it's just a dice roll."

"A club. Like a nightclub." Arthur is reporting facts. He signals to Sylvia to pour more coffee, to keep Larry in his place. "You're a fine engineer, Larry. Everyone at Transformers always thought you'd hit it big one of these days, make something useful."

Larry shoves his cup to the edge of the table. "Me, too, Art, I thought I had something going with that triode idea." He plants his elbows on the table, drops his chin to his palms. "I guess I left the company in what you might call a blaze of glory. Two months later, I couldn't generate a spark. I didn't believe it at first, when GE, Zenith—nobody wanted to hear about a triode that meant they'd have to redesign radio assembly lines. Tape recorders, handsets. I was turned down everywhere. Two years I got by—Linda, too—living off some repair work. Repair work doesn't pay a mortgage. This Insulum idea. This was make me or break me. Linda said so and, I mean, she's right. We don't have a family yet. I'm thirty-six. I guess it's time I tried my hand at something else."

Arthur grabs Larry's forearm and pats it several times. Sylvia watches, hears him deliver soothing, unfounded reassurances about the nightclub venture. She can't even wait for Arthur to finish. "How did Martin react to your decision, Larry?"

This interrupts the camaraderie between the two men. But Larry will not look at her. "Martin Parris is a realistic man. That's what I believe. He knows when to call it quits, I guess."

Arthur fiddles with his cups, relenting to Sylvia's authority on matters involving Parris.

She runs a sponge across the counter, then spots a bit of splattered coffee near the percolator, which she wipes away. "I don't know what a triode is, Larry. Perhaps I can get Arthur to teach me all about radios some day. But we are not goddamn children here, Larry." She is enunciating every word, making of her anger a staccato rhythm. "The club, if there is a club, is because you and Martin made a deal. You've signed a statement?" She speaks louder, to stifle Larry's mumbling. "You made a trade, a deal. You swear the Insulum belongs to GE after all and you don't go to jail. You go to Boston." She runs water in the sink, wets the sponge, walks to the alcove. She quickly wipes the table, picking up the cup in front of either man. "You think this isn't any of my business, Larry? This business is everybody's business now." She throws the sponge into the sink, points at Arthur. "You think he's going to jail so you can be a bartender in Boston?"

"No one's going to jail." Larry delivers this reassurance with a shake of his head, empathy for the lot of the henpecked husband.

Arthur turns to Sylvia, to calm her and accept the lead she's offered. "That's Martin's line, Larry." Arthur holds him in a friendly, interested stare. Whatever fear and rage he is producing is channeled through Sylvia's slow and steady rocking near the sink. "The one about nobody's going to jail. It was my understanding—by that, I mean I was told, Larry—you'd refused to meet with Martin. But that's your business, Larry. It's the question about the lawsuits you really should answer for me. Because, after all, my name is all over those files. You see, what I'm getting at is . . . are you saying, the lawsuits . . . that there are grounds for a suit? We're guilty?"

Reflexively, Larry says, "I'm not guilty," then adds, "Personally, I don't guess anybody is guilty, so to speak."

The only emotion Arthur can sustain on his own is pity. Sylvia's rocking is sufficient to remind him how inappropriate its expression would be. "There is a lot of room between saying you invented something and not being guilty of a crime." He draws a line along the table. "You see what I mean."

"An idea gets planted inside you." Larry finds comfort in Arthur's strong, passive presence. "I can't tell you how long I've been fiddling with the idea of more efficient transformers. Like a kid with a telephone he takes apart a million times. The kid isn't thinking about the guy who invented telephones. I was bowled over. Martin Parris thinks he can put together financing for Insulum? I all but shit my pants." He swings his heavy head and waves to Sylvia. "Pardon my French." He picks up his empty cup, pushes it to the edge of the table, expecting a refill. After a silent exchange between Arthur and Sylvia, he is rewarded. "And you came on board, and you passed on it, Art. Linda and me, we were in seventh heaven."

"Larry, I passed on your workup of a new product. I wasn't going over it to catch you out. I was there to see if it seemed like something I could move on, something I could represent." Arthur cannot exhume his confession of ignorance. He's dug as deep as he can in the presence of a colleague.

Summoning her meekest voice, Sylvia laughs, as if she is confused about a detail. "Arthur's been at it for weeks, going over and over the pictures, the specifications. I think he's still behind your work, Larry. As an invention."

"Thanks for the vote of confidence. But I guess it's really not up to you any longer, Art."

"You mean the lawsuits. You think they can win?"

Larry drinks his coffee in a single swallow, pushes it back to the table's edge. On the question of the likely outcome he admits no doubt. It is the obviousness of outcome that impelled him to sign the papers Parris proferred. Animated by confidence, Larry's bulk commands attention. "Name a sitting judge in Massachusetts who'd let them lose. What are there? Ten thousand men at the Pittsfield plant? Fifteen, maybe?"

Arthur tries to meet this confidence with reason. "The question is your work. Is it original? Isn't your own work proof enough for you?"

"No. The question is where you draw the line. Think about this, Art. Who more than me hoped Insulum was really something new? And I can't convince myself today my work for ten years there, in the transformer department, right? You know, I can't say the basis for Insulum isn't right there, at the GE. I say the hell with it."

Arthur aims for a dismissive tone. "I would think you'd recognize your own idea." Sliding to the corner, arms crossed and pressed against his chest, he's already in retreat.

Sylvia refills Larry's cup again. Larry leans over to be nearer Arthur, his impressive stomach resting on the table. "That's where Linda was a couple days ago. Shouldn't I know my own idea when I see it? Of course I talked to Parris. What would you do? He's a lawyer. He's my friend. Yes, once and for all, I talked and talked and talked to Martin. I talked—"

"We get the drift, Larry." Sylvia unplugs the percolator. "You talked your fool head off. Are you going to tell us what transpired at your incredibly talkative, secret meetings?"

Sylvia's jab doesn't faze him. "I've always had my doubts. Look at my track record. I told Martin, not the other way around. He couldn't believe it, after all the meetings. After your approval, Art. He didn't want to hear it. But you know what he said?"

" 'Any man who is a victim of his circumstances deserves to be'? 'Sign on the dotted line'?" Sylvia is shadow-boxing.

Larry Forrester won't admit her to the arena, where he has seized command. Winning here is everything to him, the life-long guarantee he made the right decision, the certainty that vowing not to work on related projects or with competing firms for at least five years was the price he had to pay. Carbon copies of three affidavits are locked inside the briefcase on the floor beside the alcove table.

Larry retreats from his advance on Arthur. With a hand-kerchief, he wipes the sweat threading through his stubbly hair. He speaks slowly, purposefully, as if divulging sacred truths. Holding forth like this—a mode he typically reserves for explaining his ideas to nonprofessionals—Larry is an infant king, improbably compelling. "After a long silence, which you might call a sad moment for the both of us, Martin says to me, and I quote, he says, 'I guess an invention is like a kid.' "

Sylvia and Arthur absorb this analogy as a toxin shot into their veins. In unison, their defensively tensed muscles give way to postures of defeat. Arthur's arms slide down along his body and he slumps into the corner. Sylvia turns to the window up above the sink, supports her body on the counter.

Larry thumps his hands against the table. "You see what he means. It's a kid, Insulum's a kid. You have to look at it like I'm a mother, a woman who finds out she's gonna be a mother. Who's the father? Depends on when she . . ."

Sylvia knows he hesitates because there is a woman present. "Depends on when the boy bee put his honey in the girl bee's honey cup? Let's skip the biology, Larry. You said you signed something." Sylvia advances this leading lie as casually as pos-sible.

"Martin called it a remand . . . or curtailment? No. Well, it adds up to me not working in the transformer business. For a period of time."

Sylvia spots Mrs. Barker's hat in the privet hedge, keeps her eye on that while she speaks. "Nothing else? Besides what? An agreement to dissolve the company?"

Larry finally is aware he's being led, though he is not sure how much territory he has traversed. "I was never in a position to make a binding legal claim or pronouncement about the originality of my work. I was not even asked. I submitted it. . . ."

Everyone in the room completes his sentence with the words "to Arthur." The silence is conspiratorial. It suits their shared obsession with self-preservation.

"That's Mrs. Barker's daughter, Dorothy, there." Sylvia is surprised to see Larry Forrester in the alcove when she turns to Arthur. "She's with Teresa Revillio. I'm surprised Teresa would even set foot in the yard after the barbecue episode." A scream from the yard engages Sylvia completely. "Arthur? Oh, look. Teresa is turning Mrs. Barker. I mean, she just grabbed her foot and flipped her over onto her back and—I think she's dead."

Sylvia moves, to allow both men a clear view of the amateur postmortem. Yelling, her hands above her head, Dorothy runs into the house. Left alone, Teresa Revillio spots the hat in the hedge and, as she stoops to pick it up, she sees Sylvia and the two men. She waves excitedly, runs toward them, brandishing the hat.

Sylvia flings open the screen door. "Is she dead?"

Teresa whispers, to be sure their gossip and her occasional burst of laughter won't be heard next door. "I saw the old girl go out early, just about dawn, and just plop herself down there. I been keeping half an eye on her all day."

Sylvia tugs her friend's dress. "I thought she was sunbathing. She didn't move a muscle."

"I think she's been dead since this morning. Plopped down and died, poor old mean thing. Isn't it like a crime novel? Dead as a doornail and in plain sight?"

"Her daughter call a doctor?"

"She's hysterical. I hope she calms down to tell them what happened. Of course, what's a doctor going to do? It's so creepy, Syl. Right in our own backyards. For God's sake, I feel like an accomplice or something." This reduces Teresa to fits of laughter, which she attempts to muffle with the hat.

"I just hope they get her off that lawn before the schools let out. The kids will swarm her like vultures."

"I can speak for the Revillio kids. I mean, God forgive me for saying so, but my kids gladly would have buried her alive. We won't spend much time missing her."

Sylvia snatches the hat, places it on Teresa's head. "It flatters you. It's a souvenir. You ought to keep it."

"Wouldn't that pretty Dorothy collapse if she saw me strutting around in this contraption?" With a squeal, she flings the hat into the kitchen. "We're both going straight to hell."

"Dead as she is she's probably still saying nasty things about the both of us. Look, there's Dorothy. I'll come over in a minute and express my sympathies. Go on. And lose the grin, Teresa." Sylvia turns in time to watch Arthur pick the hat off the floor.

Larry Forrester is in the center of the room, his briefcase at his feet. "It can be over so quickly." He shakes Arthur's hand and turns to Sylvia.

"Oh, Larry, it took the old bird some eighty-odd years to die. That's not so fast. You'll be living forever with what you've done to us."

"Sylvia!" Arthur can't think of an appropriate apology quickly enough to prevent her final shot.

"If I were you, Larry? I'd invent some scruples." She looks at his extended hand, his face contorted to approximate his outrage. "Forget it, Larry. I'd rather shake hands with the corpse next door." Sylvia turns away dramatically, exhilarated by her recklessness, the herald of despair.

Left alone in the kitchen, Arthur assesses the news from Forrester while he washes the cups and saucers. Larry's willing disavowal of Insulum invites suspicion. But he knows Larry possesses neither the wit nor the daring to orchestrate a fraud. Larry's incessant interruption of Arthur's lengthy, if incomplete, review process—*So far so good, Art? Questions about coatings? Linda and me are hanging by a thread here, Art.*—argues for his innocence.

Though he knows Martin's motives merit examination, he twitches, blinks, or hums a favorite song to disrupt prolonged thoughts about Martin. Otherwise, Arthur ends up having to watch his increasingly vivid version of Martin mounting and humping Sylvia. So he leaves Martin's motives to Sylvia. Puzzled as he is by his wife's shifting loyalties, her nagging advice—that Arthur must confront or at least investigate his partner—seems positively brilliant in light of her exposure of the bargain struck with Forrester.

But Sylvia does not return to advise Arthur. An ambulance arrives next door, and Mrs. Barker's body is removed. Sylvia leads Dorothy inside, followed by Teresa carrying the dead woman's pale blue towel. Jane, then Alison and Artie, return from school before their mother fulfills her function as the minister of practical assistance. Sylvia sees it as her job to intervene, alerted not by the survivor's sadness but by her vast incompetence. As for Dorothy, she is consoled by Sylvia, like a woman in the breakdown lane with a flat rescued by an anonymous tow-truck operator who stops to change the tire en route to the scene of a multicar collision.

In retreat from his children, Arthur stacks all his boxes on the dining-room table. At the sound of footfalls on the stairs or the slam of the back door, he feigns interest in a randomly withdrawn file. When he is alone inside, he strains to hear the voices from the driveway, tries to give each one a name and face. A crowd of kids is gathering to view the famous spot where Mrs. Barker died. Finally, the enthusiastic observers break into song. The raggedy rendition of "Ding! Dong! The Witch Is Dead" dissipates into yelps and moans when Sylvia shoos the merry mourners and leads Alison and Artie into the kitchen, just in time to see Jane finishing a cigarette.

Sylvia sends Artie and Alison to their bedrooms, with a punishment for disrespect. "Each of you—an Act of Contrition and a decade of the Rosary for the repose of the soul of Mrs. Barker. And, Artie, if there is one thing out of place in that closet, or under the bed? You'll be cleaning your room instead of going to the picnic Sunday. Understood?" She turns to look out at Mrs. Barker's house as they run upstairs. She doesn't turn to Jane, who has her hand cupped over her ashtray, a half-full glass of water. "Let me see if I have this right. Mrs. Barker just died. Mom is helping her hysterical daughter Dorothy. My father is distracted by a particularly trying time with his business, the business that pays for my food and clothing. I think the thing to do is to smoke a cigarette. Is that it? Is that what you were thinking about?"

"It's a habit." Jane says so as if she is ashamed. "Like a tic of my personality." She does not credit this excuse. She is baiting her mother.

Sylvia walks to the alcove, sits opposite her daughter. "What do they taste like?"

"Cigarettes?" Jane smiles, sensing safety in her mother's curiosity.

Sylvia draws one from the pack, pinches the end. "Does this change the taste?"

"Filter-tipped. You can break it off if you like them stronger. The boys don't like the filters. I think they make them mostly so more girls will like them. Like you see in old movies?" Jane imitates a dowager equipped with a long ivory cigarette holder. "You want me to light that for you?"

"Does it relax you?" Sylvia pulls the cigarette from her lips, rubs her lipstick from the filter. "I hate that, the smudging. Or when someone puts one out in food? The one you just smoked, did it relax you?"

Jane pushes the floating butt to the alcove wall. "What do you think? This isn't the most relaxing place in the world for me these days. You're nervous, I guess. And . . . is Daddy in trouble, real trouble?"

Sylvia drags on the unlit cigarette. "Lots of women my age have babies, Jane. There's nothing wrong when a man and a woman are married."

Jane is caught out. Sylvia has identified the more pertinent, improbable source of embarrassment. "No one's trying to stop you."

"I wasn't asking your permission, young lady." Sylvia fits

the cigarette into the pack, which she pats, a reminder of Jane's flagrant disobedience. She is about to negotiate a truce and she wants her terms to be clear. "I think it would be good for your father's spirits, good for your brother and sister . . . it would mean a great deal, if you would agree to come along on Sunday. To the Sodality picnic. A lot of your friends from the old neighborhood will be there. It's citywide, for Memorial Day."

Jane slides the package off the table, effecting the trade. "I'm sorry for doing it right here in the open. I'll tell Alison I'm gonna quit or something."

Sylvia laughs, taken aback by her daughter's aptitude. "I'm going to tell you something, Jane. But I don't want to drag in Alison or your brother yet. About your father, and Insulum. The company is finished. There are some outstanding—"

"Mom!" Jane rolls her eyes, raises her feet to the bench. "Alison already asked me if he's going to jail. It was in the newspaper. About the patents. We're the only family pretending Insulum is A-OK. Kids who didn't even know I had a father before? Now it's like Daddy and Mr. Parris went on *Toast of the Town*. He's the talk of the town. Kids—kids who are bound to be at that picnic? They wait for me to go by them in the hall at school. Then they yell, 'Jailbird,' or sing that stupid 'Hawaiian Eye' song and tiptoe like they're spies or policemen."

Sylvia mutes her surprise at this report. She only says, "You can tell those people it is none of their business."

"They aren't exactly asking my permission."

"I know we can't help what goes into the newspaper, but anything else is just gossip. Ignore it."

Jane stops short of yelling at her mother, slides back into the corner of her bench. Tears are the price of this retreat. Annoyed with herself for not venting her anger, she forces out words, ignoring the sadness in her mother's fragile smile. "Why did you have to tell Mrs. Revillio right off you were having another baby? Now her kids tell everybody about that one, too. It just kills me how you trust her. She's the town crier."

"She's my friend." Sylvia's assertion does not conceal her shock. It registers as an accusation.

Jane mutters, aware of overstepping a line meant to prevent her wandering into the adult world, "I've got some friends just like Mrs. Revillio."

"Call your brother and sister. We're having dinner early. Sandwiches tonight. I told Dorothy I would make some calls for her later on. There isn't going to be a wake. Where's your father?"

"I'll get Artie and Alison." Jane understands she has won new license to act and speak with no apparent restrictions. She doesn't know what to make of her mother's willingness to tolerate her boldness, or how to remedy the pain she suddenly is permitted to inflict. "I can mix the tuna."

Arthur waits until his elder daughter is out of the kitchen, then noisily clears the ample table. Sylvia hears the ruckus, knows he has listened to the exchange. He joins her, and together they assemble the elements for the minimal dinner on the alcove table.

Jane arrives with her brother and sister in tow. The younger children are quiet, chastened by Jane's curt report on the disaster whose progress they must measure from the sidelines. Tin cans, flatware, plates, glasses, bottles, and trays clatter and bang as sandwiches are made. The din is amplified by the diners' silence. In the uneasy transition from preparation to meal, the three children sit still, warily shuttling their attention between their impassive parents. Squeamish as they feel, they can't stop staring. The suddenness of the meal, the mess created right at table, the awkward way their parents weave to avoid collisions—these are the riches of embarrassment. Public humiliation and sex are on display in all their sordid glory, the magnetic poles of adolescent imaginations.

Fortitude and false pride sustain the family in their routine duties, but Sunday has become a day to lay to rest pretense. Ritual has been replaced by improvisational distemper.

Feeling he's unworthy and conspicuous, Arthur has sworn off church attendance. He moans and rolls to his stomach when Sylvia prods him, leaving her to fend off the children's inquiries. Jane refuses to ride to church with the rest of the family, preferring the two-cigarette walk and a pew near the door that facilitates an exit midway through the sermon (as soon as she is confident she'll pass the oral quiz administered at home). Jane wins this independence theologically, wondering aloud if missing Mass on Sunday really is a mortal sin.

Since Easter, Artie has been seated with the other ten-year-old members of the Confirmation class. Under the kind, if myopic, gaze of the emeritus pastor, the boys in the class conduct a silent swap meet. Week after week, Artie dawdles in his bedroom, selecting barter from among his cherished marbles, baseball cards, and jawbreakers. A few honks of the car horn announce the expiration of his mother's patience; he grabs the nearest item, a choice he'll rue for days. Alison alone accompanies her mother, suffering the scrutiny previously divided among three children. Worst of all is trailing Sylvia like a bridesmaid up the center aisle. Sylvia tells Alison they have as much a right as anyone to march up to the front of church. In fact, for Sylvia the prominence is not a matter of prerogative; it is an act of penance.

The disarray of Sunday morning dooms the plan to join the picnickers by noon. At half past two, Arthur parks the Rambler in the sunny, dusty lot of the Pittsfield State Forest. Toting coolers, baskets, chairs, and towels, the Adamskis march in line behind their father, following the arrows painted on white paper plates nailed to the scrawny scrub oaks. Charcoal fires blot out the scent of blossoming azaleas. Inside the deeper pinewood darkness, family claims on tables and adjacent fieldstone grills are identifiable; venerable sheets of calico and gingham, pressed and mended for another outdoor season, serve as heraldic crests.

Lunchtime is waning. Fathers nurse their favorite beers,

scratching outsized spatulas across the iron grills to loosen clots of blackened meat. Mothers repack coolers, suspiciously regarding lidless salad bowls and sweaty jars of condiments. The children, who outnumber parents three to one, disregard the warnings about fatal cramps that cripple well-fed swimmers. Gathered on the meager, silty bank of Lulu Brook, they issue dares and threats, admiring the bravest few who aren't deterred by water temperatures of fifty-four degrees.

Marching to the center of the clearing, toward a table unprotected from the sun, Arthur nods his head and grunts acknowledgment of waves and shouted words of welcome. Conspicuously late, trailing their reclusive father into a camp of active Catholics—more than half of them supported by the company he is accused of swindling—each Adamski senses danger. Aligned in public with the family, even Artie is alert to the indictment, guilty by association.

They drop their gear on a hardwood bench. Sylvia unfolds a green-and-yellow tablecloth, waits for Jane and Alison to press the wrinkles from the middle to the edges. Arthur flips open the cooler, rearranges every item stacked inside.

"I just want to feel how cold the water is." Artie runs away, eager for the anonymity of childhood.

"Jane, hand me my wicker basket, will you, honey?"

"Dad? Mom needs that basket." She doesn't speak soon enough. Heedless of Sylvia's request, Arthur spills the bags of buns and cookies on the table, hands Jane the empty basket.

"Arthur? What are you looking for? There's a kind of order to the way things were packed." She signals Jane to put the mess to rights.

"Daddy!" Jane yells good-naturedly when Arthur dumps a bag of plastic forks and paper plates and napkins beside the piles she has made. Then she sees him turn the bag upside down, shake it several times. "You lose something?"

"I hate having the table in the sun. Nobody else wanted it." Alison leans against her mother. "Do we have to stay?"

Sylvia watches Arthur drop the empty bag and dig around

inside the cooler. "Arthur, if you're hungry, just ask me where whatever it is you're—Alison, grab the red bag, sweetie. The chips are in that bag, Arthur."

"That's mine. Give it here!" Jane swipes her large purse from Arthur.

Arthur yells, "Everybody just shut up for now." He reaches for the red bag Alison has dropped onto the bench. "There isn't going to be any picnic if I don't find the goddamn hamburgers."

"Oh, great." Jane quickly opens and closes her purse.

"I'm starving, though. Mom?"

Jane balances a large ceramic bowl on her upturned palm, proffers it to Alison as a waitress would a dessert tray. "Plenty of your favorite, Al. Juicy potato salad with onions and peppers. Mmm. Want a sniff?"

"I hate potato salad. Get it out of here." Unrewarded for her whining, she drops her arms and then her face to the table. "I hate cooking out, except for hamburgers. Everybody knows that."

"Jane, slide those cookies over. Alison, have a cookie." Sylvia joins Alison at the table, but her daughter scoots behind her to sulk. "Arthur, I made the patties last night. They must be here. They were in the freezer. You said you were—stop hanging on me!" Sylvia turns to scold Alison. "Oh, Eleanor. It's you." Sylvia kisses Eleanor Wycoff's cheek. "Organizational problems."

"I shouldn't have snuck up on you. I just came over to hear the good news. Look at that potato salad. You're amazing." Eleanor pulls off her straw hat as she bends for a quick survey of the Adamski spread. When she stands again, she swings the hat in her hand.

With one eye closed, Sylvia scrutinizes Eleanor, wondering what news she wants to hear. Three other members of the Sacred Heart Sodality are walking toward her slowly, like deferential party guests approaching an eminent hostess. "Hello, girls. Nice of the sun to cooperate today."

The three squat women, an inseparable trio, are among the most loyal Sodality volunteers. Sylvia can hardly afford to offend them, though she finds them intolerable even at their most helpful. She allows them time to creep forward. They giggle. She steps closer to Eleanor, which effectively stops the swinging hat. "I seem to be the center of attention. Was I supposed to help put up signs? Bake something for someone else?"

This elicits more giggling.

Sylvia turns to Arthur and her daughters, suspecting them of making funny faces behind her back. But the girls are on the bench, watching the encounter as if it is a television show. "Did my Artie hit someone's child?"

Mary Traponi squeals, "What a card!" Then, with her hands behind her back, she pushes her abdomen into an exaggerated imitation of pregnancy. "You've got to show sooner or later." She resumes a normal pose, but adopts a sing-song, baby-talk voice. "Somebody we know is expecting a visit from the stork. A little birdie told us so."

Embarrassed by Mary's antics, but intent on acquiring the gossip, Eleanor puts an arm around Sylvia's shoulders. "Congratulations, Syl. You look wonderful. I know the timing is bad, but we can't always be in the driver's seat."

Sylvia releases herself, spinning to see if Arthur's heard this latest news; despite their pact to make a secret of her afternoons with Martin Parris, her pregnancy is being reported with a tragic aspect—the complications economic rather than romantic. But Arthur is attending to another set of mourners by the grill. Several men in khaki shorts and sportshirts, sporting beers and rolled-up sections of the Sunday *Boston Globe*, are offering condolences. Sylvia runs her hands through her hair, hoping Jane or Alison will decipher her signal of distress. But neither girl is moved; marooned between their parents, they are savoring resentment.

"It's just like Jack Campbell said to me the day you told us you were leaving the company, Art." Phil Clary pauses to light his cigar. "He said, 'You're always gonna run up against something when you're doing business with a Jew.' He's got a point."

The small crowd of engineers and salesmen raise a spontaneous "Hear, hear." A young red-haired man Sylvia does not recognize adds, "Those people haven't got the same values we do. I worked with quite a lot of them in Albany. Real Jews over there. I mean, the kind who don't take the little caps off. Not even indoors, in my office."

Phil Clary points his cigar at the young man. "Don't get me started about those hats they wear."

Sylvia jerks her attention from Arthur's supporters, afraid she has offended Eleanor and Mary. But the women's conversation has turned to a debate about the proper age for makeup use. Sylvia takes a step back toward the table. Immediately, the women resume their investigation of her physical condition. She answers curtly, knowing everything will have to be repeated as a dozen other women wander over. Each time she delivers a dismissive answer, she underscores her mental note to ask Arthur who in their acquaintance is a Jew.

Arthur's consolation party ends abruptly. Phil Clary's son is delivered to the men, hobbling and hopping with the help of his older brother, Ron, and Artie Adamski. The elder Clary scuttles quickly out of view and Jimmy Clary's full weight falls to Artie's shoulders.

Artie is intimidated by the silence their arrival has imposed. Tentative but hopeful, he looks at Phil Clary. "He was sort of shinnying up a tree down there. He sort of lost his grip?"

Jimmy nods his assent, sanctioning his friend's introduction, then hops unsteadily and yells, "Watch it! Let me down!"

Artie lowers Jimmy to the scraggly patch of grass. Kneeling, he spots his father among the men, who seem to think this is more performance than emergency. "He made it halfway up a huge pine tree."

Jimmy yells, "Way more than half, I bet."

"Yeah, way more than half, I guess." Artie bobs his head a couple times, signaling his father to come to Jimmy's rescue. But he senses he has yet to stir any of the older men to pity, never mind to action. "His leg is broke. All the kids knew right away. We heard a really big crack when he landed. Did I say he landed on his leg?"

Phil Clary points his lit cigar as if it is a diagnostic tool. To the other men, he says, "That's no broken leg. I ought to know."

This is too much for Jimmy, who begins to cry.

Angry and embarrassed on his friend's behalf, Artie yells, "It is too busted." He waves his outstretched hands above the leg in question, which Jim is holding at the thigh. He swivels to his father, hands flailing. "Why don't you just pick him up? He's too heavy for me."

Phil leads with his cigar, circling the boys as if they are an abstract sculpture he finds both confusing and offensive. The other men edge back a couple of steps, leaving Arthur as the boys' only hope of intervention. Phil addresses Arthur directly, which effectively reduces the scope of the incident to a family affair—two boys and their fathers. "I ever tell you how I played the final quarter of a ball game—playoff game—on a broken ankle? My junior year at Holy Cross?"

In unison, Jimmy and Artie yelp, "Dad!" convinced their explanations have been misunderstood.

Arthur wishes Artie had the sense to get up, run away, and leave the Clary boy to his business. He knows Phil's penchant for mixing it up at every opportunity. He is afraid that Artie, who is kneeling on the ground beside his friend, will get caught between the Clarys when a scuffle starts.

Phil spits, disappointed with Arthur and the silent gallery of men. Then he swings his body back toward the boys and hollers, hoping to shock his son and elicit a reflex reaction that contradicts the business about the leg being broken. "Knock it off with the crocodile tears, Jimmy. For Christ's sake, it just got bruised or something."

Arthur lamely interjects a question, hoping to forestall this confrontation. "You played ball at the Cross?"

From his indefensible position near his whimpering pal, Artie is ashamed of his unvaliant father. As much as he hates Mr. Clary and his big, hot cigar, at least he is a proper tyrant. Half hoping Mr. Clary goes ahead and loses his temper and ends up hitting him right in front of all his father's friends, Artie ducks his head beneath Jimmy's arm and raises him. Jimmy's protests only amplify Artie's righteousness. "Just stand there. Good idea, Dad. Let him suffer."

Jimmy yells, "Leave off, already, would ya? It's killing me," and slips away from Artie, falls down and hollers, "Hey, my leg!"

"Jimmy, get up now, son." Phil Clary is sufficiently shamed to move toward his son.

Artie runs away, not to his father, but beyond him, just behind the ring of amused and fascinated men.

Contradicting the story of his heroic sportsmanship, Phil explains, "If he can walk on it at all, it's just a sprain." This seems to satisfy Arthur. But the sight of his young son sitting in the dirt, despondent and inert, excites Phil Clary's anger. "For Christ's sake, Jimmy, just try is all I'm saying." He clamps one hand around his son's wrist and hoists him to his feet. "Take a step or two and try it out."

"It hurts bad, Dad."

"Nothing's gonna happen, Jimmy. I'm right here. Just try the damned thing, would you?"

Jimmy screams, "Mom! Help!" and seizes his moment. While his father arches back and raises both his fists, exasperated, Jimmy hops away, yelling "Mom," ignoring Phil's command to "Use the bum leg and walk normal."

Gleeful, sensing he is on the winning side, Artie hollers, "Beat it, Jimmy! Faster!"

The great escape dispels the crowd of men, each one a private fan of Jimmy, gratified to see Phil Clary lose a round in public. After final handshakes and some easy, optimistic words to Arthur, they are gone. When Arthur turns back to his family's table, Artie is midway through the story of the confrontation.

Seeing Artie's pleasured animation, Arthur figures his performance has been salvaged by the successful, antic ending provided by Jimmy Clary's hop to safety. Just to reassure himself, he shakes his head and points his thumb over his shoulder. "That Phil Clary is a horse's ass."

Amazed by this pronouncement, the girls bend over laughing.

Artie whispers, "Hope he has another beer."

Sylvia leaves the women on the false pretense of exhaustion, convinces Arthur to give up his renewed search for the missing meat. Without an indignant demand for child voting rights or a plea for an extension, Sylvia's motion to leave the picnic is seconded by Arthur and rapidly enacted.

Sealed inside the Rambler, the family feels its retreat is less ignoble. Arthur honks the horn while backing up the car, as if they are adventurers staging an escape. The spirit catches on and before it fades, he yells, "Whoa!" and veers off the access road, parks the car in a small macadam lot. It's been at least three years since they last stopped to visit Balance Rock.

"It's so overgrown. Look, there's barely a path." Sylvia bends and turns off the engine, hands the key to Arthur. "When your father and I were young? You could see it from here. From everywhere. I mean, there wasn't even a parking lot. Just a dirt road. But people came in droves. Now they put up signs and they made this parking lot, I guess, and it's gone, really. It's no wonder people stopped coming here."

The sighing in the front seat is a cue. Alison and Artie plunder bags and coolers for a snack, then run until they overtake their sister. Their parents will arrive in ten or twenty minutes. The routine never varies.

Artie runs a circle round his sisters. "Bet they're making out again."

Jane grabs his arm. "You don't call it making out when you're a grown-up. It's called making love."

"As if you'd know." Artie lunges but doesn't loose her grip.

Jane holds him until he stops wriggling. "This is the place where he asked Mom to marry him. Otherwise, smarty, you wouldn't be here."

"Know it all. I know we're here 'cause Mom's having another baby. And I know how they do that, too." He jerks his arm free and runs to the rock.

"Is that why we stopped here, Jane?" Alison's question is defensive. She doesn't want to let on that, unlike her younger brother, she is not sure exactly what a man does when it comes time to have a baby.

"Daddy loves it here. You know how he always says, 'That's one of life's little mysteries,' when you ask him something and he doesn't know the answer? It reminds me of here. I think he wants to be happy about having another kid. I guess that's why we're here. I wonder if it will still seem so gigantic?"

Alison misunderstands this as a question about the child Sylvia is carrying. "I don't think it's so gigantic. Is it?"

"I sort of can't wait to see. I used to think it was the biggest rock I ever saw. It's supposed to weigh a hundred and fifty tons." Jane slows when the massive, freakish monument comes into view.

"It's ten times bigger than you, Artie. You should see yourself. You look puny!" Alison runs to join her brother at the small, blunted tip of the inverted cone of wrinkled rock. Isolated in a tiny glade littered with rocks that barely break the surface of the ground, Balance Rock is awesome and ridiculous. Its base is three feet, but the boulder opens like a trumpet lily to a diameter of more than thirty feet. "Jane, get this one!" Alison swats Artie's hands while she repeats what he's just told her. "He says to me, he says, it's just one hell of a big, upside-down Hershey's Chocolate Kiss, so what's the big deal. You seen one, you seen 'em all."

Jane joins them near the base, beneath the improbable rock arbor. "It does look like a chocolate kiss."

Alison is anxious to show off her greater understanding of the site. "It is so a big deal. Because it was a glacier that left it here like this, all upside-down. That's geology."

Artie leans against the rock, hands in the pockets of his shorts, staring into the sky, bored—his best imitation of a swell. "I always say, it's a big chocolate kiss and all the girls like to come here to get a big French kiss." He returns Alison's disgusted sigh, then he jumps and yells, "Watch it, it's moving!"

Alison and Jane bolt toward the clearing, stop after a few steps. They slowly turn to acknowledge Artie's laughter.

He's poised at an angle, both hands pressed against the rock. "Never fear, Samson's here. Let me know when I got it back in place. I need a break."

"I'm ten times stronger than you, Artie." Alison hates any display of her younger brother's superiority.

"Ten times dumber, you mean." He bends down, snakes around the impossibly small base, conducting a thorough examination of the illogic of Balance Rock. Alison kneels near him, hoping inspiration will allow her to deliver a plausible explanation before her brother figures it out.

Jane sits several yards away, melodramatically imagines she'll miss Balance Rock when she leaves Pittsfield. She is sure she will not miss the house on Holmes Road or St. Joseph's High School or the other landmarks of her life. She doesn't bother to invent the place she'll make her new home. She doesn't rouse the many short-haired girls she's invented in the past, girls who buy a book of poems by Jane and read them in their Continental accents. She's thrilled to be enclosed by trees and stare at Balance Rock and make of it a memory. Unlike her customary pipe dreams—fantasy escapes concocted to avert despair—this is an act of hope. She does not beg for Providential intercession, a sudden and dramatic change of circumstance to satisfy her longings. She doesn't want a miracle. A miracle, she tells herself, would be a boulder big as Balance Rock floating in the air. Instead, she claims the mystery. Ill-suited as she is to her surroundings here in Pittsfield, awkward and untenable as her aspirations are, she won't berate herself again for seeming out of place, or dream up a supportive foster family. Instead, she congratulates herself on her unique ability to balance. She finally understands she'll never be like other girls, who blend in with the scenery. She is a freak of nature. Like Balance Rock, the most of her will never come to rest flat and firm against the ground. But she finally sees her point of contact here, and sees it is the point of separation.

In the car, Arthur and Sylvia have exhausted their inventory of apologies and reassurances. As a last-ditch effort, they revive the old, romantic script. Sylvia drops her hand to her side, waits for Arthur's hand to find her arm and slowly slide up to her shoulder. They stare ahead, remembering summer evenings when the rock was in plain sight. She turns to him, eyes closed. He kisses her. She leans against his shoulder, smooths his hair.

His arm around his wife, Arthur whispers, "Oh, oh, oh," as if he has to speak to breathe. This is improvisation. "I want you back. I want to be your working man again. The one you kiss when he comes home. I want to hear about an argument you had with ladies in the neighborhood and tell you how the union's going out on strike and should I cross the picket line? I even want to bring the basket by at Sacred Heart and . . . maybe, then, you raise your eyebrows 'cause the kids are cutting up. And what's for dinner? Mrs. Barker yelled at Artie and his friends for playing ball. Remember to be home by four today. Remember to pick up Alison's bike and remember you promised Jane you'd give her driving lessons and. . . . We don't make promises in the morning anymore. Lately, it's not up to me to remember much of anything."

"I broke the promise, Arthur." She wants to take them somewhere new, beyond the crying and confessions and the resolutions to be better. She wants to shape it as a story, bring it to a satisfactory end. "I remember distinctly thinking about what a grand opportunity it was to be chosen by him. 'He's so bright,' I said. I remember saying so to you. We had nothing to lose. It was like our guarantee for the future. At last, a way to do something, really do something. We couldn't miss." She stops herself, embarrassed by her own enthusiasm. "I'm talking about the business. What I thought about Martin as a businessman." She is well aware she inadvertently, and rather aptly, summarized her extramarital affair.

Arthur's silence is a kindness they can share, a willingness to live without a detailed explanation of his wife's betrayal.

Sylvia supplies the details to herself. They will always be unspeakable. It is cruel—can it be cruel to reckon with the obvious?—and it is true: Sylvia is superior to Arthur. She is the wilier, the more resourceful player. But she's barred from entering the corporate and the social tournaments whose winners rise to prominence. And she's an ineffective coach, crippling her surrogate with complicated strategies and theories well beyond his ken. Ambition, unfulfilled but unrelinquished, fueled her infidelity.

Pressed against her handsome husband, surrounded by his love, she still longs to be admired critically, inch by inch. She wants someone to account for her, by weights and measures to proclaim her fit.

Sylvia distrusts desire, the thrall of Arthur's unqualified, uncomprehending devotion. His fidelity to her is water. It wants to be her surface and her depth. It wants to be her element. It buoys her and cools her. Infrequently, she even lets it whelm her; then she lives for weeks without regard for castles built by those who crowd the shore. But desire does not take her. She's always holding to a cord anchored on the beach; it is her tether to ambition. She intends to pull herself to land and bear a child there, protect him from the lovely, lethal water.

"Should we go and have a look at it?" Arthur strikes a chummy tone as he invades her privacy. "For old times' sake?"

"Or for pity's sake?" She poses this in earnest, as if he might yet coax her back to old, romantic times. Then, to physically shirk off the awkward silence, she gently lifts his arm and slides away. "You know, Arthur, I hate not being able to see it from here. But it's more depressing somehow, to think of us going down that path. You know? After we saw it, after we agreed it was amazing—and one of us would feel obliged to mention that, thank God, some things never change. After all that, we'd have to turn around and we wouldn't see us parked here. We wouldn't see the spot where you parked the Chrysler twenty years ago. We wouldn't even see the road."

Arthur feels the perfect fool. Though hardly without precedent, her cool and rational dismissal shocks him. He suffers twice: his own humiliation and the shame he feels on her behalf. His is the queasy pain a child feels when an adult hits him hard enough to raise a bruise.

She knows what she has done. And, once again, she's left to do the least that she can do—squelch the impulse to console or soothe him, which only aggravates the wound. Being Sylvia—articulating everything she wants to understand—involves inflicting incidental injuries. Unlike abusive parents who accuse their children of inciting them to violence, she punishes herself for failing to predict which offhand comment or retort will ram against a soft and unprotected part of Arthur.

Years of pulling punches, softening the blows, and shutting down completely (confounding him seemed less egregious than catching him off guard) did not dispose of her conviction that she was a kind of monster. For twenty years, she held herself responsible. Self-regulation, vigilance, and successfully disguising what she managed to withhold from him; those were her duties as his wife. Every time he lulled her with his innocent affection, he courted a disaster.

For twenty years she lived confined. She measured her ability to love by degrees of self-restraint. One night, in an after-dinner conversation with a friend of Arthur's, she felt herself unbridled. And Martin didn't wince. He laughed. He didn't close his eyes in bed when she began to talk. She felt him arch his back and tense his thighs as Arthur would when she rolled and, with her strong arms, raised her head and shoulders up above him, away from their fused bodies. He even braced himself as Arthur did when she looked down and spoke to him inside her. But it turned out he was bracing for the thrill of her, not to endure the interruption. He spoke to her and took her at her word. He redeemed her nature.

Six weeks away from Martin in the narrowed confines of the house on Holmes Road have dispelled her doubts about him.

Circumstantial evidence is evidence enough to support his vindication. She credits him with ingenuity and wiles for surviving Insulum's collapse unscathed. Her own obsessive reveries about their time together she interprets as the proof of his abiding love. His intelligence and insight are unimpeachable, which explains her secret habit of pointing out to him the ironies that crop up in a conversation with her husband or a neighbor. She's made a stronger man of Martin in his absence; he has become the man of her dreams.

Now she is prepared to return his love completely. She is ready to deliver him a child, as if a human life is a commemorative token, an indeterminate object defined by the significance invested by the giver and receiver. Mindful of her peculiar wifely duties, the price she will demand is Arthur's freedom. Arthur must be spared. She believes Martin has the power to protect her husband's innocence. In this way, her strength will be a salve to Arthur, the comfort she alone never managed to provide him.

She has devised a circuit, one that reapportions love and compensation. In theory, it is an elegant solution. But the transformation she intends to orchestrate defies the elemental laws of nature.

Midmorning Monday, Sylvia tells Arthur she has to oversee the counting of the proceeds from the picnic. It is a hasty lie, which even Arthur doesn't countenance. Sporting to the end, he sanctions her excuse with a transparent falsehood of his own: "I'm looking at a full day of work with the files." A fair exchange of lies-in-kind approximates a mutual display of kindness.

Finding Martin's front door locked, she sneaks in through the back, which is always open. In his kitchen, it occurs to her that Martin may not be sleeping by himself. Her plan does not account for complications, not to mention competition. To overcome reluctance, she treats the situation as a test of faith: If she finds a woman in his bed, she'll go away and never come again.

Alone and unaware of Sylvia, even when she leaves the

room and returns with a kitchen chair, Martin makes the grade. After all, it was not faith but merit she was testing.

He disappoints her, waking to her presence slowly, un-alarmed. A friendly, bemused grin wins him time enough to ascertain she wasn't with him when he went to sleep, learned behavior for the active bachelor. "Well, good morning, Miss Sylvia." He sits up, stuffs the pillows in behind his back. "What is it? Ten o'clock? Been here awhile?" He crinkles up his face, runs both hands through his hair and then rubs the stubble on his cheeks. He looks at his naked arms and chest, then coyly shrugs, admitting she has seen it all before. "Would Gregory Peck ask a woman why she's in his bedroom?"

"I've been sitting here and thinking about how much time I have on my hands these days. I sort of lost my job, too." She puts her feet up on the mattress. "And how unfair that is, since I'm the only one who really invented anything." She lays her hands against her stomach, then reaches to her knees and and smooths her skirt. "Maybe I should start a company, an all-girl business."

As often happens to a single man, he turns excessively polite when conversation turns to pregnancy. "I hope you feel as well as you look. You look awfully well. Very healthy."

"I'm not sick."

"No morning sickness, even? I've heard some women do, get sick, and—well, as you say, not you. You certainly look very healthy. Would you like a cup of coffee?" He's speaking in the patronizing tone typically reserved for invalids and aged aunts. "A glass of juice? Or tea?"

"Martin, if you offer me a poached egg on toast points, I'll do chin-ups on the doorjamb, just to prove I'm not on the critical list. I'll plug in the pot. I got it all ready. I mean . . . I figured, as long as I was breaking in through the kitchen, I might as well make myself useful." She swings her arm dis-missively when he attempts to raise himself, holding to his sheet. "Stay put. I know my way around. Please don't move."

He pulls on a pair of chinos and a once-worn white shirt from his closet, rushes through his routine brushing of his teeth and hair. Vanity dictates the use he makes of precious minutes: He forgoes analysis of why she's here, spends his time deciding not to shave or button up his shirt, opting to preserve the atmosphere of scandal. After an approving final glance at his reflected image, he heads into the living room, sits behind the table, on the sofa.

"You moved." Sylvia sets down a tray, serves two cups of coffee. She drags a wicker chair nearer to the table, sits opposite her half-dressed hero. "But the truth is, no one ever really wants breakfast in bed."

He can't focus his suspicions. "How have you been?" Even his affection for her isn't steady. He fusses with his coffee, buying time again. "It's so odd. I talk to Arthur almost daily. But, of course, we never mention you. I mean, I know he knows. But an apology would only make it worse."

"I don't think apologies are in order. We're all adults."

This is a cue he won't follow. He rates the cost to Arthur far too high to justify the joy she brings him. "I think Arthur has been amazingly decent. Embarrassingly so. I mean, Sylvia, I think I was his best friend."

"I was his wife." She is encouraged by his willingness to let the past tense stand. "Who's representing the GE? Do you know yet?"

"What's the difference? It will be a team. A team of lawyers. It's Jonty Mortimer—did you ever meet him? Anyway, he's the front man. He's not a lawyer, though."

"He used to work for you, or in your department, anyway. That one? With the straw-blond hair?"

"I guess he's very handsome to women." He can't even manage to return her smile. He's spent the weekend delivering affidavits and assurances to Jonty.

As he now understands it, his remaining duty is to see that Arthur signs an affidavit claiming sole responsibility for, and knowledge of, the patent infringement. This, and a promissory note for twenty thousand dollars—Jonty's estimate of the principals' profits from payments made by GE when initial agreements were signed—must be in hand within the week. For his cooperation, Martin will be awarded a two-year retainer. This arrangement is a concession not to Martin but to press relations. By isolating Arthur and appearing to embrace the prominent former staff attorney, the image-conscious company ensures the public view will be of justice tempered by both loyalty and mercy.

"What are Jonty's plans for Arthur?"

"He has to sign an affidavit. The truth is, he has to sign what adds up to a confession. They will not prosecute the case if he does that much. And pays some money." Parris cannot sip his coffee while he thinks of Arthur, pen poised above the paper. "It's the only way."

"They promise in writing not to prosecute?"

"We have their word." He forces down a sip, as if a drink is needed to complete the bargain.

"So we have their word. We have your word. And we have a signed statement from Arthur." She resumes her pose as an indignant wife. "By the way, Martin? On the topic of money? We haven't got it. We don't have thousands to give away. We don't have a thousand. And I have a daughter ready to start college in a year. What Jews they are, with all their millions."

He stands, cup in hand, gestures with his free hand. But he cannot speak the rational words he is thinking. Instead, he winds up, splashes coffee on the sofa as he pitches the cup against the bedroom door. It bounces to the floor but it doesn't break. "Oh, those goddamned Jews again. If I hear it one more time." He retrieves the cup, shakes it as he paces behind the sofa. "Three times, without my even knowing it, three times my name has gone in for the country club. Blackballed three times. Why? I think someone nominates me every year just so they get to use their—the voting members actually have black fucking balls they drop in the basket. And now it's time to call down the villain Jew who grabs the money and tries to run off."

Reasonably, reassuringly, Sylvia says, "Martin, no one is accusing you of being a Jew. I was talking about the company. Anyway, it's just a figure of speech."

Trying to force a laugh, he gurgles. "What a city. Ten Negroes. Four Chinamen who run a restaurant on North Street. And half the Jews are Unitarians." He sits on the sofa, leans toward the table. "You idiot, Sylvia. I am Jewish. Italian Jews? Parisi into Parris, so my family could be neither, neither wops nor kikes."

"Oh, come off it, Martin. You're telling me I wouldn't have known by now? I mean, I can understand if it's your grandparents or something. But, as in the Jewish Community Center? You're of that persuasion?" A smile lingers as she speaks, her belief that his assertion owes as much to histrionics as it does to fact. Her humor finally fades, replaced not by regret but by sheer amazement. "You are honestly . . . of the Jewish faith? Well, I take it back. I'm so surprised. I never would have guessed."

"The greatest compliment of all." He flips the sofa cushion, to hide the coffee stains. He's far away from her, staring from the distance he is used to claiming to insure civility. "Arthur knows."

"He does not know. He certainly would have told me."

"I'm willing to bet those were his very words when you told him you and I slept together. Not Martin. He would have told me." He is right, or near enough the truth to silence her. "I think you better leave. I'll deal with Arthur on the affidavit, or through Jonty. I actually believe it is in his interest to sign it and get on with things. We're finished."

"You don't want to face him."

"I can't face him. I don't know what drives you, lady, but we're different."

It is the "lady" that alerts her. "It doesn't bother me. I don't mind you being in that race, Martin, the Jewish race. I don't have any feelings about it one way or another. Don't give it a second thought." Her circuit is suffering an overload. "You are this child's father. That's the truth."

He turns the cushion over, showing off the stains. "It wouldn't be a mixed kid. Don't worry. The mother has to be a Jewess, Sylvia. We have these rules. Our race." He leans back, tilts his head, and stares up at the ceiling. "I left the last time knowing it was Arthur's and I kept you alive. What for?" He looks at her and laughs. "I couldn't believe you'd been sleeping with him. The whole time. Like I wasn't willing to be not good enough to win the competition. I wanted you back here, where you are right this minute. I wanted to be declared undisputed champion. How's that for romance?"

Sylvia is afraid to move. She needs all her energy to reiterate her story. "He is my husband, Martin. But you are the father."

Martin stands, turns away, buttons his shirt. "Do they have a parade in town today? Or was it yesterday?"

She follows him around the sofa, and then to the window. "You don't have to get there first to be the father. Martin, your seed—it's all inside me, with this baby."

The graphic image engraves itself on his imagination. It is his first encounter with the notion of the embryonic child as witness and victim of their intercourse. To release his physical discomfort, he cranes his neck and then brings his fists like bolts against his head.

She seizes silence as an opportunity. "If it weren't to cover up your tracks, I wouldn't have let Arthur near me. We conceived this thing together."

"It is a baby!"

"Yes, Martin. Bravo. Alive and kicking. And it's going to grow up. It will be a person. A person needs to know why he came into the world. You are the reason, Martin. That makes you the father." She sidles up to him, presses her abdomen against his hip.

He takes a step away, then shouts, to immobilize her. "I can get the money. That much I can do, for Arthur." Conceding slightly, he adds, "And for the children. All of them."

She tacitly accepts his financial offer with her demand for more. "That's not enough. I love you. Which is not a debt you pay off. I need you, Martin Parris, just like a child needs a father. I need you."

"I have nothing you need. You can see that, can't you? I

certainly can look at you and see you don't belong here. Or is that just a fancy way of saying I don't love you?"

She gathers up a window curtain in her hand, shrouds herself in it, spins and lets it float back to the sill. "Love doesn't go away so easily. I know better, Martin."

Her friendly tone unsettles him, though he can't identify its force. It takes him several seconds to assert the truth, which is muted by his petulance. "I am a Jew. I don't love you. And I am sorry."

She maintains her pose as Martin's warm, wise lover. "Don't be crazy, Martin. You're just overworked right now. I'm not here to scream about how much I love you. I won't start repeating all the lovely things you ever said to me. After all, you were there. You said it all. You have Jonty come and see us. As for Arthur? He'll sign on the dotted line. I'll see to that much, anyway. You think it's best for him to sign, which is good enough for me. I know we've both done Arthur too much harm to wish him any undue pain at this point." She wags her hands to halt his protest, walks by him, takes the tray into the kitchen.

When she walks back into the room, he doesn't turn to her. He will not look at her. He cannot tolerate her ability to see him, even now. Her version of the past and her predictions for the future seem patently absurd. But, untwisted and unmodified, the facts remain: She did reveal him. They recognized each other once.

He saw himself as an aspiring success with Arthur; to this he added reckless love for Sylvia, rounding out his disproportionate self-image. But failure has improved his vision. He has to face what is left.

She kisses his head, pats his shoulders. "I'll be sure to call before I come next time." In her arcane math, this adds up to a good enough beginning. Arthur won't end up in jail, so half her work is done. "Stay well, and think of me."

Martin stands at full attention until her car is out of sight, then waves goodbye as a soldier would salute the passing coffin of an officer. Imperfect as his window image is, he recognizes well the little man. Like morning haze burned off by midday sun, the spirits of desire and ambition are ascending from his body. He is left alone to live with what he's made of Sylvia and Arthur, the incarnations of the ghosts he's given up.

Flesh

I

MARTIN PARRIS CRUISED by the Adamskis' house, wove his way around the grid of culs-de-sac and residential parkways parallel to Holmes Road. For fifteen years this neighborhood, the Southeast, was his happy hunting ground; he stalked and trapped the wives of bankers, doctors, and elected town officials. But he never bagged his prey. He wasn't after trophy. He hoped to prove himself an able hunter with no interest in a woman he had conquered. He wanted to discredit his own version of the tale of Sylvia, the only one who'd seen through to his weakness; Sylvia, the one who got away.

So much had got away from him. In 1962, he was the ranking counsel for transformer operations and its many subdivisions. Fifteen months later, he was bartering for leniency with Jonty Mortimer, the spokesman for the GE in the claims against the fledgling Insulum—Jonty Mortimer, whose apprenticeship he'd overseen from a remove of several corporate ladder steps.

Martin feared the worst: Successful prosecution of a criminal charge against him would obliterate his future in the law. To stave off this possibility, he offered to dissolve the company, turn over product information to the GE, and exact sworn statements from his partners admitting culpability and vowing to abstain from work on related products for five years. Jonty Mortimer mulled over Martin's offer. Parris pressed his case with daily phone calls to old colleagues. He sent two copies of his self-serving proposal to corporate headquarters in New York. Ultimately, Jonty relented. He accepted Martin's sacrificial offering of Arthur and Larry. And, in what seemed to Martin recognition of both his shrewd bargaining and his undiminished legal reputation, Jonty offered him a two-year contract as a consultant to the Pittsfield plant.

Six months reviewing the tax benefits of small real-estate transactions from one of fifteen unpartitioned spaces in the GE Payroll Accounting Office diminished Martin's triumph. He summoned every uncollected debt—from lawyers he'd furnished with recommendations and the rabbi for whom he'd organized a building fund, as well as every state and local politician whose campaign he had supported. He wanted to be made a judge.

The total owed him was not nearly enough. But the spectacle of his demise—groveling before the men who, only months before, spoke reverentially of his ascent to power—generated sympathetic capital. By 1965, he was installed into an open slot in Berkshire County Probate Court. His friends were off the hook; they were sure it was the least that they could do.

The quibbling of greedy spouses and no-account heirs bored Martin from the first. For a time, he tempered his impatience with relief; at least he was still practicing the law.

He knew what he had done. When his career stalled in the fast lane, he lost his nerve. Panicking, he didn't prop up the hood, fiddle with the engine. He hocked the car, passengers and all, for fare on public transportation. In his judicial garb, he was traveling slowly down a side street. A while back he'd seen a couple of DEAD END signs. But, mercifully enough, as far as he could see ahead, the roadway was unposted.

In time he found an outlet for the self-pity and bewilderment he generated in his chambers. He plugged into the private world of Bertie Burns, the surgeon's wife. Bertie had long since set aside her painterly ambitions to raise four children in one of several gambrel-roofed colonials on Lincoln Parkway. In her confused frustration, she exacted retribution from her husband in appliances. Driving by her freshly painted house thirteen years after his last visit, Martin squinted, remembering the island she'd installed in her vast kitchen to display her booty: a twelve-cup stainless percolator, a portable rotisserie for chickens, two blenders—one for mixing drinks and one to whiz the children's milkshakes, three pressure cookers, the full line of Revere Ware pots and pans, and hand-held whisklike tools whose functions she'd forgotten.

Just two blocks away, Martin smiled as he passed the shingled home of Ella Hailey, whose dentist husband died two years after Martin's month-long fling with her had ended; time enough to leave Martin feeling blameless. On an adjacent parkway—their proximity revealed by the Dutch Elm blight that swept through in the later seventies—he sped by the former homes of Marilyn Matthis (her husband Bob had been promoted to a job in Boston with the Social Security Administration) and the late Peg Donahue, who'd acquired a cat or dog as each one of her seven children graduated high school. Peg and Martin lasted only two weeks. He was hastened by his queasiness. Peg had insisted Martin greet the pets by given names, like Ed and Carol Anne, the names of children they'd replaced.

He located seven homes he'd habited and knew he'd overlooked a few. He remembered Marcie Vandoling but not where she had lived and maybe to this day resided. He wasn't much dismayed by his parsimonious memory. After all, its stock was nearly spent. Lately, Martin did not attend to its replenishment. He lived too much alone.

But the neighborhood itself recalled him, supplementing Martin's fractional remembering. He saw himself arriving at the back doors, acting tough and debonair, reticent or brave, suave, and even hip, as called for by the passing social fads. He'd pomaded, permed, and dyed his hair, adopted many guises. The women, too, were interchangeable. He manufactured interest in the wives of other men by transforming his self-pity into a quality approximating empathy. As he languished in judicial robes, he felt they languished in their housecoats, overworked and undervalued.

He wooed and humped and telephoned at noon until a woman dared to mention love, which reliably incited both his irony and scorn. The routine never varied, though in recent years his spectrum of emotions shrank. He compressed affairs into single days: an incautious second glance or a chance meeting was efficiently converted to a fifteen-minute session in the master bedroom.

He'd merged affection and disinterest, made a sterile hybrid of emotion.

Martin circled back to Holmes Road, parked in front of Sylvia and Arthur's mock-Tudor house. He hastily prepared a speech detailing his suspicions about Stephen and the fire, planning to speak forcefully enough to override Sylvia's defensive interjections. He attached no sentimental meaning to his reunion with the Adamskis. Though well outside his official jurisdiction, he intended to proceed impartially and expeditiously.

He was interrupted by a small white car that sped around him into the drive. Jane hoisted the emergency brake, climbed out of her car, jogged toward the front door.

Martin saw her as Sylvia, unchanged by twenty years. As if she were a vision of his making, he opened and slammed his car door to wake himself and make her go away.

Jane turned, squatted to see inside his car fifteen feet away. "Hello?" She stood up and crossed her arms.

Martin waved, hoping to dismiss her. He now knew she was a daughter, but he could not name her. She didn't move. Embarrassed, as if he were a Peeping Tom caught in the act, he slid off his seat and stood beside the car. "My name is Martin Parris. I'm here to speak to your mother. You look just like your mother. Or do you know that?"

Jane laughed. "Uh-huh. I think someone might have mentioned that to me. Arthur isn't home. I just drove him in to work." She was juggling random associations called up by the name *Martin Parris*. "No kidding. What, were you just in the neighborhood? Martin Parris." Saying his name aloud amused her. "I'm Jane. Well."

"You write. You write well. I saw your piece in *Esquire*. Women in the military, was it? And in the *Times* again. Recently. About the nurse accused of stealing needles for drug addicts?"

She shook her head, accepting his recital as a compliment.

Then she held her hand out and wound it around a couple times, but this did not dislodge a polite response or question as she had hoped it might. She laughed again. "Martin Parris. Well, I guess you came to see my mother? I'm not even sure she's awake yet, frankly. Since you read the papers, you know we've been . . . we've been up nights lately. I don't live here."

He closed the door, walked around his car, leaned back against the hood with his feet against the curb. "I'm not here about your mother. Sylvia. I mean, we haven't spoken. . . ." At closer range the likeness undid him. "Oh well, I suppose everyone stumbles over their pasts. I know it's odd for me to be . . . well, nervous laughter . . ." He pointed at Jane, allying himself with her discomfort.

She pushed her hair back, held it flat against her head. Out of her confusion and her memories came contradictory words. *He and your mother had an affair. Don't be ridiculous.* "Come in. Or . . . what do you want? Were you really just passing by?"

"It's about Stephen. Your brother." He admonished himself for providing this clarification. Her inattention to his announcement surprised him. "Your brother Stephen."

Jane was purposefully still, allowing her earlier conversation with Arthur to come to the surface. *I am his father, after all.* She let this float by, jostling her unanchored confusion. *Don't be ridiculous. He and your mother had an affair.* "I should check? She would have to be awake. To talk to you, I mean. She had a late night. You should come in though. Or would you rather wait?"

In his impatience, Martin had vaulted his attention over her. Directly above Jane, disassembled by the framed panes of her bedroom window, Sylvia savored his gaze. Relieved when she'd heard Jane's car in the drive, Sylvia had sneaked in from the hall, past Stephen in her bed, to see what was keeping her daughter from entering the house.

"I'll wake her, then. Put on some coffee? Why don't you go around the back?" Jane waited for his assent.

Martin felt ridiculous and small. Petulantly, he said, "She's awake, all right. I'll wait here, thank you. I have some things in my car."

"Pull into the driveway if you like. You're liable to get sideswiped." Jane backed up to the porch, disappeared inside.

He looked up at the window, assuring himself Sylvia would be gone, on her way to speak to Jane. But Sylvia did not dare move, for fear of waking Stephen and losing sight of Martin. In the glass beside the pane that framed her head, she raised her hand, then waved it back and forth, a queen acknowledging attendants or a child hoping for requital from a stranger.

II

JANE SPED THROUGH the parlor, dining room, and kitchen, circuiting the downstairs twice before she anchored herself to the divan. She knelt on the cushions, hooked her hands over the stiff back, let the full weight of her body fall back until her arms were taut. She flexed her shoulders forward, to expunge suspicion bodily, as if inklings and amorphous dread could be compressed and then expelled by a contraction of her muscles. She managed only to ignite the tweezer twitching of a nerve beneath her shoulder blade. She reeled her body in, breasts pressed against a cushion, chin propped up on the hard upholstered ledge. This was Jane's receptive posture, a lookout from which dilatory cats, frantic squirrels, or the appearance of the postman merited attention. This was her open space.

She wanted out. With Regina as a ram of sorts, she'd battered at her mother and her father. The confines of the house this morning were a little less restrictive, but there still was not room enough for Jane. And for the moment, her escape was blocked. Martin Parris, in peevish retreat, refused to move his car into the drive. She could not get herself beyond the limit he imposed.

She closed her eyes, to test the likelihood of falling back to sleep. Instead, the sudden darkness dizzied her. She soared above herself and saw not Jane but Stephen, isolated on the black and tiny hollow shaped by the secret intersection of three lifelines.

To temper her lightheadedness, she opened her eyes. She did not see, though. She had appropriated Stephen's vision. She felt the unrelenting pressure of the three acute and jaw-like angles formed by the tethering of Martin, Sylvia, and Arthur.

But the horror, from where Stephen stood, was not confinement or the simple recognition of an otherwise obscure geometry. Each member of this trinity—husband, wife, and lover—each bore a scar attesting to a role in Stephen's birth, a jagged laceration of the skin beneath the heart.

Jane had heard the muffled screams and keening of the injured twenty years before. Standing in for Stephen, at last she understood those cries.

From the sides of unsuspecting men and from the unplumbed depths of her own darkness, a woman had torn ribs. In an ungodly, desperate imitation of creation, she laid them down along the lines that led to the conception. On the trilateral no-man's-land within this frame, she brought forth a son. Those bleached and desiccated bones, relics of the three forsaken lives, still bounded Stephen.

Alarmed by her own graphic vision of her trapped, tormented brother, Jane sprang off the divan, spun and faced the stairs. The stillness in the house intensified her sense of danger. She stole slowly up the steps, the gory elegance of all she'd seen seared onto her mind, as if it were a ritual she'd witnessed.

From the hall, her hip against the door frame of her parents' room, Jane saw Stephen's head pressed against his forearm, distended veins along the wrist and hand that drooped over the mattress edge. She traced the narrow rib of his blanketed hips and torso to the far corner of the bed, as if a thorough survey would account for his displacement from his own bed to this one. A paranoid suspicion that she was being watched was dismissed with a quick survey of the empty stairs behind her.

She barely breathed his name. "Stephen? Stephen." Having imagined him a victim, Jane normalized her brother for the moment. Eschewing ample evidence of Stephen's instability, she'd come upstairs to rescue him. Her notion involved nothing more substantial than a helping hand to pull him from the mean and lightless triangle on which she had envisioned him. The practical problem of translating this metaphorical assistance into physical aid only now occurred to her. More agitating, and because it entailed flirtation with a taboo, more fascinating, was his serenity in his parents' bed.

She felt herself drawn into the room and with a jerk she stiffened her back. From this slightly more rational remove, she said his name again, intoning it with disbelief. Mired in the oddity, her noble if impractical objective was obscured by her tantalized imagination. He hadn't moved, so was he dead? Was this his first visit to the double bed? Had he killed his mother, hid her body in a closet, then drifted peacefully to sleep?

Jane stepped forward, crouched behind the slightly ajar door, reached toward him with her hand cupped to catch and tug his fingers.

From her awkward perch on the windowsill, Sylvia caught sight of Jane's disembodied, snaking hand and screamed, "What?" This propelled her off the sill. She banged down on her knees and yelled, "Sweet Jesus."

Stephen pressed himself up with his forearms. He saw Jane's bent-over body and hollered, "Leave him alone. Scat! Don't do it, don't you dare lay a hand on him!"

"It's me. Just me." Jane said so as she pushed the door open. She crawled toward her mother, wincing at Stephen's piercing cries for help.

Sylvia rolled back off her knees, sat straight-legged on the floor, as if performing sit-ups. She rerouted Jane's attention to Stephen, wagging her hand. "Just calm him—Stephen! Just get him to shut up for—all right! It's all right, Stephen."

Bouncing on the far corner of the bed, with the bedsheet as a sort of toga, Stephen had achieved a weird rhythm. He was chanting, "Thieves in the night. Bite your tongue. Thieves in the night. Bite your tongue."

Awed by this display, Jane backed out of the room, which proved an instant salve for Stephen.

He yelled, "Fuck her and her lousy old girlfriend. Somebody lock the door," then lay down on the bed, hid his head beneath two pillows.

Jane heard Sylvia struggle to her feet. She leaned against the railing, embarrassed and amazed by the power of her own delusion. Cruel as history might have been, Stephen was damaged now and needed fixing. As her mother shuffled to the hall and closed the door on Stephen, Jane watched her brother move his hands against his buried face.

In Sylvia's injured presence, Jane felt all slack and see-through, a mettlesome child caught poking at her baby brother between the bars of his crib.

Sylvia exhaled and bent forward, rubbed her knees. She bobbed and bowed her head, then raised herself, laughing. "Calamity Jane strikes again. Got an encore?"

This display of goodwill intensified Jane's guilt. It also obliterated her attempts to invent a reasonable explanation for her behavior. She simply lied. "I thought it was you. In the bed. Martin Parris is here to see you. Daddy's old partner, Martin Parris?" The name provoked a charge, but Jane released it by kicking one foot against the other.

"I'm having quite a morning. First Stephen decides to bunk in with me, then I have to deal with a judge who makes house calls." Sylvia's humor was spent. Stephen in her bedroom and Martin at the door were plausible grounds for indictment. She could not decipher Jane's version of either one, so she raised her nightgown, exposing her bruised knees. "I guess they'll both survive. I do need ten or fifteen minutes, though. Would you mind putting on a pot of coffee? Maybe you should get him to pull his car around into the driveway. We've had enough accidents for one morning. Do you mind, sweetie?"

Jane was wedged between apology and accusation. "Take your time. I'll get him some coffee." To herself, in the distraught and pouty manner of a child, she said, I don't know about the bones and all, but you slept with that man behind Daddy's back, didn't you?

Sylvia reached for her daughter's shoulder, nodded toward the bedroom. "I heard him come in late last night. I heard you talking to him. Anything I should know about? He seems worse again today."

Jane didn't repeat Stephen's claim that Arthur didn't want to be his father, or his botched version of the Beatitudes. "Nothing coherent." She wanted to relegate the previous night, and this morning, too, to the two-decade-deep family grave. Stephen's speechifying, a vague sense that she owed Alison an apology, weak impulses to telephone Regina: she was willing to consign it all, let it sift down through the host of abandoned, contrary hopes she tried and failed to exhume every time she came back to this house.

III

Sylvia abetted Stephen's ruse of being sound asleep, his head and hands still sandwiched by her pillows. As best she could, she ballet-danced from vanity to closet, collecting stockings, a half-slip and bra, a vented brown plaid skirt and matching lambswool V-neck sweater, a pair of shoes, her hairbrush, and a compact. Then, sheerly for effect, she lifted the receiver from the unplugged telephone, hoping he was watching. She pranced by the bed on tiptoe, left the door ajar, and made her odd way to the bathroom, where she dumped her clothing on the floor and sat down on the tub's edge.

Martin in the kitchen: She made a prod of this but generated no emotional response. It got her up; she unsnapped and folded her thin housecoat, strapped herself into her bra, but balked when she attempted to put on her pantyhose. Martin on her lawn and Stephen in her bed and the panic Jane had triggered left Sylvia with nothing more compelling than her suddenly recalcitrant knees, which were turning purple. She plied them with her hands, then pulled a tube of muscle ointment from a nearby shelf and applied an overgenerous dollop to each joint. She rubbed the excess on her lower back, sat again, then turned and faced her mirrored self against the bathroom door.

"My God, I'm massive." She arched her back, which unfurled her ample stomach and pressed her thighs into a wider pillow on the porcelain. She reached down toward the puddle of her pantyhose and cautiously regarded her reflection. She hoped the action might streamline her shape. Instead, she managed to pass her chin across her knee, so when she stood she had a dab of ointment much like shaving cream a man might miss with a too hasty shave. She nicked the blemish off, but knew at once the mentholated scent would last for hours. She wiped her knees and back with a facecloth, then a towel, but abrasion seemed to activate the odor. Embarrassed now, she dressed and sniffed, though she well knew her sensitivity was compromised; her nose delivered faulty reassurances. She took the tube of cream in hand and cursed the manufacturer for failing to supply a large-print odor warning, tossed the tube into the tiny wicker trash pail.

The early-morning mayhem finally overwhelmed her. Somehow, the fact that now it hurt her just to walk awoke her to the hopeless disproportion: Martin Parris never was the man she had imagined.

Like air, her first clean breath in twenty years, this insubstantial clarity infused her.

Her bodily response was primal. The body felt its keeper drowning. And, as threatened bodies will, it marshaled energy into the brain, effectively anesthetizing rigid limbs and torso. Instinctively, the hyperstimulated synapses spewed forth the momentary movie of her life, the body's final, timeless record of its own existence.

She saw it all and yet she lived.

A novel, queer composure moved her to the hall. She did not return to Stephen. Was he insane forever? Should she confront his doctor? How many front-page stories would he supply the *Courier* before she would admit he too had got beyond her wildest imaginings? Was he waiting, naked in the bed, for her?

She went to Martin in the kitchen. But it was Jane, alone, anxious for relief from her uneasy post.

"Stephen." Sylvia spoke his name gravely, as if he were a contagion, a threat to anyone in the house.

"He's in your bed, you know." Jane herself wasn't sure if this was an accusation or a warning. "And this visit," she pointed past her mother, in the direction of Holmes Road, where Martin Parris sat in his parked car, "this is about Stephen, or no? This is other business? I guess maybe you've kept up with him. I just didn't know it."

"No." Sylvia got herself to move. She pulled three cups from a cabinet, poured coffee for herself.

"I had some. None for me. So he's here to, what?"

Sylvia held her cup in both hands. "Well, of course, I can read minds. What's twenty years, anyway? Let's see." She paused, hoping Jane would retract the question.

"You want me to go get him?"

"Hasten the inevitable?" Sylvia sat in the alcove. "Why is he here? Maybe he forgot something the last time he came." She knew she was speaking in code. She looked at her daughter. "I don't know. To finish me off? I made him everything he is, you know. Or, at least, everything he isn't."

Jane waited for more, hungry.

"He's nothing. I don't know what you think you're going to get out of me." Sylvia could not break through her placid surface. "I slept with him. He was so smart, you know? Maybe he ruined my life. He certainly destroyed your father."

"Stephen?" Jane prompted as calmly as she could.

"If Martin Parris were Stephen's father, I would know why he is here. And, of course, why would I be here, in that case?"

She raised her cup. "Sylvia's little secrets." Her daughter's silence worried her. "They are secrets, Jane." She wanted a vow of confidentiality.

"The secrets of my life." Jane lurched forward from the counter as she spoke. "You know me, I'm an old hand at secrets."

Sylvia wanted to seal the pact. "Your father knows, if that helps."

"When has that ever helped anything? I'm sorry." She issued the apology to Arthur, really, though already she was sorry to have new and cryptic information about family life. Coming with Regina had seemed an act of closure. Instead, she saw the many leaks and fault lines in the construct, enough repair work for a lifetime. And, foolishly enough, she felt she owed her mother something in the way of empathy. "Are you sad? Or worried? Martin coming here, I mean."

Sylvia held her hands, warm from the cup, against her eyes.

"Are you crying?" Jane the child spoke the question.

"I don't know, is this crying?" Sylvia dropped her hands; her eyes were red and dry. "Will you keep an eye on Stephen for an hour or so? I hate to ask you."

"I'll go up. Does he have an appointment?"

"At noon. I guess they don't use shock therapy anymore. Do they?"

Jane met her mother's smile. "What do you call this?" She raised her hand, then crossed her arms and backed away—the permutations of her stifled urge to pull her mother tight against herself.

She stopped before she climbed the stairs, impeded by a recapitulation of Stephen's confrontation with Regina. She walked to the couch, knelt, and sprang up right away, deciding it was left to her to deliver Martin to her mother. She walked out to the front porch, waved her hand above her head.

Martin was in the driveway already, carrying his briefcase. Jane saw him smile absentmindedly; then he stopped and rather formally returned her wave, and bowed. Jane couldn't see her mother leaning out the back door of the house. She didn't understand that he was bowing to the unaged visage of the woman who'd defeated him.

Before Jane made her way upstairs, Stephen retrieved a number of his hanging photographs and brought them to his mother's room. He found his grasp was loosening on what he had determined about Arthur and his motives. His outburst on his mother's bed convinced him he was unreliable. Despite intentions, he could not control himself and make her see that he wanted to be good. He'd even put her watch back in the vanity, in hopes that she would overlook his theft of her white robe. But every couple of minutes, he would hear the laughing girls at Burgers Plus. He was counting on the pictures to remind him of the ideas he'd had in mind before the summer, when what he thought was private and didn't make him swear or run around the city causing trouble.

The photographs, unforthcoming even in the hands of their creator, reminded him of nothing but the darkroom, his home on campus. Seeing it was early, and remembering he could be alone there any morning until after lunch, Stephen telephoned the university and asked to be connected to the darkroom in McKenzie Hall. He heard the ringing of the telephone that hung above the white Formica table inset with yellow plastic tubs for bathing photos. He saw the gallon tins of fluids underneath the table, clothesline strings of drying prints and the curling, taillike negatives, their undeveloped see-through shapes and faces painted by the blood-red light bulb overhead.

The rhythmic ringing was a chant. It became a music, and it soothed him while he hid inside that darkroom, safe and far from home.

In the open doorway, Jane admired Stephen from behind. He'd wrapped the bedsheet round his waist and held two corners in one hand. His fragile bare back and his hairless and unmuscled arms were flawless. He had achieved a calm that made him stand erect, with what Jane thought was aristocratic bearing. He was beautiful like Arthur, and absurdly so. His lank blond hair fell flat aginst his neck and drew a line that paralleled the straight edge of his shoulders. She recognized the frame as Arthur's, but it was a spare geometry, his thinness glorified by the excessive drape of white sheet piled up around his feet. Jane knew this was a rarefied version of a man, not powerful but strong, too elegant to be regarded highly by a woman Stephen's age. But there he was. This was Stephen, and as long as he was still, she admired the exotica that was her brother.

Stephen's gaze met hers in one panel of the mirror. He hung up the telephone and pulled the sheet around himself like a cloak. "I'm just trying to get them to change my major, you know. Mom said I could call. I'm asking about psychology."

Jane couldn't help herself. She said, "How about drama?"

Stephen was humiliated, caught out again in a moment of lonely intimacy. "Don't you think you're sort of invading my privacy? Is Mom mad at me?"

"No one's mad at you, Stephen." Jane was shocked to find how easy it was to mark her allegiance with the others, to distinguish herself from Stephen. "You look like you could still use some sleep." She spoke softly, coolly. It was not an observation; it was a suggestion. For the first time, she was speaking to a patient, a sick man. To her surprise, he obeyed her, retreated to the bed and stuck his head beneath the sheet. His disappearance made it easier for Jane to find emotion deeper than estrangement.

Still, as she sat down on the wicker chair and watched his shrouded form relax into a dream, her sympathy—that is, her interest in her brother's illness and its cure—was tempered. Whether it was Sylvia's confession or the solace she believed inhered in such hereditary beauty, Jane claimed a healthy distance from her brother. She turned her thoughts to Lenox and how much she would tell Regina.

IV

Martin made it to the alcove with his sense of mission. The building of Beth Israel was Martin's claim to generation; to protect it, he'd convicted Stephen of a second act of desecration. He had predicated preservation of the temple on the sacrifice of Sylvia Adamski's younger son. Of course, the symmetric serving of a personal revenge compromised his purity of motive. In fact, the poetry of his solution had kept him in his car and argued for retreat. Even when he freighted his assessment of his duty with potential loss of life in unchecked fire, invocation of his ethical and civic duties as a member of the bar, the balance wouldn't budge. Then, impatient with his reticence, he let fall the weight of a reunion. Like a butcher's thumb against the scale, it tipped the balance in favor of a confrontation and he went about his business.

Sylvia had met him at the back door, let him pass. He had not grown or shrunk; he'd grayed completely without altering his part (fifteen years of fussing with his hair returned him to a plain and unaffected style); he smelled a bit hygienic, or was that just her ointment? He wore an expensive tailored glen plaid cotton suit more appropriate for the spring, and carried what appeared to be a new red distressed-leather briefcase; he might be skinnier by several pounds (or was it years? anyway, she felt her sense of measure was confounded by her meeting with the woman in the bathroom mirror); he never had been handsome (Arthur always stuck his face in at such moments); he was nervous to be near her, which explained his inability to speak her name or even utter a "Good morning" or "Hello."

This was Martin Parris in the flesh, Martin unadorned by her illusions. And for the second time this morning, she was made lightheaded as she rectified the disproportion. But this time her body wasn't fooled. It allowed her distorted and distended hopes to be expelled, responded to the momentary vacuum with a slightly quickened pulse, and then restored her balance to her when she registered his presence on a human scale.

She had missed the man.

"I was waiting for you, Martin." She moved slowly, left foot, right foot on each stair, then walked across the kitchen without bending her sore knees.

Martin incorrectly diagnosed her as arthritic. Her weight, he guessed, was an added torment. "Some things in my car." He mumbled, feeling less inclined to strike out while she limped.

"I meant, for twenty years. Early-morning humor. Coffee?" At the counter, she refilled her own cup, filled one for him, too, but did not sit down on the bench across from him. "You're a judge. I think that's all I know. I don't know if I should be proud or embarrassed, but that is all I know."

"Probate judge. And that's the apex."

This information countered even her most banal assumptions. Not only did this put him well outside the realm of Stephen's mercifully brief involvement with the courts, it meant his salary was well below her husband's. "Private practice, too?"

"Just the probate court. Oh, and a little real estate. I bought some property in Allendale. Six or seven years ago, with all the talk of building the mall."

"The mall." This was a local synonym for Pittsfield's economic renaissance. Initially, the notion was to scrap debilitated downtown shops and bring in upscale retail chains. This was meant to coincide with a return to small-scale manufacturing and successful wooing of a dozen high-tech firms (the reasoning was insular and shoddy; successive mayors won election claiming that the high-tech exodus from major cities to the suburbs was the inception of a pattern that would lead the companies to Pittsfield and its legion sister cities). What remained was a promise of a mall which, by virtue of being the only unaborted feature of two decades' worth of ill-considered planning, became the bête noire of residential life. Bankrupt local merchants who'd not changed their merchandising

schemes in twenty years, laid-off union welders, teachers made
redundant by the shrinking population, bankers holding worth-
less mortgages on empty condominium developments, and
insurance salesmen staggered by the overhead of their neo-
Georgian headquarters—all voices were resolved into a chorus
of abuse, defaming greedy out-of-towners who'd descended on
their hometown and attempted to displace the downtown, the
very heart of Pittsfield, with a mall.

"The mall. My one major venture into real estate. Of
course, you have children." Martin had decided to make his
way toward Stephen. He knew the segue was awkward. "I met
your daughter. Met her as . . . well, all grown up. I read her
articles in the *Times*. She's very talented. You must be proud."

Sylvia was put off by his solicitous manner. She reached for
her cup, leaned back against the counter. "She's a lesbian,
you know. I saw you chatting. Did she mention she has a
two-hundred-year-old lover?" She saw the effect of her revelation had been spoiled. Martin was distracted, twitching his
nose. "I apologize for the odor. It's me, though. Rest assured."

He blushed, then raised his gaze, friendly and conspiratorial
concession to the age they had achieved. "Ben-Gay?"

Sylvia was swallowing when she laughed, which produced a
gurgle. "A generic brand." She filled her cup again, then
limped to the bench. "Muscle rub. I didn't even know I had
muscles till I turned fifty." She scuttled toward the corner, to
relieve the oddity of being close.

Her genius, he decided, was her sense of timing. Her friend-
liness just now made of his motive—which, after all, was really
just an accusation—an unseemly, melodramatic pretense.
What happened next surprised him. He confessed to her. "It's
as if there's no one I ever talk to." He looked away, to spare
them both, but he continued. "Can that be true? I don't know
why I'd say so if it weren't. I don't know." He'd hoped to
strike a casual, dismissive tone but failed. He looked to her
again. "Well, I don't know. Anyway, hello."

She stretched her legs out on the bench, then shrugged her
shoulders.

"I'm sorry. It's just never occurred to me. We were friends. Formidable friends, I suppose."

She let herself be drawn in by his intimacy because she sensed in it no present threat. "Maybe it doesn't even qualify as an affair, in the end. It was more like, what? It was more like going to summer camp. A day camp, strictly speaking. Camp Can't Shut Up."

The camp name made him laugh. "I wasn't young though. Even then." He'd meant this as self-recrimination, but he did not rescind its force as accusation. He watched her struggle to retract her legs and sit up straight, assume a more defensive posture. And maybe she was right. He'd fallen for a friend and she had, too. Perhaps that alone explained her bitter, punishing withdrawal of affection. They'd shared a thrilling and peculiar mastery, but it was sterile. Sex was not the origin of their attraction or itself a goal. It had legitimized their standing as a couple. Or was that the script for love, the relegation of their bodies to supporting roles? "Well, in fact, it was an affair, Sylvia. It certainly wasn't a marriage." He was recodifying the experience to diminish it. "It certainly wasn't a life."

"That seems an odd gripe. You had a life, Martin. And, as I recall, a career, which is more than you left for Arthur and me."

"I was supposed to be the caretaker for his career because I slept with you? And, if this is for the record books, it cost me several thousand dollars. I paid off your share of the business debt."

"So? That's to say I was broken twice. Financially and . . . otherwise." His words had finally reached her, tapped emotion. He'd hit a virgin vein, connected not to what she'd made of Martin, but to the memory of what it was like to have been broken by her father, to need the simple certainty of Arthur's gracious love, and then recognize in Martin what she might have been and soon enough to hear herself speak words to drive her lover out and learn that she was powerful enough to make him go but powerless to bring him back, strong enough to carry her crime to Arthur but too weak to submit herself to Arthur's care completely, finally punishing him by issuing a lie about an unborn child, retribution for the weakness in herself she could not redeem. "Of course I wanted money from you, Martin." She slid past him, stood against the counter. "I would have taken anything you'd given me. You think you paid me off? Change from daddy's pocket to shut up the little girl? I took what I could get from you. You think that makes me rich? I've been sucking those coins for twenty years. I didn't get rich. I've got a mouthful of canker sores." Her knees buckled, but she held herself from falling by turning quickly to the counter. Gracelessly, she lunged toward the table, laid her torso across it to reach her empty cup. After she'd poured herself more coffee, she backed off further, struck a surer balance, with less pressure on her knees. She sipped from her cup, lifted her eyes to gauge her total effect. "The aftermath of love."

But Martin did not travel with her back in time. He had nothing to recover. He'd carried his defeat at her hands with him daily.

In a perfect imitation of himself before an exercised and feisty plaintiff, he explained the narrow purpose of his presence. "That's all well and good, I'm sure. But we had a terrible fire last night at the Beth Israel. As you may or may not recall, I am on the board of that congregation. It was arson, as the police confirmed just hours ago. I suspect you can appreciate why we don't believe this is an isolated incident, or one that we can very well ignore."

His voice was alien, and he'd assumed a prim and slightly scornful posture, which made her feel that anything she said would be excessive. She suspected for a moment he was purposefully acting pious to deflate her anger. But she'd heard him charge her son with arson. "Was anyone hurt?" She was stalling.

"No one was physically harmed. The property damage is extensive, an order of magnitude beyond smashed windows and anti-Semitic graffiti." He hardly recognized her, which enabled him to maintain his querulous expression. "I can assure you Rabbi Sisitkin intends to pursue charges this time.

I think it's only fair to tell you. And in your son's interest, of course. I should think you'd want to retain a lawyer, Mrs. Adamski."

"Mrs. Adamski? When did she stop by?" Sylvia was frightened and amused by this performance. She reacted as if he were a petty foreign customs agent digging through her suitcase. "Why are you telling me all this?"

"I'm not sure myself." He stood, immediately regretted this, which brought him back within her range. "Because it's a tremendously serious crime?" He realized he'd issued a rhetorical question. "I felt it was the decent thing to do, to tell you, to assume you didn't know."

"How would I know your church was on fire?"

"I didn't mean you knew!" He sat, to regain his composure. "I mean, I intend to prosecute. Frankly, I wish I'd been allowed to prosecute the last time. I really think it would have served everyone's interest. That includes your son."

"Prosecute my son?" She nodded her head, acknowledging her own inversion of the facts of Stephen's quick release from prison. "This is all without any proof, I assume. Prosecute!" She yelled, venting anger for the goodwill she'd attributed to him. "Did you get elected sheriff, Martin? Is that what brings you by this morning? What you have overlooked is that it is patently impossible my son Stephen was involved. Setting fires. Really." She could not make it sound implausible. "Stephen is under a doctor's supervision." Again, she knew she'd missed the target. "Besides, my son-in-law is a lawyer."

"If Stephen and you were to go to the police, we could discuss a way of dealing. . . ."

"Stephen. Of course, this is aimed at Stephen."

"You don't believe that. We're talking about a young man who sprayed aerosol paint—"

"I told you he was here last night. I was not the only one. My daughter, Jane . . ." She regretted having labeled Jane a lesbian, which seemed to impugn her reliability as a witness. She now suspected the story of the fire was an elaborate trap, though she could not imagine what he meant to catch. "For

God's sake, there are plenty of people who would set fire to your temple. And Stephen was with me." This sentence inspired her. "I mean, he was in my bed. He actually crawled into my bed last night." Her astonishment at these words was heightened by the ease with which she drew the line leading from Stephen to the burning building and back to the safety of her bed. "In my bed. For reasons unknown, of course."

Martin chastised himself for not proceeding directly from the temple to the courthouse, where he could be filing official charges. He doubted even Sylvia would bring her son to trial with incest as his best defense.

"And what time last night?" Sylvia struck a relaxed and interested tone. "No witnesses."

Martin grabbed his briefcase, stood and walked by her to the door.

She turned, to follow him, but blasts of pain withheld her. "People do not make false accusations and then—should I call your rabbi?"

Martin didn't turn or slow his pace to accommodate her hobbling. He left Sylvia in silence, that she might have a momentary share in the life sentence she'd imposed on him.

V

SYLVIA'S INJURY CONSPIRED against her haste as she headed up the stairs; the rumbling woke Stephen. When she finished climbing, she rested in the hall. She called blindly from her post, "Jane? Jane, wake Stephen. Is he awake?" She shuffled to the threshold.

Stephen rolled to the far side of the bed.

Sylvia would not address him. "What time did he come home last night? This is important. Jane?"

Jane stood up, a soldier caught at ease by a commanding officer. "What time was it, Stephen?"

"I am asking you!" Sylvia slapped a hand against her side.

"He doesn't know what time it was. He doesn't even know what he is saying half the time. Answer me."

The yelling scared Jane. She figured it would soon enough ignite her brother. "After midnight?"

"What time!"

"What the fuck is this? Stop yelling at me. What's the matter with you? He was fine. He was asleep. Just calm down for a minute. He had your goddamn watch on—ask him what time it was." She sat down, hoisted up her feet to the seat of the wicker chair. "Nobody in this house can ask a question in a normal tone of voice. My God. Now you want me to remember what time he came in last night? As opposed to a week ago when he was on his temple rampage? Or maybe I'm supposed to take notes when he starts again with his 'Blessed are the poor 'cause Jesus will give them a sack of potatoes.' "

Stephen was affronted by this representation of his words. "I said they inherit something for being good. Not a sack of potatoes by any means." He turned to Sylvia, to assure and advise her. "Not a word about potatoes. She's nuts."

Jane tried to appease him. "It was a joke, Stephen. I only meant to say—"

"When I only mean to say something I get tossed in the slammer. That's the difference between you and me, young lady. Now." He sat up here, imperiously wrapping himself in the sheet. "Your mother asked you a question. What time was it last night when you so rudely interrupted me?" He smiled, sensing he'd done something funny. "Any time now, young lady. We've got all day, if that's what it takes."

Sylvia was being won over by this performance; not into an allegiance, but toward the idea that he was well, not sick. "I'm missing the humor here, Stephen."

Stephen whispered, "See, Jane? You made her mad. Pretty soon she'll start crying and we'll all feel bad."

Jane was appalled by her mother's calm, as if Stephen's behavior were not extraordinary.

"Stephen, leave your sister alone." Sylvia sat on the bed's edge, feeling she'd struck a conciliatory tone.

"Why can't you be on my side for once?" Stephen let his back slap down against the mattress.

"Where were you last night? When you went out, Stephen." Sylvia would not face him. She was half expecting a confession of the crime. She steeled herself, prepared to mimic Martin's legalistic manner.

"I never lie to you." Stephen stroked her back. "I'm not the one who wants to make you cry. You always do this, like it's my fault Dad is mad at you or staying late with that old Hetty at the office. I put the watch back in the drawer. Girls laughed at me last night. Like I didn't know it was a lady's watch."

"I have to go." Jane wanted out.

Sylvia spoke quietly, stared at Jane to hold her in the chair. "There was a fire last night. At the Temple Beth Israel, Stephen. A set fire, Stephen."

"You think those girls set it? They're the type, all right. They're tough."

"What's your game, Stephen?" Sylvia stood and leaned against the threshold. "What exactly are you thinking about? What gets into your head that you think you have a right to come in here and be in this bed?" Confusion's only vent was anger. "What is it you want me to say that I haven't said already? What do you want me to say?'

"What does he want you to say?" Jane dropped her feet to the floor with a bang, then crossed her legs. "He's going to explain to you why he set a fire? He set a fire last night? What is all this all of a sudden with this temple, anyway?" Jane had relegated Stephen to an uncomprehending distance. She expected Sylvia to answer for him. "Is this like a lifelong obsession of his? Has he done things before, things like the windows last week? He's supposed to see a therapist once a week and, what? Figure out he's not supposed to go around setting fires and delivering snappy late-night wisdom from the Sermon on the Mount?" Her excitement raised her from the chair. "What are you waiting for? A sign from God maybe?" She held out her hands, palms up. She flexed them into fists and then continued. "Do you know you've been acting as if this is just standard fare? There's a fucking cyclone in here and you say, 'Alison, dear. Could you check the windows? I feel a draft.' Meanwhile, the door's been blown in. Do you get it? He is twenty years old and he is lying in your bed and you walk in here and yell at me about what time it was when he came in last night. What? Are you going to ground him for the week? What does he have to do to get your attention? Put on a goddamn crown of thorns and ask you to dance?"

Jane had pushed Stephen into frightened retreat. He hoped a calm word might dissipate the angry silence. "Don't ask me what's going on now. I think we should say a prayer for her, Mom. You and me, together, Mom. She's all worked up."

"Perfect." Jane bent to the window. "Who drives a blue Chrysler? It just pulled in." She continued to peer down, watched as Regina trundled out of the driver's seat. "She must have rented a car this morning." She faced her mother. "It's Regina."

Sylvia felt betrayed by Jane. She paused, thinking Stephen might have something to offer on the topic of Regina.

Stephen was waiting on his mother's words.

"Did you want me to invite her up, Jane? Now that we're all one big family, perhaps she has something to add to our little discussion." Sylvia went to the window, a feeble threat to call down to Regina. "She's wearing a hat."

Jane didn't know how to extricate herself. "I know she looks ridiculous in that cap. A student sent it to her. She thinks it's funky. I think it's more of her Forever in a Bus Terminal look."

Sylvia laughed, rubbed her hands briskly up and down Jane's back, winked conspiratorially. "We'll see the doctor this afternoon."

"I should cut her off at the pass." Jane reached behind herself and seized her mother's hand, then left the room.

"I know what you're going to say." Stephen sat up in the bed. "I know you're gonna say I should've known. Dad was having a bad day or something, and he didn't know what he

was saying. And I think he might have been drinking even."
He wanted her forgiveness now, believing she could rescind
the seriousness she'd attached to his misbehavior, if not the
acts themselves. "I know he's my father, right? I don't know
why I let him get to me. I should know better."

Sylvia recognized the sentiment as hers, a line she'd utter
casually after a shouting match with Arthur witnessed by her
younger son. She understood the mimicry as a plea for sympathy. "What is it Daddy said to you?" This was a prologue
to the futile question she posed to herself: What could Arthur
have been hoping to achieve?

"I've been bad. You don't have to tell me that. And the
hardest part is I can think of a million incredibly bad things
to do every second. Not fires, Mom. Things like saying things
that are incredibly sexy. Or else doing something that will
just upset everybody. And no one's ever there to stop me.
That's the saddest thing of all. I say to Jesus, 'Jesus, make
me think of you,' or maybe, 'Help me.' " He clapped three
times, but he could not dispel the urge to weep. "Right now,
I'm just praying nothing happens that will get you mad at
me." He straightened his legs and kicked them, like a swim-
mer. "If you don't say something soon, something is about
to happen. I can just feel it in my bones."

She didn't yet completely trust him to be sick, though his
defenseless posture coddled her conviction: Arthur's senseless
sudden intervention had destroyed their son. She saw in this
her simplest route to blamelessness. Not only could she claim
the high ground publicly, but she felt there was mercy for
herself in knowing she had never lied to Stephen on this score.

"It's okay to be sick. And we can get you better."

"I'm sort of lonely at U. Mass. I don't want to go back
there right away. I know nobody said it was gonna be easy,
but the difference is Jesus got to pick out his apostles." He
was still kicking up his sheet. "If I had twelve friends I'd be
sure to be good all the time. I'm not bad there ever, I mean,
it's all in going through life, I guess."

She was indicted as he echoed her own pat and silly maxims. "Stephen, no one expects you to be perfect. Jesus was perfect. I don't expect that of you."

His legs stopped. He raised his hands, let them fall slowly to his sides. "Oh boy. I'm sorry." He was defeated. She'd given up on him.

"Maybe we can figure something out together, Stephen. With the doctor." As if the light had brightened in the room, she saw his pain and abject confusion. She saw that she had work to do. This raised her mind above the mire of her own emotions. "Are those your photos on my vanity?"

"Don't look at them. They're not what you think." He stood up, shrouded in the sheet, collected his pictures, headed for his bedroom. "Jane is really mad at me. Don't tell her I said so."

"It'll be our secret, Stephen." He turned to her, startled her with his glee. "You and me, we understand each other, mister. Stick with me." She watched this last inducement swell him up with pride. He closed himself inside his room, and Sylvia began to word a plea on his behalf to Rabbi Abraham Sisitkin.

Jane's exasperated diagnosis was confirmed. And a sickness in the family would invigorate the best of Sylvia, her dauntless and pragmatic zeal for reinstating order. She did not doubt her own capacity to generate solutions. But Stephen had laid bare the core of their connection. In open-air exchanges, precious energy was wasted, released in outbursts of electric charge with force enough to spark a fire. Her first task was providing insulation.

VI

JANE AND REGINA had seized the relative peace, appropriating the two ends of the divan, to refine their mutual impression of the goings on. Regina refused to doff her cap, proof of her resolve to drive herself to New York City before nightfall. Jane knew her protests would not change her lover's mind;

they both were meant to travel to a conference in Miami for the weekend. Still, Jane punctuated her efficient summary with exhortations: *This will change your mind. Who'll keep me sane? There isn't any food at home; wait a day, fly out of Hartford. Give me the goddamn hat.*

Contrariness in matters of ideal arrival and departure dates was endemic to their travels. Regina trusted schedules devised well in advance, and felt she'd honed a useful skill, which enabled her to estimate the optimal duration of a visit to a friend, an appearance at a conference, or a holiday in Portugal. Jane typically arrived a day or two behind her partner, finding in the days before her leaving an uncompleted application for a grant (just two weeks overdue and "worth a shot") or that she had forgot to cancel dinner with a friend from Cincinnati who'd rearranged her business travel plans to make it to New York. Overstaying everywhere was a less complicated pleasure; Jane indulged a childish sense of luxury with late-date extensions of her stays away from home.

Here they were served by the generous difference in their ages (they were themselves acquainted with the math, though everyone who met one or the other made a calculation and furnished the results, as if subtraction were a relatively arcane skill). They were not less alike than any two adults who couple. But they had reason to assume that differences, like dates of birth, survived the transcendental moments in each other's arms. Eccentricities and simple preferences met with accommodation, not dismay, distemper, badgered compromising, or any of the standard bludgeons favored by adults to hammer out relations.

"I'll call you tonight. In Lenox. You're not going to keep up this night watch, Jane, are you?"

"I looked at myself this morning and I thought, I'm too old for this. So where does that leave her?" Jane glanced at the staircase.

"Energy seems to be the least of Sylvia's problems. I don't even think, in the end, Stephen will prove much of . . ."

"A threat? Is that what you were about to say?" Jane was

amused, but edgy, as if Regina might be withholding a theory about Stephen's mania. "Say it."

"No, I stopped. Not because I don't countenance Stephen as a threat, though I'm not sure that is exactly a helpful casting of his role. Sylvia." Regina trilled her name. "What a woman. I mean. Really. Did you ever see, on television, a woman, or some producer's insane idea of a woman, a talk-show host? She had one of the very first television talk shows, but a real talk show. A gabfest of a show. Everyone who appeared was a hopeless chatterbox. A lady's show. Her name was Gloria Graham? With one of those magnificent Miami hairspray waves, and a huge turquoise necklace and rings. Sylvia reminds me of her. On my life. But so damn unhappy— as if there's a thwarted, silent woman lurking inside this big, turned-out, overproduced lady." Regina was ecstatic. She'd adopted a hyperdignified, limp-wristed pose.

Jane was uninterested in the performance. She also felt the characterization was off the mark. "She's not exactly bejeweled."

"You miss the point. I wasn't poking fun at her. It's only I find it so difficult to resolve—to understand, frankly—why such an unusual woman should be so entirely consumed by a family and positively nothing else. With a good friend, one of those terrible little diaphragms or something a little more reliable than a genuflection or two, she might have, I don't know . . ."

"Had a television talk show, presumably." Jane still resented the characterization. Inadvertently, she let on she knew the woman Regina had described and misnamed. "Since I never heard of this Virginia Graham, I'm no use here."

Regina backed off. "Whatever. It's enough to say to me, 'Leave my mother out of this for now.' That's fair enough." Regina meant this. She didn't like being silenced, but she was willing to grant an exception occasionally.

"I hate what happened last night."

"Jane, I hardly think it's necessary for you to feel, to start wondering how I—apologies are not in order. I'll yell when

I think you owe me one." Regina pulled her hat off. "Only so I don't go bald. I'm still leaving in ten minutes, I swear it."

"I shit on that hat, Regina. I hereby curse that hat. The next time you wear it, the House of Chang will forever cease to serve you cashew chicken and my tits will be lopped off by a madman. Give me that thing." She swiped it while Regina laughed. It was basically a khaki golfer's cap, but the oversized visor was translucent green plastic and was blunted rather than rounded at the front. Jane pulled the hat onto her head. "Only people with embarrassing scalp ailments or big, fat guys with safari jackets can get away with wearing such a hat. I forbid it." Jane pointed to Regina. "You laugh. Of course, I look ridiculous. Laugh. I will buy you a mink hat. I will buy you a hat made of caviar. You can wear a sturgeon on your head. In my abundant generosity . . ." Regina's cackling almost undid her. "Still she laughs. I will go as far as to allow you to retain the wretched thing as a memento of your past. But should you ever so much as think about . . ." Jane burst into laughter at the sight of Regina standing up and stomping her foot.

It was only after several stomps that Regina had breath enough to say, "You look twice as bad as I do in that thing." She deftly stole it back. "I promise. Never again." She jammed it into her handbag. Then she reached for Jane's head with both her hands, pulled her face close, kissed her. "Another new trick learned, so mind what you say about old dogs."

A sharp knock on the front door startled Jane. She twisted away from Regina. Alison led her friend Liz Halstrom into the living room. "You're still here? Hello, Regina."

Regina recovered first. "Good morning, Alison. I came to relieve the night shift."

"Jane? We met a few times, but you might not—you remember me, don't you? I'm Liz Halstrom. I think every time we've met I've been in the midst of a domestic tragedy." She stuck out her hand. A bit taller than Alison, she resembled her blonder, prettier friend. But her features were sharper, as if something in her manner forced one to hold her face, and even the frame of her body in blue jeans and a yellow sweater, in a perpetually tight focus. Her short, straight hair was darker than normal, still wet from her morning shower.

Jane reached for her hand, an incentive to stand. "You stay long enough," she turned to Regina, "you meet the family friends who redeem us." She held to Liz's hand, tentatively reeled her into an awkward embrace above the coffee table. "Your hair's so cool. You'll have to forgive me. I've forgone the usual amenities—bathing, washing the face."

"Hello. I am Regina Ellington."

Dispirited by the reunion she'd witnessed from behind her best friend's back, Alison added, "A doctor."

Regina shook Liz's hand, stumbled a bit as Liz leaned to kiss her cheek. "Yes, a doctor, so feel free to pass out or break a limb."

"Alison's told me everything." Liz pivoted, ran her hand along Alison's arm. "I'm the great family fan." She walked to the hearth, pushed one of the overstuffed chairs toward the table, bent her head as she sat and scrabbled it with her hands. "Someone should invent a hairdryer. Make a million dollars." She swung her head up, smoothed her hair. "Well, the *Times*, for God's sake. And Sylvia showed me the two stories in *Esquire*."

"My publicity agent." Jane backed into the sofa, knelt.

"Hardly. Everybody here is very cool about these things. You know, 'Oh, a small piece in the Sunday magazine.' I send photocopies to everyone I know. Is that bad? Photocopying? Write a book. I'll buy a dozen." Liz was surprised not to find Alison beside her. "Hey, Al?"

From her pose near the mantel, Alison attempted to mask her jealousy, which was compounded by lingering embarrassment about Liz's announcement of having been told everything. "How about fresh coffee?"

"Just put a kettle on." Jane recognized the signs of retreat. "We can drink instant. I can do it."

"It will take me a minute. Stay where you are. Regina?"

"The doctor will have a cup." Liz propped her feet on the table. "It's medicinal, isn't it?"

Alison left for the kitchen.

"What about this painting?" Jane was excited, almost breathless in the presence of Liz Halstrom. Here was evidence of her sister's soul. Liz triangulated the distance between Jane and Alison, made it navigable. "Al says you paint now."

"Since David died . . ." She smoothed her hair again, spoke quickly to Regina. "My husband? Ex-husband, but he was in my house when he died. I mean—not breaking and entering or anything. He turned out to have a tumor . . . we have a child. Lizzie. I was a lawyer and got myself a job at the museum in Williamstown before he discovered—"

"Jane's told me." Regina patted her hair, interpreting Liz's grooming as a polite hint. "You're part of the family lore."

"How great. I can just punt on the histrionics, then." She laughed. "What a family. Proto-family. Everything is bundled up, held together. Sylvia with the News of the World, recapping events. How the family survived this election or earthquake. Anyway, the news is, I am actually selling paintings these days. Or, at least, I did sell some. A whole stack. What do you make of that?"

"Liz? Is that you down there bragging?" Sylvia hollered from the top of the stairs.

"Yes, ma'am." Liz went to the bottom stair. "What's this with the one step at a time? Am I supposed to offer to carry you the rest of the way?"

"Who else is down there? For some reason I'm in a housecoat again, although I distinctly remember being dressed once already."

"Everybody's here. It's like a world conference of women. What have you done to yourself?" Liz dragged the other overstuffed chair from the mantel, to complete arrangements for the forum. "Oh, God, Sylvia, you smell so great." She offered her arm, led Sylvia to the chair.

"I feel like a grease monkey. If my knees get any worse I'm

going to start drinking liniment. Hello, Regina, and pardon my gripes."

Feeling at home, Regina adopted her assigned role as medical authority. "I'd prescribe several shots of a fine brandy. Those are some bruises."

"I didn't want Stephen hogging all the sympathy. You and Alison bring the girls?"

"School day." Liz moved around Sylvia's chair to pull a cushion from the divan section that separated Jane and Regina. She set it on the table and lifted Sylvia's feet. "Alison's making fresh coffee. We came to take care of you."

Jane admired Liz's dexterous graciousness. She did not castigate herself with her own unsolicitous behavior. The mindless fun on the divan with Regina had freed her. She was happy to know Liz was such a capable, willing stand-in for the daughters Sylvia deserved but was denied. "How are your knees, Mom?"

"How are you? You're not leaving today, are you?"

"Just I am leaving, Sylvia." Regina smoothed her hair again, convinced the hat had left it in a state of disarray.

"To New York?" Sylvia was genuinely disappointed. The preponderance of women pleased her just now, and Liz's scattershot chatter defused the oppressive, coupled quality of Jane and this strange, fascinating woman. "Won't you stay at least until dinner? I have a doctor's appointment," she nodded her appreciation to Jane, "but I'll be back by one-thirty. Lunch? You've had a rather bad welcome. Suppose I invited you back?"

"Suppose you came to New York? We'd love that." The pronoun passed without causing any perceptible discomfort. Still, Regina sensed the levity could not long support the added weight of their novel union. "We'll all reconvene at some future date. A second conference." Regina stood, fumbled with her handbag, to secure the hat.

"I'll organize it. Mandatory attendance." Liz turned to the kitchen. "Alison? We're losing members. The doctor requires a cup for the road."

"The doctor had a pot for the road this morning." Regina inched toward the space between Sylvia and Liz. "Stay seated, everyone. Liz, I'll keep abreast of your careers and—please, Sylvia." She put a hand to Sylvia's shoulder to prevent her rising. "We'll have other chances to say goodbye. Other visits. Take care of those knees." She bent down, pressed her cheek to Sylvia's. They both pursed their lips, and when Regina tried to straighten up, Sylvia grabbed both her hands and pulled her close. "Stay well, Sylvia."

Alison was watching from the kitchen doorway. She had a clear view of her sister's puzzled face.

Sylvia said, "That's my girl, you know. No matter what she thinks, I love everything about her." She let Regina go.

Jane hurried past her mother, opened the front door and held to the knob, twisting it as if it might be broken. Before she followed Regina to her rented car, she shyly reached with her free hand and brushed her mother's shoulder.

Sylvia received this wordlessly, then sighed to mark resumption of the public fare.

Disconcerted, Alison feigned ignorance, rushed to the porch, and shouted her goodbyes. She quickly ducked her head as Jane looked back, then headed for the kitchen, where she arranged a tray for serving coffee.

"Hah, you're so funny with her, Sylvia." Liz had her feet on the table, too. The two women might have been old pals bored by the half-time festivities of a televised football game.

"When your Lizzie brings home a girlfriend, call me up. I think I did pretty damned well." Sylvia wasn't annoyed; she was interested in Liz's assessment.

"You did great. You're just so reluctant to admit you don't give a shit whether Regina's a man or a woman." Liz always cast Sylvia in this benign and forgiving light, as if she recognized the uncomplicated woman disguised by an outdated sense of her maternal duty. "I grant you, I might find the age thing a little weird."

"You? Isn't there some twenty-year-old college student running around your house with his shirt off? Or was Alison tell-

ing me about a prowler you caught? You're all crazy, the way
you live."

"Coffee." Alison slid the tray between their propped up
feet. "Where did Jane go?"

"Saying goodbye to Regina." Liz had her eyes closed, held
her arms around her waist. "Perfect right now would be that
cranberry coffee cake you make, Sylvia. With the nuts?"

"There's white bread and some frozen English muffins."
Sylvia helped herself to coffee. "Otherwise, you're on your
own. You girls could have stopped and bought a doughnut
on your way."

"We're selfish." Liz reached for coffee as Alison poured.
"Just a little cream, Al. Is there any of the lemon meringue
pie you made last night?"

Jane was standing on the porch, staring at the empty run
of Holmes Road. "I had the last piece for breakfast. You're
too late, Liz. It was fantastic. The meringue was bleeding."

Sylvia craned her head toward the porch. "Meringues don't
bleed. They cry. They weep."

"Yeah, well, I ate the sorry little thing anyway." Jane re-
took her seat on the divan. "So, you made it home safely last
night, Al? I came in to look for you but you'd vanished."

Alison was ashamed of her juvenile act of retribution.
"I walked down to Elm Street. I still half expect to see Mrs.
Collins in the all-night drugstore. She sold it though. Now
it closes at ten, one of those chain stores with your prescription on computer. And remember the beauty parlor?"

"I never thought anything in this neighborhood deserved
to last forever, anyway." Jane was annoyed about the cool
reception and the lazy send-off Alison had given Regina. "It
was silly, walking home alone."

Alison felt she'd been unfairly ostracized this morning. But,
having been at home all night, Jane had insider information,
the black-market currency of their long rivalry. "Oh well. It's
a woman's prerogative, as Mom would say."

"You say the wisest things, Sylvia." Liz poured coffee all
around. "An epigram for every occasion."

"Another sign of age—take this down, Liz—is when people start to quote you and you can't remember if you ever said it in the first place. Not to mention what you might have had in mind."

"You don't forget a word. I know that, and I'm not even related." Liz passed the cups back to their owners. "It's just that you don't believe half of what you say. And that," Liz posed with one hand on her hip, the other fanning her face, "is a lady's sacred duty."

VII

JANE KNELT ON the sofa, waiting for Liz and Alison to pass through the short stretch of Holmes Road over which she kept watch. A few seconds' waiting was sufficient to prove they'd turned to the right instead, the more direct route to Alison's home. "She's a good egg, that Liz. Are her paintings any good?"

Sylvia jiggled the dishes on the tray, hoping to rouse Jane to service. One round trip with the morning's debris seemed more than her share.

Jane stretched a hand toward the window to ascertain the late-morning temperature, but she could not reach the cool panes. "I imagine they're odd, obscure. She's so direct. Whatever that directness of hers can't accommodate. I bet that's what she paints. Did she say they were big or am I just making up that part?"

Sylvia picked up the loaded tray, shook it. "You were mean to your sister." She headed for the kitchen.

"Alison?" Jane drummed her hands on the sofa's back, a conclusion of sorts. "Just leave the dishes."

Sylvia returned from the kitchen, hugged the back of one easy chair and dragged it to the mantel. Aggravated by Jane's unhelpfulness, she puffed a few times, dragged the second chair back into place.

Jane was not unmoved; she was impressed. "You going to vacuum the rug, too?"

"I'm going to have a cup of tea and then take Stephen." Sylvia credited lesbians with a patent uninterest in maintaining a household. Otherwise, she could not have explained her elder daughter's obliviousness.

Jane followed to the kitchen. "Leave the dishes, okay?"

"Didn't I mention firing the housekeeping staff? Ingrates, all of them."

"Regina and I hired a maid. I was appalled at first, of course, but not sufficiently appalled to buy myself an electric broom instead. Her name is Natalie." She slid into the alcove. "She's Haitian."

Sylvia stood several feet from the sink, daring herself to leave the dishes undone, as a test of her daughter. She accepted the dare, pulled the kettle off the stove and lit the rear gas burner. "Tea?"

"No." Jane filed the Natalie stories for later. "You nervous about the doctor? You seem distracted."

Sylvia filled the kettle with water, placed it on an unlit front burner. She watched the back burner's crown of blue flame. "Do you think Stephen is dangerous? I never found out what time the fire was set. Am I supposed to call the police or something?" She twisted a knob to extinguish the flame and shoved the cool kettle to the hot metal stand. "If it came down to that, a person could set a house on fire."

"A version of *Charity begins at home?*" Jane still attributed to her mother the lightheartedness she herself was enjoying.

"What would I do?" Her mind was used to leading her to Martin Parris, a sentimental reflex which nonetheless prevented panic. She'd long since ceased expecting intercession. But rubbing up against his absence was a stimulant to action, a satisfactory trigger of her self-reliance.

But Martin wasn't missing any longer; he'd come and gone away.

"What would you do if what?"

Her aimless thoughts accelerated. "I should call your father,

that's what I should do." Announcing this intention calmed
her, as if the tiny space she saved for Arthur in her heart
could comfort her, contain her hopelessness, and thereby give
her room to move. This was the function of her faith, to receive and entomb her despair. Twenty years before, she'd got
down on her hands and knees and, scrabbling at the unforgiving contours of her life, she'd made a place for faith. That
grave was full now. And this morning she had sealed it, rolled
a rock across the hollow hope of Martin. For the moment,
Arthur's absence served her, though Sylvia could see this was
a shallow, temporary harbor.

"Are you all right?" Jane wanted Sylvia to take a step or
cough. Her mother's stillness frightened her. Like the parent
of a sleeping newborn, Jane cleared her throat, then faked a
cough, subversions of the urge to check her mother's pulse.

"Would you see that Stephen is ready? We should leave
soon. I want to telephone your father." She waited until Jane
began to climb the stairs to dial Arthur's number at Spectronics.

Several secretarial rebuffs failed to put her off. She asked
one of the young women for her name, which she promptly
forgot, then asked to be connected to Hetty Marshall.

"Sylvia? Hello, this is Hetty."

"Arthur's idiot secretary won't tell him I'm calling." Her
vociferousness embarrassed her. She toyed with the option of
simply hanging up. "Listen to me. Forgive me, Hetty."

"Is this an emergency? With Stephen?"

"No. Yes, on the Stephen question. I am not in any
danger."

Hetty closed her eyes, to quell her reaction to this drama.
But in the ensuing silence her impatience erupted. "Are you
likely to be endangered in the next half hour? Arthur is finishing a conference with the domestic ad reps."

Sylvia was affronted and impressed by this riposte. Her
impulsive turn to Arthur clearly was misguided, but it had
got her going. She stemmed the urge to trade a barb or two

with Arthur's pretty woman boss. She let the facts speak for themselves. "Oh, Hetty, please don't interrupt a meeting with advertising representatives on my account. Please just let him know I called. In fact, just take a message, would you? Could you ask him to call me. . . . Better yet, do you know when he'll be able to make it home tonight?"

Hetty held herself in check, spoke as if she were reading from a printed agenda. "I know he has the meeting, which ends in half an hour. And I do know he'll have to swing by the 1886 Shop to pick up a tuxedo for the dinner tonight."

Sylvia ignored this, the first mention she'd heard of a black-tie dinner. She had Stephen. "Well, the simple message you could leave him, if you don't mind . . ."

"I've got pencil poised on paper, Sylvia."

"Let him know his son—that would be Stephen—let him know Stephen's been accused of setting fire to the Temple Beth Israel. I suppose there is some chance he'll be arrested. Thank you so much. Goodbye." Sylvia replaced the receiver, walked to the bottom stair. "Stephen, let's not be late, son."

Stephen appeared at the top of the staircase, crossed his arms, then shoved his hands into his trouser pockets. He was dressed in a sport coat and tie, a demonstration of best intentions. "How do I look?"

"Like a man I'd be proud to be seen with. Do you want to wait in the car while I change?"

He clapped twice, headed outside.

VIII

WHITE NOONTIME LIGHT held buildings and pedestrians in sharp relief. The city seemed both far away and larger as they threaded through the Park Square rotary. Stephen played piano on his thighs, drowning out the questions he assumed he would be asked about the temple incident, questions he earnestly believed were his to answer, as would any guilty child rhetorically assigned the task of explaining what had possessed him.

"Will you get mad at Dad someday, for lying to me?" Stephen hoped to spread the blame, diminishing his portion. Sylvia could not sustain a correlation between Stephen as he was today and Arthur's contribution. "What exactly did your father say?"

Stephen leapt ahead of her, knowing he was moments from a room alone with yet another stranger. "What do you think about this? That maybe at our house we had bad male bonding?"

The catchphrase boomeranged. It was a glimmer of the young man with an Amherst address. Sylvia was silent as it shot by, allowing it to circle back unimpeded to the little boy who'd let it fly.

Ten minutes after Stephen disappeared inside the office, Sylvia could not remember what he'd said to make her feel so maudlin.

Stephen's disappointment was complete. Not only had Daye lied to him about the meeting with another doctor, but he was asking questions about temple windows, rocks, the color yellow. What did each one mean to Stephen? Instead of answering, Stephen pulled off his sport coat and draped it over his shoulders. Then, with his elbows pressed into his waist, he stuck his hands into the armpits of the jacket sleeves.

Daye asked him why he did that, folded his arms to look like wings, and then launched an analysis of the gesture.

Stephen interrupted Daye. He had things to say and he found the doctor boring. "We have an idea at our house, a place you have never been, I might add. Unless you beg to differ?" Stephen flapped his jacket twice. "This is more important than my arms. In case you haven't noticed, they are arms." He flipped the empty arm sockets. "I bet you would be happy to know my father is a pathological liar. Just about like a kleptomaniac—you've heard about them—except he lies instead." Stephen wanted terms to reinforce the illness aspect of his father's lying. "Some people who have visited our house call him a fanatic. You could call him a hypochondriac, Dr. Daye." He laughed here, a strategy of self-defense he'd recently adopted, to anticipate any inadvertent humor.

Daye didn't fashion a response. He relegated Stephen to the Assessment/Intensive Treatment form he would fill out within the hour. His duties as the court-appointed clinical psychologist of record provided for referral to the Jones II psychiatric clinic at the Berkshire Medical Center. It was a bureaucratic washing of the hands, though Daye was not an eager Pilate. He had a disaffection for the soap: Referrals of this sort required him to make a stab at diagnosis. He preferred to minimize the scrutiny of his technique by private psychiatric peers. Frequently, he issued full releases to his patients with obscurely worded reservations. These amounted to as many indirect referrals, but they allowed for verbose, optimistic hedging of his bets. His reliance on this option had earned Daye a reputation in the mental health community; to avoid conviction as a maladept, he essentially pled guilty to the lesser charge of pedantry.

Stephen waited in the car while Sylvia was interviewed about his patterns of behavior. She blamed her son for this transfer of attention. Feeling she'd been set up, she betrayed him as best she could. On the strength of Sylvia's secondhand account of Stephen's Sermon on the Mount, which dovetailed with his stint as Solomon and glamorized his temple turn, the doctor forged a brief but tenable history of a delusional post-adolescent with sociopathic tendencies. This painted Stephen outside the jurisdiction of the courts, the final outpost of the world of willful and responsible adults.

Sylvia supposed this rendered arson charges moot. She vowed to visit Jones II with her son before the week was out. She accepted several booklets and some photocopied information Daye said would facilitate arrangements for evaluation, insurance reimbursement for outpatient consultations, and "what pharmacologic aids my medical counterparts might deem relevant." These documents, she felt, constituted Stephen's passport. It was a victory of sorts, an imprimatur for his volatile state of mind as a sovereign state. The high seas had become his home.

Stephen formulated several apologies as they drove home. He figured it was best to tell the truth. "I didn't know he could drag you in if I didn't use up my time." He shook his head, ruing his misunderstanding of the rules of Paramount. "I could've kept going, but they don't tell you. Next time, I'll talk my head off." He added a short laugh, just in case. "We're a team, like tag-team wrestling." In his enthusiasm, he tagged Sylvia's right arm.

"They give up. That's a fact, Stephen. Dr. Daye surrendered. And I am going to give up soon." She paid his hands attention, prepared to fend them off.

Stephen was quiet until they passed the high school and the recently refurbished site of St. Luke's Residence. The bankrupt hospital, where Sylvia had given birth to Stephen, recently had been converted to a subsidized home for care of the elderly. The transformation pleased him, designed, it seemed to Stephen, to assure his personal welfare. "That's where it all began, and before you know it, that's where I'll end up." He sang this to amuse his mother.

Sylvia seized his song as if it were a piece of Stephen she could grab and shake. She tried to string together synonyms for the term "asylum" to list as residential destinations for a wayward son.

Stephen rolled his window down, stuck out his head, yelled, "They use dog food! There's human hair in their french fries!" as they passed the Burgers Plus on Elm Street.

Sylvia rescinded her plans for intervention. Instead, she made a late, swerving turn into the parking lot at Sacred Heart, eliciting loud squeals from three uniformed young girls a few feet past the driveway. She waved and backed the car into a space near the side door.

The peace of being still and at a safe remove from passersby she credited devoutly to proximity to church. She recast her rather dangerous decision to bring her son to church as inspiration. She was here for miracles, to pray him back to health.

It was her last resort, to find within the massive empty space a dimly lighted corner she could appropriate for storage. Exhausted by the prospect of interring yet another twenty years of doubt and disbelief within herself, she hoped she still had rights to use this church as a sarcophagus, though it had been erected for the use of the less inventive faithful.

Suspecting Stephen would appreciate her empathic suggestion, she simply said, "Let's go inside and pray for us."

Stephen grabbed the dashboard. He had a few things hidden in that church himself. Forewarned was not forearmed just now, though he was grateful he'd been sent the vision of his mother's robe fitted to the huge crucifix suspended above the altar. "Don't go in there. Anyway, it's locked."

"What do you mean, don't go in there? You like it here. Noontime Mass ended an hour ago, at least. We'll be the only ones." Sylvia unplugged the car-door lock and lifted the thin handle.

Stephen panicked. "Jesus says, Stay out of here! He's talking to us now. Stay out! Beware!"

Fear drove her away from him. But as she slid her sore legs out from underneath the steering wheel, he screamed again, "Don't do this to me, Mom!" With this he reached for her, to hold her back. But she had tried to turn to him and slipped. Her feet had reached the parking lot, but her back and head flopped down against the seat. She had her right hand on the steering wheel, and held herself in place, which left her unprotected as Stephen tumbled toward her. His outstretched hands hit her stomach first, then slid along the polished cotton runway of her dress. Afraid he otherwise would crush her, he worked to hold his body up above her face—until he saw his hands had landed in her crotch. The only option he could countenance was immediate retreat. Convinced he was about to smother her, he slid his hands along her inner thighs and performed a push-up.

The burst of pressure and release occasioned by his awkward calisthenic elicited a howl from his inert mother. "The knees, Stephen, my knees!"

"My hands! My hands!" Stephen screamed to preempt any further accusations.

"Just pry me up, just get me out of here, for God's sake, Stephen. Get me upright." But while she hollered, Sylvia was slithering along the seat. When she got her breasts just past the steering wheel, to which she held throughout, gravity ceased to oppose her leverage operations and she pulled herself upright.

Stephen chanted on about his hands while flipping them against the windshield, palms to backs to palms.

She wanted nothing more than to go home, and preferably in silence. "Your hands?" The insult of the tumbling was foremost in her mind. "You nearly broke my legs in two and now you want to talk about your hands? Keep them to yourself. I'll give you something to do with your hands." She accelerated suddenly. She didn't pause to check the traffic; a long blast of the horn was all the warning she felt anyone deserved. Her bravado pleased her twice: as compensation for the clumsy, painful pawing she'd endured and as a surprisingly effective palliative for her unsteady son.

IX

Two HOURS IN his empty house had made a mockery of Arthur. Unable to reach Alison by phone, and finally convinced that a third search of the kitchen drawers, the vanity and bureaus in his bedroom, and the pantry walls and cupboards would not yield the name of Jane's elderly companion's cousin, he talked briefly with his son-in-law, who denied knowledge of the fire. Arthur reluctantly adopted his mollifying theory of a family-wide conspiracy devised to lock him out of Stephen's fate. It didn't stand the test of time. Martin Parris called and happily contracted Arthur to revoke his accusation and apologize to Sylvia for any inconvenience caused her by his visit. Three teenage girls had been arrested, though they protested the anti-Jewish implications the authorities assigned their late-night (and, in retrospect, ill-planned and dangerous) investigation of the fuel and fabric needed to burn a member of their ninth-grade class in effigy. Before the conversation's end, Arthur managed to envision Martin, dressed in his robes, suspended on a pole and set afire.

Arthur fanned these flames. At first, he did so nonchalantly, to temper culpability. He opened long-locked doors and let in blasts of air—the winds of his resentment held at bay these twenty years. The ranging, yapping flames snapped greedily. Arthur liked the noise. He stoked the fire with the curtains hung to hide the family from their neighbors, excitedly flung open windows which had rattled in their frames, what with persistent rumors and recriminations whirling through the city. The flames leapt up and slithered down and leapt again until the walls were black, then blazing white and orange. The ceiling fell away in one great heave, and bedroom floorboards smoked as varnish vaporized and cracked. And that's when Arthur saw that he was safe outside the house in which his family slept. He was rooting for the fire.

The dream collapsed before the house. Arthur, in the alcove, staring at the telephone, was seized not by remorse but panic: He knew his wife and Stephen would soon be home. His crazy bastard son would have to be discussed. He'd make a feeble fuss about the private meeting Sylvia had held with Parris, and try to extricate himself, tuxedoed, without an explanation (not to mention invitation) to his wife. He worried words would fail him, as if he had worn out the one about the man denied a father's closeness to his son.

Arthur wanted out, and his fear of being dragged back inside the burning house occasioned an unprecedented fit of the imagination. It had him up and moving. He poured two fingers of his maple syrup into his glass, swirled it around, and pressed his lips into the liquid. He emptied out the contents in the sink and, running only cold water so as not to rinse away all proof, he barely cleaned the glass, then inverted it on the stainless counter. He backed away and blinked. This proved the emblem of his failure and remorse was in plain sight. He licked the bottle neck before he sealed it shut, insurance he would reek of what he'd done. Then he climbed the stairs two at a time and fell down on the bed.

The slamming of a car door in the drive was all the warning Arthur had before his younger son shot by the bedroom, kicked his own room's door, then yelled, "Now you've really done it."

Sylvia spotted Arthur's glass right off. Aloud, she said, "Of course. Why not?" She held the glass against the window Arthur had fixed the day before, then ran hot water to remove the residue of syrup. She figured he'd be on the divan, so she limped in that direction. Surprised to find the divan unadorned by Arthur, she called his name out several times, slowly climbed the stairs. Her black-and-yellow knees produced a new sensation, a threat, as if an overzealous step would send her kneecap through the skin. She thanked Arthur for this latest permutation.

The actual sighting of her husband quelled her anger slightly. In an amateurish twist, he'd reversed the normal, sober inclination and lain down on his back, one big, black wingtip propped on either pillow. Sylvia ignored him as she undressed, though once or twice she gave in to a smile or a snort, a delayed and fond acknowledgment she might accord a television farce.

Arthur didn't move, though he'd begun to rue the placement of his feet. His face was hot and he suspected blood was lagging on the uphill course along his legs. As soon as Sylvia headed downstairs in his robe, he curled into a more sustainable pose. He plotted alternate escape routes, though he still doubted he could formally outfit himself in utter silence.

Half an hour passed before the kettle whistled, followed by another tedious ascent. Sylvia went past the room and drew a bath. She came by for one last look at Arthur, envied him the peace she guessed he had achieved. Forgiving him the midday binge and overeager swigging of the cure—she'd realized he must have downed the morning-after syrup as soon as he had finished with the rum—she thought he deserved several hours undisturbed. Achieving rest by any means was something of a feat. She dialed Alison's home number and then Jane in Lenox; neither daughter answered. Surprised and rather sad to know that no one else would likely place a call to the Adamskis, she unplugged the bedroom telephone and headed for the bath.

When he heard Sylvia submerge herself, Arthur checked his watch. He had two hours yet before he stopped at Hetty's for "a cocktail or a Coke or something on the Holmes Road unrestricted list." Mindful of the fantastic story he would have to dream up later for his wife and possibly his daughters, Arthur scooted off the bed, grabbed his garment bag from the downstairs closet, snuck out the back door. He wondered if it was unfair to leave his wife with Stephen and no car. The simple proof of fairness he derived delighted him: He wasn't Stephen's father but he was the owner of the car. "So screw your doubts, Adamski," as he guessed his dinner partner would advise.

Failure of imagination led him straight to Hetty's condominium, a modern townhouse in a series built just two miles from the new campus of the community college, where the Berkshire Commerce Council dinner would be served. He parked discreetly in her little carport, his fender touching the white door of her attached garage. Tux in hand, he pressed her doorbell, fairly certain she was still at work. He wouldn't mind the wait.

The door swung open wide, revealed a slightly startled Hetty Marshall. "Adamski! I was betting on the paper boy. Come in. I had my niece's daughters here for the weekend and I finally got around to watching the ends of two movies I rented for them. Had them so long now, I may as well buy them. Comedies. I haven't laughed yet. Ha." She led him up a flight of stairs to her large combination dining and living room. "Ha. I've got pajamas on, don't I? Let me turn that thing off."

Arthur knew he should explain himself, apologize, or at least tell her not to interrupt whatever she was watching, but he hadn't quite got over her appearance. Not only was she wearing nothing but a pair of yellow silk pajamas, loungewear he knew only from the movies of his youth, but her top half was secured with only two of five available buttons. Finally, he laid his garment bag across a little half wall near her dining table. "I'm on the early side."

"Two hours on the early side. I left the office early, though. I figure this affair—last few years, I just skipped, you know—this will be a duty, which is a good enough excuse. . . ." She'd lost her thought. She'd even lost the force of her good cheer. "I'd ask you how things went at home, but you look so damned good I guess things went all right."

"A false alarm, the fire thing." Unself-consciously, he added, "Funny how you could just call that." He was impressed.

"A drink?" She hoped he'd want one, just to get her moving.

"Honestly? I think a glass of water. I can get it. I remember where everything is in your little kitchen." He'd been here for a couple of Christmas parties years before.

"You haven't been here since . . . since who cares? Nineteen seventy something. Before I got wise and rented out the Rosa Restaurant." Hetty took a single step.

"I can't tell. Have you changed things?" Arthur looked around, annoyed he couldn't spot a ringer like a fancy modern lamp or an oriental rug.

"Your coat. Hand it over. Ha, what a hostess." Hetty had herself in gear again. "Water. Ice?"

"Please."

"Sit."

He followed her instead.

"I've got seltzer, too, and maybe tonic, somewhere."

"Water's fine."

She pulled a crystal glass from an open shelf. "Water, then, is what you'll get."

"That's great." He backed away, until he felt the dining room table with his hands. "Just thirsty, I guess."

"Ice water." She handed him the glass and walked to his garment bag, which she picked up and carefully laid out on the table. "This the tux?"

"Thanks again. I never would have thought about reserving one. I guess I ought to own one."

"Renting's better. Like a car, though I don't lease mine. I tried that once." She brought her hands up to her hips and looked up at the ceiling. Then she smiled. "I'm all of a sudden nervous? Ever since you walked through that door."

Arthur stood, ashamed he'd noticed and not offered to leave her alone till six. "I'm sorry. I should have called."

"No, no. Good nervous. Not rough on the insides. Good for the soul. Not like, What's he doing here? and What am I supposed to do? Though, since I brought it up, what am I supposed to do?" She held her pose.

Arthur put his glass down on the table, saw that it was sweating, picked it up. And in those seconds, the faint and often unattended warming of his lower back and thighs did not drain off. Her silence was the confidence he needed. He set his glass down in the ring of water, stepped close to Hetty. He tugged the bottom of her yellow shirt. "The buttons have been sort of bugging me since I first got here."

"They're a nuisance to me, too." She ran her hands along his arms. She looked at his white shirtsleeves, squeezed her hands around his forearms.

Arthur didn't want her to let go. He slowly raised his hands and undid the buttons of her soft shirt. Then, with her hands leading his, he traced her sides and let her step back, twirl his body toward the stairs.

He let her pass and held her hands behind her back. Beside her bed, she turned and deftly worked his shirt off. Arthur slid his hands around her hips and up along her back. He felt his belt pulled tight and then released and he tugged at the drawstring round her waist. Hetty took the string in hand and stepped out of the pants. Arthur pried his shoes off, then

244 Mother of God

tugged off his socks, kicked slacks and underwear aside. When Hetty shook her shoulders from her shirt, he put a finger to his lips.

"Not yet." He drew her close, his open palms pressed in below her shoulder blades. "I like you here, your shirt against my arms. Like something's holding us together. Something soft."

Her hands inched down until they rested on his buttocks. She raised herself onto her toes and slowly dropped back to her heels, to feel her breasts across his chest, the width and coarseness of his arms beneath her own.

There was no moment of transgression, no clutching bravely to each other's bodies or defiance of untimely memory of other vows or voices. They were nowhere in the world. It was early. They had time.

Hetty raised a foot and rubbed her sole along his calf. Arthur drew his hands around her torso till his wrists were soft against her breasts. They carried on elaborate introductions until Hetty sat and Arthur knelt before her, hands against her middle, fingers stretched apart to make a measure all his own.

He pulled his hands away, two stars, and submitted them for her approval. Hetty ducked her head and kissed his palms. This made him laugh.

He sat back on his heels. "I'm just so glad it's you." He sprang forward, wrapped his arms around her waist, and stood up with her in his arms. "Now, take your shirt off. I can hold you by myself."

She shook it off, held to one sleeve. As he laid her on the bed, she rubbed the silk across his back, then tossed it overhead.

The aftermath was long and slow in coming. They agreed they were officially late when Hetty grabbed a small alarm clock from her bedside table and said, "Seven-thirty-five."

Arthur checked her reading, held the clock close to his face. "I have a tuxedo and all." He handed her the clock, which she replaced. Arthur knew it was the hour now for declarations and exemptions, possibly assessments and predictions, too. "Hetty?" He knew his body had explained itself to hers. The words he had were lumbering and indistinct and, he guessed correctly, not altogether true.

Hetty pulled his hand until his forearms rested on her belly. "Hetty. That's good. Arthur. Arthur, Arthur, Arthur. When we make it back here, first names only." The Spectronics senior partners were excused from making sense of one another's hips and torsos and monosyllabic moans.

They were not haunted by the precedents of love affairs encompassing whole lives. Desire had been whittled down to this, the wordless ritual of consummation, the sacramental instinct. Of course, both Arthur and Hetty had to reckon with the oddity of silence where convention called for speeches. Words long have served as lovers' recourse, the compensation they provide each other in the absence of more substantial proof of transformation. Silence here was wisdom, though bewilderment was present also, to stifle any lapses.

Clothing restored their common senses.

"I can't find my top." Hetty walked around the bed, shook the satin comforter.

Arthur stood before the mirror in the bathroom, fumbling with the studs and cuff links, upholstering himself, protecting Arthur with Adamski's rented garb.

"I'm almost ready. How are you?" Hetty held her shoes, still interested in the fate of her pajamas. She walked across the room to have a look. "You're so handsome all dressed up that it actually makes me jealous. I wish they made a uniform for women. Instead we get accessories galore. Let's go."

Arthur followed Hetty's car through intermittent rings of light on West Street's rural run. He let her lead the way into the crowded gallery where cocktails still were being served. He lost her only seconds after handing her a plastic glass of wine he plucked off a passing waiter's tray.

The spirit of the room was quite subdued, though a large contingent of young men occasionally erupted into laughter. A second waiter told him they belonged to Berkshire Mutual,

the insurance firm whose nationwide expansion would be honored with the Council's John Frederick medal after dinner
which, since Arthur asked, was steamship round and roast
potatoes.

An almost constant nodding moved him through the crowd
of men and women whom he recognized and many more who
clearly felt he ought to if he didn't. He didn't want to stop.
Circulating kept him several steps ahead of Stephen's story,
which he knew was his most recent public accomplishment.

At last the room's design defeated him. He got stuck at
one end of the narrow, arching space, and from this vantage
could see it was a lobby. On a wall shared with what he
guessed was an auditorium were hung paintings he could not
make out. The ceiling was forty, maybe fifty feet high. The
outer wall was lined with huge frosted white glass windows,
through which parking lot lights were diffused. At the concrete sill beneath the nearest window—illuminated only from
his cummerbund on up—a man was waving. Arthur looked
away, but when he turned the man was pointing with a drink
in his extended hand. He did not approach, and with his hand
held high above his silhouetted girth, he might have been a
stained-glass patriarch who'd slipped from his exalted perch.

"Arthur—well, I'll be—Arthur Adamski, you don't even
recognize me. What is it? Fifteen, twenty years?"

Arthur was not five feet from the man and still he couldn't
rouse a name. His features and proportions were remarkable
enough to make Arthur feel his failure to remember was an
insult. The man was all but bald, with one band of hair
combed across his pate. He was nearly Arthur's height, but
his heft belied this correspondence. His torso was an inverted cone, descending from a long, unwrinkled neck into
his banded, bloated waist, which the tuxedo pressed and
spread around his hips to form a hoop.

The man seemed pleased to have stumped Arthur. "Packed
on a few extra, of course," was all he said.

Arthur dropped his gaze to the man's feet and only then
did he recognize the voice of Jonty Mortimer, executor of

the General Electric's will regarding the interment of Insulum, Incorporated.

"You remember now, I can see it."

"Hello there, Jonty." The name itself seemed a slur, considering the shape of him. "Must be too long in Dalton. I've
forgotten all that now." Arthur expected this would serve as
both apology and excuse. "I'm here with Hetty Marshall. Still
at Spectronics."

"Who wouldn't be? You're doing pretty damn well up
there. New magazines every time I turn around. Now England, too? What's she like? We've never met. She's a damned
sight prettier than any of the gals we've got working for us,
if her picture's on the up and up." Jonty bobbed his head.

"She's beautiful." Arthur blurted this assessment. He added,
"Sylvia and me—my wife, you might remember—we're both
crazy about her."

"Sylvia, of course. She ever go to work, Art? Unusual lady.
Pretty tough, if you don't mind me saying so. I guess you
know what I mean. Quite something."

Arthur turned away, wishing Hetty or even Sylvia was lurking near enough to wedge him away from Jonty.

"I left the company. Of course, you probably knew that."

"When?" Arthur couldn't walk away without a reason.

"Old news, Art. Just a few years after you closed up shop
with the insulation business. With Allen Drecker. Used to
be in company relations? Older guy? He died. Still, it's Mortimer and Drecker. Public relations. If you ever need some
image boosting." Jonty bobbed his head vigorously.

Arthur said, "Closed up shop? That's one way of putting
it."

"Best face forward, Art. That's my job."

"Allen Drecker? He died a long while back, didn't he?"
Arthur's sense of time was compromised by the transformation
Jonty had undergone.

"Ten years, at least. Hold it, it was seventy-two. I can't tell
you how badly I felt."

"You know what you could tell me?" Arthur looked at

Jonty's shoes again. "It's ancient history and you probably don't remember much about this." He stared at Jonty's shoes with such apparent interest that Jonty finally kicked his left shoe up to have a look. Arthur's courage was abating, but he was stumped for conversation. Jonty leaned forward, lifted his right foot, just enough to prompt the question Arthur had formed. "I watched and read for about five years. Oh, maybe longer. Watched pretty closely, I mean." He raised his gaze. "After we'd closed up shop, the GE never seemed to do a thing about that patent, Jonty. The whole thing kind of disappeared."

"What did they want with a better insulation? Save some electricity? Back then? Who'd ever heard of the A-rabs?" Jonty swigged the last of his scotch. "But nobody wanted a couple of ex-company men telling customers the product line was inefficient or too costly to operate."

"But they must've spent a fortune on redesigns. They had a model every year, with lighter castings, space-age this or that and—"

"Well, come on now, Art. We weren't out there trying to make junk. Everybody's got an idea—a compound for the coils, seamless joints. You close out the other suppliers' options and then forge ahead."

"Who wants efficiency. Of course the company wants efficiency. Jonty, that's just double-talk." Arthur was happy to leave it at that.

"So, what if we'd decided to make this stuff—what was Parris's name for it? Terrible name, by the way. Incubus? Anyway it always sounded like that to me. What happens if we'd have tried?" He handed his empty glass to Arthur, an impatient chess master about to explain his game-winning strategy to a novice. He relied on repeatedly turning his palms up to convey the simplicity of his logic. "We get a counter-suit? I'm winging it here, Art—hypothetically speaking—but cut me a little slack. People get a little more proprietary when they see there's some real, practical dollars at stake. Am I out in left field here, Art? Imagine this for me, and gimme your best guess: A year or two down the road, you see this Incubus stuff—for the sake of argument—you're watching in the trades and you see us bring it out with a better brand name. Don't you think you might've had a second thought about who invented what? Anyway, that was my guess. It was also my guess, a hunch, we had to get to you before the profits started rolling in. Raise some doubts, right? And Parris always had an eye on something political, or in the courts—hard to court a scandal when you want the public to trust you." Jonty stuck his index finger underneath his cummerbund. "Could've gone either way, of course." He stuck his other fingers underneath the pleated sash, to relieve the pressure. "What ever happened to that Forrester guy, Art? You still in touch?"

Arthur was awed by what he'd heard. He didn't mean to lie when he said, "See him every year, at Christmas. Get together with the families." He made it up, half believing it was what should have happened. Jonty had shamed him. He tried to salvage what he could. "Course, there were other damned good reasons for closing down that particular business." He hoped Jonty understood from this he'd been involved in many more successful ventures.

"Always are. Nothing's simple. Turns out, it was what got you to Dalton. Am I right?" Jonty pulled his hand away from his waist.

Arthur incorrectly guessed he wanted to shake hands. His offer met with some confusion, though Jonty finally engaged him. "It was my job, you know. Product Supervisor, way back when." Arthur had conceded victory long ago. His tactic here was retribution of the lowest order; he wanted Jonty to admit he'd picked a fight with a weakling. Arthur was infused with a familiar swell of self-pity. "I just didn't know enough."

Jonty saw a handsome man in a tailored tuxedo, second in command at one of the few firms in the Berkshires certain to survive the century. Watching Arthur pull his cummerbund up the inch it had fallen from his thirty-three-inch waist, Jonty was convinced his jealous fantasy of Arthur in bed with the woman in the outdated *Courier* photograph was accurate, or

near enough the truth to warrant contemplation. Jonty saw
what any man would see: Arthur Adamski amalgamated.
"Patent suits are costly, Art. No one ever wins one, really. Did
I read you'd had some trouble with your youngest? Hope he's
feeling better." Jonty thought it was a car crash he had read
of, involving alcohol or drugs. Like every parent, even those
with better recall, Jonty registered the story primarily as the
latest in a series of embarrassments teenage children foisted
on their families.

"He's alive. I'll say that for him." Explicit mention of
Stephen empowered Arthur to offend propriety. "I have to
leave now, Jonty." Arthur put Jonty's glass on the concrete
sill and dodged back through the crowd.

Hetty was standing near the exit with two younger men.
"Adamski. These youngsters are lawyers. Can you believe
that?" She wanted rescuing.

His surname belonged to Stephen at the moment. "It's
home. I've really got to go."

Hetty caught his forearm in her hand. "Can I help?"

"I'll talk to you tomorrow."

"Or Friday. Take a day off if you need it."

She had reached him. "I'm getting a little better at that,
knowing what I need. Good night."

"Yes, indeed. Good night." She let him go.

X

Stephen passed the evening proctoring his mother's mood.
He knew she wasn't feeling well; she begged off visits from
both daughters, inviting Jane, and Alison and Roger, for
Thursday lunch instead, "Or tea and sympathy," she'd said.
"I'm frankly out of patience. And ideas. But the larder's holding up, what with Stephen never eating." It occurred to him
to vomit up the hamburgers from Tuesday, but he settled
for another night of fasting. The conversations Sylvia con-

ducted from her bedroom revealed her fear he'd start a fire in the house, her self-diagnosis as a "temporary cripple" (which Stephen figured was a way of saying he'd not only touched her private parts but ruptured something down there with his hands), and that Dr. Daye had punished her for Stephen's misbehavior, assigning her a stack of reading which, as she said to Jane, "makes me wish they'd lock me up. I'd let them feed me, change the linens for a week, and charge it up to Arthur's insurance plan."

He occasionally shuffled the photographs he'd taken off his wall, studying the ones that surfaced, as if they might be tarot cards. But he learned nothing of the future. The pictures were his evidence of past failures, a few so badly out of focus he could not recall the images he'd meant to represent. This nixed his notion of presenting his collected work as reparation to his mother. What would she make of them? The only way to prove she shouldn't give up on him, Stephen knew, was doing something nice for her that didn't get him thrown in jail. His memory did not turn up a temple other than Beth Israel, and churches, if he had this right, didn't count—the distinction still evaded him, but he smugly dismissed an impulse to check out Sacred Heart again as foolish. To himself, addressing the instinctive Stephen he no longer trusted, he said, "Don't waste your breath. I'm not going anywhere. The body is the temple of the Holy Spirit." The words surprised him, but he screwed up his face, twisting consternation into an approximation of amused disgust, as if anybody worth his salt would know as much. He repeated the catechism maxim with conviction. "The body *is* the temple of the Holy Spirit."

He could not assimilate this insight and the urge to move, though he now expected it might be fairly easy to redeem himself. Still, he was cautious about any hope. Lately, if he so much as touched his mother, it turned into a fiasco.

Arthur returned and interrupted Stephen's concentration. He and Sylvia were silent, until she said she wouldn't mind an explanation, which alerted Stephen.

"The dinner was an awards thing. To give Berkshire Mutual

a medal of achievement. I got there late. I should have said something, but . . . I knew you knew what happened. I'm sorry, I fell down again, I guess. When I left—while you were in the bath? I'd decided I still do need help. I went to a meeting, an A.A. group in West Pittsfield. I spoke. It's the first time I've actually spoken at one of these meetings. I explained things here, to some extent, why I can't go every evening. The group agreed I could manage myself if I made it frequently— certainly more than once a week, of course. I see it now, see I have to help myself before I can be of any help to you. Or even Stephen. Please forgive me, dear. I know it's early, but if you don't mind, I'd like to crawl in next to you and get some sleep. I left so much at work. I have to get a very early start. Are you all right, dear?"

"It's calm enough. Just waiting for the other shoe to drop. We have some decisions . . . it can all wait until tomorrow. I might read downstairs a while. I think Stephen is asleep."

Stephen was interested in her suggestion of dropping a shoe, but his father's noisy undressing confirmed his suspicion that this comment was not aimed at him. And, as evidence of his intent to please his mother, Stephen slipped beneath his bed-sheets. He felt his torso tighten and give way as he let out a yawn, a happy prelude to a good night's sleep.

XI

Sylvia slipped into Arthur's robe and cursed her husband's cavalier decision not to wake her when he left. The only consolation she admitted for having slept until ten-thirty was the improvement of her knees, which resisted negotiation of the stairs but no longer balked at straightaways.

The first irregularity she noted was the swinging door between the living room and kitchen, which for ten years had been pinned against the wall with a fabric-covered rock she'd won as fourth prize in a Sodality raffle; the door was closed. She observed this detour, circled through the dining room toward the pantry. Another underutilized oak door had been unhooked and jammed into its imperfectly aligned frame. Whatever Stephen might be hiding in his private galley, she sincerely hoped it would include a relatively recent pot of coffee. She wasn't up to him in her preconscious state. He'd already set the dining table with the china plates and silverware typically reserved for holidays. As place mats and, she guessed correctly, trivets for warm dishes, he'd arranged pairs of his photographs. The queerness of this spectacle was amplified by its suggestive, stark appeal. Its plausible intentionality acted on her like an omen, a foretelling of the unreliability of any boundary she might claim between herself and Stephen.

Coffee was the least of what awaited her. She found Stephen hard at work, preparing an elaborate lunch, involving soup and boiled eggs, vegetables—both fresh and canned, sliced apples, cheese, two bowls of shredded lettuce, and a pound of frozen bacon thawing on a window sill.

Sylvia accepted coffee in a china cup. She hadn't dared move into the convulsed confines of the kitchen. She drank it black, staring from the pantry.

All Stephen said was, "Good morning, lazybones. I don't have time to chat. You enjoy your morning coffee. Leave the rest to me."

Sylvia was sufficiently startled to obey him. She did not oppose a lunchtime demonstration of his state of mind. Her research had turned up the necessary forms and several medical opinions on the process of commitment. She'd decided she preferred a voluntary term, which made it possible for her to have a hand in Stephen's length of stay and therapy. She knew she couldn't risk the revelations that might follow on involuntary installation at Jones II. It was clear her safest bet would be to strike a deal with Stephen. The lunch he was preparing would be apt, exotic fare; a meal which even Jane could not accuse Sylvia of cooking up.

Alison and Roger arrived, were shown the table, and retreated to the divan. Their hushed and frightened awe turned
somber, then morose, after Jane arrived and pronounced it
"absolutely funereal. It's like a coffin. And," she advised her
mother, who was standing at the mantel, where she watched
the still-closed swinging door, "if you think I am going to eat
anything served like that . . . you can just tell Stephen to
drop mine on the floor. I am not about to eat his insane idea
of lunch."

A guilty thrill circuited the living room as all gathered wondered if Stephen wouldn't try to poison them.

"I ought to see what his plan is, though." Sylvia pressed
the door ajar.

He heard her intrude, grabbed the frozen bacon from the
sill above the sink. "It won't thaw. I made too much lettuce.
And I put something in the soup that doesn't even belong
in soup. I don't know how the restaurants do it. So I put in
two pieces of bread for every person. And it melted. It was
supposed to float." He was addressing the pound of bacon,
which he finally dropped into the sink. "I don't remember
even the first course." He turned to face his mother. "Does
this happen to you sometimes? I think it was the perfect
appetizer. I have to admit I don't know what I can do for
you. I'm so tired of thinking about it." He retreated to the
alcove.

Sylvia slid into the kitchen. She saw he had the four gas
burners fired up, full throttle. "I can clean this up, son. You
could have a rest."

He yelled, as if she were taunting him with his failure. "I
have to do that. I have to wash my stupid hands and you know
it." He clapped several times. "Somebody better say they're
sorry."

"I'm sorry it didn't work out, Stephen. The table. It looks
so nice." Sylvia shuttled her attention between Stephen and
the stove, certain either one might spontaneously explode.

"Okay, okay. The whole problem is, I don't know what
you really mean by the body is the temple. And for your

information, since you think I made it up just to be extra-special bad—the temple, and I don't mean my body, whatever that means—the temple is just about next door to Redfield, as in school, as in when I was in kindergarten, since Catholics don't believe in having their own kindergartens, so we had to walk over to Redfield, if you remember correctly. I don't know any other temples except my own body and, for instance, why do you keep looking at that oven, anyway?" He was not yelling; he was complaining. He'd settled in for a long gripe. "I can't think of anything to tell our guests. You know me. I say one wrong word and Jane and her girlfriend show up. I didn't think you'd know what I meant. Just what I expected, by the way."

"I'll talk to our guests, Stephen." Sylvia hoped a practical appeal would win her freedom. "They'll understand."

"Wanna bet?"

"You might want to turn off a few of those burners while I speak to the crowd."

"If I wanted to I would."

Sylvia was unsettled by the coincidence of his reawakened interest in the temple. "Gas isn't free, Stephen. We don't want to run up the bill."

"What a cheapskate. In a restaurant, you know, this lunch would cost about a thousand dollars."

"Well, at least be careful. I don't want anything to happen to you, son."

Her move to leave the kitchen calmed him. "Hey, should I just off that bacon? I think there's something wrong with it, like it's got so frozen it wouldn't taste like much."

"Good idea. I'll check in with you in a bit. Okay?"

Stephen felt he might just get away with this one—clean up the kitchen and pretend the whole thing never happened. He shooed her out good-naturedly. "Scat, then, scat. Get out of my kitchen."

Sylvia was happy to see Jane had pulled the chairs out of place and set up a space for conversation. She sat in the chair beside her elder daughter, facing Alison and Roger.

"We heard all that." Jane dispensed with summary. "I say we lock him in and go have lunch."

"Yes, well, before we leave, we may as well torch the furniture and beat him to the punch. He's got the stove going full blast."

"Weren't you relieved, at least, to read about the girls, then?" Roger thought perhaps she'd missed his point. "You did see the *Courier* story? They found the girls who set the Beth Israel fire. Juveniles, so they can't release the names. But girls."

"Arthur must have taken our paper to the office. Are you sure it's the same fire?" Sylvia's relief was excessive; she was about to grant her son a full reprieve.

"The great part of that story . . ." Jane regretted her choice of words. "Could you believe the way it was reported? As if, because the teenagers said so, there probably was no reason to think it was anti-Semitic?"

Roger assented enthusiastically. "Just happened to be in the neighborhood."

"Do you think, then, that what Stephen did, it was because he had something special against the Jewish people?" Sylvia resented the implication.

Jane hesitated, waiting for her mother to emend the question. "You don't?"

"You're as bad as that Dr. Daye fellow. He thinks Stephen has delusions of grandeur. He said he thinks the whole problem is mixed up with religion."

"You don't?" Jane drew her feet up onto her seat cushion.

Alison looked to Roger, recalling his explanation. "Religion isn't the whole problem. It's just, well, not the symptoms, exactly, but . . ."

Sylvia saw through to their private conversations diagnosing Stephen and her own blindness to his fundamental problem.

"Regina said something interesting last night." Jane waited for her mother's full attention. "It was when we still believed Stephen had set the fire, granted. But anyway, she said it didn't seem as if he had a messiah complex so to speak. It isn't as if he thinks he is the first one, or even the second one who—"

"Why would he want to hurt the Jewish people?" Sylvia was anxious about the answer she might receive.

"Why would he want to clap his hands? What did he mean by that setup?" Alison directed attention to the dining-room table. Then she turned to Roger. "Right?"

"Isn't the point—at least his point—not why? The point is how do you help him." He giggled. "Not assist him, like an accomplice, of course. Get him helped."

Sylvia considered her flirtation with danger a failure; she was not convinced that accusations were not being withheld. She spoke very quietly. "I don't want my son committed. I won't let that happen, mark my words. It will be voluntary." She paused, soliciting dissent. She hoped this new consensus on the need for intervention might yet serve her aims. "I know he'll agree if it is presented correctly. By me. The psychiatric wing at the Berkshire Medical Center—Jones II—yesterday a report was sent to them by Dr. Daye. I haven't said anything to you . . . well, one holds out hope. It's very sad." Despite her instinct for self-preservation, she had come to sorrow over Stephen. "And, if I'm as frightened as I am, imagine him. Imagine being Stephen."

Roger put his arm around his wife. "What if he won't?"

"He will." Sylvia guessed no one would press the point. Each one had a horror-movie version of a forcible commitment to stifle further speculation. "I want to wait until tomorrow. This lunch has him so scared and frightened." The rabid consensus sparked defensiveness on Stephen's behalf; she was afraid he might be treated meanly. "I was given a form. For a voluntary—I don't want to say it again. I'd like to protect him, best we can."

"Where's Daddy, anyway?" Jane wanted to leave, call Regina for advice and information about the procedures involved in such a drastic decision. She did not think she could leave her mother alone.

"At work, but it's odd you should ask, Jane. What's interesting about your father in all this . . ." Sylvia limped toward the kitchen door, turned around immediately. She stood behind her chair, to stretch her legs. "He's cleaning up after himself. God love him, he'll be at it for a week."

"What about Dad? You were about to say something interesting about him?" Alison pressed Roger's pant leg, thigh to knee.

"He went to a meeting last night, an alcoholics meeting. He'd had a few when he heard about the fire. It's only relevant because I was reading—that Daye character might do well to read the things he gave me. They claim that mood swings—severe swings, what is known as manic-depressive mood swinging? Mood swings makes it all sound old-fashioned and harmless, doesn't it? Like whimsy."

"You think Daddy's got those?" Alison dragged her husband's arm down from her shoulders, held his hand.

Jane said, "Yes, well, we're all crazy here."

"No!" Sylvia reared her head back, mocking Alison's suggestion. "Some doctors believe they're genetically related. The genes for alcoholism and for manic-depression."

Jane absorbed this affirmation of lineage, displacing the elaborate theory Regina had forwarded, in which Martin Parris was cast as Stephen's father.

Alison thought of her two genetically endangered children, reacting to the information as a threat of violence against the girls. "I have to be home soon. The kids. I have to be aware; it's so easy to lose track of time."

Sylvia shrugged off her first foray into genetics. "It's easy to theorize."

"I can drop you home, Al." Jane stood, immediately sat. "We're not leaving you alone."

"I'll stay." Roger patted his and Alison's joined hands. He wanted to protect her, and at last he had his chance.

Sylvia assented to this plan with promises to call both daughters within the hour. While her three relations confusedly agreed upon a system for exchange of information,

Sylvia went to her room and found the form she figured she might have to sign for Stephen. When she completed her round trip, Roger helped her toward a chair. "I'm actually still mobile, Roger, but thank you." She waited till he sat, then walked to the front door, pressed her back against the cool glass. "Now, I'm not going to have you spending an entire afternoon holding *my* hand, Roger."

"It's nothing. I can call in to the office later."

"It's nothing, just like acting as his lawyer, shuttling your children here and there, and—it's anything but nothing. And you know that as well as I do."

"It's hardly worth discussing, Sylvia."

"Not until I think of something I can do to pay you back. But first things first. And I can only say this because, well, because exhaustion makes one shameless." She held up the pink form and shook it. "A witness is required. I don't want to ask the girls to do it. Maybe that's unfair." She flirted again with accusation. "Let's not mince words. I don't feel I would be perceived as entirely objective. I do seem to be a principal part of the problem."

"That's just crazy." Roger giggled, held up one hand. "I know, wrong word. But, Sylvia"—he edged forward on the divan to demonstrate compassion—"it does neither you nor Stephen any good to blame yourself. He's your son, and I know how we like to think we can control our kids and make it come out right. Don't do this to yourself."

She lowered the paper to her side.

"I don't mean you should be the witness. Not at all. Of course I'll come here when he's agreed to sign. I'm certain you're right, not involving Alison. Or Jane, for that matter."

"I wanted them both not to worry. Especially Alison. She's so apt to feel responsible." The facility with which she baited him shamed her into silence. She looked into the dining room and then managed to find more words. "I don't think he will sign if you are here, though, Roger. That's the problem as I see it now."

"He'll have to, in order for me to legally witness . . ." Her implication caught up with him. "He will have to, Sylvia. Sign in my presence."

"And if he won't? We wait until he does start a fire, or tries to hang himself? And then we let some doctor sign him up for the lifetime program?"

"The point of voluntary commitment is that he knows he needs attention. It's therapeutic, asking for help."

This speech recalled Parris's performance. "That had occurred to me, Roger. But we haven't always got the privilege of perfect options. I'm slowly learning that."

He was busy formulating this encounter as a story he could tell his wife. He couldn't cast it to elude her knee-jerk accusation of him and his overstimulated sense of legal niceties. Alison would fault him there, of course. "I actually think you can present it to him in a way Steve will . . . I'm convinced we can, or you can . . . I have his good in mind, I'm not standing on principles here. It's more of a law I'm up on. Don't you think you can elicit a consent?"

"The beauty of this whole process is just that, Roger. What a farce, really. What do you rate as his ability to consent to anything today? Tomorrow? It's absurd. Voluntary commitment. It's like self-abuse. You'd have to be crazy in the first place to do it, right? I'm sorry. I realize you didn't write the law." She folded the form. "I'm so afraid we'll lose him." This was true. Whatever part of Stephen she managed to preserve would be the remnant of her arcane, unrewarding faith. She cried to think that she might find, at last, no refuge from the life she had invented for herself.

Roger heard his wife, driven to defend Sylvia or Arthur by his unrelenting, unforgiving criticisms. *I can't say what you say I should say, Roger. I can't do what you say you'd do to them. I can't hurt them for the sake of being right.* "Is it worth a try? Before we break any laws, I mean?"

"I'll do it right now." She drew a pen from her skirt pocket. She didn't trust his sympathy to last. "I'll go in there. He'll listen, I think." She was prodding herself now. "I don't see any use in making up a speech in advance. I'll know what to say. It's the best I can offer him." This moved her.

Roger stood. His sense of propriety called for fair play, given the concession he had made. Already, he was certain he had promised nothing, only promised to consider. But even this revised agreement made him uneasy, considering his partner in this enterprise. He followed her until she stopped, just inches from the swinging door.

"You can listen from here, Roger." She was annoyed he didn't step away a bit. "I'll even get him to turn the water off. You'll hear every word. Please."

He took a backward step. "Of course. Oh yes, yes."

Sylvia knocked, then let herself in, closed the door. She found herself beside her son.

"I was spying. I heard every word you said. Even with the water on. Is he still there?"

She drew a quick breath. "Who?"

He backed up to the stove, spread his arms to hide the flames. "What's this about a witness? What's so bad about what you want me to do? What's a witness for, anyway? I been that bad?"

"Stephen? Bad?" He was ahead of her.

"I want you to be my witness." He drummed his fingers on the oven door. His voice betrayed him, breaking toward a higher register. "I'll say whatever you say. I'll do it, whatever it is. But you be my witness. Why are you so mad if I want to do what you say?"

"Mad? Stephen."

"Sign it, then," he whispered. "Sign the part that says you saw what I was doing and it was okay by you."

"I'll do it now, right over there. We'll go over to the table."

"Simon says, Don't move."

Sylvia obeyed.

"Not you, Mom! Me!" Her confusion convinced him he could not be heard. He banged his hands against the oven. "Just keeps getting worse."

Sylvia sat on the bench. She pressed out the fold and flattened the page with her left hand. "I am doing this to prove how much I love you. Do you hear me, son?"

"Okay, okay, okay. Are you the witness yet?"

She poised the pen, but watched him turn away. She didn't move. She had her heart in hand and choked it off just as he grabbed the bald, red, glowing centers of two burners. He pulled them slowly off the stove and raised them high above his head, like free weights pressed against the law of gravity. She held herself in place, displaying even greater strength. She was beyond even Stephen now. She had time to spare, to wonder how he managed yet to stand, and wordlessly. At last, he howled and she saw the door swing open. Then she signed his name as if it were her own.

Roger knelt as Stephen's legs gave way, then screamed his name.

Stephen's open mouth gave out no sound.

Sylvia saw his hands still tight around cast-iron burners and she screamed, revived and horrified. She dived to the floor and crept to him, pushed Roger's flailing hands away, pulled the twitching body of her son into her stronger arms. Her fingers cupped beneath his chin registered a pulse. She held on to his jaw and with her free hand wiped the sheet of sweat off Stephen's face. "He's breathing." She reached for his left hand.

Sitting on the floor, his head and shoulders hard against the oven door, Roger screamed, "They're hot!"

She held the metal, pried his fingers loose. The center rings had bored into his palms, so she tugged gently, peeled away one burner without plucking off the enormous puff of purple skin. She reached for Stephen's other hand. "Roger, you're in shock. Stand up and drink some water."

Miraculously, he found he could obey.

She worked the second hand free of the impressed iron. "The table, Roger." She looked up at him. "We have to go now. He needs help." She screamed, "Now!"

Roger hopped, lifted by her voice. But he didn't move again. He efficiently rejected as a symptom of his mental shock the absurd idea that she was ordering him to sit down and sign his name. "I'll call the police? Or should we drive?"

Stephen was whimpering. Sylvia whispered, bowed her head toward his and blew softly on his face. She laid his hands on her lap, hoping to relieve the pain a bit. She turned to Roger. "You haven't seen enough yet?" She grunted, thrust her head, and raised herself up to her bruised knees, her arms still bracketed around her son's electric body.

Roger understood this as a threat. He believed she was capable of dropping Stephen's body to the floor, just to impress him.

"I can't stand up." Sylvia was irate Roger hadn't sense enough to help her stand. "Help me, Roger. Help me, please!"

Roger scrawled his name and began to fold the form. He was jerked to the floor. Sylvia had crept to his side. Without a word she rolled the cool and nervous body into his arms. She took the form, completing the transaction. He followed her to his car in the drive, laid Stephen on the backseat. "I can't drive."

She held her hand out. "Give me the keys. Check pockets, Roger. In your pants?" She grabbed his leather key case. "Get in the back now. On the floor, if there's no room. Hold his head and get his hands above his heart. You understand. His hands have to be held higher than his body. You know how." She ran around the car and within seconds they were moving. "Keep his hands high, Roger. Brace his head. You can do that, Roger, right?"

"I think I've got him. I'm okay." He couldn't shut up, frightened as he was. "He's breathing little bits and there is some color in his face. He's gonna be all right, I know he is. I know he will be fine. I'm so sorry. When I thought you wanted me to sign and all, even at the same time I knew it was not you caring about forms. I had it on the mind. You were lifting him all by yourself, what with his hands and all."

"Roger! Roger, honey, that's enough. Listen to me, son. It's just five minutes more and we'll be at the hospital with the doctors. Stephen, can you hear me? You can hear me. Oh my God, your hands." She saw him, backed by fire at the stove; she watched him turn and reach and turn and reach until she could not tolerate the sight. He had impressed her more than any man had ever done. She couldn't sound the depths he'd opened in her. Neither her despair nor intermittent doubts he was alive at all in Roger's arms could sound the depths. "You can hear me, son. You can hear me and we're going to get better. You just rest now, baby. I've got faith enough for both of us, you'll see. You hear me. You've got someone here who loves you. You can't help but just be better."

But he would need her help.

The blue and white flames strobed again. She saw Stephen turn again and reach, but this time, and forever, she could see it all, see herself react before he turned completely, watch her body bolt instinctively to save her son, feel her weakened knees give way and drop her to the floor, short of Stephen, helpless as he grabbed the burners, raised them up triumphantly, and then collapsed.

When Stephen woke, he would have to live with this, his history.

Third Trimester

A SILLY, GENTLE MAN walks Pittsfield's well-lit streets by night. Others dream. He isn't mindful of the city's centuries. He doesn't mourn the spring receding with its promises in tow. He heads for daylight with two safety pins, twelve bottle caps, a yellow rose barrette, eight pennies, and a length of copper wire.

He has an age, but it is indeterminate—well beyond the rightful age for his uncrenulated skin and silk-cord-muscle step, and short by five or ten the years a person ought to live before his hair begins to shine, white, fading toward translucence. He lost his name, or else succumbed to popular demand for local legend; today, he's known as O.B. Joyful. No one speaks to him, except polite, astonished children who will mutter, "Thank you, sir," and run to ask their mothers why the old man said they'd lost the roofing nails and coins he pressed upon them.

"That's O. B. Joyful," mothers say, pleased to have an opportunity to teach the youngsters history and its lessons. Depending on the neighborhood, and vagaries of mothers' moods and dispositions, another generation comes to terms with O.B. Joyful, no-account or celebrated poet incognito: descendant of Thoreau, town drunk, half-Mohawk Indian, or Harvard-educated black sheep of a ranking Berkshire family; resident of Balance Rock, molester, herbivore, deaf mute, or warlock; millionaire, pauper, or the coot who keeps a beaver as a pet.

"He's crazy if he thinks I'm gonna wear a mask." Jane twirls a patch of gauze above her head, holding to the cotton laces.

Sylvia waves a hand behind her back. She's squatting near the foot of Jane's bed, watching Dr. Cahill through a window screen. "Keep your voice down, Jane. He isn't gone."

"At least you'd think he'd buy a car. Admit it, Mom. A grown-up doctor on a bike is loco. You know who he looks

268 *Mother of God*

like? He looks like O.B. Joyful." Jane's implication here is sinister. The story she inherited involves elaborate schemes by which the white-haired wanderer offed several wealthy wives. In his ironic and abbreviated name, the "B." is short for Bluebeard. "I think I deserve a real doctor. I am ill."

"Stop it." The illuminated fenders of the doctor's bicycle disappear. "He's more doctor than the most of them. If you would get down off your high horse for a minute, you might realize how fortunate we are Dr. Cahill is willing to go on treating you and your sister. Some pediatricians wouldn't bother." She sits near Jane's knees on the bed. "I know you don't feel well." She grabs the mask, examines it. "Lord knows, you've made that clear to all of us this week."

"You heard him, I'm infectious. Give me my mask." She knots it into place, pleased when she hears her muffled voice. "Shouldn't Alison sleep somewhere else?"

"Please stop doing that with your voice. And I forbid you telling Alison about all this. She isn't going to get mononucleosis. You heard the doctor."

Jane says, "What Alison doesn't know might hurt her," but Sylvia cannot make out the words. "I'm still going to the J.M.S."

"Either take the damned mask off or don't try to have a conversation. It's getting on my nerves." Sylvia moves to the matching bed a few feet from her daughter.

Jane unties the laces, leaves the mask to flap and shift as she enunciates her vow. "I am go-ing to the Coun-try Club Jun-ior Mem-bers Soi-ree next Sa-tur-day."

"If you're well enough to dance, you're well enough to vacuum and clean your room. Dr. Cahill said only bed rest will help."

"What do you think I am do-ing?" Jane holds her body stiff and speaks mechanically. "I am rest-ing. Am I or am I not?"

"Keep it up, young lady. You'll dance a merry tune."

Jane is not courting her mother's temper to amuse herself. She is seeking intervention. She wants parental law to arbitrate against her date with Ronald Clary. She feels he's served her well, proof positive of social viability, even if he is a year behind her at St. Joseph's High. "Am I sup-posed to wait un-til it is next June and I have the Jun-ior prom to go to? Is Ron sup-posed to wait?"

Sylvia refuses to answer the stuttering.

Jane sucks the gauze, administers a practice French kiss. She knows a boy's tongue in her mouth would be much worse.

"You'll have to call the Clary boy and tell him, Jane. I know it must be disappointing. It won't help, but I promise you, there will be other dances. Don't do that with your mouth. You'll catch a cold on top of all of this if the mask is wet."

"All right, already." Jane draws the mask across her brow and ties it as a hairband. "I'll call him up tonight."

"You could ask him over." Sylvia regrets the failure of the first and long-awaited full-fledged date. "Show him the poem you're working on."

"I showed you 'cause you promised. . . . Ron Clary couldn't care less about the Diocesan Poetry League. He's got the country club. Anyway, you're going to jinx the contest talking to everyone about it." Jane is pleased to have her mother's full attention for the moment. She wouldn't mind if all July and August passed this way, herself in bed, her mother stopping by with trays of food for literary conversations. "It *is* a sonnet. I made up my mind."

"You're good at those. I think the judges will appreciate you trying to . . . poetry ought to have a form, I think. It makes it more like science."

"And music. Here's the thing, though. Don't tell anyone. But listen. A sonnet, right, is supposed to have just fourteen lines, but fourteen exactly. Right?" She rolls onto her side, to face her mother, "Mine will have only thirteen. There's a missing line, at the end. The couplet—that's the two lines at the end that rhyme?"

"The couplet? Right. But why not two lines there?" Sylvia's

dim interest in poetics is supplemented by a renewed commitment to her family. When she leaves Arthur, marries Martin,
she will need a strong alliance with the girls.

"Since it's about a dying young girl—too young to die, you
see? Cut off from life before her proper time." Jane rolls her
eyes, the only gesture her exhausted body will allow for a release of pleasure. "And the title. I even have the title now."

"I know. I swear myself to secrecy upon my father's grave.
What is it?"

"It's my best poem yet. I think this being sick is good for
something. The title is"—Jane needs a long intake of air to
calm herself—" 'Save the Last Line for Me.' Wait till you
read it. It's a real poem, like you might read in a book."

"Oh, Jane. It's wonderful." Sylvia bends and pulls the mask
from Jane's grooved and greasy hair. She holds the mask
against her mouth. "Won-der-ful." She folds the mask into
her palm. "It's sad and funny both." She's broken through the
pretext of her patient bedside vigil, or maybe Jane has pulled
her through. They've made it back together.

But Sylvia cannot relax, indulge the luxury of still and simple moments. She moves ahead, bounding from the point of
contact with her daughter to the month or year of Martin's
reappearance. This separates her from the minor tragedy of
Ronald Clary, whom she figures hasn't brains enough to comprehend his loss. She guesses Martin knows a more sophisticated class of people, maybe Europeans, whose teenage sons
or nephews—young, serious, dark-suited men, all willing to
convert to a more popular religion—will have a way with
words.

Having watched her mother slip away again, Jane lets herself retreat to sleep.

A sudden breeze infests the elms and lifts the dotted-Swiss
curtains from the sill. Sylvia stands up to test the nighttime
temperature against her body, the indicator she will use to
mark the proper warmth of milk before a midnight feeding.
The air incites no chill, so Jane is safe. The humid July sweetness seems more salve than threat, in fact; just what a less

prosaic doctor would have ordered. She tucks the mask into a pocket of her skirt.

Cultivated curiosity hastens her descent; she's after explanation for the shuffling of papers she hears each time she approaches Arthur lately.

Arthur holds his hands atop a stack of magazines. "Just paging through some more Spectronics information. Seems to be a pretty healthy business, Mrs. Marshall's laser magazine."

"Well, lasers. A person can hardly live without one these days."

Arthur reaches with his far arm, alerting Sylvia to Alison, who's curled into the corner of the divan, hidden by her father's body.

Alison senses Arthur needs defending. She lifts up the latest issue of the magazine he gave her. "This new job Dad got is swell, much better than the General Electric. They've got things in here for laboratories and maybe space explorers. How come we never got this magazine before?"

Sylvia knows there is something noble in her younger daughter's recent ministrations to her father's pride. But she cannot tolerate the form it takes. Her impulse is to wedge them far apart. She will not credit Arthur's exoneration of their proximity of late. He says they don't have such an easy time saying what they feel. "Where is Lisa Revillio, Alison? You two finished playing early tonight. It won't be summer forever."

"I'd rather read. She's retarded, anyway. Says her dad made a laser. She's just jealous. Daddy says her father can't even start a fire in the grill. Look at this one." Alison displays a full-page advertisement for an electro-optic vacuum process. "Supposed to be a vacuum, I guess. Is it for eyeglasses, Daddy?"

Arthur reaches back and pulls his daughter in against his side, then drops his head against her shoulder, reading the small print aloud.

"Stop it, Alison. Of course it's not a vacuum cleaner for eyeglasses. Don't act as if you understand nothing. It's not attractive. And I hope the dinner dishes have been dried and put away."

"Jeez Louise. I wish I'd get a contagious disease." Unable to untangle shame and anger, she hands the magazine to Arthur, whimpers, "Save my place," then runs into the kitchen. Sylvia has made her cry, but indirectly. She can withstand a sudden scolding, but she can't accept her father's failure to provide defense.

"I'm quick with her, I know." Sylvia says so mechanically, to defuse Arthur's indignation.

"You must be tired." He squares the edges of his pile with his palms. "Have a seat, why don't you?" He pats a cushion as an invitation. "How's Jane? Doctor seemed to think the bed rest would do it for her."

"Why isn't Artie home from the game yet? It's after nine." She belatedly accepts his offer of a place to sit.

"I suppose maybe the game ran late?" Ever sporting, tactful Arthur, always shagging balls from deepest left field. "You feel all right tonight?" He savors this, the one invasion he allows himself. He speaks the same words nightly, after stern reminders of the need to find the right, apologetic tone of voice, to make it clear he hates to pry and yet he doesn't mean to shy away from duties he'll inherit in the absence of the father.

"No major changes to report since last time you checked in. I'm fine. And Insulum? Is it all cleaned up yet?"

On to serve and volley; Arthur's ready with his backhand. "Another day or two. I give myself till then. It's an awful lot to digest. I don't want to be corralled into another bad decision."

"Is that what you were burying just now? Before I came into the room?" She eyes the pile. "You must have memorized it all by now. It won't clean itself up."

Arthur hates this euphemism she's adopted, as if he's dirty. "I like to know what I'm signing."

"Oh for God's sake, Arthur. Since when?" His obdurate position fuels more than her frustration. The disproportion in his caution, which she measures against reckless willingness to sign his name to patent applications and a host of other legal forms, defies all logic. His irrational behavior distends the close, familiar boundaries of their interactions, and such inflated contours easily accommodate her misplaced faith in Martin.

"It is my name, Sylvia."

"A name you've been kind enough to share. I don't think Mr. Mortimer is likely to forget you haven't signed them."

They do not tire of this dance, the abstracted ballet of their embattled marriage. Artie slips into the kitchen, late again. He takes his place against the narrow stretch of wall beside the threshold to the living room. Experience has taught him that his awkward words of solace are of no use to his sister Alison. Even if he puts away the dishes, she won't tell him why she's sulking, she won't be coaxed out of the alcove. She points a finger at the copper-kettle wall clock and all but shuts her eyes before she turns her face toward him. His scheme of incremental tardiness is thus recorded. His sister's silent accusation is the only vestige of his role as a featured performer in the artful orchestration of complicity and compromise that is family life. It is not sufficient. Artie knows he is no longer the object of parental love and worry. So he choreographs his own entrances and exits and his brief and graceless onstage appearances. Some days he hangs back, standing in the wings, memorizing the repetitive and circumscribed steps that fall to the man cast in the role of the father.

Artie waits until his mother says "That's perfect, Arthur" or words he recognizes as a prelude to a protracted standoff. Then he shuffles toward the stairs and yawns, says something to remind his parents Alison is lurking in the wings. He means this to imply he has an alibi documenting his arrival in advance of the curfew limit. It wins him easy passage, without fail. But its effectiveness is as recrimination, as if he'd said, "We heard every word again."

Each member's guilt, or fear of full exposure, guarantees complicit observation of eviscerated family rites.

Even Ronald Clary's unannounced arrival, two days after Jane received her mask, incites no particular concern, though Sylvia wonders if her daughter's illness soon will be reported as an invention, another symptom of the family's fear of being seen in public. The house is big enough—if just—to accommodate a tantrum or a few days' private mourning, which follows on the rare intruder from the outside world.

"I'll tell Jane you are here. Have a seat."

The too-tall red-haired boy screws up his courage, opting for the spacious sofa, hoping Jane will take the hint. He hears the tenor of an argument above, which he assumes is his fault. He guesses Jane is now afraid to let herself be seen in her unkempt, early Saturday disguise. This he counts as an advantage. He needs some leverage to convince her they should travel to the dance next week with his best friend, whom Jane refers to as "the big dope with the ears."

"Ron?" Jane speaks before she is in view. "I'm sick. Mononucleosis." Just as she steps down onto the carpet, she sees that she is barefoot.

"The kissing disease, right, Jane?" Alison scoots from the kitchen to the dining room, back toward her hideout in the kitchen. "Hello, Ronny. Goodbye, Jane."

Ron is on his feet. "Hello, Alison. Jane?"

"Ignore her. She broke her leash." Jane takes to a chair beneath the mantel, several yards from Ron. "I'm contagious."

Ron does not doubt this. He steps back, bumps the divan, steps around the arm. "Wow." This applies both to the condition of her hair and to her arrival in a knee-length bathrobe. "You must be sick as a dog. What happened?"

Jane jettisons her prepared apology. "It's the latest fashion fad. I quit washing my hair. Don't you like it? It's catching on."

"I mean, I'm real sorry for you. What about the dance?" He is appalled by her apparent unconcern for the practical problem she poses to his plans. "You just figure on staying sick till then?"

"I happen to have mononucleosis. It takes forever to get better. I said I'm sorry, didn't I?"

"This is really not good. Wow. This may be bad." Ron knows well this brief trip to wit's end. He has both hands atop his head. "What about your sister? You think she'd go with me?"

Alison braces both hands against the alcove table.

Sylvia straightens her arms, pushing her breasts off the banister upstairs.

"She's an eighth-grader!" Jane is awake for the first time in a week.

"She's gonna be a freshman in September. Not as a date, I mean, as friends." Ron is oblivious to the implicit insult. He's defending his integrity. "You gotta admit she's pretty. She always says hello to me. She might say yes."

"You can't ask my sister on a date." Jane is certain his idea flouts several rules of social conduct.

"I know she's just a kid." He sees no refuge but retreat. "I was joking, just a joke. I just wanted to see what you'd say."

Jane speaks for Alison and Sylvia when she says, "I know a joke when I hear one. Why don't you just go with your best friend there, Mr. Ears?"

"It was a joke."

"It was not."

"Can't you even take a joke?"

"Why don't you just find a date who gets your jokes, then, if that's all you want." Jane does not find any excuse to sink into a less excited state unwelcome. "I'm sorry. I guess maybe you should just leave. I'm catching."

"All right, then. I'm real sorry we can't go together, though. Say you believe it was a joke." He hangs by the door, actually expecting a reprieve.

"Get lost." Jane restrains her reflex to stand before he leaves. Alone, she appreciates the spacious room, the unobstructed vantage it provides of intermittent street life, and the embracing contours of the chair.

"He leave?" Alison sits on the lowest stair. "What a creep." She'll say anything to hear about the boy who asked her out. "I wouldn't go with him to the biggest ball in town."

Jane relinquishes her claim on social life. She sees now as

she figures Ron must see: the unaggressive posture of a blond and quiet girl with shoulders small enough to get an arm around, a habit of locating herself just below the object of her interest, a knack for crying, no offending features, and a smile for the asking. "You are pretty, you know. But you can do much better than any Ron Clary."

"Are you sad, Jane?" Alison is stunned by the display of goodwill. "Aren't you mad he asked me out?"

"He didn't quite ask you out, Alison."

"He would've, if you'd let him. I mean, I'd have said no, even if he didn't ask you first."

"Alison? Are you deaf? He said it was a joke." Jane stands, driven to her bed. "You're so gullible."

Sylvia steps quickly to her bedroom. The failure of her daughters to achieve a lasting peace is not a situation she can rectify. But Jane's bad luck with boys does seem to be worsening. And Ronald Clary sounded an alarm, a warning bell alerting everyone to Alison's impending debut as a teen. Time is not benign. The hollow hope she holds for Martin is her only place of safety in the claustrophobic home. The house is crowded, and bruises are no longer rare. Her faith in his return acquires a peculiar aspect of benevolence just now: If nothing's done on Holmes Road soon, there's bound to be a damaging collision.

The Adamskis do their best to minimize the accidental injuries. The children tend not to issue invitations to their few but loyal friends. Sylvia turns down an offer of a baby shower, extended on behalf of the "trio at Sodality," by Mary Traponi. But morbid curiosity drives Sylvia and Arthur to an open house next door. Dorothy hosts without the help of Mitch, her handsome husband hovering about in photographic shrines adorned with mounted brass and silver medals, commendation letters from the Speaker of the House, as well as postcards written in a perfect Palmer hand.

Teresa Revillio approaches Sylvia, who pretends to read a letter issued on behalf of "the Kennedy brothers, to the brave men of Berkshire." Teresa hasn't spoken to her best friend in the neighborhood since Mrs. Barker died. "No evidence of the old girl."

"Teresa. Why, hello." Sylvia fits her empty glass in among a field of standing frames. "What's new with you? It's been a while, hasn't it?" Her fast and too-high speaking voice is a parody of false excitement. "Very little new on our side, what with the baby—you know all about that, though. And, from what I'm told, you even bothered to let everyone else know as soon as possible. So sweet of you."

"Sylvia! Don't tell me you thought you might keep it a secret? You're showing." Teresa hesitantly credits Sylvia's bad manners to the pregnancy. "I had to come today. The place still spooks me."

"You mean poor Madeline Barker and the way she died? Dorothy?" Sylvia bellows the name, which acts upon the small crowd as a muffle. "Can you make it this way for a moment, dear?" She waits until their hostess is beside Teresa. "Of course, you know your eastern neighbor, Teresa Revillio. She was just asking me about your mother, Dorothy. What is it you were wondering, Teresa?"

Teresa successfully resists the urge to scream Sylvia's name. This occupies her for the moment.

Dorothy is keen to repair the past. "It was a shock. I can't tell you how I wish she hadn't had to go and die in the backyard. You two were so amazingly composed. I have to tell you, God rest her soul, she wasn't in the best of shape. You know. Up here." Dorothy points a finger at her head. "A cranky neighbor can be hard, I know, with children." She rescinds her finger, then lifts a hand to either shoulder, works her thumbs into her pleated epaulettes. "I say, soon as Mitch gets back from Indochina—where'll they send them next? The moon, I guess. Anyway, I say, me and Mitch? We'll do our part for the American family, if you get my drift."

"Drift? You're looking at an avalanche." Sylvia pats her stomach, annoyed with Dorothy for spoiling her exit with her imperturbable good nature.

Dorothy's hands leave their nests and flutter toward Sylvia, flapping dismissively. "Who can blame you? Pardon me, but your Art ought to have a whole brood. He ought to be on television, far as I can tell."

"Let's hope not." Sylvia is not grateful for the indirect suggestion of her husband as a story on the network news.

"Not that your Phil isn't . . . well, Teresa, you don't take offense at anything."

"Not among friends, Dorothy." Teresa directs this at Sylvia, through Dorothy, to jolt her old friend back to form.

Tapping Dorothy's shoulder, Sylvia completes the circuit. "As my own mother used to say, When among strangers, check your hat; when among friends, check your purse. Where's Arthur got to?" She walks away, ushers Arthur toward the door.

Teresa does not follow her old friend. Obligingly, she submits herself to a review of Mitch's seven-year career with the Marines. Sylvia's performance leaves her feeling queer. She isn't put off by an innuendo of misconduct or even blurted accusations of betrayal. It's the scripted quality of Sylvia's delivery that most affects her. Their casual relations hardly merit the dramatics. If Sylvia is waiting for a formal letter of apology, Teresa thinks, as Mitch receives his first promotion, it'll be one hell of a wait.

By shedding friends and social obligations, Sylvia relieves the pressure in her shrunken sphere, but only temporarily. Before the end of August, the child she is carrying is a distinct and burdensome presence. Her bulkiness embarrasses the children. She has to back into the alcove. Every time she bends to look inside the oven, or stops and counts the stairs she's yet to climb, she is appalled by her own weakness. Several visits to the doctor do not satisfy her curiosity about the child's penchant for migrating well beyond the boundaries familiar as her womb. At night, it wiggles toward one hip, threatening to break out through her skin. The unhelpful explanation she offers to her frightened husband does nothing to assuage her, either. "It's too alive, Arthur. It feels like a boy, but a grown boy, two or three years old." This only restores to Arthur his invented, cinematic memory of little Martin squirming on his wife.

The low-level, constant buzz of worry for her unborn child drives Sylvia's determination to impose a perfect order on the routine household operations. Stray socks, an unmade bed, or even slight resistance to a preplanned trip to procure uniforms and school supplies earn Alison and Artie several afternoons in their respective bedrooms. Alison is apt to cry on these occasions. The stricter, new regime demands a standard she cannot achieve. Her misery at being singled out for an infraction is compounded by the certainty that soon enough another feature of her hygiene or her grooming will be judged a failure.

Artie, too, anticipates the worst. So, he smuggles to his bedroom a book of dirty jokes, some comics, and a sampling of the cookies from the family larder. He is no victim when he's banished to his bedroom. He's the mayor of Fat City. If he is released for dinner, he acts beleaguered and admonished. The immediate gratification of playing two adults for chumps is transmuted over time into a more sophisticated pleasure. While imprisoned in his rather cushy isolation cell, he can force his parents back together. He sees them as the mean but inattentive wardens of a sly and hardened inmate, the sort of guy who runs a gambling ring from his oppressive prison-movie cell.

This plot line leads inevitably to escape. And when Artie finally claims a greater distance from this house, the space between his parents will seem inconsequential. With wary backward glances he'll see his mother and his father, apparently together.

Though she is deemed well enough to resume light housekeeping chores, Jane wins an exemption from her mother's aggravated rigor. She credits her poetry for this envied, special status.

By the end of August, Sylvia has ironed out the wrinkled schedules of summer. Two days before the school year starts, Arthur reminds her of the matter of their dirty linen. "I stopped by at the GE this afternoon, Sylvia."

"I don't suppose you've finally cleaned up the whole mess, once and for all?"

"I went to see Allen Drecker. He's in public relations—which is Jonty Mortimer's territory, or at least it's supposed to be. Allen claims he hasn't heard anything, not a word. He'd know if they were about to market it."

"I have two skirts to hem and I don't know what you mean by 'market it.' Market what? You mean, advertise your failure to make a clean break with the company?"

"Insulum. I can't understand it. I don't know, I just can't stand to think it's going to just sit there, never used."

"Arthur? Has it not occurred to you they may be proceeding with their case against you? As we speak. It has occurred to me. Did Mr. Drecker tell you Jonty had withdrawn the suit? I'm sure Mrs. Marshall would be terribly impressed to see you up on charges. Arthur? What are you waiting for? You want miracles, I suppose. You, who can't even see his way clear to go to Sunday Mass with his family?"

From the far end of the divan, he can see she is right. He also sees she has become unnaturally huge; with her legs on the coffee table, her hands immobile on her stomach, she looks unflappable. "I thought going there would do it, put me over the edge, that I would sign the affidavit and be done with them. If I was sure they wouldn't prosecute—but how can I be sure?" He knows the question is rhetorical. He doesn't want an answer; he wants Sylvia to make the question go away.

"You have their word." She sees his disappointment; her unimaginative response is not what she has taught him to expect.

"Martin Parris is back there now. At the General Electric. They've given him a job." It is a shameless prompt. Arthur twists his mouth into a querulous smile.

The news does not surprise her. She admires Martin's wiles. And she knows Martin is as good as his word; he promised Arthur would be spared. "Arthur, you can imagine, I hope, how awkward this is for me. And I know I'm not up to . . . well, all the details, sordid and otherwise. But, well, take my

word on this. No one's coming after you. I can guarantee it, if
you sign. . . . Well, you have my word."

This establishes the terms of faith, for Arthur and for Sylvia.
As long as Arthur is not served with papers, Martin's word is
good and so is hers.

Sylvia believes she has negotiated wisely. The tacitly adopted
contract acknowledges her ties to Parris. She interprets this as
insurance. She can delay arrangements with her silent partner.
Her option won't expire.

Presently, she can't sustain her romantically expectant posture. She must concentrate on carrying to term. Her due date
is October 23, but she is not convinced she can withhold her
eager, volatile child.

After a week of petulant resistance, the children quietly submit to early morning breakfasts and the other rigors of the
school year. Sylvia ranges round her home, preparing checks
for monthly bills for both September and October, muttering
about the geniuses at Corning Glass who make it possible for
her to bake and freeze a week's supply of casseroles and stews
in serving dishes that Arthur can return directly to the oven.
Midmorning, the last Tuesday of September, while she paws
around in Arthur's closet, searching for the little yellow suitcase she has carried to St. Luke's with every child, she spots
the crinkled, stained manila folder in which Arthur's overdue
confession still resides.

It intrigues her, as might a photograph of Arthur with a
group of people she has never met. She recognizes him—in
fact, the likeness is astonishing. Still, she can't resolve the
context. Is it a part of his life he would rather hide or is it
insignificant, a misplaced memento of his wasted youth?

She takes it to the kitchen, lays it on the counter, opens the
underlying drawer. She pulls out a blue steel combination-lock
cigar box. The lock was busted years ago, the first time Jane
was left to babysit her brother. It was a tandem crime; Artie
held the screwdriver, Jane hammered it into the catch, expecting to expose a wad of cash or secret adult tools and
games. Now, as ever, the box safeguards nothing more exotic

than the mortgage on the house and term-insurance policies on every family member.

Sylvia studies Arthur's uneccentric signature, though she has often signed his name to checks and credit applications. With a ballpoint pen one of the children left beside the sink with several wide-rule sheets of paper, she draws a suitably dramatic "A" on the generous line of hyphens Jonty's typist made for Arthur. She follows with a fairly accurate rendition of his name.

She immediately regrets the thoughtless, hasty choice of blue ink, where black would be appropriate. Worse, she feels the operation was a bit of whimsy, where ceremony would have better served her.

Her disappointment in the aftermath is complicated by the child's drumming. Aloud, to recover something of the pleasure she relinquished to expedience, she says, "It's official. Congratulations, one and all."

Unsatisfied, she circles through the downstairs twice. Inspiration spares her a third pass. She dials Ellen at the GE switchboard, asks to speak to Martin Parris. "Hello, Ellen. Let him know it's me, Sylvia Adamski."

"This is Martin Parris's line. May I ask who is calling?" Martin whispers, which only heightens interest at the nearby desks.

"Martin?" Sylvia laughs at his inadequate disguise.

"No, this is Harmon. This is Stephen Harmon."

Sylvia giggles, teased by her own confusion. She can't decide if Martin is being coy or if he intends to carry off this ruse. "*Who* is it? This is Sylvia Adamski speaking."

"Stephen Harmon. Mr. Parris is away for several weeks." He is staring at the tiny months of a laminated two-year calendar, the border of his unblemished cardboard blotter.

"Really." Sylvia pauses, still happily imbalanced. "Really? Stephen Harmon. Can I trust you, Stephen Harmon? Are you a close friend of Martin's?"

Martin's humiliation seeps through his badly acted impatience. "Is there a message?"

The unflattering motive for his absurd behavior is lost on her. She is amazed by his puerile dedication to the blatantly unsuccessful scam. "You might tell Mr. Parris he can alert Mr. Mortimer. The papers are signed. Really, Martin."

He concedes, restoring volume to his voice. But he will not engage in conversation. "Jonty Mortimer's office has a telephone."

Before she can assimilate his return to normalcy, Arthur's car rolls up into the drive. "Speak of the devil. I can't speak now either." In her eagerness to end the conversation, she supplies Martin with a similar motive. "I won't call you again. At the office. Oh . . . oh well. That's all."

Arthur lifts up a bag. She can't suppress residual laughter, even staring at the open folder on the counter.

"Hello, dear. I thought maybe lunch?" Arthur shakes the white bag. "Sandwiches, and chips, and extra pickles—just for the heck of it."

It's accidental, but he's gotten through to her; something in his still expectant voice, the paper bag, the pleasure of proximity to his reliable and prepossessing body.

She is crying as she shoos him toward the living room. She brings the folder. "It just seemed like this was my job, in the end. So I signed it. That is the truth. I just up and signed it. You can burn it, if you like. Thank you, Arthur, for the lunch."

"Oh, you found it! I've spent about a week emptying my desk out every day at work. They're gonna think I'm crazy up in Dalton. I didn't know what I was going to do. How could I say I lost it? What do you mean, burn it? Oh! You signed my name. Now, that looks good. It's a great job, Sylvia. Just like I'd signed it myself." His relief is compounded by the intimacy her forgery suggests.

"I was getting out my yellow suitcase—"

"Already? Like, today?"

"Advance planning. You know me."

"I'll drop this by to Jonty on my way out this afternoon. It'll be all cleaned up, finally." He puts the folder on the floor, beside his blazer.

"I don't really know what got into me, thinking it was up to me to sign it, before—"

"Before I lost it again. Sylvia, listen, I don't think anyone at GE is going to care if Alison signed it. Just another folder for their files, right? I'm getting me a glass of water. You?"

"Right. Yes. I can get it, though."

"You sit and eat. A pickle, maybe?"

His return is not sufficient in itself to interrupt the silence she courted in his absence. Not even casual assessments of the choice of sandwiches are issued to interrupt the quiet lunch. Fifteen minutes reimagining her abortive chat with Martin, and she is years away. She berates herself for being dull and self-possessed, instead of catching on to Martin's coy flirtation. She's sure it was a joke. After the baby leaves her body, she will get her humor back. A woman has to learn to take a joke.

Arthur speaks her name three times without success. He scrunches up the paper bag, disposing of the four half-sours.

"What, Arthur? Me?"

"Just, did you want more water, maybe? I should be heading out."

"No, nothing. Lunch was lovely."

"You feel all right today?"

"No drastic changes to report."

"Well, never mind. You stay right there and finish up your sandwich." He bends to grab the folder and his blazer, kisses her still uncombed hair. "You know where to reach me."

The temptation to call Martin fades as she stands up. The child has been still since Arthur's arrival. The heft of it has changed. She feels it deeper, lower. She dismisses her ascendant panic as benign confusion, brought on by the unfamiliar comfort she's achieved. "We'll give Mr. Parris a call after we've got you on your feet. Agreed? Now, let's pack that suitcase."

She finishes her packing, despite the spiraling of her suspicion that the child isn't well. Uncertain on the stairs, she is glad to have her suitcase; the child's weight has been displaced inside her and she can't rectify the balance. She sets the suitcase near the back door, goes to the counter, dials Ellen at the switchboard once again. "Give me Mr. Mortimer. Jonty Mortimer, please. I don't have the number, but I know he has a telephone. It's terribly important." She senses that her child's near enough to birth to merit reassurances. She breathes deeply, reminds the fetus it is weeks before the due date, that the ruckus is a false alarm, a too-old mother out of practice.

"Mortimer."

"It's my husband, Mr. Mortimer. I wanted to speak to him."

"Might I ask who is calling?"

"Let's not play games. This is Sylvia Adamski."

"Hello, Sylvia."

"Arthur. Is he there? Are you awake? Is Arthur there?"

"Mrs. Adamski, please. He was here not fifteen minutes ago, but I am afraid—"

"He's gone." The child moves, not fighting to get out but rolling listlessly. "For God's sake, just say it. He's not there."

"He's not here. Are you all right?"

"Of course he's not there. The goddamn car. This is what I get. Lunch but no car."

"Should I send someone by? Could I help . . ."

Sylvia stares at the receiver, which she has laid down on the counter. Ignoring Jonty's shouting, she cuts the connection, calls the operator. "This is absurd. My name is Sylvia and I need a cab, I think."

"Hello, may I help you?"

Sylvia hangs up the telephone. She estimates the time of a round trip to Dalton and eliminates Arthur from her calculations.

"Hi, Mom. I'm home."

"Jane! Come here, sweetie. On the double."

"What is it?"

"Come here when you're called!"

"I'm here." Jane stops several feet short of her mother. "You're gonna have it, aren't you? You gonna do it now?"

"Not if I can help it. Find the telephone book. Call a taxi."

"You're amazing. You're so calm. I'll get the phone book." Jane drops two notebooks on the floor. "Can you move? I don't mind, but the book is in the drawer. Is it bad to move?"

"Let's see." She can move without pain. She sidles toward the sink, holding to the counter. "I can't believe it's time."

Jane is stunned with admiration. "How far apart are they?"

"The taxi, Jane. What?"

"The contractions. Don't you use a clock or something? Any taxi company. Who cares which one? I'll dial now."

Sylvia is laughing, recognizing her own trick of speaking to rouse herself to action. "Address. Make sure you tell him our address. And I'm pregnant, and I think he better hurry."

"On the double, mister! She's just about ready to have a baby." Jane slams down the telephone. "Sit? Or stand? I'll get the bag. Same one you used for Artie."

"I'm not having contractions. The baby moved today. It's lying, or it seems to be, on its back. That isn't very likely, is it? Head to toe, right across the bottom here, from hip to hip?"

"I'm going with you. Think of all the calls I can make from the hospital. Be there any minute. You a little scared, too?"

"We'll take it easy, get ourselves out front. I can use you if I need some help just walking. Let's make this easy on ourselves, real slow." Sylvia leads Jane around to the front door, avoiding stairs.

"I got the door. Here's my hand. Want it? Lock the door? No, Alison and Artie."

"I don't think I have any names picked out. Well, that's the least of my problems."

Jane knows it falls to her to keep her mother calm. "We'll come up with some good ones. That's what we'll talk about right now. How about Emily for a girl? I also like Clara."

"You read too much. How about Mary? That was my mother's name."

"That's good, then. But don't make any decisions yet. You're under pressure."

"Well, you won't hold me to anything, will you?" Sylvia pulls Jane against her side. "I wouldn't want to do this without you. Oh, and look at that, Jane. Our savior's here already."

Sylvia sprawls out across the back seat of the taxi, one hand beneath her hips. Jane snuggles into the well behind the driver's seat.

"Seat up front, young lady."

"Just step on it, mister. St. Luke's, right, Mom?"

"She's right again." Sylvia negates the dangers of the journey by calculating that a ride to Pittsfield General Hospital would be fully three times longer. A primitive, unyielding concentration precludes awareness of their progress. At the hospital, she watches Jane bolt inside and then return with two nuns and a wheelchair. A doctor greets her at the door.

"Just happened to be in the neighborhood, Sylvia."

"Dr. Shore. Prompt as ever."

"Is this Jane? My first delivery of—"

"Four. I'm the oldest. I'm Jane. Now I'll move away, so you can help her."

"The baby's low, Dr. Shore. It's wrong. No contractions, and suddenly not discomfort. But it's time."

Jane impatiently allows the doctor to digest this information, place a hand against her mother's stomach. She interprets this as a display of doubt. "She ought to know."

"She's the pro." He puts the back of his hand to Sylvia's forehead. "I'm not surprised, Sylvia, if that's any consolation. After the last two visits? I figured you for a cesarean this time. We'll take a look, have you sign yourself in upstairs. Right impulse, getting here. Let's go, sisters."

"Jane?" Sylvia holds up her hands to slow the pace of the nun behind her wheelchair.

Jane runs to catch up. "Hi."

"A friend in need. Right?"

"Good luck. I'll call Daddy, right?"

"And Jane? What about Stephen?"

"You mean, if it's a boy."

"Maybe even if it's a girl?"

"Well, I won't hold you to it or anything, but I sure hope it's a boy then, for his sake."

Sylvia is pushed past Jane into a waiting elevator. As she is spun around, she catches sight of her pale, bewildered daughter, slouched against the wall. "For *whose* sake, Jane?"

Jane smiles slyly, aware she is being granted a share in naming her new brother. "For his sake. Stephen's sake, of course. For Stephen."

The Light
of the World

I

To RECTIFY HIS FRAUD of signing on as Stephen's witness, Roger passed the afternoon casting aspersions on the Jones II induction process and the "inefficient, no, downright danger- ous referral process between you people and Paramount." Be- fore he returned to Sylvia, he'd bullied Bill Daye into reading his report aloud to Berkshire Medical's chief of psychiatric intake services on the telephone. Daye also had a copy of the initial diagnosis of delusional behavior delivered by taxi to the hospital. The staff at Jones II was instructed to prepare the necessary voluntary commitment forms. The head nurse in Emergency was to notify the treating physician that transfer to Jones II had been arranged. Roger credited his profession's pursuit of malpractice claims for the capitulation of the doc- tors involved.

After the initial paperwork, Sylvia's only distraction for three hours had been a single, brief consultation with the woman doctor treating Stephen. Sylvia politely acknowledged the doctor's intention to administer mophine and, unable to absorb the brief report on the condition of her son's dermis and metacarpals, volunteered to sign a morphine assent form. The doctor assured her this would not be necessary.

She was similarly unimpressed by Roger's triumph, though no less grateful for his assistance. "Everyone's so helpful. Thank you, Roger. Dr. Allegretti stopped by about an hour ago or so. She'll be back. You'll like her." Sylvia tugged on Roger's hand and cajoled him into the seat next to her in a small abandoned wing of the waiting room. "I'm very im- pressed by this operation, I must say. Click, click, click. No one misses a beat. Makes you feel like you live in a big city. They brought me coffee. I should get out more often. Imagine

291

how much better the restaurants are since Arthur and I stopped having dinners out. This is bound to be good for Stephen, too, you know. I can see that now."

"I called Arthur, and Alison. I thought Arthur should wait at home, though it's past seven now." Roger giggled, less confident in the sphere of the family. "Maybe I should call him again."

"And Alison will call Jane and Jane will have spoken twice to Arthur by now. We have to wait. So do they."

"Sylvia, would you like to lie down?"

"Here? I'd be afraid to! Where would I wake up?"

"Why don't I get you another coffee, then?" Her manner unnerved Roger. He suspected she was in shock. "Sylvia?"

"Just sit, dear. I'm fine. Unless you want some yourself. I'm just amazed by . . . does it seem possible that it was only a week ago he was arrested?" Sylvia could not compress her retrospective insights and revisionist understanding of Stephen's performance into a time frame of days.

"Mr. and Mrs. Adamski?" Dr. Rachel Allegretti had donned a hairnet since her last visit.

Sylvia did not immediately recognize the short, thin woman. "May I help you, young lady?"

"I'm Roger Hibbard, son-in-law." He stood, helped Sylvia up from her chair.

"Dr. Allegretti. Why don't you come this way. Mrs. Adamski?"

"Call me, Sylvia, please. I'm afraid you look much smaller and—don't mind me saying so—less pretty without your hair. Don't ever cut it." Sylvia took a single step, waved to her confused companions. "I'm coming. Knees. I'd almost forgotten them." She lurched forward and followed the doctor into a spare, bright examination room.

"Stephen is sleeping. I've spoken to Nurse Durant about his status next door." The doctor let this reference to Jones II register, observed no worrisome increase in emotional pulse. "Please have a seat, both of you." She backed away toward the vinyl examination bed. "There is no metacarpal damage, nothing serious there. Most of the epidermis is destroyed, and there is a good deal of dermal damage here," she held one palm up and pointed to the heel. "That is the area of third-degree burning, on either hand. Silver nitrate, antibiotics, we've done what we can. I wrapped the hands, and the dressing will be changed every few hours through the night. Certainly, he has some nerve damage, though the extent is unclear at this point. He has severe muscle tremors in the extremities. I don't think he caused permanent ligament damage. Now, this was self-inflicted?"

"Of course." Roger was insulted.

"Oh yes. He thinks he's Jesus. It all follows from that." Sylvia delivered this with such aplomb that its novelty was obscured. Roger admired her succinct analysis; it seemed a fair conclusion to him. Rachel Allegretti nodded, finding in such a delusion a more convincing motive for grabbing two cast-iron burners than any she'd imagined while exploring the canyons burned into Stephen's palms. Sylvia's relentless reimagining of the previous week during her spell in the waiting room proved a sufficient gestation for this idea. It was born of received suspicions of lurking anti-Semitism, a disbelief of her own stupefied inaction, and a desire to raise Stephen's behavior to disturbingly original heights, well above the level of parental culpability.

"He'll have to spend the night here, in a private room. Supervised, of course. We can effect the transfer tomorrow, late morning." Rachel Allegretti interpreted Sylvia's composure as surgical calm. "If no one's told you, Mrs. Adamski, you're holding up very well. I would like to prescribe . . . It does catch up with you, and I could see to it you get something to help you sleep. For tonight."

"I suspect you're right." Sylvia felt the doctor's sympathy exonerated her. "You've been marvelous. God bless you."

"His hands will heal. We'll watch out for him." The doctor raised her gaze to the ceiling, as if the limits on her time were spatial. "I'm afraid I have other patients. You can always reach me here."

"The prescription?" Roger thought a Valium for him would not be out of order.

"I'll have it set up before you leave. Stay well. I'll see you tomorrow. Late morning, Mrs. Adamski."

"Call me Sylvia, dear. Ten-thirty?" She followed the doctor to a counter and shook her hand. "They'll fill me up right here?"

"Please read the labels, all of them. Tomorrow." Dr. Allegretti jogged down the hall, sped through a set of swinging doors.

"Sylvia? Wouldn't you like to just look in on Stephen?" Roger considered this another hospital oversight.

"While he's asleep? Oh no. I wouldn't feel right. God knows, he needs his rest." Seeing Stephen, she knew, would defeat even drug-induced sleep. She figured she could brief Arthur and Jane, take a pill, and call the doctor in the morning. It was the most anyone had a right to expect of a woman in her position.

II

THERE WAS NO Friday-morning sky. A crust of arid arctic air had edged in up above autumnal humus; a tarnished silver mist was lifted up, displacing daylight and dissembling the hour. Sylvia stood watch, her hands against two bedroom window panes set off by shrinking silhouettes of steam.

She felt constrained. This feeling had survived misattribution to the grim, restrictive weather, and a second trip downstairs for extra coffee followed by an entirely cold-water shower, which washed away the residue of Nembutal. Even her performance of a fairly painless plié did not assuage her sense of limitation.

Her range had been reduced. There was little left for her to do. At last, she dressed and called the hospital. But she hung up before the operator located Rachel Allegretti. She forced herself to walk downstairs without succumbing to the urge to limp or balance on the handrail.

"You look more awake this time."

"Jesus, Mary, and Joseph!" Sylvia slapped a hand against her chest and stumbled off the bottom stair toward the mantel.

"Watch it!" Jane yelled but did not jump up from the divan. "Thank God. Sit down before you kill yourself. Sorry if I scared you."

Sylvia had ended her maneuver with both hands against the back of a chair, bent over the seat cushion. She straightened her back, dragged the chair close to the coffee table.

"You ought to leave that damn chair over here, instead of moving it every day. You all right?"

Sylvia did not look at her daughter. She sat, then got her feet up on the table. "You're a menace."

Jane laughed. "Oh well, you didn't hit your head or anything."

"I mean it, Jane." She raised her gaze to meet her daughter's. "It doesn't make things any easier, being crippled. You could've called and let me know you'd be here. Or rung the bell."

"I said I'm sorry."

"Sorry solves everything. When did you get here?"

"What time is it now? Half past ten? An hour . . . I watched you come down with your cup to get a refill. Imagine what you would've done if I'd said hello that time."

Sylvia was indignant. "You were not here."

"You had on Daddy's robe."

"And you just sat there?" Sylvia did not appreciate her daughter's unofficial, self-appointed status as observer. "What if I sneaked around your apartment in New York?"

"You'll never come to New York. Why pretend?" This brought the episode to an uneasy close.

"I have to go to the hospital soon."

"I thought I'd go with you."

"If you think that's a good idea." Sylvia tugged her nylons, smoothed them up along her thighs. "Don't ask me."

"Daddy called me up. Said you were still asleep. He was going to see him early."

"So you came by to spell him? Arthur wasn't going to the hospital. He went straight to work, trust me. I was awake. I heard him on the phone in the kitchen when he spoke to you." Sylvia shrugged. "So, I guess we're even. Born spies."

"To his credit, he only said he might go. Or he was thinking he might go. You want more coffee?"

"We should go soon." Sylvia relaxed into her chair, crossed her ankles on the table. "I don't know, maybe it's the sleeping pill, but I can't make myself move."

"It's all been exhausting. Then you find out there's no bottom to it. There's jail, there's the court, and did he set a fire? And then this."

"This is the end. You were right. All along. The Sermon on the Mount, the whole—"

"You said that last night on the phone. I never said he said the whole thing, the Sermon. Or even meant to. It was only what I made out from his babbling that night, the one thing I recognized." Jane did not enjoy the proximity to credit for her brother's swift commitment. "He never said to me he thinks he's Jesus."

"We have to wait until he's got a crown of thorns? Those are your words." Sylvia had not intended to adopt an accusatory tone. "What's done is done."

Jane figured this was true enough for Stephen, though she did not accept this as the final word on her complicity. "I want a drink of juice. Anything for you?"

"I'll follow you." Sylvia shuffled slowly after Jane. She headed for the alcove, where she'd left her coat and purse the night before. "Find the juice all right?" She turned as Jane poured from a yellow carton into Arthur's morning-after glass. "Don't use that one. It's old."

"The glass?"

"Just take another. Where did you find that one?"

"It was right here. Daddy must have used it. It's clean. Don't worry."

"I would have seen it there. Don't, Jane. I'll get another."

"Mom. You didn't even see *me* this morning."

Sylvia sprang up. "Just use a different glass."

"Would you sit down? This glass is fine. What?" Jane watched her mother reach. She drew her arm away reflexively, but Sylvia had two fingers hooked around the glass's lip.

The glass banged down and spurted juice across the floor. "You broke it, damn you!" Sylvia felt the liquid splash against her shins and run down toward her shoes.

"I what?" Just for effect, Jane threw the open carton into the sink. "What is it? Stephen's baby cup or something? Look, I'm soaked." She looked down at her splattered slacks. "What's with you? Just sit down. I'll wipe this up."

"Oh, Jane, I'm sorry. But take a look. Right there." She pointed to the floor beneath the table. The unbroken glass rocked itself toward rest. "It's your father's favorite glass. That's why I yelled. I'm sorry, sweetie."

"What's it made of? Plexiglas?" Jane wet a sponge and bent to clean the floor. "Between the two of us you'd think we could break a glass." She looked up at her mother. "You're going to want dry pantyhose."

"Would you believe these are stockings?"

"No wonder you're such a klutz. Go up and lose the girdle. Or are you sweet on Stephen's doctor?"

"She's a woman!" Sylvia slid backward, making room for Jane, who worked despite the slip in etiquette. "I don't mean that rules her out."

Jane tilted up her face, then knelt. "I tell you what. In that case, you put on a pair of slacks and bring your girdle down for me."

Sylvia reached down and grabbed the sponge from Jane's hand, rinsed it in the sink, and tossed it to the floor. "If you're still thirsty, have a glass of water. Please." She headed for the stairs. "You intend to just let that juice sit there in the sink? I'm not cleaning up after you, young lady."

Jane yelled, "I'm bringing that along. The whole half gallon. I'm gonna tell your doctor friend you never let us use cups at home."

"I've already told them all my kids are nuts."

Jane ran the sponge along the sticky floor, teased back toward a conspiratorial good humor. "Well, Stephen. If you really think you're Jesus, then I must be the Queen of Sheba."

III

JANE, SYLVIA, AND ARTHUR sat together on a purple sofa in the sun room on the second floor of Jones II. Stephen lay in a white private room just halfway down the hall. His transfer had occurred at ten o'clock. Arthur saw him wheeled in from the elevator, his bandaged hands immobilized by metal crutches rigged up to the chair; his eyes were closed. A young man wearing blue jeans and a khaki chamois shirt had asked Arthur not to look in on his son until he'd finished an initial interview.

Arthur reported these events to his agitated daughter and his disbelieving wife. "He's a good-looking young man, with a full head of black hair. Joseph Johnson. It's almost two hours since I spoke with him, though. It's a good sign, I'm sure, that they could move Stephen. Though his hands are . . ."

"His hands will heal. Dr. Allegretti said so." Sylvia felt Arthur coming to the hospital was a grandstand move. She resented his awareness of the facts.

"I'm sorry about the stove, by the way. I should've left a note." Arthur found relief in conversation. He wanted confirmation of the sighting of his glass, the alibi for his escape to Hetty Marshall's home. "I'm going to buy a new set. The gas company must sell them downtown. They have a showroom near Park Square."

"Arthur, what note did you leave?" Sylvia eyed Jane, accusing her of not reporting this among the morning's oversights.

"You think I know about a note?" Jane was insulted by her mother's readiness to fault her on this score, which seemed related to the credit she'd accrued for diagnosing Stephen. "He wants to buy a new stove, and you think I hid the note he left? So it would be a surprise?"

"Just two new burners." Arthur spoke dismissively. "Not a brand-new stove."

"New burners? Why?" Sylvia shot her hands out, then drew them slowly back; she could not retract her words. "Well, of course, but we can't . . . we do need an oven, after all. Well, new burners, if you want them. I don't know. Did you throw away the ones . . . the ones he used?"

"I put them underneath the sink."

"My God, the burners aren't the problem, though, Daddy."

"The center of the—the burns. Well, he lost some skin." Arthur watched his wife and daughter edge along the purple cushions.

"It's disgusting. Stop it, Arthur. Of course we will replace them."

"Mr. Adamski?"

Sylvia was up before her husband. "And I am Sylvia. I am Stephen's mother. I want to see my son."

"I'm Joseph Johnson. Certainly you can look in on him. I'd like to speak to both of you. And you are?" He held a hand toward Jane.

"Oh, me? Apparently the only reason Stephen's here. No one else thought anything was odd. I'm Jane." She waved off his hand.

Joseph Johnson dragged a metal folding chair toward the sofa. "It will be useful to speak with you, all of you, later on. I've read Bill Daye's report and the reports on Stephen's injury. What I haven't done is spoken yet to Stephen. He won't speak. Not just to me. Dr. Allegretti, all the nurses. And I noticed he would not acknowlege you, Mr. Adamski, when we came out of the elevator."

"With his eyes closed?" Arthur hoped this information would exonerate him. Defensively, he added, "I wasn't at home when he did this to himself."

"The event is, believe it or not, it's not really what I'm concerned with. I'm concerned about it, yes." Dr. Johnson found it difficult to attend to the three impatient, disparate reactions his words elicited. "He shut his eyes after he saw you. The point about his self-inflicted wounds is that he clearly has a history, however brief—" He raised a finger to silence Sylvia as she jerked forward. "I can tell you my initial sense. I believe he's had a manic episode, at least. I don't think anyone can guess the long-term implications. But even accidents have histories, Mrs. Adamski. Not just the skid marks leading to the crash, but highways, side streets, years of incidental travel. But until he speaks—"

Sylvia disregarded the young doctor's wagging finger. "He will speak to me. He'll look at me, at least." She wasn't mindful of the jolt she caused both Arthur and the doctor. "I want to see him now, alone. Jane, you drive Arthur up to Dalton. Or have him drop you at home. I want to be alone with Stephen. I'll see you later on, at home. He's afraid of all of you." She refused to be subdued by Dr. Johnson's hand signals or Jane's ironic, quiet laughter. "I watched it happen. I want to be with him. Can't I just see him, sit with him until he falls asleep? Is that so awful?" She stood, took hold of Dr. Johnson's hands. "You, of all people. Can't you imagine how scared he might be about what's going to happen to him next? It's not as if he started the day hoping to sear the skin and nerves. He didn't wake up wanting that."

"I want you to see him, Mrs. Adamski." The doctor shook his hands free. "I only want you not to think I don't worry how he feels, as well. I do. I don't want anything upsetting . . . questions he can't answer. I can't imagine he knows why he ended up here."

Sylvia stepped back toward Arthur. She turned to him, then Jane, then faced the doctor, pleaded. "But I just want to see him. Stephen. After all, just see him. Maybe sit with him, let him know I love him. Couldn't you just take me to him now?"

She'd converted Joseph Johnson. He felt officiousness was misplaced, given her traumatic role as witness. As she spoke, the defensiveness exhibited by Stephen's father and this sister sparked his suspicion. Only the mother seemed to have the normal, consuming interest in establishing her own sense of Stephen's precarious condition. "Come with me now. Dr. Allegretti wants to see him later on this afternoon, about the tremors in his arms and shoulders. He should be fairly coherent. Even if he isn't speaking yet. I think, for one more night, he will have the morphine. He'll sleep comfortably that way." He led her from the sun room, his hand against her back. "They've just changed his bandages, and they seem to feel his skin will come around. They're using—"

"Rachel said his hands will heal."

"If he should ask, the bandages he has will stay on till tonight, or tomorrow midday. The constant changing—they've been at it every two hours—that's no longer necessary. A good sign. He's responding. And he's on a higher dose of antibiotics to insure—"

"I doubt we'll talk about his hands, Doctor. I just want to see him. Can I sit down in there?" Sylvia stared at the door separating Stephen from the world.

"There's a chair or two. I'll look in on you both a little later." He put his arm across the doorway. "I'm here because I want to help him, Mrs. Adamski."

"Sylvia, please."

"Sylvia, then. Just so you believe that. For his sake."

"We're all going to make it." She pushed by him, limped into Stephen's room. She smiled at her son but didn't speak. She knew the doctor was still holding the door open. As a test, she whispered, "I love you, Stephen. I'm awful happy to be here."

Stephen flashed a silly smile, which he meant as invitation to the doctor. The door swung shut. They were alone.

Stephen drew a breath and held it as she ran her gaze along his quivering arms up to his white gauze boxing gloves. His

lower arms were balanced on padded ramps, to keep his hands
above his heart, weakening the pulse of blood, and still his
hands twitched rhythmically, every shot of blood a shock of
molten lead, burning bone and then hardening and adding to
the heft that he believed was threatening to overtake the muscles in his arms. The nurse who'd changed the bandages had
hid his hands with her soft, rippled back, but Stephen had already memorized the colorful topography the burners raised.
He'd watched the swelling, smelled the roasting of his skin
like human hair held near a match. He recalled the hours holding tight while she sat on the bench, unmoved. He remembered Roger coming to the kitchen later in the day, and how
his mother had made Roger sit down on the bench and shut up
and just sign his name.

He was terrified to speak. She didn't want to save him. Did
she want to do more damage? Hit his hands or push him off
the bed?

"It's okay if you want to act like Jesus. It's the right idea."
She stared at his two hands until he blasted out his breath, to
distract her. She turned to him, expecting words. "You can say
anything to me, son."

Stephen wanted her to leave or tell him why she'd come. He
refused to speak and give her yet another chance to say she
couldn't make out what he meant, or how he was so mean, or
how she loved him and he always made her cry. The morphine
and the red-hot metal in his hands conspired to compound his
dislocated, overbearing dread.

Sylvia was weeping.

He felt this was unfair. He couldn't understand her. He'd
figured out that when he talked, he might upset her, so he
had sworn himself to silence. When he'd discovered that he
couldn't trust his body either—his hands had got him into
trouble more than once, which made everybody mad, which
also made her cry—he shut his body down, clamped his hands
around the burners so she would see he didn't want to hurt her
anymore. She didn't try to stop him; she let him ruin his
hands. The very least she owed him was a thank you.

Instead, she wept.

What did she expect? What was she looking for today?

She dried her tears by ducking down her face and rubbing one cheek, then the other, several times with either bicep, as if her hands were useless too. She stained her white silk sleeves, not with her tears, but with the impress of her reddish makeup powder.

Stephen concentrated on his hands, hoping to divert her gaze from the damage to her blouse. If he had made her cry, he was responsible for that mess, too.

She cried, but hers were tears of absolution. All she saw was Stephen, her own son, in pain and all alone. She recognized him finally. The tiny contours of the unlit room approximated her revised assessment of her proper sphere. They'd come to the same end. In her son's mute and tortured state she saw the incarnation of her broken faith. She had nothing left to say. No one could be taken at his word.

Her memory and faith were complementary. She had relinquished her expansive and ecstatic future. To compensate for this, Sylvia forgot. Bereft of faith, she found her past was unredeemable. She would no longer seek redemption for her trinity of men—her father, her husband, and her lover. She believed only in her son; not the unborn child, or even the amazing vandal wrapped up in her robe. The past was limited to Stephen's pain, which had delivered him to this clean, private room. The future was his comfort, day by day and by her side.

She smiled when the doctor made his promised momentary visit. She had achieved her peace with Stephen. She saw him plainly now. She recognized her son. That is, she loved him.

And this was love. It was not declarative; it was ineffable. It was eternal, as measured on the momentary human scale. It was no more. Healing miracles did not attend it.

Love's presence was as soft light, kindest in its play against their faces. Stephen registered the change. It was not that he felt better. Blood still blasted in his hands. He hadn't yet found out what city he was in, though Dr. Johnson's clothes had made him think of farms, so he remained alert to clues

pertaining to the Middle West. But when his mother tilted
her head to the left and smiled, he recognized something fragile; he knew love was here.

This didn't change them, either one. It heightened possibilities.

Sylvia reached for her purse and Stephen jealously regarded
her nimble fingers twisting free the clasp. He watched her pull
out three felt-tip pens with a single hand; she held one beneath her thumb, tipped her palm and rolled the others to her
purse. He could not imagine what she had left to sign, so he
just closed his eyes, the sole defense in his depleted retinue.

Sylvia believed she'd had an inspiration. She could prove
her faith in Stephen, win him back, no matter how insane his
sister or the doctors made him feel. She would take him on
the craziest of terms.

He heard her pop the cap and felt her body, warm beside his
naked forearm. He let his breath out slowly as she walked
around his feet, then took a bite of air when her silk sleeve
began to dance on his other arm. He kept his eyes closed until
she capped the pen and sat again.

He looked at what she'd done. He saw the circles she had
painted on his palms. Instantly, he felt his fingers plunged
into an outlet, which yanked his head and snapped his shoulders toward his spine. But soon he understood he'd only tried
to raise his right hand to his forehead, an aborted reflex gesture
to express his impotent dismay: Stephen was convinced the
nurse would chew him out for messing up her artful windings.
He turned to Sylvia, and in the fragile light he saw her raise
her eyebrows, hopeful but restrained.

He looked up at his hands. The circles were resolved into
irregular and, he thought, rather unconvincing drops of blood.
He closed his eyes and hoped she had a better explanation
than the only one he had: As far as he could see, his mother
thought he'd turned himself right into Jesus. This meant trouble. He was well acquainted with the fate of people who got
mixed up with Jesus. Dr. Daye and Dr. Johnson threatened
Stephen with Him constantly. If anyone found out his mother

had become a true believer, they would both be in steel beds, maybe hooked up to machines to make them talk. The old guy with the cane would swipe the laces out of all her shoes. Once they heard you were confused, they never let up.

Afraid she had exposed him, Sylvia whispered, "No one's going to be mad. This can be our secret."

He opened his eyes, warily turned to her. His empathy for her confusion was mixed up with embarrassment on her behalf; since she'd cried and used her sleeves instead of her two healthy hands, her face was striped. He wanted to protect her, so he smiled his approval for her drawing. Then he closed his eyes and let the pounding rhythm of his blood beat him back toward sleep.

Sylvia stole out as a young nurse backed in, dragging her array of medicines and tools.

Dr. Johnson waved to Sylvia from the counter of the nurses' station. "Holding up?"

"We'll make it, best we can."

"Still silent?"

"Yes." Sylvia smiled apologetically and pointed to the waiting elevator, held her hand against the door. "All he would say is that he's sorry. And, of course, how much he loves me. What could I say?" She stepped inside and shrugged. "He doesn't have to be sorry. His job is getting better, and I love him. Right? What else is there to say? Should I come by tonight?"

"Why don't you give him until morning? I'll look in on him and call, if there's a problem. Which there won't be." Dr. Johnson doubted every word she spoke. This didn't rile him. In his experience, a mother was incapable of hearing anything an adult child said. Sylvia displayed the classic symptoms. He saw her as an ordinary, frightened mother begrudgingly surrendering her son.

IV

"ARTIE'S COMING HOME TONIGHT. I mean, your brother. Did I mention that already? He called me late this afternoon." Sylvia sank down again, well below the surface of the silence.

"I spoke to him as well." Jane put her arm up on the divan's back, her finger pointing to her mother's hand an inch or two away.

"He called us, too. Maybe that's why I thought I should drop by." Alison was several feet away, marooned in the upholstered chair beside the mantel. She did not pass on Roger's confession of having left a message on Artie's answering machine to prompt the call. Nor could she imagine why Artie, of all the Adamskis, had prompted her to reveal Roger's increasingly appealing determination to move her and their children to Brattleboro, Vermont, where he intended to establish a private practice. She was nurturing her weakened faith in Roger, and checked her habit of exposing him as barter for admission to the inner sanctum of this home. Too much time with Jane and an overdose of Liz Halstrom left her groggy. She could not keep pace; she felt perpetually late, left out in the lobby while the plot was being laid. As a countermeasure, she began to tell a story of her own. "Becky—that's your niece, Jane, though you haven't seen her for a couple years; she's a second-grader."

Jane said, "Yeah, Becky?" and waited for her sister to complete the thought. "What, was that just a tic? Saying a kid's name in the middle of a conversation?"

"Conversation might be going a bit far." Sylvia withdrew her arm and sat forward, feigning interest. "What about Becky? Were you going somewhere with her name, Alison?"

The second silence was too much for Jane. "Well, for God's sake, give her my regards and let her know her name came up."

Alison was satisfed. She suspected it would be easy to elicit

proof of her older sister's militant dislike for her. "I'm sorry I
don't talk a mile a minute. I was just making a point about
how hard it is to tell children about something like this." She
shuffled in her chair, to face her mother more directly. For the
moment anyway, Jane could be excluded.

"Try something really wacky." Jane smiled as she spoke.
"Tell her the truth."

Alison had steeled herself against her sister's interruption.
"Roger was great, explaining how Stephen had really chosen to
go in, to help himself. For all intents and purposes, I mean."
Here she played her trump at last. She bowed slightly to her
mother. "He told me about the form he signed for you. I
agree, it's best that way. Why should the hospital decide when
he is ready to come home and get on with his life? So Becky
wanted to know—"

"Can I break into story time here? What form did Roger
sign?"

Sylvia was still unmoved by the detour in the conversation.
She sensed no danger. "For voluntary commitment to Jones II.
Is that the one you mean, Alison?"

"Roger signed him in as if he . . ." The hesitation brought
Jane to her feet. "They think Stephen's in there by free will?"

Alison reflected her mother's calm. "Roger is the lawyer. In
fact, it's just a technicality."

Jane backed up against the door. "Did you really sign him
up as if he signed himself in there?"

"I was speaking with him, showing him how it was up to
him that way, to admit himself, to leave when he felt better."
Sylvia was unconvincing in this pose as a bewildered mother.
"I'd signed his name, just on the copy I had here, for Dr. Daye
at Paramount. He gave it to me. Stephen had agreed to sign.
But then there was the lunch he wanted to prepare for all of
you. He got himself distracted." Sylvia ignored Jane, telling
this to Alison directly. "Then, as Roger probably told you—
after you'd all gone and he was kind enough to stay—then it
all began. And, I guess, in the confusion—"

"In the confusion, Roger signed it." The story approximated Roger's dismissive account. "Let's face it, Jane, it's much better this way."

"Roger signed a legal form witnessing an act he didn't see."

"Stop repeating it as if it was a plot." Sylvia resented this badgering.

Alison spoke very slowly. "In the confusion, Roger signed it. Is that good enough for you?"

"Old Jane, that nitpicking old maid. Me? Of course it's good enough for me. I mean, after all, confusion is nine-tenths of the law, isn't it?"

Alison attempted an appeal to reason. "I don't know about you, but I don't claim to know what happened to him, what snapped. No one has all the answers."

Apologetically, wryly, Sylvia said, "Along the way you make up a few."

Alison was relentless. "But, Jane, you're the one he talked to that night, after running out of here with Mom's watch on. The Sermon on the Mount? Come off it. You don't think it's a little odd, odd enough to let the rest of us know?"

"Let who know, exactly, Alison? You and Roger? When were you elected to the American Psychiatric Association? Who?" She kicked her foot in the air, to attract Sylvia's attention. "I'm catching it coming and going on the Beatitudes. I want it known I never said—"

"Stop it, Jane!" Alison had expended her rational reserve. She didn't understand the aside Jane had passed to her mother, but she knew it was proprietary, designed to keep her out. "The point is, if I'd known half of what you knew, I'd have done something."

Jane turned on her sister, but managed to withhold a sharp response. She stared at Alison, framing her for memory: the polite posture unmodified by anger; the simple slate-blue smock splashed all about with streaks of yellow, accentuating the color of her generous hank of hair tied at one side in an intentionally casual braid. Jane watched her sister tightening her grip on the chair's thick arms, fearing retribution. Her defenselessness brought Alison, the younger sister, alive for Jane. She looked back at her mother, silent and inert. "As if you didn't know enough," Jane smirked, "you had to make things up? You're as bad as I am. I've had Stephen hanging by a thread, to cover for myself, I guess. For my staying here. I was supposed to be at a conference in Miami with Regina. Something about news coverage of women's medical issues. Anyway, I want to go look in on him. I'll drive to Hartford tomorrow, fly from there, try to catch the last night, maybe lunch on Sunday." She knew she was talking herself out. "I'll call you tonight, okay? Is that all right?"

"That's fine." Sylvia's regret at Jane's announcement of departure was tempered by relief.

"Maybe I'll see you tomorrow morning, Al? The three kids having breakfast in the alcove?"

Alison refused to speak. She'd been consigned to the periphery again. She tried to calculate the mileage from Pittsfield to Brattleboro, but the distance defeated her calibrated tether. She accepted Roger's gleeful estimations: The hour's drive was too brief to justify overnight excursions, and day trips from Vermont would be too exhausting for the children.

What she didn't know would always haunt her. But her children wouldn't have to face their crazy uncle, the specter of her past.

Her sister's sulking presence triggered Jane's reliable intolerance for self-pity. "For God's sake, Alison, don't waste any more time worrying about what I knew when. Had you known a fraction of what's been going on in this house forever, you'd be a different person altogether. Look at me. And count your goddamn blessings."

V

ARTHUR USED HIS BODY as a wedge to pry into his son's dark room. Stephen was asleep. He didn't move. Arthur couldn't

wrench his own attention from the hands, though this de-
volved into an abject admiration for the ingenious rigging job
the Jones II staff had done. He'd almost acquiesced to Dr.
Johnson's diagnosis of a long-term stay when an elderly, short
man tapped a cane against his ankle. Arthur backed out into
the hall.

"You know that kid in there?"

"Stephen is his name." Irrationally, Arthur attributed a sixth
sense to the visibly deranged old man, suspected he might
guess he wasn't Stephen's natural father. "Stephen Adamski.
I'm Arthur Adamski. And you are?"

"Whadda ya sellin'? Shoelaces? They don't allow 'em." He
tapped Arthur's ankle twice, a prelude to a secret. "Nurses
got a thing for shoelaces. They take 'em from the patients—
off your shoes or sneakers, they don't mind. Then they eat
'em."

Arthur glanced down at the man's leather slippers.

"Mind your manners. Whadda ya got against me?" The old
man ambled toward the sun room.

Arthur headed for the elevator, convinced the least he could
do for Stephen was to hasten his release. He wished his word
was worth more.

VI

ARTIE SAT ALONE in the kitchen alcove. He'd stopped along
the highway heading home, and slept until the sun rose. His
nose was runny, coffee hadn't warmed him, his mother was
asleep. He'd walked halfway upstairs and heard her snoring,
which made him laugh and back away, embarrassed. He'd
seen his father's car on East Street, heading west toward Park
Square; Artie had waved and honked his horn, but only managed to upset a mother midway along a crosswalk with a
stroller.

He heard a knocking at the front door, found his sister Jane
outside, wrapped in her own arms. "You knock now?"

"It's fucking freezing out here. Nice car. At least they pay you." She held her hands against his cheeks, kissed his forehead. "Welcome home. Or, what? How's tricks? Let's have some coffee."

"Hi, Janey." Artie let her pass. "Seems a little crazy we have to come to Pittsfield just to see each other."

"Crazy? You ain't seen nothing yet. My God! He even makes a pot of coffee. Want a refill?"

He joined her in the kitchen. "Please." He sneezed. "Slept for a couple hours in my car."

"Someone ought to invent a motel, make a million dollars. She's got Kleenex everywhere."

He pointed to the alcove. "Found some in the dining room. Do I get an update?" He trusted her above them all to tell the truth. He felt related to the family through Jane, the likeness of his mother fashioned as an outcast. He could approach her.

"I saw him last night. He's got a shrink, Joseph pardon-the-pole-up-my-ass Johnson. Seems smart enough. Stephen isn't speaking. No one seems to think he can't. His hands are just amazing, apparently. Everybody's saying they'll be fine, but the nurse who was going in to look at his bandages? She said she's never seen such a thing. Not just the bandages, which are impressive. She said something about they look like casts— plaster casts people write their names on?—which they do. But the hands, she couldn't even describe the damage. 'Never seen anything remotely like it,' she said. Given where she is, you figure her relative standards are pretty fucking drastic. How's that for starters?" She slipped in across from him, nestling into a corner of the alcove. "There's a sort of rumor going round that Stephen thinks he's Jesus, which is absurd, of course. I don't think he knows enough to think he's anybody. How are you?"

"Here I am."

"You look tired." She made a quick evaluation of his short brown hair, his sallow face and light brown eyes. The blue turtleneck showed his flat chest and smooth torso. "Are you thin?"

"I never weigh myself. Do I look skinny? You do."

She poised her elbow on the table, held her coffee cup as daintily as possible. "The virtue of the black knee-length dress. Feel a little weird to be here?"

"I don't know yet. I drove by Dad on East Street, oddly enough."

"New burners." She pointed to the stove. "To replace the two Stephen used. It's all pretty grisly."

"I'd like to see him."

"You can't get to him until after ten. I don't mean, Please hang around. But they won't let you see him. Would you rather just take off and wait there?"

"Is that a warning?" Artie sneezed again. "Sorry. Maybe I'm allergic."

"You want breakfast?"

"Should we wait for Mom?" He watched her slide along the bench, then stop abruptly, disappointed. "Or would you rather eat right now?"

"No, you're right." She stood, hoisted herself up onto the counter. "If you're here for more than a couple of days, you either lose your manners or your mind. More coffee?"

"Not yet." Her caustic wit was an electric wire she used to stake out private territory, adjacent but inviolate. "Should I call Alison?"

"For what?"

"Let her know I got here. I guess it's such a rarity I want the full exposure. I don't know, breakfast with the nuclear family once every five years?"

"It's a nuclear family, all right. Hold on to your seat. It's a particle accelerator of a home. Call her up. I'll go get Mom." Jane leapt off the ledge.

"Shouldn't we just let her sleep?"

"Of course we should. And she'll be mad as hell we didn't wake her half an hour earlier. Welcome home." Jane raced from the room.

His sister bolting from the room woke Artie to the oddity of being in this house, as if he'd dreamed eight years in Erie.

In fact, he'd got to Pittsfield half asleep and let himself be led through the city by burnished memories of downtown and Park Square. When he retraced his route, he saw that where he had endowed the range of North Street's clothing stores and banks with a soft patina, the legacy of a stagnant local economy and the odd case of bad luck was evacuated shops, yellowed cardboard CLEARANCE SALE signs taped to display windows, and an abundance of fine gray sand swept up at every traffic intersection. The desolate downtown was like a funnel, drawing him down into this house.

VII

SYLVIA STOPPED SHORT of the kitchen, undid the buttons of her cardigan, fussed with her hair, then entered. "It's half past eight already? This is the first Saturday in years I'm missing morning Mass. What next?" She ignored her husband at the stove, stooped to let her elder son quickly kiss her cheek.

Artie pulled away to sneeze.

"God bless you. Whoops!" She shrugged, turned to pour a cup of coffee. "Everything you say these days—why are you staring at me, Arthur?"

"I thought you'd sleep a little longer, with the pills and all." With a pliers, he twisted off another metal clip, a feature of the burners he'd procured that had prevented easy installation.

Sylvia allowed his eager publication of her two-pill prescription to go unchecked. "Is your sister coming, Artie?"

"Roger had to go to work. She can't."

The second sister's absence proved a liability when the Adamskis were all seated in the alcove. Not only was the natural alignment of women versus men a failure conversationally, but Artie found he could sustain no alternate arrangement. In the operation of the family, he'd played the substitute; the fifth wheel, but not useless. He was the spare, filling in a bit of funny reportage on school if Jane was sick in bed; asking disingenuously about the butts he'd found while shoveling if Alison was absent; serving up a youth-group dinner at the parish center; even bringing to the table a handy magazine or the business page from the *Courier* while Arthur traveled to Orlando or Los Alamos on business.

He was too far away from Alison to know what she might say. When he finally asked about his brother, he was provided with additional retellings of the recent past. Not even Jane would venture an opinion on the future.

"Has anybody thought about what's next? I mean, in terms of therapy, or bringing in another doctor to evaluate his state of mind?" Artie managed to recover the sense of urgency depleted by his restive roadside nap. "He needs to hear about our hopes for him. Not expectations, but our willingness to help."

"This *we* business. You really ought to have a chat with Alison, you know." Jane carried her plate to the sink. "It hasn't occurred to her either that we are the problem."

"Have some respect." Arthur's sense of place within the family had ascended. He wanted to get Stephen home, and he wanted to impress his elder son.

"Oh, Arthur, really. For what?" Sylvia pushed her plate aside. "It does no good to get yourself worked up. I mean this, Artie. As a sort of warning, I suppose. Of course, you're upset. As we all are. But nobody has a panacea. Your brother isn't even speaking to the doctors yet, so all the talk of therapy—"

Artie yelled, to save himself from smothering beneath her words. "Not miracles! Not panaceas or some crazy drug. I see enough people on the streets in Erie. I'm not here to whip up false hope."

"Good for you." Sylvia was unaware she had offended Arthur, even after he pushed her hand away as she attempted to refill his cup. "Artie?"

He accepted, which he knew his father interpreted as capitulation.

"Maybe all I want to say to you is, Don't hurt him. Don't you dare. I'm sorry for the way that sounds. But listen to me,

son. You've been away a long time. Your brother didn't have
an older brother or a sister"—she turned her face to Jane, who
whirled water in the dishpan, raising suds—"while he was
growing up. Don't tell me about Erie, Pennsylvania, or New
York. We all live with our choices. Don't bring your problems when you visit Stephen." She allowed the awful silence
to amplify her words. "You think you know a thing or two,
I'm sure. I'll tell you this, son. You walk into that room and
you'll see there's no such thing as false hope. There's just
hope. It's all we have."

Arthur seized his chance. "I only know this one thing. We
have to get him home." He looked to Sylvia, whose interest
was inspired by agreement and suspicion. "I don't mean me. I
don't mean I can do him any good. I know he doesn't want to
talk to me. He shut his eyes, you heard the doctor say so."
Arthur was offended by the failure of his confession to raise
a protest. He persisted, emboldened by the shameful consensus he'd created. He had underestimated his position; he was
below consideration. He retreated past his daughter at the
sink, held himself inside the doorjamb. He lingered just long
enough to acknowledge his mortification. "I've never understood. A slow study, that's your father, children. Never won a
passing grade. I failed. Flunked out." He headed for the stairs,
agitating his humiliation with the pliant rod of self-pity. In
Arthur's mind, this constituted a whopping big down payment on the twenty-five-year right of way he'd signed with
Hetty Marshall.

Sylvia said, "He's right." She paused, to make it known her
assent was unqualified. For purposes of emphasis, she added,
"Stephen does belong at home. I thought I'd go see him soon.
I want to change my clothes, though. It's cool this morning."

"I'd like to go alone. Just for an hour, maybe?" Artie soft-
ened his appeal with a quick recitation of the lesson he'd been
taught. "I'll be gone tomorrow. Work and all."

"I'll plan to wait until eleven, then." Sylvia winked her appreciation.

Artie sneezed. "Excuse me."

"You won't give your cold to Stephen, will you?"

"Jesus, Mom, leave it alone." Jane twisted both faucets, shook her hands, and wiped them on her dress. "Artie, turn your head before you sneeze and don't wipe your nose on your little brother's blankets. Understand?"

Sylvia accepted the rebuke. "And you, my dear? Are we allowed to know your plans?"

"I might stop by to see him later on. I have to pack and pick up around the house in Lenox. Though Regina's cousin Jessica's a slob. I have to be in Hartford by four."

"Should we say our goodbyes right now?" Sylvia drew her daughter to her.

"I'll call you up every couple of days and make sure you're all following my orders." Jane was released before she'd finished speaking. "You all right?"

Sylvia twisted toward her son. "You get to be my age and they start feeling guilty when they leave you. It's such fun." She touched Jane's hair. "We'll all be fine. Please call. I'm missing you already. I'll have to get that Liz over here and make her talk to me."

Jane heard her mother's muffled steps erasing her omission of a polite word about Regina, and the novel, and the spurious vow to travel to New York. Jane joined Artie in the alcove. "Home, sweet home, huh?"

"It's worse than ever. Everything is—all stripped bare. I've never seen anything like it."

"What? Did you grow up blind?"

"It's worse, Jane. I mean, just driving down North Street this morning. It's everywhere. Land of decay."

"Look, if we'd grown up in New York City we'd just have a better variety of choices. One day we'd be in Times Square, Riverside Park, then Brooklyn Heights. You sound like Alison. Of course we see ourselves here, in Pittsfield. Here we are. But that's all there is to it. It's not so ironic. It's just a city, a lot of people hiding out at home, watching television or working on the pipes. Stephen didn't grow up on North Street."

Artie laughed. "I wasn't thinking of Stephen, Jane. I had in mind just you and me and Alison. And Mom and Dad. Nothing we heard in school, nothing we ever saw driving around at night or playing ball . . . nothing contradicted anything right here. At home. It was all so unmixed up."

"Maybe you're right. What do I know? I certainly always hated it here, this house. The old neighborhood had its charms."

"It's that sort of thing. The old neighborhood? It's a slum. It's not that I object to shanty old row houses, it's the euphemisms. Downtown? Down where? It's not there, it's all boarded up. The GE fired half the people in this town. Have you gone up by the lakes? They don't even put up docks. Three years ago, or four, I drove by—"

"Who cares? Let them drain the goddamn lakes. Pittsfield will survive us all."

"Right." He was aware he had protested too much. Jane didn't need the pull of a larger, longer-lasting home to draw her back here. The little house she hated had attracted and repelled her without fail. "Let the lakes be drained." Artie granted his too-long withheld permission. And he knew Pittsfield would survive the autumn of its industry. When the final blasting fire at the General Electric was extinguished, the leaf-like canopy of blue-gray smoke would fall away. Genetic engineers or couples dining out would stare through factory walls of checkered glass restored to their prewar clarity, and they would wonder what in God's name was the purpose of preserving the stand of limbless chimney trunks outside. Those furnaces would be another curious memorial. They would have no function, really, unless as grossly outsized lightning rods discolored by an acid rain. "On top of that, I can all but guarantee that Stephen's gonna catch my cold."

"His hands aren't good for much else. He might as well use them as hankies."

"What do you really think about him? What will happen?" If we do survive, he meant, will we be saved?

"Misconceived Stephen." Jane said this reflexively, silently completed the phrase as if it were a line of poetry she'd long since sewn into her memory: Tiny as he was, we could not accommodate him.

"Misconceived in what sense?"

The word had greater resonance spoken as a question. Jane smiled. Seeing Stephen as an infant, she caught a glimpse of Artie as a ten-year-old boy in shorts. "I can still see Mom holding Stephen. At the time, I was appalled, of course. She seemed so ancient near a brand-new baby. As if time were unaccountably long. When she'd talk to him? Or, especially when she'd sing? They were sad old songs. Or maybe they were only Irish drinking songs. Anyway, she sounded sad. Like she could see she'd never make it to the future."

Artie was too anxious to endure a further recollection. "Except . . . well, here we are. Except for Stephen. What about his future?"

Jane relented, though she was wary of making any public diagnoses, considering the currency of her version of Stephen's Sermon on the Mount. "I guess I think three out of four of us is pretty good, given the odds. And I think even Stephen will heal, or come to rest, at least. Isn't that a law of physics? Nothing lasts forever?"

Artie distrusted Jane's benign assessment of her brother, but he felt ill prepared to challenge her. His own image of insanity was nothing more original than abstract splatter painting. He saw Stephen's actions as random and incautious and, finally, successful; they stimulated rational critique and passion.

Jane was ready to be gone, to walk away a little farther this time. "What's the worst that can happen?"

"I frankly can't imagine."

"Really?" Jane slapped her hands against the table. "I must be getting old. The worst that ever happens is we all endure."

VIII

ARTIE WAS BARRED from Stephen's room by a young nurse beside the door. "It's bandage time in there. We're a little late this morning."

Artie held the door ajar but could not see to Stephen. A light flashed as the young nurse grabbed the metal handle, swung the door shut tight. "Was that a strobe?"

"Just a Polaroid. They keep a photographic record of his hands. It's the sort of thing we send around to burn clinics." She was experienced enough to keep her eyes averted. She leaned against the wall and tucked the skirt of her blue uniform behind her, flattening her thighs. "I'm sorry you have to wait."

"How is he?"

"He's a very good patient." She inched the inner edge of her left shoe into her right shoe's concave arch. "You'd have to ask the doctor. I can find the name, if you like." She smiled at the intersection of her shoes, raised her hazel gaze at last.

"I'm Artie. Stephen's brother. I don't live in town. I didn't even know this place existed."

"Jones II? It's one of the best in the country. The doctors here are very intelligent. And we aren't overcrowded. It's friendly here, I mean, professional and all, but I think there's something special, too." She pulled another tuck in her taut skirt.

"Coming through." A nurse and two young interns pushed by Artie with a cart.

"You signed in at the desk, I guess?" The young nurse stood up straight.

"I did. Is it okay to go in now?"

"I'm sure he'll be happy to see you." She drifted down the hall, backed in beside another door, pressed herself into place.

Artie walked directly to his brother's side. He didn't dare

say anything. Stephen wore all their words as wounds—fresh, open wounds and smooth, insensate scars.

Stephen drew his head and neck back deep into his pillow. He guessed his brother had been sent for, perhaps as a replacement for his father. His arm ramps had been lowered—Dr. Allegretti hoped a lesser angle would defuse the twitching in his shoulders—and Stephen felt more helplessly supine than ever. He could not see his hands.

Artie backed away, indicted; he sensed the tensing of his neck and shoulders was the only self-defense his brother could eke out of his constricted state. Space between them did not soothe Stephen. Artie backed up to the wall, then sidled toward the plate glass, reminiscent of a window, moved back to the bedside chair and sat, soon stood and strolled around the foot of Stephen's bed, his fisted hands inside his trouser pockets. His affected casual demeanor could not long support what Artie brought to bear: The stories of the clapping, broken windows, jail, and the most memorable of Stephen's speeches weighed on his shifting point of view.

Ten minutes reading Stephen's scrambled mind precluded *Hello, there. How are you doing?* In the astonished, momentary hesitation that attended his first view of Stephen, he'd dropped his tether to the world of words, banal or probing. Artie felt his able mind and body constituted prowess. Stephen's silence was an intimate permission, as if Artie had been allowed to strip his brother, tie him to the bed. As the intruder, Artie had no recourse to redemptive actions. Passive Stephen transformed every random thought, a snort to stifle back a sneeze, and glances at the mummy hands; everything became a violation.

He was the first to come without a word; Stephen worried silence wouldn't serve him as escape. Silence was his last resort and Stephen had been unprepared for uninvited guests.

Artie sneezed.

Stephen was heartened. He hoped this was his brother's prelude.

Artie sneezed again, then issued three more, which he managed to repress except for little snorts.

Stephen was indignant. He suspected Artie was teasing him.

Artie moved closer to his brother, but concern for spreading germs stopped him beside the hands.

This alerted Stephen: Artie had been sent as an inspector, to check out his mother's story of his Christlike hands. He wondered where they'd put his mother in the meantime. He made a simple plan: He would claim he'd painted on the dots himself, which would account for Sylvia's confusion. He'd even tell her he had done it—tell her to her face—if they brought her, unharmed, to his room.

He squeezed his eyelids tight, tapping his depleted reservoir of courage, then blindly left his final resting place and spoke. "I did that myself, you know. Look pretty real, don't they?"

"Stevie!" Artie stepped past the ramps, pressed his hands against the mattress.

The yelling of his nickname made Stephen angry. "Use my real name. Who do you think I am?"

This question buffered Artie's thrill at hearing Stephen's voice. He would not speak in terms of the delusion; instead, he tried to edge around the name of Jesus, toward his brother. "I don't need anybody telling me who you are, Steve. Not that anyone would bother. I came to see you, Stevie. After all, you are my brother."

Stephen rejected this pledge of allegiance. It had never served him. "What makes you say a stupid thing like that? You think I wouldn't know if I had a brother?" He stretched the wrinkles from his eyelids, raising ridges in his brow, which was as far as he would go to make his point. He refused to see. "Be careful what you say, 'cause you'll disturb me. And I've got the scars to prove it."

Artie let himself be led. "Anything at all, I tell you. Anything you say. I just want to hang out here with you."

The casual and friendly "hang out here with you" caught Stephen out. While Artie watched, he smirked, repeated the phrase several times, effecting something of a swagger with his shoulders as he spoke. "Like brothers. Just sort of hanging out."

"Right. Talk or no talk, depending on how you feel." Artie knew he'd gotten through. "There's a nurse, the one with hazel eyes? I bet we can get her to bring lunch for two."

"Just eatin' lunch or hangin' out?" Stephen loved the sound of this.

Artie carried on, unfazed by Stephen's lidded eyes, which he'd accepted as the arcane precondition of this conversation. "The idea is just to be together."

Stephen showed a sudden huge and silly grin. If Artie really wanted to be brothers, maybe he'd be willing to watch out for their mother—protect her while she was confused, even convince her Stephen wasn't Jesus. If he didn't have to bear the cross of being Jesus for his mother, he could finally figure out what city he was in, get himself back to Pittsfield. He was certain he could land a job as a photographer of hands. He began his background check on Artie. "Do you really love me? Like a brother, now, that part's important."

"Of course I love you, Steve. We are brothers." Artie regretted glancing at the door, as if to say *In case of an emergency*. He had forgotten Stephen's blindness, feared his brother might have noticed. "Coast is clear. Never know when a nurse might stick her head in."

Stephen cut to the quick. "Tell the truth now. Am I Jesus?"

Artie slowly transferred body weight, from his two hands on the mattress to his lower back and knees, rocked away without disturbing Stephen. "No?" He concentrated on the bandaged hands, proof of safety.

"You ever wish I was Him? Jesus?"

"Stevie, no. No, never."

"Would you hurt somebody who thought so? If you knew somebody, and say you were related, maybe? You wouldn't mind if that somebody believed I was really Him? Jesus?"

Artie shook his head dismissively. "No, never. Absolutely

not. I love you. What about some lunch, though?" He hoped
to sneak back to the brothers business.

"You swear on a holy stack of Bibles you can keep a secret
for the rest of your entire life? 'Cause if you ever tell I told
you, I'll fire up those burners and stick 'em right inside my
eyes. I know a trick or two."

Artie did not want to be the keeper of Stephen's secret identity as Jesus. He let the offer pass with nothing but a reassuring smile.

Stephen's haste was fed by Artie's warning about interfering
nurses. "I've got two big ears for a reason, mister."

"All right, I promise. But you didn't need to make me promise. You can tell me anything." Artie recalled his mother's
strictures against upsetting Stephen further. He'd been convinced he could avoid confronting the delusion, step behind
the splatter painting, find the artist. Now he understood the
artist was at work. The crazy masterpiece was wet. He was
standing in the studio.

Stephen wanted one last reassurance. "You did hear what
I said about my ears? Or was it my eyes? Say yes."

"Yes. I won't tell. Ever."

Stephen was relentless about this condition. "I remember
things, so you really better mean it. Or say goodbye now to my
eyes. Okay? Like how you said Mrs. Hammerstone was a pretty
snazzy chick? And how about I come visit you in Erie, Pennsylvania—which reminds me, by the way. Is that Erie city
somewhere on the middle of a map? Forget it. What about it?
Can you keep a secret after all of that?"

"You have my word." Artie figured, at the worst, his word
would end up as a squiggled line on Stephen's crowded canvas.

Stephen raised his head and shook with pain. Annoyed, he
sucked in air and hissed it out. "Go up there for yourself. I
can't see that far today. Well, what about it?"

Artie hadn't planned to understand. He ventured a good-
natured guess, to establish his willingness. "The bandages, you
mean."

"Well, I didn't mean my feet." Stephen had to open his eyes, to see if Artie's calm was true. "Mom did it, Artie. She believes. I mean, she really believes."

Artie was unsure whether Stephen was blaming Sylvia for his injury or crediting her with the new, clean wrapping. This seemed a crucial point of reference for the future. "She put the gauze on them?"

"The dots." Stephen rolled his eyes.

"The dots?" Artie bowed until his face was only inches from his brother's hands. He hesitated before issuing a contradiction. "I don't think I know what you mean by 'dots.'" He smiled plaintively at Stephen, though he was alarmed to meet his brother's disapproving stare.

Stephen enunciated every word, ruing his decision to enlist his brother. "The big and little blood dots. The ones that make me look like Jesus."

It fell to Artie to remember the unremarkable detail of the redressing of his brother's wounds. But in the suddenly electric interplay, he grounded himself, held to his professional belief: The less attention garnered by disturbing or disturbed behavior, the briefer its duration. In deference to his mother and her warning, which he wished he'd heeded, he said, "Mom loves you, Stevie, very much."

"I know all about that. But that doesn't make me look like Jesus." Stephen spoke sternly, admonishing his brother. "And that explains the stupid dots!"

"If anyone could see dots, I'd see them, okay? I promise you, if you could see, you wouldn't see them either. It was just a big mistake. It's not your fault." Artie felt harangued. Stephen's intransigence had flustered him.

"I have to see." Stephen closed his eyes. It was clear to him once he'd performed the math, a perfunctory piece of business. He announced the results. "Artie equals Arthur. He doesn't mean to make me cry." He understood his brother's motive. He was here as an ambassador of Arthur. Artie was going to torment his mother for her confusion about Jesus, all because she loved Stephen and she didn't love Artie or his equal, Ar-

thur. Stephen bounced his back and shoulders, readying himself for lift off.

Amazed, Artie pleaded, "Just open your eyes and have a
look. Just open your eyes."

Stephen issued a low, animalic grunt and slid his elbows off
the padded ramps. Then he rested.

Artie was on unfamiliar ground. He hoped to silently wait
out the minor tremor, avoid the urge to run or scream, which
he was certain would provoke a greater quake.

Stephen sucked in air and jerked his head and neck, creat-
ing the momentum to effect a sit-up and to fling his arms outside the ramps. His hands swung near the criblike metal side-
boards. He tilted back his head, twirled his hands in little circles, humming his great satisfaction. Then, he dropped his
head and briefly raised both hands, registered the whiteness of
his palms. He knew just what he had to do, once he was brave
enough. He'd give his mother something to believe in, something even Artie equals Arthur couldn't doubt.

Was Stephen finally done? An exhausted athlete loosening
his strained, retracted muscles? Artie watched his brother's
face relax. He could believe that Stephen was relieved to finally
extend his arms. The first thud of the bandage on the metal
sideboard might have been an overly enthusiastic arc. The
beating of his brother's hands was sudden, a preening bird's
unprompted hammering of wings. Before he moved, Artie
screamed, "There's nothing on your hands!" Then he dived
at Stephen's head, pushed his shoulders to the bed, and shut
him down.

A woman in the doorway yelled, "His hands, the nurses!
Get the nurses here!"

Artie felt his brother's head fall, wet and heavy. He gently
tugged his forearm free, laid Stephen's face against the pillow.

The woman screamed again. Artie reached for Stephen's
hand, but the young girl with the hazel eyes pressed her hands
against his chest and pushed him back. From this remove, he
saw two women and a man, and someone said, "Contusions."
Artie watched the women lift the bandaged paws, one hand

beneath each wet magenta crown, and rest the forearms on the ramps. He stepped forward, dipped his head to see what they were cutting. He said, "Watch out! I think that might be blood on Stephen's hands."

One of the women said, "Get him out of here."

The nurse he knew grabbed Artie's shoulder, put one arm around his back. She did not hand him off to Sylvia, who was standing by the door.

Artie said, "My mother's here."

"We're going to the sun room. Your brother will be fine. The doctor's with him now. Come on." The nurse set Artie on the purple couch. She left as Sylvia lurched in, relieving her of duty.

Artie told her everything her son had said. He added only this: "You mustn't ever let him know I told you, though. If ever anything did happen to his eyes, or anything at all . . . I hope he isn't badly hurt."

Sylvia said nothing, though she kept her lips apart.

The girl with hazel eyes appeared and bowed to Artie, apologetic and forgiving. "The doctor said to tell you they have stopped the bleeding, Mrs.—"

"Sylvia. Call me by my first name, dear."

"He will have to be restrained. His arms. At least—"

Sylvia had interrupted her with nothing but a slight twist of her head. "Restraints."

"For now. You should speak directly to the doctor, though. I'm afraid I have to leave you now." She pirouetted, ran away.

Sylvia was staring down the hall. "What do you think got him started with the dots?"

"He doesn't think he looks enough like Jesus?" Artie felt her question as an accusation of his laggardly response. "I was amazed enough to hear him speak at all."

Sylvia did not assume responsibility for having invented this latest plague. The problem, as she saw it looking at the nurses and their skittish patients, was Artie's intervention. She believed she could not safeguard Stephen's body until she had him home alone; strangers threw him into jail, his own brother threw him into fits of self-abuse. She did her best to curb her anger. "When he whispers to me, it's about how sorry he is." She paused to watch her son receive this lie.

Artie accepted the rebuke. It confirmed Stephen's insistence that she alone believed in him.

She went on. "Not anything about dots." She crossed her arms and fended off a short man in a bathrobe who was carrying a plastic bag. "Clearly, Artie, talking to you upset him."

He waved his hand, surrendering. He hadn't even kept his word. It little mattered that the promise as he understood it— not to tell the world Stephen believed he was Jesus—followed on the widespread publication of this suggestive notion. He had invested her with his word; she could keep it for him. "I'd just like to see him, just look in. Before I leave." He meant forever.

Sylvia was distracted by another interloper. She crossed her arms, then backed off quickly. "Oh, I am Stephen's mother."

"My name is Dr. Colleen Hague. Stephen is asleep. Mrs. Adamski, we've got a brace around each arm, for now. As much to hold down the bleeding as anything. The palms are so delicate at this point, we don't want to take any chances." The emphasis on fragile physiology subverted nascent protest. "We have to help him keep his hands so absolutely still. I think even conversation makes that hard, you know, how we all get excited, feeling better. I think, perhaps, if we were a bit more restrictive about visits. For the time being."

"I do want to see him."

"Of course you do. I'm a mother, too. I hate to ask so much, but maybe in, say, fifteen minutes? We've given him something just to help him rest. I'd like him to be quiet for today."

"You ask nothing. You're an angel of mercy, Dr. Hague."

"Perhaps, just you alone for now." She winked at Artie. "Your brother's really fine, okay?" The doctor left.

"I think I'll just go home. I guess you have a car, Mom?"

"I'll be there soon. Drive safely now." She waited until Artie stood, then took his place, as if it was the only seat available.

"I'm sorry, Mom."

"Artie, it's too hard to understand. And it's too easy to sound harsh. I don't like that. For now, you go home. And let's not tell your father. He's not handling this well at all. Your sisters either. I'll tell Alison to hold off visiting, she'll understand. Jane's gone by now, I guess." She'd accounted for her other family. "Stephen has enough to live with."

He swore himself to secrecy, which served him after all. From his upended point of view, this bound her not to repeat what he had said about the dots, and sealed the gash he'd opened in his solemn vow to Stephen.

Words create and words destroy, and that was the truth of this and of all matter. Artie believed at last that no one could arbitrate the bloody force of what was said. The truth hurt, too. And so he took his chances. And it did not seem unlikely that this chaos might explain why so many vows of secrecy were sworn and broken: the hope of minimizing damage.

Artie stopped to drink a cup of coffee in the Berkshire Medical cafeteria. Eavesdropped reports of staff romance and surly patients ripping out their intravenous tubes provided the foundation for inventing a complex, humane milieu in which to place his brother. His terrified replaying of Stephen's self-destructive fit provoked a moment of paralysis. Temporarily inert, his body was overtaken by the words he'd always held at a disdainful distance; now they reached him: He believed the legion parents, humbled and afraid, confessing impotence as children left their homes with guns and packaged drugs and fire in their eyes.

He wandered through the breezeway, signed his name at the reception desk, and climbed the stairs to Stephen's room.

"Your mother left a while back. Were you supposed to meet her?"

He stared into her hazel eyes and recognized her willingness. She saw what Artie needed. "If you came in along with me? Just so I can see for myself?"

"You're from out of town? You have to leave today?" She kicked the heel of her left shoe. "Someone might see us. And

I'd have to say I tried to stop you. They might throw you out for good, I mean. It happens."

"I was just standing there when it happened. It wasn't anything I did to him."

"Sometimes that's all it takes. We got a black girl works with us. Some of them won't have a thing to do with her. They scream, knock things over. We get all kinds here, all shapes and sizes. I always say, though, It takes all kinds. I'll follow you."

Artie had expected she would make a point of exempting Stephen from the general population of Jones II. He allowed her time to draw a distinction.

"If you're nervous or anything, this is probably a bad idea."

This moved him. He slid past the door and held the handle as it closed. The nurse held the door at the other side, keeping it a few inches from the frame.

He tiptoed toward the window, aiming wide of Stephen. The young girl stuck her hand inside the door and waved him back. He obeyed, but stopped beside the brackets holding Stephen's arms in place. The bandages were smaller, a pair of cotton mittens. Both palms were decorated with red teardrops.

IX

"Your mother's resting upstairs, son." Arthur stood beside the front door, turned his head and looked through the paned glass to the street. "Got a taxi on the way. I'm going to a meeting."

Artie pushed his knapsack off the divan cushion. "A meeting on the weekend? Business must be good." Or bad, he thought.

"Not a meeting meeting." Arthur put one hand around the door knob. "A.A. Instead of waiting out another night alone, trying to avoid the Legion."

"Good for you, Dad. That's tremendous." Artie's inflection sagged beneath his vocabular enthusiasm.

"One day at a time." Arthur salvaged honesty with this, the answer Hetty gave him when he'd asked, rhetorically, how he might repay her. "Your mother tells me you'll be leaving early in the morning, what with Erie such a drive. I hope we'll see you. . . ." Arthur didn't qualify the sentiment by naming date or place. "There's my cab."

"I could drive you, Dad." Artie stood up. "I don't have to leave so early."

"The meetings can go late. There's nothing anyone can do for Stephen. It was good of you to come all this way. 'Course, he can't let you know, but he'll remember you were here." He reached across the table, held his son's hand for a second. "You wouldn't think so but, believe me, he remembers." Arthur took his hand back. "Get some supper, now. Drive carefully. I like your car. We'll let you know how things with Stephen go. I hate to leave." Arthur waved and left the house.

Artie credited his sister's theory of endurance; he also gave a nod to Pittsfield, ambivalent host to both the Legion and the local A.A. chapter.

He watched the dimming of the day from a corner of the divan. Stephen was secure. Artie braced himself against the impulse to assume responsibility for Stephen's actions or his future. His work with juvenile offenders was often enough complicated by the effort he expended extricating parents, pregnant girlfriends, naïve teachers, and astonished siblings. Isolated from recriminations and apologetic histories of abuse and sheer neglect, a teenage prostitute or vandal could be made to see the simple truth of his or her behavior. Working backward from the action, it was possible to re-create the faulty process by which an urge to get attention or to revenge a series of humiliations had been transformed into a self-defeating criminal offense. He did not dismiss the action; he advocated restitution. But he believed the words *I didn't mean to do it*. The phrase was a linguistic instinct, uttered every time a child spilled a glass of milk, past punishments and warnings notwithstanding. He believed it was the universal cry for help.

"Does that make sense? That's what I meant about the dots. There's no use denying what he did to his hands, or even who he might have thought he was. But you can't believe that's what he was after? That's what Stephen wanted all along?" Artie pressed a finger to the cap of the prescription bottle Sylvia had placed before him on the coffee table. He made the single pill inside the amber plastic vibrate, confirming her rebuttal of his father's implication. The typescript label specified two capsules only, not to be renewed, under penalty of law.

Sylvia looped a double knot and snapped the length of thread below the collar button she'd replaced. She dropped the white shirt on the rug, beside her chair, pulled a pillowcase from her lacquered mending basket. "What about your sister Jane? I was the monster who believed she was confused, remember? Now, I grant Jane a special nature. I mean, she clearly wants to sleep with women, right? She seems well aware Regina's older than Methuselah. Or is Jane right? That Alison is the crazy one, that she can't be happy raising two kids, giving up her job?" She stuck her hand into the pillowcase and pulled it inside out. "You tell me. I'm all ears. Apologies? A birthday card to Stephen every other year? You didn't *mean* to miss another Christmas?" She raised the material, searching for the flaw. The hemline sagged and she ripped it clean away, smoothed it into place, and stitched. "I don't like it. I don't even understand it. But I know you mean it. Not to hurt us, not because you're not a good son. It's your way. But, Artie . . . I guess I don't believe I *didn't mean to do it*. I don't think people ever say exactly what they mean. We can't. Your brother hurt his hands—and twice now. That's what I believe. I think he meant it."

"And next?" Artie resented the equation of his and Stephen's actions, though the point was moot; he would have to grant her Jane's behavior compromised his notion of intentionality. He was not convinced the history of Jane opting for

Regina was linear and undistorted. Even if he argued for a spectrum of sanity, assigning everyone a spot, the placement of Jane nearer than himself to Stephen could only seem self-serving. "Really, though. What next? What if he wants a manger? Or a cross?"

She stuck her needle through a fold and put the pillowcase into her basket. "He has his cross. He asked you was he Jesus, you said no, and he drew blood. They tied him to his cross. Or am I deluded?" She opened her mouth slightly, pressed her tongue against her teeth. Then she tilted her head, querulous and calm. "You really can't imagine what he'll do if he wakes up and sees his hands are clean?"

Artie was awed. He understood that Stephen need never speak again. She'd sing to him and whisper "I know just what you mean, son," when he grimaced or rolled over in his bed. The bandages would be unwrapped, revealing not a man's prehensile fists but a newborn's twitching starfish hands.

"No one, not even the doctors, have anything left to say, Artie." She believed this was a fitting final word.

Artie wished his father hadn't left. He wanted one more picture of his parents in one room together. He'd frame it generously enough to accommodate an image of his little brother, which could be slipped in surreptitiously, while Artie wasn't watching. From a distance, he could manage to resolve that image.

Instead, he had to live with this solitary portrait of his mother, almost smiling, attended only by the ghost of her self-sacrificing son.

Hoping to cast her in a better light, he blurted his frustration. "Okay, so I don't have the answers. I don't think I know more or better ways. The doctors . . . there are drugs. I want him to get better." Then he closed his eyes and seized his brother's hands, at last believing Stephen would hurt himself. He trusted Sylvia to read his mind. "What good does my believing do him now?" He'd yelled his question, which he recognized as a rite of exorcism. He smiled wryly. "I'm sorry."

Tapping his fingers against his chest, he said, "It's me, of course. Because I didn't stop him. I hurt him. I can't save him. And I'm sorry."

Sylvia stood, limped to the table. She sat on a corner, rubbed a hand across his hair. "I think that's his job, salvation," she waited until he raised his face and met her gaze, "with the doctors, maybe, and let's hope without involving any more lawyers." She stood, retrieved her basket. She rested one hand on the chair's back, leaned and watched her son. Then she shrugged. "I just want to get him off his cross."

X

ARTIE THREW HIS KNAPSACK in the back seat of his car. The night was dark, watched but hardly lit by stars. Though Artie had warned her of his idea of leaving without waking her, his mother knocked on the glass of her bright bedroom window, waving both her hands. He yelled, "I really will come back. I'll call this week." She must have heard him, or seen his hands and trusted that he had his reasons. She lifted her wrist, and he waved when she completed her exaggerated double take, confirming his departure time as two o'clock. He backed out with his headlights off, to better see his mother, one hand against a window pane, the other lost in shadow on her face. He accelerated quickly. His tires squealed when he braked before the red light at the Elm Street corner of Holmes Road. The only other car, a yellow compact idling on Elm, did not move ahead on green. Artie waited out the red light, speculating on a host of minor automotive problems he was prepared to solve. The green light blinked above him. He proceeded slowly, steering his car near enough to see inside the compact.

In the driver's seat, Arthur followed Hetty's forearm to her hand against the window, and he saw his spying son.

Artie did not stop, but he drove slowly enough to be overtaken at a normal speed, should Arthur have decided to pursue. He watched for Hetty's yellow car in the rearview mirror until he was a mile past the city's western limit.

Though the streets had been untrafficked, his hopeful backward glancing made this Artie's slowest trip through town. All he remembered, though, were stationary street lights blinking as he rolled beneath them, one by one resolving, receding, waning, then briefly reappearing as he headed up a hill, the downside dotted with electric circles of confusion.

About the Author

Michael Downing teaches writing and literature at Wheelock College in Boston.